The Colossus Conspiracy

By

Ron Delpit

ISBN: 978-0-7596-8657-1 (sc)
ISBN: 978-0-7596-8658-8 (hc)
ISBN: 978-0-7596-8656-4 (e)

Print information available on the last page.

This book is printed on acid-free paper.

1stBooks - rev. 02/15/2021

For my family and friends who always believed.

Especially for Nan and Gene

For whom I can do no wrong,

For Ken, for his constant encouragement

and M.

Thank You all.

Chapter 1
Juice

God he loved Vegas.

The feel of it. The smell of it. The pulse of it.

It was more alive than any place he had ever been. It had everything, and it had it 24 hours a day, seven days a week, 365 days a year.

Las Vegas was a city without a conscience or a last call. It was unfazed by war, recession or the Dow Jones.

Opulence. Decadence. Opportunity. Those were the operative words.

Brian Powers loved Sin City.

He saw it as Paradise Found. A place where dreams came true and lives changed with the turn of a card or a roll of the dice.

It was odd how the whole world came to Vegas to vacation and Vegas natives went elsewhere. It was March, and Las Vegas was in the midst of what Brian kiddingly referred to as its "three days of winter", which consisted of some showers and gusty winds. Rather than fight the winds he had hightailed it to Mexico, figuring to spend a week in the sun, enjoying margaritas, sans phone calls, on his first trip to Cabo San Lucas. He had brought his cell phone, but had promised himself he would not turn it on other than to check messages every other day before going to bed. Still, he knew someone would find him. Someone would need something. There would be a crisis.

There always was.

This one plopped itself into his lap just three days into the trip. The call was simple and cryptic, and disturbed his poolside siesta at the Royal Indios Hotel.

And it came from one of the last people on earth he'd expect to chase him down. He recognized T.J. Fitzgerald's deep, resonant voice as the first "Is that you Brian?" crackled through the static of the dated cordless phone which had been brought to him post haste by a young, skinny Mexican pool boy.

Fitzgerald's somber tone jarred him to alertness.

"Yes, it's me Fitz, what's up?" He didn't ask how Fitzgerald had found him. Only his travel agent knew where he had gone, and he hadn't decided on a hotel until his arrival, but Fitzgerald's sleuthing powers weren't the issue at the moment.

Whatever it was must have just come up because there had been no word from T.J. Fitzgerald the night before when he checked his cell phone for messages.

"Something of a situation has developed," Fitzgerald said calmly. "I could use your help."

The evenness of T.J. Fitzgerald's tone did nothing to calm Brian's suddenly racing heartbeat.

Ron Delpit

"I'll come back just as soon as I can get a plane. I'll check the schedules and get back …"

"That won't be necessary. I have a jet waiting for you at the Cabo airport. It'll take you right into the main terminal at McCarran."

He didn't ask about the problem. He didn't need to.

T.J. Fitzgerald was the Vice-President and Chief of Security at the Colossus Hotel, Las Vegas' biggest and most exclusive resort, and not someone given to jumping to conclusions.

"The engine's running," Fitzgerald said softly.

And so it began.

Fitzgerald did not call during the three-hour flight and except for the flight attendant and two pilots, Brian was alone on the impressive new Colossus Hotel jet. For a short period his mind wandered, wondering what could be troubling his friend, then he drifted off to sleep.

It was useless to try to imagine. He knew no matter what scenario his mind envisioned, the real problem would be something different. No sense worrying about imaginary monsters.

There were enough real ones.

The baggage claim area at McCarran International was crowded and the wide-eyed tourists were buzzing. A gorgeous showgirl from Bally's long-running "Jubilee" show was vamping on the huge overhead screen, welcoming the latest influx of visitors to the Entertainment Capitol of the World.

A minute later the showgirl was magically replaced by a video of Siegfried and Roy inviting the newest arrivals to their spectacular production at the Mirage.

It was all part of the never-ending flash, trash and hype.

Slot machines jingled all over the airport. People of all ages, races and religions fed coins into the mouths of the airport slots as they waited for their slow arriving bags.

And Brian smirked a knowing smile as the non-discriminatory machines swallowed up coins by the hundreds from players who were playing more for pleasure than treasure.

At the airport it wasn't about winning. The suckers played just to be playing. For the "fun" of it. For the "Vegas Experience". They were so anxious they couldn't wait until they got to the hotel.

Brian had lived in Vegas more than half of his life, and after twenty-two years he never for a minute regretted leaving the escalating prices and traffic grids of Los Angeles for the Vegas lights and desert nights.

Vegas represented hope for everyone. That was the unwritten lure of the city. It may have been a town without pity, but it would never be called a town without hope.

2

Stories of down on their luck gamblers who went from rags to riches in one lucky session were commonplace in Vegas. And for good reason.

With every new roll of the dice, the hope of winning provided a mega-kilowatt adrenalin rush, better than the first snort of blow. Life was wonderful and time stood still for those few seconds the dotted red cubes tumbled from the shooter's hand across the green felt and came to rest at the far end of the oblong table.

It was the same glorious high a blackjack player felt when he called for a hit and turned a thirteen into a 21, or watched the dealer bust out.

And every weekend another 150,000 Pollyannas landed at McCarran or came rolling down Interstate 15 from all points North, South, East and West, looking for cheap rooms and two for one buffets. They were armed with their weekly paychecks and ATM cards with a change of clothes as their only baggage.

A more elite, silver spoon set of invaders touched down in private Lears, GS 8's and hotel chartered Challengers at McCarran's Executive Air Terminal with limos on the tarmac anxiously waiting to whisk them to ballroom sized suites with butlers and maids at their beck and call.

It was all part of a weekly ritual and it didn't matter if the visitors won or lost. They'd keep coming back, and next time they'd be just as optimistic.

The reason was simple.

No other resort spot in the world could offer the same payoff. Not Disneyland with its Magic Kingdom, not the Virgin Islands with its sunshine and glistening white beaches, not even New York with all its hustle, its Broadway plays and the famous lady holding her torch.

Those places offered some nice memories and assorted Kodak moments, but that wasn't the point. Tourists who came to Vegas all wanted the same thing. A chance to hit it big. A chance to win and change their lives. Hit mega-bucks and send the boss a telegram telling him to find himself another flunky.

An e-mail go fuck yourself.

Brian remembered doing the same thing two decades earlier. Before there was e-mail. He had gotten lucky, gone on a streak and made what he thought at the time was a fortune. He was feeling so good he didn't even call. No call. No show. No more job. No regrets.

The money ran out before long but his attraction for the town never waned. It was where he wanted to be. It was his town.

One with its own special language. A native tongue not found in a Berlitz language book.

It was "gaming" not gambling, and the slots were referred to as "the machines", as in "Does he play tables or machines?" It had an innocent ring and the jargon carried over to the money too.

A five dollar chip was a nickel, a $25 chip was a quarter or green, as in "green plays", and a hundred dollar token was never referred to by denomination.

It was always "black" or a buck. A guy making a sports bet would say "Gimme a buck ten on the Lakers minus the seven" and the ticket writer understood the bet was for $110. A "dime" or "large" meant a thousand as in "I had two dimes on the Cowboys, or he's up forty-seven large.

The city could make your heart race like the engines of an Indy car on Memorial Day.

You could put casino chips in the collection plate at Sunday mass, find a sports book to make a line on whether the end of the world would come on a weekend or weekday, and visit the best parts of the most fascinating cities in the world for the price of a cab ride up and down the famous Las Vegas Strip.

And even though the new billion dollar mega resorts kept putting in roller coasters, motion rides and arcades, Vegas was not a place for kids, no matter what the Chamber of Commerce said. Not unless casinos started giving kids credit lines or setting up booster seats at the blackjack tables.

It was a town of wise guys as much as it was a city of lights. In Vegas everybody had a scheme, a dream or both. Most of the time merit had little to do with your ultimate success. It was more important who you knew or who you blew.

The natives called it "juice", and in Vegas "juice" was more important than money. If you had "juice" you didn't wait in line to check in, or to get into shows or restaurants. And you didn't pay for squat. The acronym, "RFB", stood for Room, Food and Beverage, and it meant all your charges were compliments of the casino.

Players with huge credit lines had juice, however the real juice was reserved for the wise guys who knew someone or something. They didn't need credit lines to get juice. They were the guys who not only knew where the bodies were buried, they knew who buried them.

Brian had a friend called "Chicago" who had serious juice. He was an old-timer who either couldn't get licensed or who didn't want to have his entire life laid bare before the gaming control board and the media in order to get a paycheck and health insurance.

Still, "Chicago" could get anything he wanted at any major hotel.

Once or twice a year he'd clue certain casino bosses in on a fixed horse race, or provide one of them with inside information on an IPO because he knew a Wall Street suit who was jammed up and more afraid of his bookie than the S.E.C. The result meant a tax free hundred grand or more to the casino man, and his gratitude.

When "Chicago" wanted a primo booth to see Danny Gans, Siegfried and Roy, the Bellagio's "O" show or two ringside tickets to a championship fight, no one ever told him to try another night. There was no such thing as a sellout for a guy with strong juice. If the show was sold out, two waiters brought in a table

4

from the wings and made another row or somebody already in a booth was told he had to move to a table.

And the wise guys had their own code of ethics. They didn't abuse their power. They didn't ask too often, and they never raised their voices. Their most sensitive requests were handled in a tone no louder than a whisper, like an eight-year old making his first confession.

If you had enough "juice" even your call girls were compliments of the house. Call girls, not hookers. The difference was style and about $500 an hour.

The upscale Strip hotels dealt only in U.S.D.A. Prime and your casino host or friendly bellman was usually your contact. You told him what you needed and he made it happen. Every major hotel had a few girls on the line. Girls they could trust to be discreet. Working girls who were allowed to hang out at the hotel bars without being bothered by security. If they weren't on property one phone call could get them to your room in fifteen minutes. Domino's couldn't deliver anything as hot, or as fast.

A slightly above average looking working girl ran about $250 an hour for straight sex, but a drop dead gorgeous top of the line honey could demand as much as $1500 an hour or 5g's for an overnight stay. A square might wonder what a hooker could do that a girlfriend or wife couldn't and Brian Powers knew the answer.

Guys treated call girls like rental cars. They were there to be used and abused. To try everything they couldn't try at home. They could get kinky without feeling guilty. For the right price a call girl was fair game for just about anything. After all you didn't have to live with her every day.

The main difference was attitude, and the pleasure was a one-way street where the customer came first, last and always. For the right price one of those pro lovelies could take you around the world, make you think you'd celebrated New Year's Eve in Rio de Janeiro with fireworks and have it all seem so real that when you regained your senses you'd have gunpowder on your hands and speak with a Jamaican accent. She could touch you in places you wouldn't even touch yourself. She'd put her tongue somewhere for a second or two, and you'd swear on your grandfather's grave it had been there for an hour.

"Mr. Powers?"

A buff looking guy in a tuxedo with an "Eric" name tag was asking.

"Good choice," Brian answered, recognizing the gold Colossus shield on the man's breast pocket.

"Mr. Fitzgerald sent a car for you."

"That won't be necessary," Brian smiled. "My car is here at the airport. Just tell Mr. Fitzgerald I'm going to run my stuff home and I'll meet him at the hotel in about half an hour."

"I'll let him know," the driver said, forcing a half-smile as he turned and walked away.

A minute later he was back, extending his cell phone toward Brian.

"Mr. Fitzgerald would like to speak to you…"

"Brian, the hotel isn't such a good idea. I'd rather if we met somewhere else. How about the Mirage, in say forty-five minutes? Lagoon Bar."

"Deal. See you there."

After first settling down in Vegas, Brian hooked on with a local magazine as an entertainment writer, then struck out on his own, publishing his own magazine. It was a slick tourist publication that also gained immediate acceptance among local casino honchos for its content and inside gossip.

They liked seeing their names and pictures in the magazine and Brian saw to it every issue carried an interview with one of Vegas' most influential casino heads. He personally wrote the pieces and the on-going series helped him forge some lasting ties with the city's most powerful gaming bosses.

The Editor's badge also got him backstage with Vegas' superstars and he quickly crafted friendships with the One Name Gang. Sammy, Sinatra, Cher, Elvis, Liza and Engelbert became his pals. He was running with the Big Dogs. He exchanged Christmas cards with golden voiced Robert Goulet, and became buddies with Paul Anka, whom he considered the most consummate performer this side of Sammy D.

All of that seemed like another lifetime.

Now he free-lanced as a "Gaming and Security" consultant, which was a fancy way of saying major league trouble-shooter.

He was part public relations man, part lobbyist, part detective and all about business. Brian's street and political connections ran deep, as did his relationships with the entertainers.

He tossed his duffel bag and suitcase onto his bed, brushed his teeth, pulled out another pair of tennis shoes, found a clean shirt and headed for the door. The entire exercise took less than five minutes.

Ten minutes later he was turning into the Mirage valet parking lane. He ignored the "full" sign in the middle of the driveway, maneuvering around it as an agitated valet parker tried to wave him off.

"Hey buddy, we're full. You'll have to pull around to the…"

The kid stopped in mid sentence.

"Sorry Mr. Powers. I guess I blanked. I wasn't paying attention to the car." Brian smiled.

"No problem, Danny. Take care of it for me," he said, pressing a nickel chip into the kid's hand.

Brian Powers had rubbed elbows with Howard Hughes, played $5 blackjack with Kenny Rogers when the country gambler was down on his luck, and sat in a suite with Elvis when the King was at the peak of his comeback fame.

Between shows one night he was downright stunned as he watched the King of Rock 'n Roll point and fire one of his pearl-handled .45's at the screen of the television set in his dressing room, blowing the 19 inch Sony to smithereens.

"Sumbitch can't sing a lick," Elvis deadpanned, a slight curl on his lip.

The sound was deafening and reverberated in Brian's ears for days but it made for a great "I was there when it happened" story.

Sammy had cooked for him in the kitchenette of the Candyman's two-story Caesars Palace penthouse and he had consoled Joan Rivers following the suicide of her husband, Edgar Rosenberg.

He'd exchanged insults with Wayne Newton, Shecky Greene and Diana Ross, gotten to know and admire country sweetheart Barbara Mandrell, cut birthday cake with the late George Burns and shared private laughs with funnyman Don Rickles.

And one night he tried not to act shocked when he was making small talk in a Riviera dressing room with Dolly Parton when the Queen of Dollywood unholstered her eye-catching size 42 double D's, turned to him with her hands cupped under them and declared:

"I wish people would quit asking if I've had breast implants. Look at these things. They were the size of softballs by the time I was 10 years old and they just never stopped growing."

Brian Powers was as Vegas as neon and green felt, and like the city, he embraced mobsters and priests with the same fervor. They were all his people.

The late afternoon heat was oppressive, and Brian could feel the beads of perspiration on his forehead as he stepped out of his car and headed for the cool of the Mirage lobby area.

He made his way through the congestion of tourists just inside the casino's glass doors to the Lagoon bar to meet T.J. Fitzgerald.

It was almost two and the bar was quiet except for a couple conventioneers enjoying an after lunch cold one and a young couple making goo-goo eyes at each other in the far corner.

The cocktail girl was at his side almost as soon as he slid into a booth. Fitzgerald had not yet arrived.

"What can I get for you?" she asked as she deftly slid a napkin on the table.

"Crown and seven..."

"Coming up."

Her nametag said "Shauna, California" and her costume said there ain't much more to see. In some joints the girls complained about how revealing their outfits were, but in the classy strip hotels the young pretties were too satisfied with $300 a night in tips to piss anyone off.

Brian Powers was 43, with thinning hair and soft, caring brown eyes. He had a quick wit, a still fiery temper that was getting slower with age and an admitted intolerance for incompetence.

He had been divorced since the eighties, spent the nineties looking for love in all the wrong faces and was either optimist or fool enough to believe it would all turn out okay in the end. He liked Christmas, betting football, 60's music, Leroy Neiman artwork and milk shakes. He also liked a certain type of woman. A kind of repressed Catholic school product. A woman with kindness in her heart, shyness on her face, seduction in her eyes and a whole pool of unleashed lust sitting just below the surface. It didn't matter if she could cook.

He took a long sip of his drink and looked around the main floor of the Mirage casino. He had an unimpeded view of the high-end blackjack tables from his seat in the Lagoon Bar and he could see the steady stream of passersby pausing to gawk as they passed the table where someone with an uncanny resemblance to former Bulls superstar Michael Jordan was playing. The gleaming bald pate and dangling gold earring were enough to make people wonder if it was really His Airness, but once he unleashed that boyish, light up the room smile, his identity was no longer in question.

For the most part celebrities could go about their business in Vegas without being bothered. People were used to seeing them. They came for DeLaHoya vs.Trinidad, Holyfield vs.Lewis and Tyson vs. anybody.

A championship fight was an excuse for the town to get even crazier than normal. Behind closed doors casino bosses cursed Don King but he was their P.T. Barnum. He was a huckster and a hustler but he controlled most of the big fights and the big fighters. He commanded huge site fees from the hotels to put his fights in their arenas but people came.

Not just people, but players with money. On a fight weekend every casino in town knew they'd have an increased drop and plenty of action.

A Don King event had the economic impact of a Super Bowl for the city. No one really cared how much he stole from the fighters, nor did it really matter. As per the norm in any Don King promotion, the boxers got their biggest paydays, the hotels brought in their best customers and King and his electric hair smiled all the way to the bank.

High profile celebrities rubbed elbows with the masses at the fights, and they all cursed their own gullibility when the result turned out to be an outrageous verdict, a first-round knockout or an ear-biting fiasco.

But a questionable decision seldom put a damper on anyone's weekend. Hotels bought almost all of the $1500 ringside seats and used them as bait to lure in high-rollers for the weekend.

"Hey Joe," it's Lou from Mandalay Bay. "Just wanted to let you know I have two ringsides for you for the Tyson fight if you can make it in next month." That was the telemarketing technique and every hotel used it. And the higher your credit limit the better your seats. There was a pecking order and the customers knew it.

Casino Marketing Departments spent hours upon hours trying to come up with Special Events special enough to make the big spenders come calling. Slot tournaments, baccarat tournaments, the Three Tenors, Nascar races, Ricky Martin, Streisand, The Stones or the National Finals Rodeo.

It didn't matter. Book it and they will come. Hype it and they will call and ask about it. You had to spend money to make money, so if Don King or Bob Arum wanted a $7 million site fee you anted up. Then you went to work selling it.

And Vegas was an easy sell, because the city itself was more special than any of the Special Events on the king-sized marquees.

A dapper, well-dressed man in a dark suit slid into the booth alongside him and Brian turned his gaze from The Jordan Show to T.J. Fitzgerald.

His real name was Travis John Fitzgerald but Brian had never heard anyone refer to him that way. Probably no one but his mother had called him that in a hundred years. The only reason Brian knew was because he had once seen T.J.'s driver's license.

Brian knew whatever prompted Fitzgerald to ask for a sit down was important, and also confidential, otherwise the meet would have taken place on Fitzgerald's home territory at the Colossus.

"I appreciate your coming Brian," Fitzgerald said routinely and Brian could see the concern in his friend's eyes. T.J. Fitzgerald's title was Chief of Security at the Colossus but that was only on paper. In reality he was the second most powerful man at the 6,000 room hotel because his best friend owned the joint and Fitzgerald was his most trusted confidant.

"What's up Fitz?"

"I'm not exactly sure Brian." He was carefully measuring his words. "There are some things that just aren't right at the hotel, and even though I can't put my finger on it, I smell something."

"Like what?" Brian asked softly, privately wondering if Fitzgerald was in any danger.

"There's a chance the Colossus might just have a problem with a chip scam which might also involve some heavyweight money laundering," Fitzgerald said without hesitating. "And I don't think anything this big could fly without inside help. The scheme is much too sophisticated. Hell, I wouldn't have noticed it myself except for a fluke."

"What kind of fluke?"

Fitzgerald hesitated slightly.

"Look, Brian. I could be all wrong on this..." He paused again, and then began.

"Somebody's been passing off some perfect counterfeit chips, and we're getting overloaded with some very shaky markers. And last week a Chicago gambler hit us for a million two in forty-five minutes."

9

"That happens," Brian said. "Players get streaks too."

"I understand that," T.J. said quietly, "but I looked at the tapes. The guy seemed to vary his bets too perfectly. Like he knew what was coming."

"Did you change dealers?"

"Three times. Even changed the cards twice."

Brian was going to ask a question but he let it pass not wanting to interrupt Fitzgerald's train of thought.

"The blackjack losses we'll investigate, but the other stuff is more complicated," Fitzgerald continued. The force of his suggestion hung in the air like a threatening storm cloud.

"I don't know how high it goes, but I do know we're talking about some serious money. Very serious money."

"How serious?"

"Maybe as much as three or four million a month…"

"And you think maybe the rigged blackjack shoe, the counterfeit chips and the phony markers are all connected?"

"That's what has me worried," Fitzgerald answered as he folded and unfolded the napkin in his hand.

The wheels in Brian's head were in overdrive.

"Have you talked to Forrester?" It was the most logical question.

Adam Forrester was the owner of the Colossus and a former Chicago businessman who seemed out of place in the Vegas casino industry. He had virtually come out of nowhere three or four years earlier, built the Colossus from the ground up and turned it into one of the most profitable and spectacular hotels on the Strip.

"Not yet," Fitzgerald said evenly, and the hesitation in his answer did not escape Brian's attention. Granting major markers to players with questionable credit was something that usually went over the credit manager's head. Sometimes only the boss could give the okay—and the boss of the Colossus was Adam Forrester.

"You need to," Brian said firmly.

"I will," T.J. replied, "but I want you to do some checking first. Before I approach him. Do it quietly and discreetly."

"I don't know any other way," Brian laughed.

Brian didn't ask if T.J. thought the conspiracy reached all the way up to Adam Forrester.

He had to be entertaining the thought, which probably explained why he didn't push Adam Forrester about the shortage. It definitely explained why Fitzgerald thought it important enough to track him down in Mexico.

Fitzgerald's next statement may have answered the question.

"I'm afraid someone might be squeezing Adam, and he's trying to handle whatever it is on his own," Fitzgerald said heavily. "I've dropped some hints and given him the opportunity to tell me if something's on his mind, but so far nothing.

"Maybe I'm imagining things. I mean. I know he's got a lot of things on his plate, but he's been jumpy and real moody and that's not like Adam. I've known the guy a long time Brian. Something's up."

Brian also knew Fitzgerald had excellent instincts.

"I'm afraid it could be something serious if he doesn't want to tell me."

T.J. Fitzgerald and Adam Forrester were old Chicago buddies and had known each other for over fifteen years. Fitzgerald had been Chicago's Chief of Detectives when Forrester convinced him to join him in Las Vegas as his right hand man. Fitzgerald had his twenty years in, and no family to speak of so he took an early retirement and made the move.

He had not regretted it, and he was the perfect man to watch his friend's back. From all he'd heard, Brian had Adam Forrester pegged as a man of character and integrity. But then again, when it came time for show and tell you discovered a lot of surprising things about a person's true colors.

Fitzgerald had said on previous occasions that he was concerned because he thought Forrester might have made some enemies by refusing to play ball with the unions.

One thing was certain. Adam Forrester didn't back down when he had the hammer. He was a man of his word and he expected you to be the same.

He'd had run ins with the Culinary Union, some independent contractors and the Teamsters in his four years in Vegas, but all of those battles had been resolved. And in each of the skirmishes Adam Forrester had come out a little the worse for wear, but clearly the victor.

Maybe someone was jealous.

He was a shrewd businessman who knew how to turn a buck, and he had a hot young wife who looked as good in neon as she did in a bikini.

"Any chance your problem ties into the murder of that Colossus employee a couple months ago? You know, the guy they found in his car?"

"Who the hell knows? Fitzgerald said roughly. His friend's frustration was evident. "In light of what I know now, I can't rule it out. His name was Jimmy Santo. He was our graveyard cage manager."

"I didn't know him well, but he seemed like an okay guy."

"Anybody do a background check on him?" Brian asked. "I mean after the homicide. Could be he was into something that went sour."

"I'll look into it," Fitzgerald said, jotting it in a notebook.

"Cops wrote that off as a car jacking gone wrong. Maybe it was more than that," Brian suggested.

"At the time I had no reason to question that theory," Fitzgerald said as the lines on his forehead deepened." Maybe it's just a coincidence…"

Both of them knew it wasn't.

T.J. Fitzgerald's voice trailed off.

By nature he was an extremely cautious guy. If he admitted to having a hunch, chances were he had more than circumstantial evidence. T.J. Fitzgerald didn't believe in coincidences and neither did Brian.

Fitzgerald hadn't mentioned the mob in so many words but the implication was clear. And if some Eastern or Midwest crime syndicate had its fingers in the pie Fitzgerald had good reason to be concerned

The mob wasn't visible in Vegas the way it was in the 70's and 80's, but it was still a big part of the town. Once upon a time nearly every Vegas hotel had a tie in with organized crime.

But corporations had changed the look of Vegas. Howard Hughes and his Summa Corporation had started the clean-up trend in the mid 70's when he bought the Desert Inn, Frontier, Landmark and Sands in one fell swoop.

Hughes treated Las Vegas like a Monopoly game and the gaming control board was so anxious to have him as a property owner, it bent over backwards to expedite his licensing every time he got a hair up his ass to buy another hotel. After all, the eccentric little trillionaire was doing what the sheriff, the gaming control board and the feds had been unwilling or unable to do—take control away from the mob.

In the early days, skimming was a way of life, and all the families understood that stealing their own money was as close as they'd ever get to being legitimate. And with all that cash on a daily basis it was easy to launder in East Coast profits from numbers, prostitution, loan sharking and drugs.

Brian had also seen the explosion in machines, especially video poker and high-end slots. In the seventies and eighties slots were almost exclusively a woman's domain. Now even the high rollers went for the slots, which was okay with the hotels. Many properties had knocked out their showrooms or lounges to add high-end slot areas featuring $25, $100 and $500 machines. Neighborhood bars, pizza joints and grocery stores all had slots. A carton of milk, a loaf of bread and a roll of quarters were the order of the day. And why not?

Machines never called in sick, didn't require twenty-minute breaks every hour, didn't need days off to take their kids to a doctor's appointment, didn't bitch about the health and dental coverage or ask for raises. All they did was work 24 hours a day, everyday, never complain and never threaten to join a union.

"I'd like you to start your own unofficial investigation," Fitzgerald said, zeroing in on the point of their meeting. "I don't want this to turn into something really nasty. At least not without us being prepared.

"And if you do come up with something, anything, don't discuss it on the phone. I'm not sure my phone at the hotel is secure."

That got Brian's attention. Once again he didn't ask for details but he filed it in his memory bank.

"Want something hon?" It was Shauna making the rounds.

"Just a bottle of water," Fitzgerald said softly, the gold wedding band on his left hand shining as it caught the sunlight. His wife had been dead nearly five years but Brian had never seen him without it. It was the only jewelry he wore.

He was a good-looking man, a shade over six-foot with graying temples and an easy smile on his youthful looking face. Brian figured Fitzgerald to be in his mid 50's but it was hard to tell from his physique. Fitzgerald worked out in the Colossus health club religiously, played squash and a little basketball in addition to jogging. He also had a black belt in karate.

"Okay. I'll get on it Fitz. Let's see what I can dig up. Give me a few days."

They sat for a few more minutes making small talk, Brian promising to advise Fitzgerald if he got wind of anything, then they parted. T.J. Fitzgerald made his way to the hotel's North entrance while Brian headed for valet parking at the main entrance.

His cell phone had been vibrating sporadically for the last 20 minutes but he had ignored it, choosing to let his voice mail take messages rather than risk disrupting his conversation with Fitzgerald.

Brian paused for a moment near the Mirage registration desk to check his messages.

A pretty young girl with a push-up bra and a Colgate smile was punching information into a computer while an incoming couple waited at her check-in station.

Computers were the new Vegas. Brian had been around long enough to remember when hotels didn't have computers to check you in or tell a pit boss how long you'd been playing or to chart your average bet.

Veteran pit guys always kept it in their heads. Nowadays if a small bettor asked for a lunch comp, a pit clerk had to check his computer rating to see if his play warranted a freebie. And front desk clerks didn't always have PC's to let them know when the rooms were ready. In the early days the maids just called down after they finished changing the sheets and sweeping out the heartaches.

Brian's burgundy Seville was right up front when he walked out, having been pulled to the side by the valet kid. Thank God there were still a few perks that came with having been in Vegas for two decades.

The Caddy was one of his most cherished possessions. He had bought it "right", getting something of an insider deal through a dealer pal, Tony Clausi, a throwback old country Paisan who spoke softly, wore French cuffs and had been married for 45 years to a woman who had never driven a car. Tony C. was more Italian than spaghetti.

He waited as a throng of passersby walked against the light, hustling to get to the front of the Mirage in time to see the volcano erupt with simulated molten lava cascading across the water. It was a novel and spectacular little sideshow, which ran every fifteen minutes between 6 p.m. and midnight, and it always slowed Strip traffic to a crawl as drivers jockeyed for a spot close to the curb to get a better view.

On a whim Brian veered the Caddy into the Caesars Palace entryway, hoping one of his contacts there might have a tip on the Colossus situation.

David Copperfield's name almost shouted at him from the freestanding marquee, the black 12-foot letters filling the entire sign.

The seductive beckoning of the blue-green indirect lighting made the hotel look like a huge phosphorescent spaceship glowing temptingly in the dark. Caesars had undergone an 18 month $100 million makeover in an effort to keep pace with the new megaresorts and the result was spectacular.

Brian walked past Cleopatra's Barge, a scaled down version of an actual Egyptian ship moored in a few feet of water just steps away from the gaming tables. It was a popular bar and dance spot for hotel guests because of its motif and the fact management kept it stocked with live bands and plenty of pretty faces. The Barge didn't attract many locals though, because at $7.50 per, the price was a lot stronger than the drinks.

He was looking for Earl, a security guard and long time friend to pick his brain.

A moment later he spotted Earl's slick black hair near the casino cage.

A wide smile engulfed Earl Ray Bonner's face as Brian moved toward him.

"What's happening partner? Where you been keeping yourself?'

"Here, there and everywhere," Brian responded as he shook Earl's hand.

"How are the girls?" Brian asked, well aware that any mention of Earl's 10-year old twins might cause his friend to start extolling their virtues.

"They're wonderful. The light of my life," the guard replied. "Here's the latest picture."

Without looking up from the snapshot Brian went right to the reason he was there.

"You heard anything about some out of town hustlers trying some funny business at the Colossus?"

"You never were one to pull any punches, "Earl answered, shifting from one foot to the other.

"They're becoming seriously cute," he said, handing the photo back to the guard.

"I've heard bits and pieces," Earl said in a near whisper. "And I also heard a rumor that something big was coming down real soon. But you know how people talk. Nothing concrete. Just talk on the street."

"No names?"

"None that I remember."

It wasn't much help.

"I did eavesdrop a few words from a couple of muscle-types jawing in one of our bars about a week ago that could tie in…"

Brian arched his eyebrows.

"I didn't pay it much mind because it was so off the wall. Besides, how would guys like that come to get any real inside information? According to the way they were talking the Colossus was either going up for sale or somehow about to change hands. Any truth to that?"

"Not to my knowledge," Brian said honestly. "I don't think that's going to happen."

"That's good, because I've heard the man in charge over there is a pretty stand-up guy. What's more the Colossus hired a couple friends of mine recently."

Brian was ready to move on.

"These guys looked like goons in suits," Earl remembered. "I figured they were just flapping their lips. Trying to act like big shots to impress somebody. Hell, they were yapping like the Colossus changing hands was a done deal. Sounded like so much bullshit to me."

"Thanks Earl. Do me a favor and stay alert. Anything you hear call me. Even if you don't think it means much. Run it by me."

"I will if you promise to not be a stranger."

"Put this in a piggy bank for the twins," he said, handing Earl a small brown envelope with a Ben Franklin inside.

"You know you don't have to…"

"I know pal. That's exactly why I do it. Besides, it's not for you. It's for them, from Uncle Brian."

"Something else on your mind?" Brian asked, sensing there was something Earl wanted to say.

"Nah, nothing I can't handle, I guess," Earl answered, leaving Brian an opening.

It took another minute or so of coaxing before Earl got enough guts to tell Brian his dilemma.

He was into a bookie for $4500 and he was getting some heat. The mope had made a passing reference to Earl's kids and the guard was more than a little shook up.

"I'll have a word with him," Brian promised after Earl gave him the bookie's name.

"If it's too much trouble, don't worry about it. I'll work it out," Earl said, hoping Brian wouldn't back off.

"I'll take care of it," Brian said strongly. "Relax".

"Thanks."

Minutes later he was cruising along the now glittering Strip, headed for his home in Green Valley, an affluent suburb in the Southeast part of Vegas.

He had a three-bedroom 2500 square foot home with a loft that he used for an office, a pool and a spa and he had bought it for $150,000 two years earlier. In

LA or San Francisco you couldn't buy a one-car garage for a hundred and fifty-grand.

Earl Ray's problem was a no-brainer.

The bookie was obviously a small time independent operator. Connected guys never threatened your family. Fact was, once they made up their minds there was nothing left to talk about. Three o'clock in the morning was their time.

And you never saw it coming.

Brian made two phone calls, giving the bookie's number to the second man he spoke to.

"Make a settlement or make it go away, as a favor to me," he said to the voice on the phone.

"You got it. Tell your friend it's done."

Earl might have to fork over five hundred as a token for the reaching out, but he wouldn't be bothered anymore.

"Thanks."

"Fagetaboutit. I still owe you plenty."

Earl's problem was over, but the Colossus situation was the pisser.

T.J. Fitzgerald would have known if Adam Forrester had any thoughts of putting the Colossus on the market. That wasn't the kind of thing you kept from your right hand man. And he couldn't imagine anything Adam Forrester couldn't share with Fitzgerald.

Unless, of course...

He wasn't ready yet to consider Forrester being part of the problem. But money made people do some strange things. And fifty million a year wasn't just money. It was fuck you money. Tax free fuck you money and plenty of it.

Brian wondered if the Colossus was doing as well as people thought. The books wouldn't tell him. He'd have to find out another way.

More questions than answers. Two of his friends with their tit in a wringer. Not exactly the way Brian wanted to end his day, or his vacation. Especially when some of the answers might have some ominous overtones.

Chances are it was an independent gang working with a well-placed insider, somebody like a cage supervisor or shift boss. It could possibly have been mob connected, but there was no buzz on the street.

No matter which scenario was correct, for three or four mil a month the culprits were not going to go quietly into the night.

There were going to be some casualties. He was sure of that.

Chapter 2
Tiffany

"The black one or the green one?"

Tiffany was holding a long strapless black dress against her near perfectly shaped body as she turned to face her friend.

"They're both pretty hot," Valerie said admiringly, "but I think the green works better because it matches your eyes. Of course if you wear the black one the contrast will make them stand out."

"Thanks for nothing Val," she said with a smile. "You're certainly no help."

"What are friends for?"

Valerie Rogers and Tiffany Wayne were more than just friends. They worked together, shared each other's most intimate secrets and treated each other like sisters, although neither had a real life sibling.

And despite their common interests they had come from completely different backgrounds.

Val was a short, average looking girl with shoulder length red hair, a loosely connected network of freckles, which she hated, and an open all-American smile. She considered herself well adjusted despite the fact she had just celebrated her thirtieth birthday and had never been involved in a serious relationship.

Her parents were hardworking people born and raised in Des Moines and who still lived there. They ran a hardware store, attended church every Sunday, were outraged by the lyrics in rap music, still believed Lee Harvey Oswald acted alone and were convinced everything they read in the newspaper was true.

"They couldn't print it if it was a lie," was her mother's stock answer any time Val had challenged something that sounded illogical.

She had given up trying to change their opinions when she was sixteen.

Val had attended Northwestern thanks to a scholarship she won through the Des Moines Chamber of Commerce. She had begun as a political science major, switched to fashion design her sophomore year and graduated at the top of her class two years later.

At 31, Tiffany was a year older than Val and well on her way to making a name for herself in the designer eat designer fashion world.

She was sometimes mistaken for one of the models at the fashion shows she attended, but she knew if anyone looked real close they'd realize she wasn't as tall nor as anorexic as many of the runway queens.

Tiffany stood 5'7 in her stocking feet and weighed a proportionate 120, but it was her long dark hair and sparkling green eyes that drew the most attention.

And now she was suddenly one of the hottest designers in the country. People Magazine had done a short profile of her in a recent issue, mentioning her in the same company as Liz Claiborne and Donna Karan. It was heady stuff but she was determined not to let the recognition change her outlook and focus.

If anyone knew how quickly dreams could be shattered, she was the one.

Once upon a time she thought she had an idyllic existence. Her parents were a storybook couple. She had attended the best private prep and finishing schools, then moved on to Vassar where she was class valedictorian. She had majored in fashion, and by graduation time had offers from most of the top designers in the field.

That was eight years ago and her life had taken some fast and depressing directions since. *Growing up* her shrink had called it, but Tiffany wondered how many girls grew up under similar circumstances.

First, her parents "perfect" marriage collapsed without warning, her father announcing he wanted out, lamely claiming the relationship had become stale. He said he was dying a slow death and needed something different.

His remedy turned out to be a sexy thirty- year old redhead with the kind of body usually found splashed across the pages of Playboy.

Tiffany had pleaded with him at first, but Adam Forrester was too blinded by lust to listen to his twenty-six year old daughter accuse him of having a mid-life crisis and his new girlfriend of being a gold digger. Embarrassment also played a part.

He could not look her in the eye and face up to an affair with a woman just four years older than his own daughter. Tiffany had idolized her father. He had always been there for her. Been her biggest supporter and she his biggest fan. He was 54, a self-made billionaire in the stock market, and had always been her white knight. Her hero. That image was forever tarnished by the divorce, and both knew their relationship and trust would never be the same.

She was hurt and confused, her innocence lost and her secure world invaded.

But her pain was nothing compared to her mother's.

Adam and Susan Forrester had been married for thirty two years, and Tiffany had suspected her father of having had an affair on more than one occasion, but had never confronted him. If her mother knew, she never let on.

Tiffany was quite certain Susan Forrester had never been unfaithful, and she had probably never known another man. Which is why her husband's surprise revelation of ennui and the subsequent divorce struck her like a bolt of lightning.

She didn't even have a clue their marriage was in trouble.

After a little publicized whirlwind split, Susan Forrester found herself alone and humiliated. Even the huge financial settlement could not assuage the ache that ravished her body. Her life had been devastated.

She retreated into a quiet isolation, consistently finding excuses to beg off from involvement with the many social clubs and charities she had once enjoyed so much. She stopped returning calls to her friends, choosing instead to spend her days and nights in a self-imposed solitaire.

Following graduation Tiffany signed on with the New York Design House but returned to Chicago within three months of her parents' divorce. Somehow she managed to talk her way into a position with the Chicago Fashion Institute. The hours were flexible enough to allow her to visit her mother almost every day, dutifully bringing a smile and words of encouragement, even though she still could not understand her father's selfishness and lack of loyalty.

And every day she and her mother acted out their own two-person play.

She, pretending to be oblivious to her father's absence, her mother living out the ruse that she was doing well and getting on with her life. Those were lies neither of them dared address.

After a few weeks Tiffany cut her visits down to twice a week, feeling secure enough to talk to her mother on the phone the other days.

Putting a life back together was a slow process, especially in this case, but Tiffany was confident her mother was making normal progress.

Her father offered no help, and Tiffany made no attempt to contact him. Her feelings for him ran deep, but she knew she could never forgive him.

She learned of his comings and goings through the business section of the Chicago Tribune and was mildly shocked to read that he had liquidated many of his holdings and was planning to build a casino in Las Vegas.

Tiffany was intrigued because her father had never been a gambler and to the best of her knowledge had seldom if ever been to Las Vegas.

Absently she wondered about his motivation for a new start in the west, assuming it was the influence of his new companion, Diana Carter. There had even been a picture of the two of them in the Living section of the newspaper one Wednesday.

"If Judas were a woman it would be Diana," she fumed as she tossed the paper in the trash.

Four months later an article in the society section gave details of the marriage of one Adam Forrester to a Ms. Diana Carter. There was even a picture of the newlyweds emerging from "The Little White Chapel", a microwave marriage factory in the heart of the Las Vegas strip.

They were probably married by an Elvis clone in a white jumpsuit, Tiffany thought, and she knew she was just trying to fend off the sadness she felt in the pit of her stomach.

Two days after learning of her ex-husband's marriage, Susan Forrester committed suicide, taking an overdose of the drugs doctors had prescribed to help see her through the lonely days and emptier nights.

When her father was a no show at the funeral, Tiffany decided to legally change her name from Forrester to Wayne, taking her mother's maiden name. She did it out of spite and she vowed to have nothing more to do with her father.

His being in Vegas kept him from being a part of her life but she could never really put him out of her mind no matter how hard she tried. At least not at first. As the years passed he became less and less a part of her conscious thoughts.

Supposedly he was out of the country on his honeymoon and unable to be contacted. By the time word of Susan's death reached him on a remote island in Tahiti, the funeral was over.

Tiffany blamed and hated him for everything.

Ron Delpit

"You have some damn nerve calling two days after she's buried." She could remember the words, and her anger as if it were yesterday. She had literally spat the words into the phone when her father had called.

"You killed her, just as surely as if you had shoved the pills down her throat. You killed her the day you left."

She had never before dared speak to her father so disrespectfully, but the anger kept boiling over and she had no control. He did not try to respond or make her see his side, choosing silence as she vented her fury.

"She was as good as dead from the moment you walked out. I can't believe you were so selfish," she wept. *"I hope your girlfriend was worth it. I don't ever want to speak to you again..."*

"Tiffany, I'm so sorr...."

She heard him mumbling some feeble response as she moved the phone from her ear and placed it softly in the cradle, feeling as though a burden had been lifted. Her own strength and rage stunned her.

Tiffany had no idea why those heartbreaking memories were forcing their way into her thoughts on this day but she couldn't keep them from coming. It had been years and she had tried hard not to think about any of it. Not thinking and not remembering forced her to block out a sizable part of her past, but it was the only way she could breathe. The only way she could survive.

A strong breeze rattled the large, sliding glass door leading to the condo's terrace, and the force of it snapped Tiffany out of her melancholy flashback.

She and Val both looked up with wrinkled brows.

"Wow," that was pretty strong.

"Well I hope it dies down some tonight," said Tiffany, "otherwise my hair will be blowing all over the place."

"I'm sure it'll calm down, Valerie said reassuringly. "It has to. Mother Nature knows this is the night for Chicago's famous *Friends of the Arts Ball* and she knows anybody who's anybody in this town will be there. You don't think she'd be brazen enough to mess with all you VIP's, do you?"

Tiffany feigned a hurt look, pretending to be offended by Val's sarcasm, and her friend took the bait.

"Only kidding Tiff, but you know it's true. Even Mother Nature would have to think twice about raining on this parade."

Tiffany knew Val was right.

The *Friends of the Arts Ball* was Chicago's most prestigious social affair and it raised more than $2 million every year for the city's cultural arts programs.

She had been to the black tie event once before, when she was married to Dr. Jack Davenport, but the invitation was in his name and she was his guest. Since their divorce the invitations had slowed to a trickle and then stopped.

This time it was very special. She had been invited on her own merit, as Ms. Tiffany Wayne, Fashion Designer.

20

Her marriage had lasted three years and the thing she remembered most about it was not inviting her father to the ceremony. *Let him read about it in the papers like I did when he got married. Let him hurt like I do and like my mother did.*

Walter Thurston, her father's lawyer and her godfather, gave her away.

The failure of her own marriage was sobering and on lonely nights she wondered if it had been destined to fail. Had she expected too much? Had she given too little? Was she trying to compensate for the loss of both of her parents?

She still didn't know the answers, but she had learned there was more to a marriage than met the eye because everyone who knew them thought she and Jack were the perfect couple. However, at home, alone in the living room and between the sheets something was missing. There was no spark, no passion.

But Jack Davenport was not totally devoid of emotion. He had a passion for his work and more passion than he should have for one of the hospital's bottle blonde nurses who was more than willing to sample the good doctor's bedside manner.

The affair, which she learned of by accident, was the first crack in her "happily ever after marriage". Jack fell off the fidelity wagon at least twice more that she knew of and it was more than she could handle.

His "Sorry" was getting a little hard to swallow and it was she who finally uttered the "D" word and he didn't object.

It hurt, but it hurt more to be played for a fool. To smell another woman on his body or to try and pretend she believed his lies. They tried separation and it didn't work. Eight months later they were divorced.

She didn't regret her split with Jack, but she had often prayed that she could learn to forgive her father. She had come to terms with it all and she wanted to talk it out with him and move on. She wanted to tell him that she still loved him despite the pain she had endured. There was no way she could deny that. Life truly was a bitch.

"I must tell him," she promised herself on the day her divorce became final. "It's been long enough and we've both suffered enough." But two years had passed since she made the silent vow and pride had kept them at arm's length.

Adam Forrester was one up on her though, because he sent birthday and Christmas cards without fail. Like clockwork they always arrived on time, serving as a visible reminder that he had not forgotten her.

Subconsciously, it was reassuring to know he was still out there, caring about her, but she never responded. She didn't think she ever could and the more time that elapsed the more difficult it was to remember things about him. Like the sound of his voice, the curve of his chin and his disarming smile.

She wondered how much he had changed.

"God, look at the time. I have to be going Tiff." Valerie was already scurrying around looking for her coat.

"Call and tell me about it when you get home, no matter how late," Val pleaded. "I want to know every detail. And don't hoard all the interesting bachelors."

"I'm not going with men on my mind," Tiffany said, feigning indifference.

"Besides, you know the kind of men who usually show up for these things."

"Yes I do," Val giggled. "Rich".

"Old and usually married," Tiffany deadpanned while handing Valerie her coat and shooing her out the door. Her invitation had said "and guest" but she and Val agreed that if they went together people would assume they were either losers who couldn't get dates or lesbians. It was a no win situation.

Tiffany wasn't accustomed to attending major events unescorted and might have skipped this one if not for her friend's constant nagging. Eventually, she had become excited about it and was looking forward to the evening.

She glanced at the clock on the mantel above the fireplace. It was only 2:30 so she had time to take a short nap before getting ready. Before lying down she walked to the dining room table and re-checked the invitation for the umpteenth time.

"Cocktails from 6 to 8. Dinner to follow. Black Tie required."

She'd start getting herself together about 4:30 and leave the house about 6:15. She wanted to arrive at the Governor's Mansion around seven. Never let them know you're anxious.

She crossed the living room and straightened the throw pillows on the sofa. Through the double-paned terrace door she could see sailboats on Lake Michigan, their sails and flags whipping in the howling wind. Twelve stories below Lakeshore Drive stretched out as far as the eye could see.

The condo had been a smart investment even though the $300,000 price tag seemed a bit steep at the time. She had taken her share of the proceeds from the sale of the house she and Jack had owned and plunked it down on the place fifteen minutes after seeing it.

Walter Thurston had handled the paper work after re-assuring her that it was a sound business decision. It was the first major purchase she had made on her own.

Two bedrooms and a loft, high beam ceilings, a gas fireplace, plenty of closet space, formal dining room and one of the most breathtaking views in all of Chicago.

Surprisingly, despite her bundled up anxieties she had little trouble falling asleep once she curled up on her king-sized four-poster bed. She tugged the pink and white comforter up around her neck and slept soundly.

Tiffany awoke refreshed and relaxed with nothing but a long soak in a deliciously hot bubble bath on her mind. As she sat up she had a fuzzy reflection of her dream. Parts of it remained very vivid even though like most dreams the storyline was jumbled.

Everything seemed to run together. Her mother, her honeymoon with Jack, the bitter arguments that ruined their marriage, and her father. Mostly her father.

Suddenly it was important for her to make peace with him. She wanted that.

The shrill noise of the alarm startled her, turning off her thoughts as if they were a bad TV movie. She was thrust back into the present. It was 4:20, time to get ready.

The phone interrupted her trek to the bathroom but she managed to start the bath water before answering it on the third ring. It was Walter.

"And to what do I owe this unexpected treat?" she teased.

"Margaret insisted I call to be sure you were still going to the Ball and to see if you wanted us to swing by and pick you up."

She had known Walter Thurston her entire life. He had been her lawyer for the past three years and both friend and legal counsel to her family for more than three decades.

Walter would have been a Hollywood casting director's dream lawyer. He was tall, with broad shoulders; heavy eyebrows and the kind of open face that inspired trust from the moment you laid eyes on him.

Tiffany had once described him as a cross between the Perry Mason of black and white TV and Gerry Spence, the buckskin clad dispenser of provincial wisdom.

Walter always wore dark suits and his large, powerful hands were soft and fleshy, and he was instantly recognizable by his old leather briefcase. It had been a Christmas present from her father some twenty years earlier.

"I'm definitely going," she said, letting her jeans fall to the bathroom floor. "But I've already made arrangements for a ride," she fibbed.

"Thanks for checking on me though, and I hope you'll save me a dance." She wriggled out of her panties and turned off the water.

"You've got a date young lady, he said sounding very pleased.

"Margaret is looking forward to seeing you too.

"I'm really glad you decided to accept this invitation," he said more soberly.

"There'll be a lot of city leaders and VIP's at this thing and it won't hurt to have them meet you in person."

"You point them out to me Walter, and I'll take it from there."

For a moment she wondered why she had lied to Walter about having a ride, then realized it was because she didn't want to be stuck at the Ball and Walter always seemed to be among the last to leave.

As one of Chicago's most celebrated criminal attorneys he was a popular conversationalist and seemed to enjoy the rare gatherings where he was not the keynote speaker or guest of honor.

She would take a cab, and if the Thurstons noticed she would make some excuse about her ride failing to show. She certainly didn't want to hurt their feelings. She loved them both and considered them her only family.

She smoothed her dress one last time, turned out all the lights except for one over the stove in the kitchen and headed out the door. She had, in the end, opted for the emerald green gown. It was floor length and cut just low enough to turn a few heads. She carried a small matching purse and a drop cluster diamond necklace that had belonged to her mother set off the outfit.

Tiffany alit from the taxi at precisely seven o'clock after having made the driver double back when she thought she caught sight of Walter's car.

A tuxedoed doorman who barely glanced at her invitation escorted her up the walkway into the mansion's foyer.

At the coatroom she literally bumped into Oprah Winfrey who had handed her coat to the attendant and made a wide turn preparing to enter the main room.

The ballroom was alive with the buzz of voices from every corner of the enormous room. There were small groups of people everywhere.

Governor Grant Alworth and his wife Alicia were flitting from one conversation to another, politicking she assumed, even though he had an incredible approval rating and re-election was still two years away. Tiffany recognized them from television, and having seen them so often she felt as if she knew them.

Waiters and waitresses moved efficiently through the crowd offering champagne and hors d'oeuvres. Bartenders in red vests with white ruffled shirts and black bow ties were busily serving cocktails from portable bars in strategic locales. Long decorative tables, overflowing with gourmet foods ranging from Russian caviar to roast duck were sprinkled throughout the room.

Republican Senator Everett Dawson was holding court to her left and Tiffany wondered if the gossip about him being a womanizer was true. He was single but the press had no conscience when it came to digging for dirt on potential Oval Office tenants.

Dawson was tall, handsome and popular, but after the way the GOP had skewered Bill Clinton with zippergate, a Republican candidate would have to be as clean as church linen to stand a chance.

He looked up and caught her staring, and she returned his smile. What else was a girl to do?

Engrossed in small talk in other mini-arenas were notables such as Martha Stewart, advice columnist Ann Landers, designer Tommy Hilfiger and late night talk show host David Letterman.

She had not yet spied Walter or Margaret.

As she panned the crowd again, she spotted Margaret in the far north corner near the piano. Their eyes seemed to come together at the same moment and the older woman made an almost imperceptible motion encouraging Tiffany to join her.

Tiffany felt relieved. Now she would at least have a starting point to begin mingling and learning the players.

As she neared Margaret, Tiffany saw Walter, busy swapping stories with film critic Roger Ebert along with Chicago Mayor Richard Daley and a man whose face she recognized but whose name she could not recall. Fortunately Walter saved her from committing a faux pas, offering the names of his immediate circle of friends first.

"Tiffany, I'd like you to meet Roger Ebert and His Honor, Mayor Daley." The third member of Walter's select little circle was none other than Federal Reserve Chairman Alan Greenspan and she laughed at herself for not recognizing him immediately. With the Stock Market at the top of the news everyday, Greenspan's image should have been as recognizable as George Washington's.

The high and the mighty seemed drawn to Walter, which was the primary reason he had been approached so often to run for office himself. Always he had refused, claiming he would rather leave the political arena to younger, more aggressive seekers.

Privately, Margaret confided it was because he dreaded the travel, high profile and strain on his private life that would accompany public service.

"Besides, this way I can keep both my Democratic and Republican friends," he had joked.

Margaret was as comfortable socially as her husband and she was on a first name basis with most of the rich and famous. With Margaret and Walter as her chaperones, Tiffany didn't for a moment feel awkward or intimidated, although later in the evening when designer Liz Claiborne complimented her on her gown, she felt herself blush.

Val had been right. The place dripped of money, but it also sizzled with energy. These were Chicago's movers and shakers, the people who made the city hum.

"Tiffany Wayne, I'd like you to meet Roger Sanderson, Director of the Chicago Museum of Fine Art."

Margaret was effusive in her introduction and the twinkle in her eyes told Tiffany that the gentleman was single, well heeled and eligible.

Roger was tall, with wavy brown hair and a small little cleft in his chin that reminded her of a young Kirk Douglas. Tiffany figured he was in his mid to late 30s.

Not bad Margaret. Certainly an impressive start.

When Margaret drifted off, Tiffany found herself alone with Roger, which she surprisingly found herself not minding. She had expected to be gun shy in a one on one situation but this was different. He was not trying to hit on her and she did not feel pressured.

Their conversation was still in the 'nice party...would you like a drink...are you here alone' stage when they were interrupted by a trio of guests intent on getting Roger's attention.

"Hello Roger." A thin, balding man with a thick British accent was smiling at Sanderson.

"And who is this lovely lady you are so obviously trying to keep to yourself?"

Roger shifted his weight, and she sensed he would have preferred that the two of them had gotten a chance to get better acquainted, but the intrusion gave them both some breathing room.

"Tiffany, this is Sir William Judson, Director of the Chicago Ballet Company," he said evenly. "Sir William...Tiffany Wayne. Miss Wayne is a fashion designer, and from what I can gather, a very fine one."

"I'm sure she is," he said sincerely. "Anyone so beautiful must be successful."

She couldn't tell if Sir William was being facetious or speaking without thinking. She decided to accept the compliment and not over analyze.

"Now that we've been introduced, I'd like you to meet my friends," Sir William continued.

"This is Jennifer Laredo and the man with the perfect tan is her escort, Johnny Marciano. Johnny is one of the Ballet Company's biggest supporters."

"Pleased to meet you," she said, addressing the threesome.

The heat from Johnny Marciano's eyes bored a hole through her body to her soul. He wasn't looking at her lustfully yet she suddenly felt as if she were naked.

Slowly she moved her hand to straighten her gown, doing so mainly to break the spell of his gaze, and to be sure she was, in fact, still clothed. It was as if he had invaded her.

For an instant she felt as if he had slipped inside her skin and was clinging to her like the ivy vines clung to the walls of Wrigley Field. He had effortlessly penetrated the façade she so often donned in public.

Men had looked at her like that before and she had stared back so vacantly she had immediately diffused their passion. With Johnny Marciano it was different. Something had stirred inside. Something very primal and something she had managed to keep suppressed for a very long time.

"You're acting like a schoolgirl," she admonished herself silently.

A guy looks you up and down and you come apart. Pull yourself together.

Outwardly she showed no emotion, her practiced "Nice to meet you" line uttered dispassionately in an attempt to conceal the sensation that roared through her entire body. But he sensed it. She knew he did and it made her uneasy.

"Johnny is on the Board of Directors of the Ballet," Sir William continued. His comment broke the spell and was a welcome interruption.

"And Miss Laredo is one of the most sought after models in the fashion business," Sir William added, almost as an afterthought. Tiffany surmised his compliments were for the sole purpose of playing up to Johnny Marciano.

Tiffany recognized Jennifer instantly. Her picture was everywhere. She had been Sports Illustrated's Swimsuit cover model the year before, and on at least a dozen other major magazine covers since.

"It's a pleasure to meet you," Tiffany said sincerely. "You're even more stunning in person than in the pictures I've seen of you." Jennifer accepted the compliment graciously, looking Tiffany directly in the eyes. They were like two cowboys sizing each other up prior to a quick draw duel.

"If you designed the dress you're wearing I'd certainly like to see some of your other creations," said Jennifer, and when she tilted her head a certain way Tiffany could see why the woman was so popular.

Laredo had nearly perfect features including flawless skin, long blonde hair and lips so pouty they made Angelina Jolie's look thin. Tiffany wondered if they had been artificially injected. Her eyes were piercing, almost hypnotic. Quite a package.

If Jennifer noticed the eye contact Tiffany had shared with Johnny moments earlier, she didn't let on. Maybe she had just tagged along with Johnny so he had a date at the party.

Righto dreamer. Better think again..Or maybe, with her looks she wasn't accustomed to her dates looking up, down and through other women. Whatever.

She found herself hoping that Johnny and Jennifer were not a hot item, and if she didn't find out for herself tonight, she's ask Val to make a few discreet calls to friends in the modeling world.

For God's sake Tiffany, you don't even know the man...

Johnny was suave with Hollywood good looks, East Coast manners and a tan that certainly hadn't come from the artificial light of some tanning booth.

"He's too good to be true," she thought." Now what's wrong with this picture?"

A minute or two later Sir William, Johnny and Jennifer moved on and she was again alone with Roger Sanderson. He turned out to be a charming talker, with a staccato wit and an engaging smile. She liked him, but he was no Johnny Marciano.

Adlai Stevenson Jr. acknowledged Roger with a quick hello as he headed for the latest group Walter was entertaining, and the party moved on wonderfully. She was glad she'd come.

About time you got out and socialized some," *she scolded herself.* She hadn't realized what a hermit she had become. It had been four months since her last real date. Ridiculous.

She parted from Roger, separating herself on the grounds that she had to locate Margaret and find the powder room, but only after promising Sanderson the last dance of the evening and giving him her phone number. It was the first time she'd done that in a long, long time.

27

Shortly after midnight she began to deflate, having met at least 30 new faces, smiled all the smiles she had in her for one evening and danced until her feet hurt. She was silently thankful when Margaret convinced the honorable Mr. Thurston that it was time to make an exit.

She had agreed to accept a ride home with the Thurstons, seeing no good reason she should have to cab it back in the chill of the night. She had shared intimate glimpses of her life, career and future plans with at least a dozen people and in turn listened attentively to their stories of family and business accomplishments.

All in all it was a most enjoyable evening and some of the connections she'd made had the promise and potential to become valuable assets to her blossoming career.

And Valerie would be proud of her. She had given a very eligible bachelor her phone number and had a good time. She wasn't so sure she'd tell her about Johnny Marciano.

"Are you very tired, Tiff?"

It was a leading question and she knew Walter had a reason for asking.

The dark blue Lincoln Continental was kicking up fragments of gravel as he maneuvered it out of the driveway of the Governor's estate and turned left onto the icy street.

"To tell you the truth Walter, I am a bit pooped," she admitted, "but it was a fantastic party."

"Well, if you can summon up a little more energy I can promise you the best cup of Irish coffee you've ever had, "the lawyer said pleadingly. "And before Margaret can put the kibosh on the idea, I'll take a solemn oath we won't stay more than an hour.

"Sir William and some of the other guests from the Ball are going to stop by the Oak Room for a quick nightcap and I promised we'd join them if you girls weren't too beat."

She was drained, and the idea of going to the Oak Room seemed anti-climactic, however she didn't want to be a stick in the mud and it was her night out. Besides perhaps the suave Mr. Marciano might make an appearance.

"I can handle an hour," she said with genuine enthusiasm. "It should be fun."

"Good for one. And how about you sweetheart?"

"It's fine by me, "Margaret said with mock resignation. "Besides, if I know you, you already told the whole gang we'd be there even if it meant the two of us going back after we took Tiffany home."

Walter didn't contest Margaret's statement. He was pleased his wife knew him so well. And loved him so much. After 36 years she had totally accepted the fact he was a people person.

In the beginning it had been hard for her to share him. She wasn't jealous, and he had never given her reason to be, but she fiercely wanted to protect their privacy and their private time.

Gradually she came to understand how much he loved being surrounded by friends and family, and that having them around only magnified his love for her.

They had no children but lots of nieces and nephews thanks to her two sisters and Walter's three brothers.

To make up for the time he spent at the office and on various boards and charity committees, Walter planned special weekends and vacations for just the two of them.

But even those often disintegrated because he'd make new friends wherever they went and often included them in whatever they were doing. It made her realize her husband's magnetism and his love of life, and along the way she also came to fully understand his love for her. That's what made their marriage special.

The Oak Room was not so much a restaurant and bar as a tradition. In Chicago it was the place to be seen as much as New York's "21" or the Polo Lounge in Beverly Hills.

To an outsider it may not have seemed so impressive, but it was definitely the "in" spot for the rich and famous crowd. It didn't have the latest in art deco, hip music, a fancy menu or a maitre'd you could bribe.

Jimmy Langdon either knew you or you didn't get a table. And he knew everybody he should know including the recently famous and about to be famous. Jimmy read everything and heard everything.

Sometimes he knew company big shots were fired before they knew. He was privy to business mergers, insider stock tips, secret political plots and movie star indiscretions. And he was as trustworthy as a parish priest.

He even recognized Tiffany, which made her feel pretty important, however she knew quite well that if it weren't for Walter she would still have had to wait for a table.

"Hi ya Jimmy, "Walter said in his baritone voice. "Got any seats tonight?"

Jimmy smiled broadly and hugged Walter.

"For you my friend, always. Only I wish you wouldn't make it so long between visits."

The high ceiling to floor oak paneled walls were the mainstay of the décor and they were set off nicely by the lush, forest green carpeting.

The maitre'd escorted them directly to the section being commandeered by Sir William. There were three large round tables set side by side, all occupied by elite stragglers from the Friends of the Arts Ball. Tiffany had met some of them at the Ball and introductions to others were made hastily, with all parties realizing it was probably too late and too impromptu for any of them to remember each other's names.

As they adjusted their seats, Tiffany scanned the group looking for Johnny Marciano. She had presumed if Sir William was present, Johnny and his date would also show. She was glad she was wrong. He wasn't there. She could relax.

The buzz at the table was loud and it seemed like everyone was talking at once.

Sir William's voice seemed to drown out the others.

"Well Helen," he said, his heavy English accent seeming to draw the words out. "It didn't rain on us tonight, but we'd all appreciate it if you could do something about this dreadful wind and cold next year."

Helen Mitchell was the Chief Organizer and Founder of the Ball and its biggest contributor, having seen the project through from a whim to its present status as the crème de la crème of Chicago's fundraising events.

At sixty-four, she was one of the Windy City's wealthiest and most influential widows and the Ball had become her pet project. Rumor had it she personally approved every name on the guest list as well as every item on the menu. Some said she even interviewed the waiters and waitresses insisting that they be clean cut and able to speak English.

No earrings on the guys, no visible tattoos, no chewing gum during the interview and don't be late. She was as strict as a Catholic school nun, and more feared.

There were incredibly few complaints about the autocratic way things were run and none about the money the event raised every year.

"You want me to set it up for the Bahamas or Florida next year?" Helen laughed. "I'm sure that would go over big with the Chicago media."

"Anywhere warmer," someone shouted.

"Palm Springs is warm," another voice offered.

"But there's nothing to do in Palm Springs except look at the sun," a voice at the other end of the table chimed in.

"How about a cruise?" someone else suggested.

"Well maybe the next best thing to having the Friends Ball in a warmer clime would be for our little group to take a short and well deserved vacation each year when it's all over," said Helen more seriously. "We might all benefit from a little R&R and some sunshine."

There was a humming sound around the table as members of the group offered opinions about Helen's suggestion.

She was powerful enough and respected enough to make it happen, and God knew no one was more organized. And every one of them could afford it, no matter what resort they chose.

"What about Vegas?"

The speaker was a large woman sitting across from Tiffany and she had obviously had too much to drink. She was wearing an expensive blue sequined gown, and from Tiffany's vantage point she could clearly see one of the woman's boobs about to pop loose from her dress.

She's in her cups and her cup's about to runneth over, Tiffany thought, and a mental picture of the woman's boob hitting the table in full view of all the wealthy patrons brought a smile to her lips.

Adjusting herself as if she sensed danger, the woman shifted to a more upright position, straightening her dress and avoiding embarrassment.

"Maybe Las Vegas would be nice," Helen Mitchell said in a crisp voice, addressing the issue as if it were a real possibility instead of idle table talk.

"What do you think Walter?"

"I haven't been to Vegas in quite some time, Helen," Walter said without a hint of interest.

"Then perhaps old chap, its high time you consider going again before you get too old to enjoy it in all its decadence", Sir William laughed. "Friends tell me they've built some fabulous hotels in the last couple years and chefs like Wolfgang and Emeril have opened gourmet restaurants there."

"It's always warm in the desert," a man at the far end pitched in.

Tiffany squirmed in her chair. The talk about Vegas had made her slightly uneasy despite the fact no one had asked, nor had she offered an opinion.

"What's the weather like in Vegas this time of year?" asked Roger Sanderson.

"This is March and Vegas is usually rainy this time of year," another partier responded, "but it starts to warm up in April."

Again the assembled members began whispering to their tablemates and Tiffany could almost sense a mass exodus from Chicago's freezing temperatures to the sun and sand of Las Vegas.

"Are you still in touch with your old pal Adam Forrester?"

Tiffany's heart stopped.

The voice was Helen Mitchell's and the question was directed at Walter Thurston. To Tiffany all the other conversations seemed muted as Helen's question hung over their section of the table, virtually demanding an answer.

To her knowledge no one in the group, not even Helen knew that Adam Forrester was her father, and it seemed like an eternity before Walter responded to Helen's inquiry.

The mere mention of his name sent an electric shock crackling up her spine as if someone had touched her foot with a live wire. She had not heard anyone discuss him in years, at least not in public, and it slightly unnerved her. Even Walter and Margaret, despite their interest, steered clear of the subject and out of the feud between she and her father.

Helen did not wait for an answer.

"Do you think he might be able to arrange a block of rooms at his hotel for some of his old pals?"

"Great idea, Helen."

Walter shot Tiffany a perplexed look, raising his right eyebrow just a tad, but enough for her to know he felt badly about the path the conversation had taken.

She looked back at him softly, knowing they were both trapped.

God she hated Vegas.

She had only been there twice, once on a quickie weekend getaway with Jack and she had not enjoyed it. The place had no culture, and was unbearably hot to boot. What's more, there was sand and neon everywhere and no air to breathe.

It was a moment before she realized Roger Sanderson had slipped into the chair next to her after the man who had been sitting there shuffled off to the bathroom.

"Do you like Vegas?" Roger asked softly.

Funny how everyone who enjoyed Las Vegas assumed everyone else had been there.

"I'm not much of a gambler, "she replied, still a bit off balance. Vegas doesn't really appeal to me. If I were to take a vacation I'd rather ski at Vail or Gstaad. If it's sun I'm after, I'll take Tahiti or Jamaica any day."

She was trying to be pleasant with a delicate subject. She had decided on the drive from the Governor's Mansion to the Oak Room that she would attempt to re-open the lines of communication with her father. And that was before any of the talk about Vegas got started so it felt like these people were invading her thoughts.

Tiffany had no idea what she'd say if she saw her father, and at the moment she wasn't anywhere close to admitting to anyone that Adam Forrester was her father. Not yet anyway.

A few minutes later the Friends of the Arts guests began to straggle out of the Oak Room, but only after organizing a committee to explore the possibility of them going to Las Vegas en masse.

In the car, Walter apologized profusely for the indelicate situation and Tiffany assured him she realized it wasn't his fault.

"Its okay Walter," she said downplaying the whole thing. "I suppose it was unavoidable, and I know you would never do anything to make me uncomfortable. And no one there had any idea Adam is my dad.

"I'm all right Walter. Really I am. Besides, I have a sort of confession to make. I've made up my mind to try and make peace with my father, and to quit blaming him for my mother.

"Maybe we've both suffered long enough."

It was the first time she had spoken about her mother out loud and she was amazed she was able to do so with such control.

Maybe it was the alcohol. Four glasses of champagne at the Ball and an Irish coffee at the Oak Room were enough to lower a girl's inhibitions a little.

"That's wonderful Tiffany," and she could hear the excitement in Walter's voice. "I never thought I'd hear you say that. I hoped it, but I never thought I'd actually hear it, or be alive to see it."

"That makes the perfect ending to a perfect evening," Margaret said happily.

"That doesn't mean he'll accept me with open arms after all this time," she added protectively. "He could reject me completely.

"I imagine his life has changed tremendously. He's gone from being a stock market genius in the Midwest to being a novice casino owner in the neon capital of the world.

"And let's not forget there's a new woman in his life."

The last sentence was catty and had slipped out accidentally which definitely meant she had had too much to drink.

"Your father has never stopped loving you Tiffany. And he's never stopped caring about you."

Walter decided it was time for everyone to lay their cards on the table.

"Through the years he's insisted that I keep an eye on you and I can assure you he's extremely proud of your successes.

"His biggest regret is that he's had to experience them vicariously. I am your lawyer, my dear, and your godfather, but I am also your dad's lifelong friend. And in this instance, his eyes. And I will continue to be as long as you both need me."

She had suspected Walter was keeping a watchful eye on her but never accused him of it. Maybe she didn't want to know the answer if he wasn't doing it for her father.

She knew he had important clients and cases and often wondered how he always found the time to handle her menial problems.

And even though Walter hadn't personally been involved, the Chicago papers made no secret of the fact his firm and the managing partner of its Big Apple affiliate, one Lanny Sarno, were the lead defense team for one of Chicago's most violent mobsters.

According to the papers Charlie "Big Chuck" Grunzo was an absolute mortal lock to get life without parole, maybe even the death penalty after he confessed to fourteen brutal contract murders. There was talk he'd pull a Sammy "The Bull" and become an informant and for months that appeared to be his only out.

The betting on the street said Grunzo had a better chance being a corpse than a stoolie. But it never came to that. Grunzo came to his senses, pled not guilty instead of rolling over and the battle was on. Newspaper stories and the radio talk shows were unanimous in their opinion that someone had whispered sweet nothings in Grunzo's hairy ears.

Tiffany paid little attention to the case despite it being in the headlines, and had never even considered asking Walter about it. All of that underworld stuff was totally beyond her comprehension.

But she had read enough to know that Sarno was a slick piece of work. He was a well-schooled criminal trial lawyer who ran Thurston and Associates New York office and the newspaper stories said he had had plenty of success in New York and New Jersey defending upper level mobsters. He had even represented the late John Gotti on a small case during the Teflon Don's early reign of terror.

Tiffany wondered how he and Walter had wound up in bed together but never had the occasion to ask. After all, Sarno worked out of New York and Walter was almost always in Chicago. She assumed the man was a good lawyer and it was just a business relationship.

Sarno turned out to be as good as advertised. Two months into the trial he struck swiftly and lethally, presenting a motion to have "Big Chuck's" confession suppressed on a technicality. It created a furor at City Hall and in the DA's office but the damage was done.

An appellate court upheld the mistrial ruling and Grunzo walked out of court with a smile, and a slate as clean as a grammar school blackboard in the summertime.

In the past eighteen months, Tiffany had genuinely needed Walter's legal advice, and the forming of her own corporation as well as the intricate contracts she sometimes dealt with, required an experienced and trusted eye.

She had insisted on paying Walter's full rate even though she had to go behind his back and threaten his secretary before discovering that his going rate was a hefty $500 an hour.

"If all of that is true then I guess I'm almost ready to join the Vegas Express," she kidded. "That is if it ever gets off the ground."

Walter was eyeing her through the rearview mirror and she grinned back at him, unspoken satisfaction in their eyes.

"I now have the best reason in the world to get the whole thing in motion," he laughed.

"Not too fast though," Tiffany stammered. "I may be mentally ready to do it but emotionally I'm not sure. There's still a lot for me to work out. I think I need a little more time."

"Don't worry about it honey," Margaret sympathized. "No one in that group can up and leave on a moment's notice, no matter how independent they seem. It would take them weeks just to rearrange their schedules. The main thing is you've made up your mind."

"I want it to be a surprise," she said spontaneously. "Don't breathe a word of this to my father. I want to walk into his office at the Colossus and knock his socks off."

"Something like the prodigal daughter." Tiffany couldn't recall the last time she had heard Walter's tone so carefree. Margaret couldn't either and it made her feel warm inside.

"This Colossus. Is it really all that spectacular?" Tiffany asked inquisitively.

"It is pretty incredible," Walter beamed. "I was at the Grand Opening as your father's guest. It's one of the most fabulous hotels ever built. It has more rooms than any other hotel in Las Vegas, and I think it might even be the largest hotel in the world."

Tiffany was impressed, but she was also surprised to hear that Walter had been at the grand opening.

"The Trib Travel Section had some nice things to say about it," she remarked, realizing she was letting on that she knew more about the Colossus than she had previously cared to admit.

"And the Colossus has the top name entertainers in the world in its Athenian showroom. Everyone from Whitney Houston to Garth Brooks."

"I like him," Tiffany said in a barely audible voice, staring out the window as her mind tried to process a thousand different thoughts and emotions.

"One other little footnote that might interest you my dear," Walter said softly. "In the midst of all that Grecian décor the Colossus offers a five-star gourmet restaurant that critics say is the most exquisite in Las Vegas, maybe even the country."

And then Walter literally let the other shoe drop.

"It's called Tiffany's.

Her body felt hot all over. It was as if blood were rushing to all parts of her anatomy at once.

Perhaps Adam Forrester had not forgotten his daughter after all.

The Colossus. Well, it would be a colossal reunion. It was almost 3 a.m. when she closed the door and latched the dead bolt. She was too exhausted to hang up her gown, laying it carefully over a chair next to her bed. The remainder of her clothes and her shoes she shed without conscience.

She did manage to drag herself to the bathroom long enough to brush her teeth and remove her makeup with a cold washcloth. She thought for a moment about calling Val but instead fell sleepily on the bed, engulfed by darkness, a smile on her face and visions of happily ever after dancing little girl style in her head.

Half an hour later she thought she heard a phone ringing but it sounded so far away she made no attempt to move. She had just lapsed into a deep sleep and wasn't at all coherent. At 3:40 a.m. it was either the wrong number or someone who had no concept of what time it was or what sleep meant. If it was Valerie, she would have to have a talk with the girl.

Six more rings and she realized she had forgotten to turn on her recorder when she had left earlier in the evening. She decided not to answer it. In a few seconds whoever it was would give up.

The ringing stopped.

Ten minutes later it rang again.

She wondered if it was Walter. Had there been an accident?

He couldn't possibly have arranged the trip that quickly, she thought, her eyes trying to focus and her arm searching for the phone in the blackness.

Maybe it was Roger Sanderson. In her semi-conscious stupor she even imagined it might be Johnny Marciano. Wild, nonsensical thoughts bounced through her brain.

With the help of the faint green light from the small digital clock on her nightstand, she found the receiver.

Her hello was very, very soft, and very sleepy.

"Miss Wayne? Miss Tiffany Wayne?"

Yes, I'm Tiffany Wayne," she said more alertly, her brain concluding that it was not a wrong number or a crank call.

"Who is this? Is something wrong?"

Her words were coming faster, her tone sharper.

"M'am, I'm sorry to disturb you at this hour but I've been trying to reach you for the past several hours. There was no answer."

"I was out..." she stammered. "What's wrong? Did something happen to Walter?"

The man still had not identified himself, but his tone, while contrite, sounded official.

"M'am, I'm Detective Sergeant Don Sarabian with the Las Vegas Metropolitan Police Department."

It seemed like an hour before his next words.

"Is Adam Forrester your father?"

"Yes, he's my father." She was still half asleep.

"I'm sorry to have to be the one to inform you Miss Wayne, but your father is dead. Adam Forrester was murdered last night..."

The words became a blur, and anything the detective said after "was murdered" was drowned by her screams.

Chapter 3
The Other Shoe

Brian Powers heard about Adam Forrester's murder just minutes before T.J. Fitzgerald's phone call.

"Brian, did you hear the news about Forrester?"

"Just saw it on the tube. You have any more details than what they're giving on the news?"

"Not yet," Fitzgerald answered, and there was alarm in his usually calm voice.

"We still don't know all the facts. The police called me at home. I just got to the hotel. You were my first call.

"I'm still numb. I can't believe it. Adam Forrester was a good man, Brian. I can't believe he's dead!"

Forrester's murder was a shock to both of them. Ripping off a casino, even for a couple mil a month was one thing, but murdering the casino boss was a whole new ball game.

"We need to meet, Brian."

"When?"

"Maybe in a couple days. It'll take at least that long for things to get back to anything even resembling normal around here.

"I'll call you..."

"I'll be waiting," Brian said solemnly. "In the meantime, I'll see what I can find out.

"By the way, have the cops been to Forrester's office yet?"

"I don't think so. Why?"

"No particular reason. I just thought you might want to get the first look, before the uniforms start picking things apart."

"Do you think this has anything to do with the situation we discussed?"

"It could," Brian hedged. "In fact I'd be surprised if it didn't."

"If nothing else I suppose it clears Adam," Fitzgerald muttered.

"Not necessarily," Brian said. "It might only mean he was in the way. Or had served his purpose."

"I hadn't thought of it like that," T.J. said dejectedly.

"Let me know who caught the case. Maybe it's someone I know and can push for some details."

In the two weeks since his meeting with Fitzgerald at the Mirage, Brian had nosed around for clues to support Fitzgerald's suspicion that the Colossus was the victim of a credit scam or some kind of embezzlement. Or that it was for sale.

Other than the rumors Earl Ray had passed along, he had come up empty.

"I'm really sorry about Forrester, "Brian said sincerely. "I know you two were friends for a long time. Call me as soon as things have died down and we'll get together."

"Thanks, Brian. There's going to be a great deal of turmoil around here for a while. The day-to-day operation of the hotel, the employees and the public trading of Colossus stock will all be a handful. Everything is upside down and news people are crawling all over the place. The worse thing is no one has any answers right now."

An afterthought.

"How's Forrester's wife taking it?"

T.J. Fitzgerald had been in such a state of chaos since being informed of his friend's death he hadn't given much thought to Diana Forrester. And that was odd, because she was a vital part of the hotel. He knew she had a lot of input in Adam's decisions.

"I'm not sure," he answered, wondering himself. "She was out of town, but she's on her way back, as we speak. The Colossus jet went to pick her up."

"Listen Fitz, when we get together let's make it real casual. Not in your office. Maybe dinner, someplace where we can talk privately."

"Okay, I'll be in touch soon." Brian could tell Fitzgerald was preoccupied. He could hear people asking him questions in the background.

"Stay safe," Fitzgerald mouthed before hanging up.

"You too," Brian replied, and he hoped both of them could. He also knew it wouldn't be easy.

Chapter 4
Diana's Domain

Fittingly, it was a dreary Chicago morning. A vicious chill was in the air and the wind had a hard on for anyone brave enough to challenge it.

The post 9/11/01 security precautions had slowed the check in lines to a crawl and Tiffany had moved through the crowd in a daze.

United Flight #711 from O'Hare to Las Vegas' McCarran International departed almost an hour late rumbling noisily down the runway before effortlessly rising into the dark gray sky and leveling off at 30,000 feet.

"We've only been in the air a few minutes and it feels like we've been flying for hours," she said in a barely audible voice. Two Valium had little effect and Tiffany felt a huge knot in her stomach.

She fidgeted, trying to settle into a comfortable position in the first class seat, and she wondered why airlines didn't offer sleeping berths on cross-country flights. It seemed so logical. She'd heard that some carrier was now doing it on Trans-Atlantic trips.

Great. Maybe I should ask the pilot to take us to Europe.

She didn't know if the lump in her belly was from indigestion or anxiety and didn't care. She was not looking forward to all that was waiting for her in Las Vegas.

It was freaky. She hadn't seen her father in years. Now she'd see him but he wouldn't see her. She was headed for a place she despised, and she'd be forced to be civil to the only person in the world she hated.

Tiffany knew Diana Carter, or Diana Forrester as she preferred to be called, would be waiting. It was more than she could handle.

She closed her eyes again and tried to sleep.

Fortunately, she had the entire row to herself so she was able to stretch out, using two of the little aspirin sized pillows to prop her head as she curled across the two oversized seats. She covered herself with a couple of flimsy airline blankets from the overhead compartment and tried to get some rest. Her body ached, her eyes were red from crying and she was disoriented.

Walter was across the aisle, his face buried in a New Yorker magazine he wasn't reading. Tiffany felt safer knowing he was near.

Outside was a sea of dark clouds and she wished she could just walk out into them and have them engulf her. The past thirty-six hours had been a nightmare, and she had no recollection of how she had gotten to O'Hare, of having checked her luggage or having packed. Only a hazy vision of Walter standing at the ticket counter holding their boarding passes.

All she remembered of the past two days was sitting on the black overstuffed sofa in her living room listening to Walter make phone calls. She remembered

Ron Delpit

Margaret making tea and talking to her, but whatever she was saying made no sense.

The shock of her father's death had numbed her senses.

The Thurstons were her first call after she hung up with the detective from Las Vegas and they wasted no time in coming to console her. She had called them at 3:45 a.m. and they were at her door at 4:30, Walter in soft shoes, a flannel shirt, jeans and a heavy parka and Margaret still in her nightgown and slippers under a huge black overcoat.

She had opened the door and stood there looking at them, frozen in the moment. She hadn't cried yet, but when Margaret hugged her she literally collapsed in her arms and the tears erupted as if a bomb had gone off and shattered her tear ducts.

Walter had carried her to the couch while Margaret retrieved a blanket.

"Just try and relax dear. Walter will take care of everything. He knows what needs to be done," Margaret said reassuringly. And she was right.

The rest of the day Walter was a slave to the phone, operating methodically, shielding her from all the depressing little details that come with arranging a funeral, especially a sudden one. Only once did he need a direct answer and he had to practically shock her back to reality to get her attention.

"Tiffany!" He was almost screaming. "Can you hear me?" His tone had an urgency to it that jolted her out of her catatonic state.

"You must decide where he is to be buried. Do you want the funeral in Chicago or Las Vegas?"

She had stared at him blankly, not knowing what to say. But it didn't matter. Her decision on a burial site was irrelevant because Walter had overlooked one very important detail.

The choice wasn't hers to make. It was Diana Forrester's call. She was Adam Forrester's next of kin, and also the new owner of the Colossus Hotel.

Now, not only would she come face to face with the woman for the first time, she would also have to accept the fact Diana would be entitled to her father's estate.

Diana's decision to bury her husband in Las Vegas was not a major surprise, thanks to Walter. He had prepared her for the possibility, explaining it was the most logical course of action.

"They lived there, had a home there and were part of the community," he reasoned. "Most of your dad's friends and associates are in Las Vegas now.

"I know you wanted him to be buried next to your mother but this is the way it has to be honey. I'm very sorry. There's no legal way around this one."

Walter was being strong. He was always strong, but even in her pained stupor Tiffany could see beneath his businesslike exterior. This one really got to him. Adam Forrester had been more than just a good friend to Walter Thurston. He had been a god.

Later Walter would cry. A long emotional and private goodbye to the friend he had admired for 40 years, since the day they met as 13-year old freshmen at the exclusive Buckley Preparatory School. Even then Adam Forrester stood out. He was a leader. He always had the answers. To everything.

"How could he have gotten himself murdered?" The question exploded in Walter's brain, bringing reality to the fact his friend was not only dead, but also killed violently and on purpose. Walter Thurston had still not come to grips with that.

One thing at a time he reminded himself. First the funeral. Walter hated funerals. When his own father passed he did not want to go. Margaret had dragged him. There was just something about seeing people he loved so lifeless. It made him feel so mortal.

"Coffee?"

The stewardess's voice yanked him roughly back to the present.

"No thanks," he said putting his hand over his cup. "I think I've already had enough to last me for a month. How much longer until we land?"

His watch was still on Chicago time, and as the flight attendant looked at her wrist, Walter reset his Bulova, moving it two hours back to align with Nevada and the Pacific Time Zone.

"We should be landing in about 35 minutes," she answered, picking up his empty coffee cup and dropping it in the plastic waste bag she held in her left hand.

He glanced across the aisle and was relieved to see that Tiffany had finally fallen off to sleep. For that he was grateful.

The Friends Ball, her agreed reconciliation and the news of the murder were a tremendous burden. He hoped it wouldn't break her.

Other bombs were going to drop. He was pretty sure of that. It was the uncertainty of not knowing who was going to drop them or when they were going to fall that unnerved him. At any rate, he had a strong suspicion the worst was far from over.

He hoped it wouldn't be more than they could handle.

Years of dealing with thousands of cases and situations had taught him that few things ever fell perfectly into place, no matter how clear cut they seemed.

There was no such thing as an open and shut case. O.J. Simpson's murder trial proved that. The guy had done everything but leave his helmet and Heisman trophy at the scene of the crime and he walked away a free man. Walter wasn't expecting any major snafus in Vegas but he knew he had better be prepared.

He would be. Tiffany he wasn't so sure about.

A young black man holding a cardboard placard reading "Thurston" greeted them at United gate #25 in the "B" concourse and a white Colossus limousine awaited them at the airport's VIP arrival area.

"There's a slight construction delay on the I-15 so I'll stick to surface streets. We'll get there in about the same time," the driver said politely.

Walter nodded.

"The Strip won't be very crowded this time of morning and you'll have a nice view of all the new hotels." Walter wondered if the driver had any idea of who they were or why they were in town. Obviously he didn't, and there was no reason for Diana to have told him.

Walter had tried to keep up with the Las Vegas building boom through newspaper articles and conversations with Adam, but nothing could have prepared him for what he was seeing.

The driver took the aptly named Paradise Road to Tropicana, turned west on Trop and headed directly for Las Vegas Boulevard, better known as The Strip.

They passed alongside a run down trailer park then the sprawling MGM Grand with its signature green paint in keeping with its Emerald City Wizard of OZ theme and a huge Golden Lion dominating the entrance way.

The aging Tropicana with its marquee trumpeting the classic "Folies Bergere" sat on the South corner, while across the street, on land Walter remembered as empty acres of sand no one wanted, The Excalibur and New York New York climbed impressively into the sky.

Pedestrian overpasses linked the four corners together and even at eleven in the morning he could see T-shirt clad tourists, beer bottles in hand making their way across the bridge from the Trop to the Castle-like Excalibur which Walter thought looked a lot like a K-Mart with lights.

New York New York was another new property to him, complete with its Coney Island roller coaster soaring up, over and through the hotel, a replica of the Statue of Liberty and a mock Brooklyn Bridge.

The architects had duplicated the Big Apple's skyline re-creating the Empire State Building as well as the Chrysler Building and other recognizable landmarks. It was an ingenious idea and it differed from the other theme hotels because of its unique subject and attention to detail. Even the mock newspaper vending machines were spray painted with graffiti to add a realistic inner city look.

The New York theme was carried out religiously throughout the hotel. The Hilton had red limos, the MGM's were green and NY NY's private VIP cars were all painted yellow to look like Manhattan taxis, minus only the legion of abrasive, non-English speaking maniacs who passed themselves off as drivers.

Tiffany saw none of it as she stared vacantly out the window, sobbing softly as she recalled her first ever trip to Vegas, with her father.

You know, I came here with my dad years ago," she said softly.

"I didn't know that," he said.

"It was my eighteenth birthday and it was best present I received. I got to come to Vegas and listen to him give the keynote speech at a Success Seminar. I was thrilled, and so very proud of him." Tears welled in her green eyes.

She leaned closer to Walter and put her head on his shoulder, her tears wetting his sports jacket.

The Colossus occupied about 50 prime Strip acres and the fragmented outline of the legendary Colosseum in Athens stood out so impressively it was visible from either end of the three mile long Strip.

Brent, the limo driver, already had their electronic room keys so they were able to bypass the busy registration desk and head directly for their rooms.

Score a thoughtfulness point for the widow Forrester. Perhaps he was anticipating problems that would never materialize. Maybe the lady wanted to make things as easy as possible for everyone concerned. That would be a pleasant and welcome surprise. Perhaps he was underestimating how much Diana was affected by Adam's death. After all, she was his wife and he had no reason to think they didn't love each other very deeply.

Diana had done as he had requested and given them adjacent but not adjoining rooms. The mini-suites were located on the 20th floor of the impressively appointed Mount Olympus Tower and came complete with a view of the twin Olympic pools, fully stocked wet bars and comfortable king-sized beds.

It was only noon on Monday and Walter would not see Diana until the following morning at eight. He had called her from Tiffany's apartment and arranged a breakfast meeting, thinking it would give him time to go over the funeral details and get a fix on where the lady was coming from at the same time.

When he had spoken to Diana from Chicago she had not yet confirmed a time or day for the funeral.

"I think Wednesday will probably be the best day," she'd said. "We need a day or two to give friends and relatives from out of town time to arrange travel plans."

He was anxious to see if anything had changed.

Walter had spoken to Adam Forrester regularly since his friend had left Chicago and they had discussed everything from world politics to the growth of Las Vegas. The one thing they didn't talk about was Diana, probably because Adam realized how much his friend and lawyer had loved and respected Susan Forrester.

When he thought about it, Walter couldn't remember whether he was more saddened or shocked when Adam told him he wanted to end the marriage.

Adam had wanted him to handle the divorce, reasoning that since it was going to be uncontested it would make things easier.

"There weren't many things he wouldn't do for Adam Forrester but there he had to draw the line.

He had stammered when Adam first brought it up.

"I don't think that would be a good idea," he remembered saying. The request hadn't caught him completely off guard, but he had hoped Adam would simply ask him for the referral of a solid divorce lawyer.

"There won't be any difficulty over property or other assets," Adam had offered, trying to get him to reconsider. "You know I'm going to be very fair with Susan. More than generous."

"I know you will be, but I'm too close to both of you. I'll find someone you can trust and I'll be sure you're both satisfied with the outcome."

What he really wanted to say was, "What the hell are you thinking?" And remind Adam what a wonderful woman Susan was, but he didn't. He knew that Adam Forrester had not been completely faithful during his years with Susan but he also knew that none of the flings had ever turned serious.

In the end, Adam agreed to hire a neutral lawyer, and it was the best solution for all of them. Walter had not wanted to be in the middle, or have anything to do with their dissolution.

Over the years, the few times Adam had mentioned Diana he did so in a very low-key manner and always in a positive light. The only thing Adam Forrester ever seemed disappointed about was his separation from Tiffany.

With the rest of the day to kill, Walter decided to get out and explore the town a bit.

Tiffany opted to remain in the hotel.

"I'll just catch up on my sleep," she said when he asked if she wanted to have lunch. "I'm not hungry now. Maybe we'll get some dinner later."

"Okay. But if you change your mind just call room service. I'm going to wander around the Strip for a while, and then I'll be back in the hotel. Call me whenever you're ready to eat."

He could see the new Paris Hotel, with its cloned Eiffel Tower and Arc de Triomphe, almost directly across the Strip, so he decided to start there.

The mammoth Venetian Hotel, complete with gondolas and scale model Venice street scenes, was his next stop and he was impressed. Not only were the new hotels unlike any he had ever seen, each had its own shopping venues featuring stores and prices that regular working people couldn't afford.

He visited the Pyramid shaped Luxor, the Polynesian themed Mandalay Bay, and of course, the Bellagio where just for the hell of it he browsed in the Armani store. The only thing he found more amazing than a sport coat priced at $950 was the fact all of their clothes were wrinkled.

"For a thousand bucks you'd think they could press the thing."

When he realized he'd been gone nearly two hours Walter looked for a pay phone to call Tiffany. She was probably worried. He felt guilty for letting the time slip away, but he had needed some space. To clear his head. The distraction of the new hotels had helped.

He ambled over to the house phone at the Monte Carlo to call the Colossus and check messages. He didn't really expect any and was glad Tiffany hadn't needed him. He had already called Margaret, letting her know they had arrived safely even before unpacking.

Margaret's first concern was of course Tiffany.

"Has she opened up at all? You must see to it that she eats." Margaret continued without waiting for an answer. "She must keep up her strength."

"She's still keeping pretty much to herself," he said. "I'll try and get her to eat something a little later."

"Call me when you know the funeral schedule," she said firmly.

He promised he would. She had loved Adam too, although Walter had to admit Margaret was far less sympathetic about his split from Susan Forrester.

It was after three when he returned to the Colossus, and the only message was from his office, asking him to call at his convenience. He had succumbed to the temptation and aroma of a Philly cheesesteak sandwich during his tour of NY NY's Greenwich Village section, a lunch he could never have had if Margaret had been along.

He hoped Tiffany had called for room service and put some solid food in her stomach. If she was sleeping he didn't want to wake her yet, but he did want to make sure she ate dinner before too long.

Promptly at six o'clock he dialed her room.

She answered on the second ring.

"Hi sweetheart, it's Walter."

A drowsy "hi" came back.

"Are you still sleeping?"

"Not really. Just sort of resting. I had a pretty good nap," she said, "but I'm still a little tired. I'm also famished."

"Good. That's the reason I'm calling. I've made a dinner reservation for 7:15 and I wanted to give you time to freshen up."

There was a short silence on the other end.

"Walter, I'm just not ready to go downstairs and have dinner in a restaurant. Couldn't we eat in? Order room service. Would you mind terribly?"

"Of course not. My place or yours?" he kidded.

"Yours I guess. Mine's a mess. I'll throw something on and be over in five or ten minutes."

It was the most life she'd shown in two days, and Walter hoped it was a sign she was getting stronger. It might also be that the medication was wearing off.

Tiffany arrived at his door dressed in a plain gray sweat outfit and tennis shoes. Her eyes were puffy and red in the corners, but even without makeup she had a certain glow. She was a beautiful woman.

Tiffany slowly flipped through the menu two or three times before absently depositing it back on the table.

"Made up your mind yet?"

"I can't," she said weakly. "Just order. Anythng. I don't care."

"So what happens now?" she asked while they waited for the food to be brought up.

She was distraught, but bravely trying to push on.

"Well, from what I understand, the funeral will be Wednesday morning. That hasn't been confirmed yet, but it makes sense.

"I'm meeting Diana tomorrow morning at eight and I'm sure she'll have the schedule."

"I want to be at that meeting," Tiffany said strongly, her voice even and steady.

"Are you sure?" His instincts warned him a meeting between the two women would not be a good idea.

He had intended to meet Diana alone, thinking it would be the best course of action and the least confrontational. Tiffany's insistence on being part of the package was an unforeseen complication.

Walter wanted to kick himself for mentioning the meeting. I should have just gone ahead with it and let her know the details. A head to head meeting with Tiffany and Diana was potentially dangerous. And now there was no avoiding it.

He failed to convince her otherwise and she fended off his weak excuses.

"I'm a big girl, Walter. You can't protect me from everything. There comes a time when everyone has to face some things they'd rather not.

"I can't avoid the woman the entire time we're here so I'd rather get it over with quickly. Count me in for breakfast, or at least for the meeting. I don't think I'll be in the mood to eat much."

For the next two hours they chatted about a thousand stupid little things, Tiffany recalling memories of happy times she had shared with her dad, Walter reveling her with stories about her father in his high school days.

And for those moments the sadness disappeared.

It was after eleven when she pulled herself up from the small sofa in the suite's living room area and announced she was going to bed.

"I feel much better, Walter. Thank you for this evening. It really helped me. Now I've got to get some sleep so I'm ready for tomorrow's meeting."

"I'll leave a wake-up call for both of us," he said, walking her to the door.

In the morning, when the phone rang she had already been up for an hour.

"Good morning Miss Wayne. This is the front desk. It's 7:15 a.m."

Her body ached, her muscles still knotted despite having been able to stretch out in the large bed. She also felt a surge of energy. She wanted to get this done, get it over with and get the hell out of Las Vegas and never come back. She wanted to get on with her life or at least get back to trying to put the pieces together again.

She let the scalding hot shower hit her full force, then completely shut off the hot water and used only the cold spray to shock her into alertness.

The phone rang again as she stepped out of the shower. She wrapped one of the plush over-sized bath towels around her chest and another smaller one turban style around her still damp hair. She was headed out of the bathroom to answer the phone then noticed a receiver on the bathroom wall.

It was Walter.

"Just wanted to be sure you were up," he said with rehearsed cheerfulness.

"Are you about ready to go downstairs?"

"Almost," she fibbed. "Give me ten minutes."

"Perfect," he replied.

It was 7:50 a.m. as they made their way to the elevator.

The Alpha Coffee Shop took Tiffany by surprise. It was huge, and at 8 a.m. it was already bustling. There were six or seven people in line waiting to be seated, a few of them with plastic cups filled with coins of various denominations.

Tiffany assumed they were taking a nourishment break so they could get enough strength to attack the machines again.

Walter took her arm and guided her through the milling customers to the empty "Invited Guest" line and the hostess station.

"We're here to meet Mrs. Forrester," he said with an air of authority, and the words "Mrs. Forrester" exploded like a firecracker inside Tiffany's head.

There was only one Mrs. Forrester and it's not Diana, she thought angrily.

"Right this way sir. She's in the executive booth in the far corner."

It was obvious from the hostess's quick reaction that she had been expecting them. Her blonde mane and Greek-style costume reminded Tiffany of a modern day Helen of Troy.

Diana Forrester was easy to recognize.

Tiffany had seen a few pictures of Diana in the society section from time to time so the woman was not exactly a total stranger.

Diana was strategically seated in the middle of a very large tufted leather booth with a small reserved sign perched at the edge.

Tiffany swallowed hard. The meeting was going to be more difficult than she had imagined. Suddenly she wanted to turn and run away even though her legs were carrying her toward the booth.

I shouldn't have come. I should have let Walter handle this.

Her earlier energy had mysteriously ebbed. She was on Diana's ground now and she felt it.

A thin smile played on Diana's face as Walter and Tiffany approached.

"Please sit down," she offered, not bothering with any formal introductions.

"You must be Walter, and Tiffany I recognize from the pictures on your father's desk."

"I'm Diana Forrester."

47

The emphasis was hard on the "Forrester" and Tiffany knew it was for the purpose of establishing the ground rules.

A waitress with a pair of tassel-adorned menus appeared as soon as they were seated, as did a waiter in a black vest who attentively lit Diana's cigarette.

"Would you like to order first, so we can talk without being interrupted?

"I really don't care for anything right now," Tiffany said directly to the waitress.

"Just coffee. Black," Walter said, responding to the waitress' glance.

Tiffany was filled with questions, and anxious to ask them.

"I just want to know what happened? How could something so terrible have happened to my father? Who would want to kill him?" The questions had all spilled out at once, her nervousness getting the better of her.

Diana's eyes narrowed, as if she was focusing in on Tiffany.

The waitress was at the edge of the table, pad in hand ready to take their order.

"Just bring us a pot of coffee," Diana said offhandedly, dismissing the woman.

"Right away, Mrs. Forrester."

There was the name again, slamming into her senses.

As soon as the waitress turned away Diana responded, an irritable edge in her tone.

"No one really knows what happened yet Tiffany. I certainly don't have any answers. I was out of town. We're all pretty much still in a state of shock."

"I suppose the best way to handle things between us is to deal with it head on," Diana said boldly. "This isn't going to be pleasant for any of us."

Neither Tiffany nor Walter flinched. Tiffany could feel her heart thumping wildly in her chest. She wanted to keep asking questions until she got some answers that made sense, even though she knew it would be fruitless.

Instead she tried to distract herself, momentarily fixing her gaze on a small Grecian urn that sat on a ledge behind Diana. She also silently counted to ten and took a deep breath. It helped her calm down.

"The funeral is set for tomorrow morning at ten," Diana continued as if going over a board meeting agenda. Her red hair glistened in the artificial light and Tiffany wondered how often she had it colored.

Diana was only four years older but she was a hard thirty-five, and when Tiffany looked more closely she could see some miles on her, despite the expensive cosmetics. The body appeared to be in good shape, probably from bike riding or working out in the hotel gym, however the Vegas nightlife and blistering desert sun had definitely done a number on her face. She still looked good, attractive even, but in 10 years a mirror would no longer be a friend.

You party you pay, thought Tiffany, and suddenly she was curious as to whether her father had also found time to party. He had never been a real party person but maybe he had changed. Maybe breaking away and breaking out was what his leaving had been all about. Something of a second childhood or mid-life crisis.

She wondered what his life with Diana had been like, and as she did, she found herself building resentment over the fact Diana Carter had shared the last five years of her father's life.

"I know you haven't spoken to your father since he and I were married," Diana said, a hint of attitude in her voice, "but I can assure you he was never happier."

Tiffany resisted the urge to say, "and how would you know that?" and let her continue.

"We were very much in love."

Tiffany felt as if she was suffocating.

Sensing the tension, Walter intervened.

"Is there anything we can do? Any details that you need us to handle?" he inquired, looking squarely at Diana. "Do you need…"

"No, but thank you for asking. I have everything arranged the way I know my husband would have wanted it," she blurted, with the emphasis on husband. "My biggest concern will be deciding what to do with the hotel now that he's gone."

"I can see how that might be a problem," Walter replied. "I mean, without Adam here to run things…"

Diana pounced on the thought.

"I am quite capable of running this hotel," Mr. Thurston. "In fact I've run it for weeks at a time when Adam was out of the country."

"My first thought was to sell the damn place and move back to Chicago or get away from it all and go to Europe for six months or a year, but I just don't know. I'm not thinking straight right now. Your father and I both loved the Colossus," she said addressing Tiffany.

"But now it's full of memories everywhere I turn. Every time I walk through the lobby or step in the elevator to go up to the offices I feel his presence. It's overwhelming."

"And that's bad?" Tiffany said icily. Her sarcasm did not escape Diana, who ignored the dig.

"I've alerted the bell captain and the executive office personnel to handle any requests you might have so they are at your service night or day," she said coldly." I'll be in Adam's office the rest of the day if you need me."

Tiffany was put off by Diana's patronizing and didn't believe in the woman's sincerity or mock courtesy.

Diana could feel Tiffany's resentment.

"Also," her eyes boring in on Tiffany, "I've been in touch with our lawyer and arranged to have the will read on Thursday. I thought you'd want it done as soon as possible so you can get back to Chicago. No sense you two having to hang around any longer than you have to. I think the will is pretty much a formality anyway."

The one-upsmanship in Diana's tone was unmistakable.

Between the lines Diana was reminding her that all that had been her father's was now hers, and she did not need or welcome any advice about how to handle or dispose of it. Especially from her husband's long lost daughter.

At that moment Tiffany hated her. Not that she had wanted to like her. It just would have been easier if she could have seen some remorse or sensitivity in the woman.

She wanted to blame someone for what had happened to her father. For what had happened to her. For him being taken away from her just when they were about to make up and Diana was a handy scapegoat.

After all, it was Diana who had seduced him and lured him away from his marriage. And she had no doubt it was Diana who convinced him to leave Chicago. Indirectly then, it was all her fault. Tiffany knew her thinking was flawed, however, the more she looked at Diana the more she despised her.

It was hardly an original story. Sexy young girl from wrong side of tracks latches on to wealthy married man, rekindles his dormant desires, gets him to leave his wife, marries him and inherits the whole enchilada when he winds up murdered. Estranged daughter is left feeling empty and alone.

It stinks, Tiffany thought, her mind exploding as if someone had just detonated a bomb.

"Murdered..."

The word struck her full force for the first time and it hit her like an unexpected slap in the face.

"We haven't discussed who might want to kill my father, or why?" she said matter-of-factly and her bluntness caught both Walter and Diana a bit off guard.

"Since you were so close to him maybe you might have some idea." Tiffany was looking hard at Diana.

"The police have already asked me that," Diana said sharply, "and I couldn't give them any help. I haven't got a clue. I didn't know Adam had any enemies."

"I imagine the police will get around to asking the two of you the same questions," Diana said flatly. "Its all routine."

"There's nothing routine about murder Diana. At least not in my family."

Diana was seething.

"I was involved in just about all of Adam's business dealings and I believe I knew all of my husband's friends," she said evenly, "and I can't think of anyone who could possibly dislike him enough to want him dead."

Diana was aware that Tiffany was uncomfortable with the tone of the conversation and she tried to make her even more so by repeatedly referring to Adam as her husband instead of as Tiffany's father.

"About the only thing my husband agonized over were the constant offers to buy the hotel. Even though he loved this place, there were days he thought about selling. But he loved the Colossus. *We* built it brick by brick. There was no mistaking Diana's emphasis of the "we".

"But he missed Chicago. He missed the stock market and he didn't particularly like being in the spotlight the way he was here. He kept telling me he didn't want to sell, but I know he had incredible offers from money people like Donald Trump and Steve Wynn as well as from big corporations like Bally's and MGM.

"Sometimes I think he kept the Colossus more for me than for himself. He knew I loved it, but it would have been okay with me if he sold it. I wanted whatever he wanted."

Then a shift in gears.

"You know Tiffany, I wasn't quite sure how you and I would get along and I suppose in the grand scheme of things it doesn't really matter," Diana said cattily.

"I know my husband loved you very much but to me you're just another spoiled little rich girl. Of course, I would never say that to Adam, but I often wondered why he bothered with you when you turned your back on him and treated him so badly."

"Perhaps because he loved me," Tiffany said haltingly.

"You crushed him when you shut him out of your life. Or didn't you care?"

The words smacked against Tiffany's face like angry waves against a sea wall.

She didn't want to weaken, but her eyes were tearing and she couldn't hold them back. She felt them rolling down her cheeks and Diana's attack wasn't over.

"Personally I wasn't even sure you'd come to the funeral," she said, moving in for the kill.

"And why wouldn't I come?" Tiffany answered, somehow summoning up the strength to sound challenging. "I am the only real family he has, you know."

"I know you blame me for everything, from the divorce to your mother's suicide, and that's okay," Diana replied without pause. "I guess you need someone to blame. The thing is, I was there for my husband when he needed me. I was the only one who was.

"While you were ignoring him for the past five years I was his everything. He relied on me. He loved me and he trusted me. I would never have turned my back on him."

Tiffany's mouth was agape. Walter was nervously fingering a packet of sugar, squeezing it so hard he tore the paper and the grainy white contents spilled in a neat little pile in front of him.

When Diana finished there was a stony silence.

51

And when Tiffany spoke she could hear her own voice cracking.

"I'll say my good-byes to my father privately tomorrow, and I look forward to seeing him one last time. As for you, if I never see you again it will be too soon.

"I'm sure the funeral will be more emotional for me than for you. I'll have to bear my sorrow forever. You can just cash in your chips and move on to the next mark."

Walter tensed. For a moment he thought Diana was going to either throw her coffee or try and slap Tiffany across the face. If they had been seated closer he was sure there would have been a physical confrontation.

Tiffany's voice had grown stronger with each word and by the end of her tirade her tone was confident and controlled. Inside, her heart was slamming into her chest and her legs felt like Jell-O.

Diana's face was burning, her naturally rosy cheeks a deep red, but she didn't get a chance to reply.

Tiffany abruptly rose from the table leaving Diana to stare at her back, and Walter slid out from the other side of the booth as if on cue. Nothing more needed to be said.

They walked briskly out of the Alpha Coffee Shop, her arm in Walter's to help her remain steady, across the casino to the elevators at the base of the Mount Olympus Tower.

A uniformed security guard at the elevator foyer eyed them closely, then allowed them to pass when Walter dug out his suite key and nonchalantly waved it at him.

Ever the gentleman, Walter did not mention the scene at the table and Tiffany appreciated his discretion.

"I'd like to get a little more rest and maybe try to calm down a little," she said, her jangled nerves all aflutter.

Walter could tell by the look in her eyes that she was still shaken by the nasty verbal exchange with Diana.

"I also want to check with Val and see if there's anything going on at the office that I need to handle."

"I have some calls to make too." Walter was still not sure if he should address the coffee shop battle, ignore it or try and offer Tiffany some consolation.

"And I'm going to give that Detective Don Sarabian a call," Walter added. "Maybe he has some new information."

"Thanks Walter. Please let me know if he does. I don't want to leave here and have my dad's case turn into just a file number and another unsolved mystery," she said wistfully. "And no matter what Diana says, I know gambling is a rough business. People make enemies.

"One other thing Walter. I would appreciate it if you could arrange a private limo to take us to the funeral home in the morning. I'd like to spend a few minutes alone with my dad before anyone else arrives.

"Please call the funeral parlor and set it up."

"I'll see to it," he said in a fatherly tone. "Now go and get some rest. And call me when you feel like talking. I'll be in my room."

"Thanks for understanding Walter. I hoped you would," and he could see her growing up before his eyes.

It had certainly been an eventful morning. And it wasn't even nine o'clock.

She was certainly a lot tougher than he gave her credit. He didn't think she'd stand a chance in a war of words with Diana, but she had given the widow Forrester her comeuppance. He was proud of her. But he knew she was not thinking straight and he vowed to keep an even closer eye on her.

She spent most of the day on the phone with Valerie, making arrangements for a showing in Paris. It would be her first international show and it would mark the unveiling of her own "**Tiffany Collection**".

"You must have made some impression at the Ball," Valerie joked, trying to lighten the mood. She could sense her friend's despair and she ached for her.

"And why is that?" Tiffany asked with total innocence.

"Are you kidding? At least 100 people have called asking where they can see samples of the line. And the Trib had a story about you and the dress you wore to the Ball in the Arts and Leisure section the next day.

"You're a hot topic Missy."

"We're a hot topic then my dear. Remember we're in this together."

Valerie was grateful that Tiffany wanted to share the glory, but she knew her friend was the heart and soul of the business. Tiffany had vision. She was brilliant and she had a fabulous eye for what worked.

The best part about Tiffany's creations was their practicality. They would both laugh when they saw fashion shows on the E! Channel with outrageous designs they knew normal people would never wear.

"Ego," they'd shout in unison as they watched pencil thin models parade up and down in two thousand dollar outfits, many of which looked like they were from outer space.

"Promise me we'll never design anything that crazy and impractical, "Val had pleaded.

Tiffany knew if Val said a hundred people had called it was probably more like six or seven and that was okay. She knew her friend was only trying to ease the tension.

It was six o'clock by the time she got around to calling Walter.

"I'm starving counselor. Let's eat." Her mood had improved, thanks to a few hours of undisturbed rest and a relaxing bath.

"I'm pretty hungry myself," Walter agreed, even though he had ordered a room service lunch shortly after noon.

"Do you want me to call downstairs and have something brought up?"

"To be honest that was my first choice," Tiffany admitted, "however I think I'd rather go down. You're probably going to think this a bit strange, but I'd like to eat in the restaurant my father named after me.

"I hope you don't consider it too maudlin or sentimental. Thing is, this may be the only chance I ever get to eat there because I don't plan on coming back to this town, and Diana will probably change the name of the restaurant as soon as the ink is dry on the deed to the hotel."

"I don't think you're being silly at all," he reassured her. "In fact, it sounds like a good idea to me too. I'll make a reservation. Its six now. How long will it take you to get ready?"

"Give me half an hour."

"I'll make the reservation for seven. Okay?"

"That'll work," she said, trying to be light.

The gourmet room was all she could have hoped for, elegantly decorated with expensive handmade Tiffany cut crystal chandeliers and plush red velvet booths illuminated by small Greek lanterns with shades made from papyrus. The flatware was hand carved silver, the water poured into silver goblets and the service superb.

"I spoke to the detective," Walter began after the maitre'd had seen to it they were both comfortable and the bus boy had delivered their water. It was Evian, not the standard ice water with a slice of lemon most other restaurants offered.

"Funny thing," Walter continued, "Detective Sarabian actually knew your father. Seems your dad helped him out last year, providing a couple of the Colossus' top entertainers at no charge for a police charity event on short notice.

"Anyway, he's taken a personal interest in the case and promised he wouldn't let it rest without exploring every lead. I gave him my number in Chicago and he agreed to keep me informed.

"I also spoke to the funeral home director. You'll be able to view the body at 8:30 tomorrow morning, before anyone else arrives. A private limo will take us."

"Thank you Walter. Thanks for everything. You've been a tower of strength through all of this," she gushed. "I know how much he meant to you too."

"Excuse me sir," said the waiter, setting a silver bucket with iced champagne at the outer edge of their table.

Both of them looked at it quizzically.

"Compliments of the gentlemen at the center booth," the waiter explained, answering their puzzled expressions.

In the dimmed lighting Walter could not make out the donor but in a moment the man approached their table and a huge smile took full possession of Walter Thurston's face.

"T.J. Fitzgerald, you old son of a gun. It's been a while hasn't it? How's life treating you?"

"Kicking the crap out of me right now," Fitzgerald said honestly. And taking notice of Tiffany, he apologized for interrupting.

"I'm sorry for intruding," T.J. offered, studying her as if trying to place her face.

"It's just that I haven't seen Walter in so long...since we were in Chicago, maybe five or six years ago."

"Forgive my poor manners, "Walter apologized. "This is Tiffany Wayne. She's a longtime family friend, and a client."

"And excuse me for not recognizing you Miss Wayne. You've certainly changed a great deal since I last saw you."

Tiffany squinted as she eyed Fitzgerald.

"You couldn't have been more than seventeen or eighteen," he explained. "I think you were just getting ready to go off to college. I came to your home in Chicago one Saturday afternoon to meet with your dad. You brought us iced tea in his den."

She thought she remembered, but wasn't sure.

"My condolences regarding your father," T.J. said somberly. "We worked very closely and he was a wonderful person. I can't tell you how sorry I am that this happened."

"Thank you," was all she could manage.

Walter had planned on contacting Fitzgerald following the funeral, even though he was sure the Security Chief had told the police anything of importance.

But how did you wind up being murdered when your right hand man was an ex-Chicago detective? Now wasn't the time or place for that discussion, but Walter had every intention of asking some hard questions when the time was right.

Tiffany guessed Fitzgerald to be in his early 50s. She would have thought younger if not for the heavy dark circles under his eyes. Other than the eyes he had a clean-cut look and an expensive suit that made her think he was either a lawyer or some corporate big shot. He had that air about him. Not arrogant or cocky, just calm and self-assured.

"We were just leaving," Fitzgerald said, and I don't want to spoil your dinner.

"You're not intruding," Tiffany answered before Walter could object. "You may as well have a glass of the champagne you sent over."

She had found the champagne a bit incongruous considering the circumstances.

"Thanks," said Fitzgerald, sliding in next to Walter.

"Maybe you ought to invite your friend too," said Tiffany looking over the top of her menu at the man now sitting alone in the booth where Fitzgerald had been.

T.J. Fitzgerald motioned for his companion to join them and Brian Powers obliged. He was glad he and Fitzgerald had finished their meeting.

For days T.J. had been too busy to meet and their only communication had consisted of a series of short phone calls. The dinner meeting was their first chance to get together, and they had been huddled in a private booth for more than two hours, exchanging information and insights on Adam's murder and the events preceding it.

In the three days since the tragedy, Brian had been working around the clock, calling on every contact he could think of to try and piece together the who and the why. The what was easy. The what was the Colossus.

"What do you want first, the good news or the bad news?" he had asked Fitzgerald.

"Give me the bad first," Fitzgerald had replied.

"The bad news is there's no good news," he said without trying to be funny."I'm pretty sure I've gotten to the bottom of the three million a month that's been going south, but so far nothing I've heard connects it to Forrester's murder."

Fitzgerald seemed surprised.

As odd as it seems, maybe Forrester was a random thing," Brian continued. "As far as either of us knows, Adam Forrester knew nothing of the scam, so there would have been no reason to take him out.

"The money that's been walking out the door has been going with the blessing of one of your own guys. It's a credit heist. Usually it goes undetected for a month or two, and by then it's too late. You just happened to trip over it sooner.

"Your ex-cage boss...Jimmy Santos. He was in on it. He was okaying certain customers to walk with hundreds of thousands in chips every few days. And he was being well taken care of, but he got greedy and it got him dead.

"Jimmy's departure didn't slow the scam down though. They just found a new inside man. I don't know who yet, but I'll keep digging."

"What about the blackjack losses?"

"I don't have an answer for you on that yet," Brian said honestly.

"By the way T.J., there were some rumblings that Forrester was approached a few months ago about selling the joint. My sources say he turned the offer down cold. You know anything about that?"

"He mentioned it, but that happens every day at hotels along the strip. Why? Does it have any significance?"

"It could. And then again it might not mean a thing. But sooner or later somebody will hear something. The street is the first to know. Stay tuned."

Fitzgerald was impressed.

The report he had just heard told him why Brian was the best. He had the contacts, he was thorough and he got the facts without raising dust clouds.

T.J. Fitzgerald knew he had to keep a lid on the info Brian had just divulged. That wouldn't be difficult since, at the moment, he had no one to share it with. The police wouldn't take him seriously, and Diana hadn't officially been named hotel president yet. Besides, Brian had asked him to wait until he could get an "all clear" on Diana before confiding in her.

Introductions were made all around as Brian sat at the opposite side of the booth from Fitzgerald, causing Tiffany to slide to the middle closer to Walter.

"If there's anything either of you need to know about Las Vegas, Brian's the man to ask," Fitzgerald said, complimenting his friend. "He's a private consultant and one of the sharpest guys I've ever worked with."

"That's pretty high praise coming from an ex-cop," said Walter, with an eye on Brian. "Fitz usually tosses around compliments as if they were manhole covers."

Fitzgerald chuckled.

"I would have been lost when I moved here if it weren't for Brian," Fitzgerald continued. "He showed me how to tell the good guys from the bad guys and clued me in on some of the scams that go down in this town."

Brian was a bit uneasy listening to Fitzgerald sing his praises.

He had liked T.J. Fitzgerald from the moment he met him, and had been happy to give the former lawman information whenever he needed it.

A few months after Fitzgerald joined the Colossus they had worked together to bust a baccarat cheating scam involving dealers who were ripping off the casino by running in rigged decks, then dealing winning hands to players with whom they were in cahoots.

It was difficult to catch them in the act, even with all the hotel security cameras because they'd only do it five or ten minutes every couple of hours, but with the amount of money wagered on baccarat, those few minutes a night cost the casino more than $800,000 in a ten day period.

Brian had dogged them around the clock and put heavy pressure on his street sources to get a line on the outside partners.

Eventually, he was able to make them through a Paris Hotel cocktail waitress he had once helped beat a solicitation rap. She had a girlfriend who cocktailed at the popular "Rum Jungle", and had waited on two guys with big bankrolls and bigger mouths.

D.P., his contact at the club, directed him to the girl.

"Yeah, I remember them," she said. "You don't forget creeps who order Cristal and leave you a dollar tip. They were bragging about putting a whipping on the Colossus baccarat game."

Moral of the story: never stiff the hired help.

In the end, one of them caved in and all four wound up doing serious prison time. Nevada did not take kindly to cheats, and the judges loved to make examples of them. Brian had worked in the background, doing all the legwork and feeding the information to Fitzgerald. When the bad guys were nabbed Fitzgerald got the credit and Brian earned the security chief's unconditional respect.

The faint aroma of Tiffany's perfume tickled Brian's nostrils. It was light and powdery. She turned her attention to him as his mind tried to recall the fragrance.

"So Brian, how long have you been in Vegas?"

Walter and Fitzgerald were immersed in their own conversation, reminiscing about old times, and catching up on the recent past. They paid no mind to Brian and Tiffany's small talk.

"Just moved here, about twenty years ago," he joked.

She smiled. "Where'd you come from?"

"California."

"I take it you like it here?"

"Never want to live anywhere else. There's always something going on here and everything's new."

"I heard Mr. Fitzgerald say you're a special consultant. What exactly does that mean?"

"I work with hotels on special projects. Everything from security breaches to public relations problems."

"What do you do for fun?"

"Watch sports, play a little basketball and write."

"The great American novel?"

"Hardly," he said a little non-plussed. "Just some notes about my experiences in Vegas. One day I'll put them all together and see what I come up with."

"Sounds interesting. Might make a good book. I had the impression everyone who lived here worked in the casinos and played with those neon yo-yos for recreation."

Brian laughed.

"You'd be surprised how many people really think that way. Actually Vegas is a pretty average town except for the gambling. We have banks, churches, grocery stores and people with regular jobs. Kids even go to school out here in the Wild, Wild West," he deadpanned.

"Of course they learn to count a little funny...ace, deuce, craps three, hard four." Talking to her was easy but her swollen eyes told him she'd rather be somewhere else. Any place else.

"Well, I'm sorry, but how can anyone take a city seriously when it has streets named after Wayne Newton and Sonny Fremont?

"Touché," Brian surrendered. She'd touched a nerve. Brian had no use for Newton because the singer was an egomaniacal bully who had gotten away with all sorts of hijinks because of his political clout. He was always willing to do a fund-raiser for a high-powered political figure, especially one leading in the polls.

But Vegas and the 90's had caught up to Wayne and his curious ways. He'd filed for bankruptcy, been forced to sell most of his fancy Arabian quarter horses and lost a good deal of the respect he had commanded in the 70's and 80's. His former lawyer sued him for five million for non-payment and his once good buddy, Tony Orlando, filed papers claiming Wayne tried to cheat him out of millions in a Branson, Missouri theater scheme. Wayne, of course, came out of the bankruptcy fiasco smelling like a gallon of the Paco Rabane cologne he loved to splash on after shows.

At least Newton was no longer the city's Golden Boy. He'd worn out his welcome at most of the top Strip hotels, barely managing to save his career with a patchwork deal at the rundown Stardust. The press releases said he'd get $40 mil over ten years, but the numbers didn't add up.

Sonny Fremont was something else again.

His name was on the marquee at the MGM, even as they spoke, and Brian had pegged him as an opportunistic sleaze-bag with more balls than talent.

He'd met Fremont on two occasions and nothing the singer said or did had changed his opinion. He was all about "me" and getting over on any attractive woman who was the least bit star struck by his celebrity. And he wasn't bashful about it. Brian had a hunch it was only a matter of time before Sonny Fremont bit off more than he could digest.

"And how long are you going to be in Vegas?" Brian asked, not yet aware that Tiffany was Adam Forrester's daughter.

Walter interceded.

"I'll be leaving right after my father's funeral," she said looking away.

"Adam Forrester was her father," T.J. explained as he saw Brian's furrowed brow.

"I'm sorry," was all Brian could muster.

"Thank you."

She seemed too innocent to be mixed up in the gambling world, and Brian wondered how close she had been to her old man.

Tiffany glanced around the table and felt at ease. She was comfortable with all three men.

Fitzgerald seemed like a nice man, and Tiffany had enjoyed exchanging barbs with Brian. The conversation had been innocuous and it had temporarily taken her mind off the problems at hand.

Brian and Fitzgerald departed just as the waiter returned to take the order.

The meal was sumptuous, Tiffany nibbled sporadically at an entrée of Trout Almondine, baked potato and salad while Walter finished his steak and Maine lobster along with three dinner rolls.

They avoided any discussion of her father, or Diana, perhaps not purposely, but Tiffany was sure they both enjoyed their meal more because of it. They talked about the weather, Margaret, T.J. Fitzgerald, Brian and the superb food.

Paul, one of the three waiters who had attended their table, brought the check in a black leather sleeve, setting it near Walter with an almost imperceptible motion.

Walter scanned the bill, signed his name and room number and left a $25 tip.

"I really enjoyed dinner Walter. Thank you for taking me."

"My pleasure, but remember it was your idea."

Earlier she had blushed when Walter had informed Brian and Fitzgerald that the room had been named in her honor, yet inwardly she was pleased and proud.

"The restaurant is every bit as special as you my dear," Walter said as they walked toward the elevators.

The casino was busy. It was almost 10 p.m. and it seemed like almost every table and slot machine was in use. In half an hour it would be even more of a madhouse as the current crowd would be joined by another 1,000 people coming out of the showroom.

That was the idea.

While many of the ladies headed for the powder room, the men would try and get in a few hands of blackjack or a few rolls of the dice. It was a temporary rush, some nights lasting as long as half an hour, and every casino with a showroom depended on the extra infusion of traffic each night to help make the nut.

Tiffany felt her eyes getting heavy as the elevator silently whisked them to their floor.

She wasted little time slipping into her nightie. Snuggled cozily in the big bed she turned and reached for the phone.

"Operator. This is Tiffany Wayne in room 2106. I'd like a 7 a.m. wake-up call please."

"That's already been arranged, Ms. Wayne."

"Thank you." And thank God for Walter.

She fell into a sound sleep, not stirring until she reached gingerly for the ringing phone at seven. She would have killed for another half-hour.

She tried to collect her thoughts, as she got ready, her nerves getting the best of her. Three times she dropped her brush and accidentally dumped the entire contents of her purse searching for her lipstick.

Tiffany ached to see her father once more. To touch his hand. When she did, she knew he'd feel what was in her heart. Somehow he'd know she had been planning to come and see him.

At 7:45 she dialed Walter's room.

"Good morning Walter. I'm ready. It was her most authoritative tone.

"The car should be downstairs," he replied.

He had been dressed for nearly an hour, having awakened at 5 a.m., a full ninety-minutes before his scheduled wake-up call.

"I'll be in the hallway," he said.

As she walked out of her room their eyes met and they exchanged a sympathetic smile, like two soldiers set to engage on a solemn mission.

A black limousine with "Colossus" etched in gold letters on the door sat idling at the hotel's front entrance, its driver at the curb. He opened the door as he caught sight of them.

"Diana insisted," Walter said apologetically while guiding her into the back seat. "Someone apparently informed her that I had asked the bell captain to order a private car for us."

She felt her neck redden.

"Its okay Walter".

The ride to Carlton Brothers mortuary took less than fifteen minutes even though the driver elected to motor down the heavily traveled Strip instead of using the expressway.

"The freeway is jammed with morning rush hour traffic," he explained.

Real people going to work did not jibe with Tiffany's image of Las Vegas and it reminded her how Brian Powers had described the town away from the lights and glitter.

Still, the whole place looked strange and out of whack in the daylight, as if the morning sun had caught it by surprise.

As the limo turned off the Strip and cruised past a 7-11 Tiffany caught sight of a woman in a wrinkled evening gown, with last night's good times still playing in her sleepy eyes. The brightly colored dress, with the revealing slits up the sides made the woman stand out like a pimp's purple Cadillac.

Lost in her thoughts, Tiffany did not notice their arrival at the funeral home. It was a stately building with towering white columns, reminiscent of an old Southern plantation.

Charles Carlton, the senior member of the Carlton Mortuary staff, met their car. As they alit, he greeted Tiffany and shook Walter's hand.

"Good morning Miss Wayne," he said in a deep voice.

Then, looking at Walter, "Mr. Thurston, if you can spare a moment, I'd like a word with you. Its rather important," he said, turning his eyes away from Tiffany's.

As Walter stepped inside the funeral director's private office Tiffany looked for the signboard indicating which room had been prepared for her father.

"Adam Forrester, 2C." The arrow pointed to the right.

She moved cautiously down the carpeted hallway, and she could feel herself beginning to breathe faster and faster. Outside the room was a huge wreath of red roses with a large silken banner, "To My Beloved Husband".

She was glad Walter had been called aside. She wanted the moment to be private.

At the outer door she hesitated a full five seconds, trying to compose herself. Did she really want to see him again, or to did she choose to remember him through the fond memories of happier days? She knew the answer. She would never rest if she didn't see him again.

Time to make peace daddy...

She pulled on the heavy oak door, paused at the back of the room for a split second, then with head bowed, walked directly to the casket. Abruptly she spun and charged out of the room, almost running over Walter and Carlton as they entered.

"It's closed Walter. The damned casket is closed!"

She glared at Carlton, half in anger, half-pleading.

"I want the casket opened, Mr. Carlton. Please open it. I want to see my father."

Carlton looked at her wide-eyed and began to stammer. Before he could say anything Walter took her arm and pulled her aside.

"Diana ordered it sealed," he said holding her arm firmly. "She called Mr. Carlton at home this morning and demanded the casket remain closed. She said under no circumstances was it to be opened. Not even if you insisted."

"She did this to hurt me," Tiffany hissed, her nostrils flaring. "She knew how important it was for me to see him one last time. I told her when we met yesterday."

"I'm sorry Miss Wayne, but by law Mrs. Forrester has the final word," the funeral director said in a way that let both of them know he was sympathetic to their cause. He was a deer caught in the crosshairs.

"The casket is permanently sealed," he apologized. "It can never be reopened."

Tiffany bolted for the car.

"I can't believe anyone could be so heartless and vindictive," she screamed, tears streaking her makeup.

"Tell me she can't do this Walter. Tell me you'll find a way." She was slumped in the seat; feeling helpless and she could feel herself coming apart.

"I wish I could," he said with unmistakable exasperation, "but that's why Mr. Carlton called me into his office. He was advising me of the Nevada law. This was not his doing, Tiffany. He wanted us to understand that. He was on your side. It was simply out of his hands."

It took every bit of persuasiveness he could muster to convince Tiffany to relent and attend the funeral at all. Never, not even in court on his finest day had he been so eloquent and convincing. And he did it while setting aside the disgust he felt for Diana Forrester's despicable and vengeful actions.

Still he didn't win her over completely.

Tiffany watched the entire proceeding from the rear seat of the rented limo. She did, however, have the window down. Walter and T.J. Fitzgerald were the only pallbearers she recognized.

After the procession of funeral cars and mourners departed, Tiffany stepped out of the car, a black lace veil concealing her face and the tears that soaked it. As she walked across the freshly cut lawn toward her father's grave, the heels of her patent leather pumps created a wobbly trail of spike marks in the damp grass.

The casket was still suspended above the open grave, its gleaming mahogany exterior almost completely covered with flowers. Large wreaths, many from rival casino owners, gave the area around the gravesite the aura of a flower shop.

"I didn't want it to end this way," she whispered, as she stood alone in front of the casket. "I love you daddy, and I always will.

"Please forgive me for my anger and my immaturity. You were always in my heart and I will miss you...more than anyone will ever know. Thank you for everything you did for me and for everything you were to me. I know you can hear me and that you always knew I still loved you. I only wish there were a way you could tell me that, so I could rest easier. Goodbye, daddy."

She laid a single white rose on the coffin, then turned and strode quickly back to the car. Returning to the back seat she sat erect, totally numbed as she waited for Walter, who was exchanging goodbyes with the last few mourners.

She felt small, and almost totally helpless. Her father was dead. She was in an unfamiliar city where she knew no one, and his business was something she didn't understand or even want to understand.

Still, a fire burned in her soul, and she wanted it to consume whoever was responsible for Adam Forrester's death.

"I can't let go like this," she said as Walter joined her in the backseat. "I don't know what I can do, but I have to do something. I have to do what I can to find out what really happened."

Walter was dismayed. He knew the situation was dangerous and he didn't want Tiffany in harm's way.

"We have to trust the authorities," he started. "I think they are going to do everything possible to bring whoever killed your father to justice.

"Besides, what would you do? What could we do? Why don't we wait and see what happens? For now, I think the best course of action is to leave the investigation in the hands of the police and the homicide experts."

She knew he was right, but it didn't matter.

"I owe it to him," she mumbled. And she owed it to herself. She wasn't afraid of the truth. In fact, she honestly believed it might set her free.

What she feared most was living the rest of her life without knowing.

She was torn. It was imperative she return to Chicago immediately or it would be impossible for her to meet the production deadlines for her fall design show.

Ron Delpit

Tiffany knew no one in Vegas, but still she had to make an effort.

And since she was sure Walter would try to dissuade her from getting involved, she simply wouldn't tell him.

Back in her suite at the Colossus, she searched through her purse for the business card Walter had given her earlier.

"There it is," she said aloud as she looked at the plain black and white card.

"Detective Sergeant Don Sarabian, Las Vegas Metropolitan Police Department."

Hesitantly, she dialed the number.

"Sarabian." The voice sounded gruff.

"Hello, detective. My name is Tiffany Wayne. I'm Adam Forrester's daughter."

He knew who she was.

"I just wanted to talk to you about my father…I mean about the case…I mean about any progress with finding out who killed him." She was nervous. She really didn't know what she wanted. She felt silly.

"I understand, Miss Wayne. And very I'm sorry about your father." The voice didn't seem as intimidating as when he first answered.

"We're doing all we can, Miss Wayne.

"We have committed almost every available man to this case. It is our top priority. I can assure you we are doing everything humanly possible to catch whoever is responsible.

"There are hundreds of leads to explore," Miss Wayne, "and we're going to explore every one. There are no shortcuts in something like this," he said bluntly.

"Is there anything more I can do?"

"Not really. I know it's a lot to ask, but you have to trust us to do our job."

She wondered if she could.

"Do cases like this usually take a long time?"

"Sometimes they do," he answered, trying to be patient. "You never know when you're going to get a break in a case. I told Mrs. Forrester the same thing a few minutes ago.

"In fact, I told her I'd keep her informed of our progress. You say you're going back to Chicago, so it might be a good idea if you kept in touch with Mrs.Forrester. I'm sure she'll keep you in the loop."

Fat chance of that.

There was nothing she could do. Calling Diana was out of the question. There was no possibility the widow Forrester would cooperate.

She'd have to find another way. Maybe Sarabian's superior. Or a private eye.

The Chief of Police was no help.

Stan Marksbury, Las Vegas' top cop, had already handled six calls regarding the Forrester case, plus been to a briefing with the mayor, by the time Tiffany got through to him. In addition the press was all over him.

64

A hotel owner being gunned down, in his own home, was a public relations nightmare. The national media portrayed it as a mob hit, and wondered if it could be the forerunner to a gangland war, while the local papers editorialized that crime might be out of control in Vegas. It was no-win situation.

He forced himself to listen politely to Miss Tiffany Wayne.

Marksbury was as puzzled by Forrester's death as anyone. He'd been on the force twenty-one years, the last eight as chief, and never, in his memory had such a prestigious citizen been murdered without the police later discovering he was into something shady. Usually drugs or the mob.

A few years back Lefty Rosenthal, the notorious bookmaker and an exec at the Stardust Hotel, had survived a car bomb. He had worked the case. No one was ever arrested because it was no more than a message from the mob to Lefty to mind his p's and q's. Lefty got the message, toned down his very public image, and moved to San Diego.

He couldn't help but think that maybe this was another message. None of it made sense unless Forrester was somehow involved in the mob. That was the only information he really needed to know. If it was a mob hit he'd ease back on the investigation.

He couldn't afford the manpower and they'd probably never solve it anyway. He'd said as much to the mayor, but in the meantime he'd have to deal with the family and the press.

"I understand," he repeated two or three times, in answer to her comments.

"We're going to continue to do everything we can," Miss Wayne. "I'll keep an open line of communication with your step-mother, "Mrs. Forrester.""

Tiffany's ears were red.

"Give me your number in Chicago, Miss Wayne, and I'll call you if something turns up." He didn't pick up a pencil. "There's nothing more you can do here."

"If, Chief Marksbury? Or when?"

She knew he was pacifying her.

The police were a dead end.

Maybe she'd hire a private investigator out of Chicago, but first she had to get there.

She spent the next hour making travel arrangements, managing to reserve first-class seats for both she and Walter on an 11:40 p.m. red-eye flight later that night.

"I shouldn't leave before the will is read," Walter said apologetically. "You must be represented. And I don't think it's such a good idea for you to leave tonight. You know how uncomfortable it was coming out here. Even in first class."

"I really wish you would wait until tomorrow. Please do me a favor and allow me to try and book you an early morning flight. That way you can get a good night's sleep and be well rested."

She couldn't argue with his logic. She could stay in the hotel and get a decent night's sleep in a regular bed instead of twisting her neck and body in a cramped airplane seat for five hours.

It wasn't necessary she be there for the reading. She did not want to sit idly by and allow Diana the satisfaction of gloating over her new empire. She was a non-violent person, but after what had happened at the funeral home, Tiffany was not sure she could maintain her cool if she came face to face with Diana again.

Walter made a reservation for her on a morning flight and she thanked him.

She stayed in her room the remainder of the day, sitting in front of the television long into the night while old black and white movies unfolded tired story lines in deafening silence. Hour after hour she stared at the tiny images, the TV sound muted so the words wouldn't run together with the dialogue already playing in her head.

Thirteen floors above, in the exclusive thirty-fourth floor penthouse suite a sleeping Diana Forrester turned toward the middle of the bed in an effort to shift into a more comfortable position, her bare left arm reaching out in the night, a contented smile on her lips.

A muscled arm enveloped her, pulling her naked body closer. She felt the warmth of his hardness as she nestled against his firm torso. He gently caressed her breasts and kissed her deeply. Her senses were immediately awakened, and in the dark his fingers plunged tenderly into her familiar wetness.

"Make love to me again," she whispered. "I need you. Tonight I need you more than ever."

She pushed back the sheets and in the darkness a satisfied smile crept across Sonny Fremont's slightly stubbled face. Funny how things worked out.

"I need you too baby," he moaned as he moved on top of her, his manhood responding to the sensuous beckoning of her soft hands massaging his inner thigh.

Things were going to change. Nothing could stop him now. Everything he had ever wanted or dreamed about was finally within his grasp.

Who said you couldn't have it all? He would. It was just a matter of time.

Chapter 5
Sonny Fremont

Sonny Fremont was guilty of a lot of things, but forgetting where he came from, and how much dirt had been kicked in his face on the way to making it in Las Vegas, was not one of them.

The dry, hard-baked oil fields of Oklahoma were thousands of miles from the Vegas Strip but only a heartbeat away in his mind. And there were still a lot of nights when he awoke in a cold sweat, dreaming he could hear his mother's loud and piercing voice calling "Sonn-ee, Sonn-ee." His given name was Harold Rainmaker. His father was part Cherokee and he was proud of his heritage even though he was really only one-fourth Indian. He was named after his uncle and hated the name Harold. He much preferred "Sonny", a nickname he acquired because of his penchant for "Sonny Boy", a cheap syrupy concentrate that was their main lunch and dinner beverage.

His mother would mix a twenty-nine cent bottle of the thick red liquid with two quarts of water and they always had something to wash down the red beans and rice or her special once a week pork chops. As a kid he drank enough "Sonny Boy" to turn his insides red. Still, he never seemed to tire of the sweet taste it left in his mouth. And the "Sonny" tag was a lot easier to deal with than Harold, especially for a pudgy thirteen-year-old with a squeaky voice and cheeks that looked like they were stuffed with jawbreakers.

A month after his seventeenth birthday he had run away, because there was nothing for him in Broken Bow. The town was almost deserted, the people were mainly living out their days and he had bigger dreams.

Sonny Rainmaker was just 14 when he watched his father die in the oil fields he had stalked for 43 years, collapsing from a stroke as the hot Oklahoma sun baked the mud and oil into his dark skin. The other men in the field tried to make some shade, but there was none, save for their own shadows.

They dabbed at his crusty face with his own dirty bandanna, dampened only with the tepid water from their canteens. They had called a doctor, knowing there was little chance he would arrive before Seth Rainmaker exited the planet.

Sonny had watched helplessly, his own mud caked face wrinkled, but otherwise emotionless as he saw the life slowly slipping from his father's body, his parched lips cracked like the dry pancake dirt of the Oklahoma panhandle. Sonny didn't have to fight back tears, because none were pressing to break loose. All he felt was fear. Fear he'd end up the same way.

"Give him some room," the foreman yelled as an old Chevy pickup carrying the town doctor rumbled across the dusty road. All but two of them moved back to their jobs. Sonny crept closer, until he was standing directly over his father.

They exchanged a look Sonny would never forget.

"I'm sorry kid. I did all I knew how to do. Get the hell out of this godforsaken place if you can."

Seth Rainmaker used what seemed to be his last bit of strength to cross himself, even though he wasn't Catholic.

He was dead before the truck stopped rolling.

Sonny swallowed hard as the men wrapped his father's body in a worn army blanket and laid it in the back of the truck. It was at that moment he knew he had to run. He ran all the way home but didn't go in. He stopped under a huge elm tree fifty yards from the house. No one had come to tell his mother, and he didn't want to be the one to break the news.

Sonny worked in Jake Fisher's Pawnshop the next two summers, doing odd jobs and sweeping up. Old Jake really didn't need any extra help but he felt sorry for the family after the tragedy.

Of all his chores it was the dusting he liked most because it allowed him to hold and polish Cowboy Joe Foster's guitar.

Everyone in Broken Bow knew the story of the guitar, and how it had belonged to Cowboy Joe, one of the Midwest's biggest radio stars. Cowboy's widow Mattie had taken a loan against it after her husband died and never come back to claim it.

From the day he had first run his chubby fingers across the strings and held the scratched two-tone hull to his chest, Sonny knew he would one day make it to the stage. He had to. The guitar would make him famous. He could feel it when he held it close to his body. One day people would clap for him.

Out of every $20 paycheck, he gave Jake five bucks as an installment on the guitar. He kept five bucks for himself and gave his mother the remaining ten.

Working for Jake, Sonny learned a lot about heartbreak, because the people who frequented the shop were desperate. Most were so down on their luck they were hocking wedding rings and family heirlooms to pay rent or buy food.

Two days before the start of school and his senior year, Sonny Rainmaker threw some clothes in a backpack and headed for town.

"I'm getting outta here Jake. There's nothing for me here."

Jake Fisher knew Sonny was right. He had run the pawnshop for 36 years and he knew not many local kids ever made it past the city limit signs.

"Good luck to you boy," Jake said wistfully. "Here's a little something to tide you over 'til you get work," he said, slipping a faded $20 bill into Sonny's palm.

"I suppose you ought to take this with you too," the old man said, pulling Cowboy Joe's guitar off the wall hook where it hung behind the counter. You've just about paid for it anyway."

Sonny smiled broadly, then hugged Jake Fisher. Quickly he backed away and stuck out his hand. The older man shook it.

Ten minutes later he was walking west along the two-lane blacktop frontage road that eventually intersected with Interstate 40, his head down, his spirits up and his thumb pointing toward Nashville. His mother was at work, waiting tables at the Broken Bow Diner, and he didn't stop to say goodbye.

A trucker in a gleaming silver cab hauling overnight freight roared to a stop at the highway on ramp, the powerful air brakes of his sixteen wheeler letting out a blast that almost blew Sonny off the shoulder of the road into the bush.

"Where ya headed kid?"

"Nashville, I guess," Sonny said, sounding none too certain as he slipped his right hand into his jeans pocket to make sure the $20 bill was still there. He was scared so he clung tightly to his guitar, looked out the window and watched silently as the flat, barren Oklahoma countryside and its ugly oil derricks faded into the background.

He made it as far as Memphis, arriving two days later feeling as if he had been on the road for a month. He was tired and sore from sleeping at odd hours in uncomfortable positions. He smelled of sweat, and the stale smoke of the trucker's cigarettes clung to his clothes and hair.

Nashville was still his preferred destination and he'd get there, but first he had to deal with Memphis. He had never been away from home before but he was no longer frightened. He learned where to get a shower, a meal and a cot without answering too many questions and picked up a job washing dishes in a truck stop restaurant. He worked nights and spent his days hanging around the music district gathering all the information he could about singers, songs and record companies. He was also honing his guitar skills.

He had written to his mother, explaining his leaving was something he had to do, and he suspected she wasn't too upset, since it meant one less mouth to feed. He apologized for not giving her the $20 Jake Fisher had given him. Afraid she might send his older brother Cary to find him, he had a trucker mail the letter from somewhere in Texas. A week later, with money from his dishwashing paycheck he sent her the twenty. This time the postmark was Baton Rouge.

It was three months before he hit Nashville where he lucked into a job as a stagehand at the "Wild Blue Yonder", a roadhouse dance joint that featured touring acts four nights a week. It gave him a chance to see how different performers prepared and how audiences reacted to what they said and did. Sonny Rainmaker was learning firsthand how to work a crowd and his musical skills were growing by leaps and bounds thanks to the tips he was getting from the visiting musicians.

On occasion he would get to jam with the new bands and he lived for those times. He knew music was what he wanted to do with his life and that he wanted, make that needed, to be on stage.

Four months later he got his chance, and it was a disaster.

"Why don't you go out there and warm them up," said Red Brewster, sucking down a long-necked bottle of beer backstage. Brewster and his band had just pulled into the busy parking lot a few minutes earlier. They were an hour late and their equipment had not yet been unpacked.

"Go ahead boy", Red urged, as much because he wanted to quiet the restless crowd as take his sweet time getting ready.

"You can do it. It ain't no big deal." He had jammed with Red's band at rehearsals two or three times and held his own. "Five or ten minutes should do it," Red whispered. "And don't be nervous."

It was the break Sonny had dreamed about.

"Wild Blue" owner Bucky Gray introduced him, explaining to the packed house that Red Brewster had run into foul weather and needed another few minutes to get ready.

He strummed the opening bars of a popular country tune, then began to sing the words he'd heard a hundred times on the radio. His high-pitched voice seemed to come out an octave higher than normal and he sounded like a frightened girl. Instead of applause, they began to laugh. He didn't make it past the first verse, tears rolling down his cheeks as Red walked on stage to save him.

Backstage, they took turns trying to console him.

"Hell, I sounded like a cat in heat until I was about 19," said Bob Hodges, Red's bass player.

"You still do," someone laughed, but the hurt in Sonny's stomach wouldn't go away. The memory of the polite applause as he first took the stage burned in his memory. The humiliation, however, made him leave Nashville.

He bought a one-way bus ticket to Los Angeles and along the way he made up his mind that as soon as he got enough money he'd have an operation to fix whatever was wrong with his vocal chords. He could never have a career as a country singer with a falsetto voice.

After days of sleeping in a $12 a night flophouse room, which he shared with two other teenagers, and eating McDonald's or nothing at all, he was practically broke. Finding work in Hollywood was a lot tougher than getting a job in Memphis or Nashville.

"Hey Oklahoma, there are all kinds of ways to make fast money in this town, provided you're willing to do what it takes." The speaker was Jamie Barnes, a handsome blond youngster about the same age. Jamie was a cut above all of the other street kids he'd met on Hollywood Boulevard. He was articulate, didn't do drugs, to Sonny's knowledge, was always well groomed and never without money in his pocket.

Sonny eyed him suspiciously.

"I won't steal," he said to the well-dressed youngster who sat across the table.

"I'll find a job soon."

"Whatever you say man. But this ain't stealing," Jamie said calmly enough to arouse Sonny's curiosity.

"And I don't want to get messed up in drugs or anything illegal."

"This ain't illegal either," Jamie promised.

Seven months and three porno movies later, Sonny was sitting in a doctor's office in Beverly Hills. He had enough money in his pocket to pay the bill and enough guilt in his heart to fill the Grand Canyon.

The porn money was good and he had to admit he liked the work but he quit cold after saving up seven grand. His decision wasn't popular with the producer's moneyman, a good-looking guy in his mid 20's who wore silk suits and expensive Italian shoes.

It was also Sonny's first encounter with Mario Torino.

"You can make a lot of dough here kid. One or two more pictures and you'll be able to afford anything you've ever wanted."

Saying no was something he'd have to handle delicately.

"You're probably right, Mr. Torino," he said trying to downplay the whole thing, "but I just don't want to do this anymore. I want to be a singer."

"I don't think you understand," Torino said slowly, "it would be in your best interests to finish this out. A couple more pictures and everybody's happy. Then if you want to be a singer I'll do my best to help you."

The slow, deliberate tone of Mario's voice conveyed his threat. He was trying to intimidate him into doing a few more movies.

He knew he couldn't give in. If he didn't walk away now he might get too comfortable with the money. And if the flicks started to get major exposure and somebody recognized him, Sonny knew it might ruin his career as a singer.

His knees were shaking and he didn't want a confrontation with Mario, so he tried to buy time. He didn't have the guts to say "no" to Mario's face.

"Maybe one or two more pictures wouldn't hurt," he said not meaning it. "Give me a day or two to think it over. Okay Mr. Torino?"

"That's better." Mario backed off a bit, thinking he had gotten through. He clapped his arm around Sonny's bony shoulder and reassured him, "Don't worry, everything will work out, and before long you'll be able to move on and do whatever it is you want."

Mario was only a few years older and Sonny wondered how a guy so young had worked his way into a position of power so quickly. He didn't learn until later that Mario was just an errand boy for some Chicago hoods.

He'd made three movies and socked away seven thousand dollars. It was more money than he had ever seen at one time in his life. In a good month even Cowboy Jake didn't make that much.

His savings, coupled with his obsession to be a singer, gave him the courage to walk away from Mario's little studio. He skipped out of the flophouse and was a "no-show" at the production meeting for the next movie.

He knew Mario would be furious.

A week or so later he ran into Jamie.

"Mario's plenty pissed at you man. You'd better either come back or stay the hell out of his way."

"What will he do?"

"Are you stupid, or what?" The guy could hurt you big time."

"Maybe I ought to call him and explain."

"I wouldn't if I were you. If you're not going to come back you'd better just get the fuck out of town."

He intended to take Jamie's advice, but not until after his doctor appointment.

"I'm afraid there's nothing wrong with your vocal chords, young man," the doctor said as he came to rest in the high-backed chair behind his desk.

"Then what's wrong with me? Am I just a freak or what?"

"Not at all." A small smile played on the doctor's lips. "The procedure is very simple and can be handled on an outpatient basis. Quite simply you have an inverted testicle. When it is properly lowered your voice should be normal."

The operation was as easy as the doctor had suggested, and before long he was picking up jobs in little clubs and piano bars all around the San Fernando Valley and the Hollywood Hills. He made friends with some other musicians around town, including a few studio players and backup session singers. They encouraged him to try his luck in Vegas.

"That's the place to go," said Jackson Carter, a black singer who seemed to know more about Vegas than anyone else in their crowd.

"I'm telling you man, Vegas is off the hook. It's a happening place. Broads, booze and money. And the brightest lights this side of Broadway. Besides, there ain't nobody in LA waving a record contract at you."

Sonny wasn't sold.

"Don't you want to see your name in lights?" Jackson taunted. "Man, with your talent you won't have any problem getting a lounge gig over there. You gotta at least give it a shot."

He wanted his name in lights more than Jackson or any of their friends could possibly know. It was his dream.

He didn't own a car but the airfare to Vegas was cheap enough and there were flights every hour from LAX. He felt good about Vegas. So good he only bought a one-way ticket.

A one way ticket to Paradise.

And Vegas had turned out more than okay so far, but it was going to get better. He wanted it all. Power, fame and respect.

He had headlined almost every big showroom and was in a position to be a principal in a casino if things went as planned. Diana Forrester was his express ticket. When she officially took over the Colossus she was going to make him the biggest star on the Strip. That was her promise to him.

And everyone knew he had paid his dues.

Shortly after blowing out of LA, he'd hit the downtown casino lounges, like Jackson had suggested, the theory being it would be easier to get a job in joints featuring round the clock entertainment. Those clubs were like cable TV. They had plenty of hours to fill and were always looking for performers to play the dead morning gigs.

He spent his first three days in Vegas trying to get past the secretaries in various Downtown Entertainment Directors' offices.

It was a slow and frustrating process. He didn't have a demo tape, an act or a set of 8x10 glossies. One thing he did have was time, and he used his idle hours to check out the lounge acts that played the early morning shifts, studying the way they handled themselves on stage.

He also kept his ears open for names and knocked on as many doors as he could during the day, hoping to catch an entertainment director willing to give him a break.

As Sonny Fremont thought back on how it all started, he was amazed he had made it at all.

I really didn't know shit when I came here. It's a miracle I am where I am today. Headlining on the Vegas Strip and sleeping with the Queen of the Colossus. Life had been good despite the rough beginning.

He even remembered his first gig and how he got it.

It was a Thursday night, around midnight. He had tried three times during the day to meet Mint entertainment director Eddie Morrison, finally deciding the best time to catch him would be late night when he came in to check on the evening lounge acts.

Morrison was a skinny little man around sixty with a bad rug, tobacco stained teeth and an open-collar shirt. Sonny figured the guy had seen better days and better hotels. He had probably landed at the Mint because someone owed him a favor. He was typical Old Vegas, sporting a diamond pinkie ring and a large gold medallion around his neck.

It was a few ticks after midnight when Sonny peeked his head in the partially open door to Morrison's office.

Morrison was on the phone, but waved Sonny in. It was a cramped little room with eight by ten headshots and newspapers spread over most of the floor. There was only one chair and Eddie pointed toward it as Sonny squeezed inside.

"Whaddya mean he can't be here," Morrison screamed into the phone. "His fucking show starts in two hours. This is the last time he screws up. He's not a fucking star anymore you know. He can't keep getting loaded then look for someone to wipe his ass. He bangs all the waitresses in the joint then calls in sick because his dick is sore. Screw him. I'm tired of having to scramble to cover his ass, and you should be too. Let him stay in bed. He's through here."

The man slammed down the phone and turned his piercing eyes to Sonny.

"And who the hell are you?" Before Sonny could answer Morrison continued his tirade.

They say timing is everything and in this instance the axiom proved true.

Sonny listened patiently while Morrison vented. When the little man's rage began to subside he became more reasonable.

Morrison quizzed him about his background and Sonny embellished his resume by lying about his experience. Morrison also tested him on the lyrics to a dozen different songs in various music categories and he impressed the older man with his versatility.

"You got an act? You got backup singers?

"I can sing anything," Sonny replied, "but I don't have a band or backup singers." Sonny shoved a dog-eared clipping from the trade newspaper *"Variety"* across the small desk. It was a favorable review done when he played a small lounge in LA.

"I don't know," Morrison hem-hawed. "You're a good looking kid, but this is hard work. Sometimes there's no one in the audience at 4 a.m. and you have to play anyway. It isn't all fun and games.

"What's your name, anyway?"

"Sonny Rainwater."

"Boring fucking name...What are you, some sort of Indian?"

"Part Cherokee," Sonny mumbled.

"Ya gotta give 'em something with pizzazz," Eddie Morrison said pensively.

"Make people think they're seeing the Second Coming of Jesus. Or at least Louie Prima.

Morrison rolled out names like Sonny Gold, Sonny Silver, Sonny Day and Sonny Sky before settling on Fremont.

"Fremont works," Morrison said as he stared out his second-story window at the Fremont Street sign." He was proud of his brainstorm. They'll remember that, and you know what kid? Even if you don't have a lick of talent you already have a street named after you." The man laughed out loud and Sonny hoped he wasn't laughing at him.

Harold Rainwater was so *"not cool",* he had no idea The Mint was on Fremont street, or that the street which bore his name was at that time the heart of Las Vegas.

"And don't ever forget who named you kid. Eddie Morrison named you. I created you." And so Sonny Fremont was born.

It had been a long and not always pleasant journey from Oklahoma to Vegas but he had finally arrived. Along the way he had bussed tables in Memphis, washed dishes in Nashville and pumped gas in Arizona. He wasn't proud of those jobs, or of sleeping on park benches and in three-dollar flophouses, but they were not memories of which he was ashamed. He had plenty of those.

"Are you any fucking good?" Morrison asked again, then added in a nasty tone, "You'd better be. I'm going to give you a chance kid and I don't like to look stupid. You're on in two hours. Three days a week you'll play from 2 to 8 in the morning, three days you'll play from 3 a.m. to 9 a.m. You'll do 50 minute sets, six times a day and you start tonight.

"I'll have a house band ready to play backup. Bring your own music and be here by 1 a.m. so you can meet the guys.

"One more thing kid," the agent said as he stared at Sonny's now six-foot frame and his jet-black hair. "If you bomb here you can forget about working anywhere else in this whole town. If you can't make it here you just can't make it."

They hadn't discussed money and Sonny didn't care. He was going to get another chance and somebody was even going to pay him.

That couldn't happen today Sonny mused. Everybody's got to get a piece. My manager, the band, my agent. Everybody's got their fingers up my ass.

He had left Eddie Morrison's office in a daze. Across the street he bought two brightly colored satin shirts, one turquoise, the other fire engine red. They would be his costumes.

For fifty minutes an hour, six times a night Sonny Fremont gave everything he had, and he never cheated the sparse audiences. He played to drunks, to losers just looking for a place to sit before hitting the sheets or the streets, to hookers and an occasional high-roller. He and Cowboy Joe's guitar were soon the talk of the downtown lounges and he developed a strong local following. When dealers and waitresses stopped by it was a form of tribute, and Sonny ate up the attention. He loved the fame.

Women admired him and he knew how to turn their vulnerable admiration to his advantage. Sometimes he'd keep a notebook detailing how many he'd slept with in a week, then try and top his own record the following week.

On his twenty-first birthday he smoked his first joint, had too much tequila and wound up passed out on the king sized bed in his apartment with a pair of identical twins cursing him in frustration. The roller coaster ride of notoriety and the increasing applause was more than he had dreamed when he was back in Oklahoma. This was for real.

It didn't matter that there were nights he played to an empty lounge, or that no one was coming around offering him jobs in the main showrooms. Morrison had moved him into a better time slot and he was happy right where he was. People knew his name. They knew who Sonny Fremont was and he was confident it wouldn't be long before he'd see his name on a Strip marquee.

But headlining took longer than he anticipated.

Ron Delpit

He sweated it out for three years in the downtown lounges, moving from the Mint to the Horseshoe to the Four Queens and back again. He learned the business and the town. Finally, the call came, but not quite the way he expected.

"Hey Sonny, there's a guy out front who says he's got some business to discuss with you if you've got a minute."

It was 4 a.m. and Sonny had just finished his last show. He was toweling off his hair when Mint stage manager Bobby Glenn gave him the message.

What's he look like Bobby?"

"Looks like money," Glenn replied. "Nice suit, expensive watch. He's sitting in the back row. Could be an agent or maybe just some rich guy trying to sell you something."

Sonny peeled off his white satin shirt in favor of a pullover sweater, ran a comb through his hair and walked around the back of the stage to the small lounge. It was nearly 5 a.m. and the room was almost dark.

The man smiled as Sonny approached the small booth in the rear of the deserted lounge.

"Hi Sonny, great show. I'm Oscar Bento, president of Four Star Talent Agency in Los Angeles," he said extending his hand and offering his card.

"My pleasure," Sonny said shaking the man's hand.

Sonny had handled all of his own contracts and been his own agent. He'd sold himself short a few times but at least he didn't have to pay a commission and had no one to answer to. His career also had no upward direction and he was aware of it.

"Third time this week I've caught your act," the man said. "I like your style. You really know how to work a crowd and you have a great repertoire."

"Thanks." Sonny was eating up the praise.

"I'll cut right to the chase here Sonny. No sense beating around the bush. I'd like you to give our company a chance to represent you.

"I understand that until now you've represented yourself and handled all your own business, but I'll guarantee you that if you sign with Four Star, we'll get you booked on the Strip, in a main room within six months."

Sonny sat up a little straighter in his chair.

Oscar Bento's eyes were serious. Sonny guessed he was in his 40s, but he could easily have passed for younger if not for the heavy pouches under his eyes. He was well spoken, appeared sincere and was holding out the brass ring Sonny had been waiting for since arriving in Vegas. Was it the next step?

Sensing Sonny's hesitance, Bento kept talking.

"Once you're a headliner, the next stop is records, then the big screen," Oscar said confidently. "You have the looks and charisma to make it in the movies, no doubt about it." Bento's words were like helium, filling up his senses. Some of it Sonny had dreamed. Some of it he had not dared imagine.

76

"All of that sounds great Mr. Bento, but I don't know." He had seen and heard enough scams to know not everything came out the way it sounded. He didn't want to get suckered by something in fine print.

He had two more meetings with Oscar Bento over the next month and each time he liked what he heard. The promises all sounded good. And Oscar was saying what he wanted to hear.

"How about giving me a copy of the contract so I can show it to my lawyer."

"Sure. No problem," Oscar said. "Everything's on the up and up. Have your guy look it over. We want you to be comfortable. We're going to be working together for a long time."

"Everything seems to check out," his lawyer reported. "Four Star checks out okay." It was the green light Sonny had hoped for. "They're on the level, but their contract will be tough to break if you decide you want out. It's pretty binding, so be sure you're comfortable with them directing your future."

Sonny only heard half the warning. The loudest words ringing in his ears were Oscar's promises of a record deal, a Strip headlining job and a possible movie deal. If Four Star could make just one of those happen he'd gladly sell them his soul.

He flew to Los Angeles and signed the papers in Oscar's office. They celebrated with dinner at a fancy Beverly Hills eatery where Sonny saw some familiar movie stars. Frank and Barbara Sinatra came in as they were finishing their meal and on the way out Oscar stopped by their table and said hello. Oscar called Sonny over and introduced him to the Chairman of the Board, erasing even the smallest doubt Sonny might have had about Oscar's credibility.

The contract called for Four Star to handle all of Sonny's business dealings and manage his money. Oscar even promised to try and arrange a guest shot on a couple of network variety shows, which he did within three months. Suddenly, Sonny was living large.

He had a renewed energy. He had met Sinatra, Oscar was going to open the right doors and had promised he wouldn't be doing lounges very much longer.

He went home on a high. The shows had gone well and he was sure he had made the right move by signing with Oscar and Four Star. Soon he'd be on the Strip with a big star on his dressing room door. That night he dreamed of the applause. Of sellout crowds giving him standing ovations.

He awoke about noon, to a loud banging on his apartment door.

It was a kid from the French Bouquet Flower Shop holding the largest floral bouquet he'd ever seen.

` "You Sonny Fremont?" the delivery boy asked, unimpressed.

"The one and only," Sonny smiled.

"Then this is for you."

Sonny grabbed a five-dollar bill from the small table next to the door and handed it to the boy.

For a minute Sonny sat at his dining room table staring at the flowers, then he plucked the card from the little plastic holder stuck in the arrangement.

"Sonny,

I'm so happy we're working together. We're going to make you the biggest star in Las Vegas and I already know you can make it in the movies. I'll be in touch real soon."

The card was a little confusing but he didn't give it a second thought.

Things were falling into place. Oscar was moving him up in the world. He had made the right decision.

As he set the large vase on the counter he glanced again at the signature card.

The flowers weren't from Oscar. The card was signed "Best wishes, Mario Torino, owner, Four Star Talent." Sonny Fremont's face turned to stone.

This time he knew Mario Torino wouldn't let him get away. This time Mario owned him. And so went the uneasy relationship over the next few years, as Sonny's star rose and Mario and his gang reaped huge profits.

The years passed and Sonny lived in a limbo of ambivalence. His sensory being was enjoying the fame, fortune and pleasures of success while his tormented inner-self constantly devised plans to break free and rid himself of Torino and Four Star.

He was building strength, through money and maturity. And he was always on the lookout for the type contacts that would not be afraid of his underworld partners.

But he knew Torino was ruthless. And worst of all Mario knew his darkest secret. A secret Sonny had hoped would never surface. It was a chapter of his life he wanted desperately to keep hidden. Now he would be forced to remember it because Mario would never let him forget the dirty little movies.

He knew running was not an option.

Chapter 6
Family Business

When Dominic "The Donut" Donato rose from the high-back leather chair at the head of the long oak conference table an immediate quiet came over the room.

The other four men gave him their full and undivided attention, and with good reason.

At 66, he was still a strong stump of a man with powerful shoulders and the solid build of a wrestler or retired football lineman. And despite his sagging jowls his huge hands and massive arms proved he was still as strong as a bull.

Legend had it that he had earned his nickname in the 50s when he had single handedly murdered three men foolish enough to try to double-cross him. After killing them with his bare hands he sat at their table and gorged himself on the freshly baked donuts they had brought from the corner bakery that same morning.

"The Donut" had done nothing to diminish his reputation as a cold-blooded killer in the ensuing years, and now, as the senior member of the five major Cosa Nostra families he commanded respect. Donato had risen through the ranks, and had the support of virtually every capo and foot soldier on the street, which is why he had been elected chairman of the family heads by unanimous vote.

Donato had also learned to change with the times. He knew the families could no longer solve all their problems through violence or gang wars, and he had demonstrated on more than one occasion that he could mediate disagreements and bring about compromise without bloodshed.

It was that rare combination of ruthlessness and reason that made him the perfect choice to cast the deciding vote when necessary.

"What we do is a business," he said looking around the table. "It's like any other business, and we must do whatever we can to keep things running smoothly.

"We must always explore every option before we take physical action," he warned. And when we're dealing with a problem that affects someone out of your own territory it must be discussed before you are allowed to move.

"You can deal with problems in your own cities however you want to. The council will never interfere. Anything else we must talk about.

"Is that understood?"

The men in the room nodded.

"We don't visit someone just because we don't like them," he said slamming his fist hard on the heavy, newly waxed tabletop.

"There are times when we must set an example, but that doesn't happen unless the majority of us in this room agree. Capish?"

There were whispers but no rebuttals.

The Donut knew not everyone agreed, and he knew they would still make their own rules when they saw fit but that was the nature of their business. Besides, it was a violent world. Storeowners didn't pay protection because they liked your personality.

The assembled family heads were secure in their privacy because the meetings were always at different locations, and the conference rooms were always swept for bugs, bombs and monitoring devices. Still, it paid to be careful, and none of them ever called one another by name during their conferences. Being careful was how most of them had managed to survive.

None of them wanted the notoriety of John Gotti, nor did they want the consequences. The less the media knew about them the better.

"Your attention, gentlemen. We won't be long today."

"The main purpose of this meeting is to formally announce that the situation in Vegas has been handled, and there'll be no more battles over that territory," Donato said roughly.

"The Kansas City, New York, St. Louis and Detroit families will hold on to what they have. The Chicago family is in the process of gaining control of the Colossus, which should more than make up for them losing the Stardust and Fremont Hotels.

"I'll let Mario fill you in on the details."

Mario Torino stood and faced his peers.

At 36, he was the second youngest man in the room. Only Tony Andreolli, who had taken over the Cleveland organization following his father's fatal heart attack, was younger.

Torino's jet-black hair sported a fresh razor cut, his fingernails were recently manicured and he exuded confidence. He had smooth dark skin and soft hands, and his expertly tailored $2,000 Armani suit and silk Kenneth Cole shirt gave him the look of a corporate executive headed for the boardroom rather than the head of the Chicago mob about to address his counterparts.

"As most of you know the Colossus owner, Adam Forrester, is now out of the picture," he said slowly, as if gathering his thoughts.

"However we must wait a respectable amount of time before we make our move to purchase the casino."

"Who decides what's a 'respectable' amount of time?" Joe Bonito asked almost before Mario stopped speaking.

"And what makes you think the new owner of the Colossus will be any easier to deal with than Forrester?" The questioner was Andreolli and his high-pitched voice always grated on Mario's nerves. "I hear Forrester's widow is a tough broad, almost as tough as him maybe."

"She may be," Mario said calmly, not wanting to let on he was offended by Andreolli's unspoken insinuation that Chicago might have trouble taking care of its own business.

"Our contact has everything under control,' he replied, "and he's already assured us that when the time comes, the lady will be all too happy to take the money and run."

He had not been around as long as some of the other bosses but Mario had quietly solidified his reputation as an effective leader.

When Paulie Giovanni died of natural causes two years earlier, everyone assumed it would be Mario's cousin who would step up as the Chicago boss. Only Mario and his cousin knew why it didn't happen that way.

They had made their own deal, with his college educated cousin opting for a high society profile and legitimate business interests, leaving Mario to oversee the loan sharking, bookmaking and drug trade.

Mario Torino had been raised on the streets and he had a sixth sense about what worked and what didn't. If he had a fault, it was being too quick with his temper but he had learned to control his emotions. He now realized that revealing what he was thinking and feeling was a luxury he couldn't afford.

Still, despite all the power he wielded, Mario would never make a major decision without checking with his cousin. He knew better.

For a moment there was disorder as several of the men spoke at once, some of them directing questions at Mario and others talking amongst themselves across the table.

"Quiet!"

There was no mistaking "The Donut's" booming baritone.

"This is Chicago's problem. The Colossus is what they bargained for and it's up to them to complete the deal. If they don't, their family is shit out of luck.

"They're not going to horn in or get a piece of anyone else's action in Vegas." It was the assurance the others had been waiting to hear.

"Just a minute…" The challenger was Alfonso Gambino and all eyes turned toward him. He was the new boss of New York, and he was as shrewd as he was vicious. His red, ruddy face was drawn tight as he pulled himself to his feet.

"I think there should be a definite time limit on how long Chicago has to take over the Colossus," he said defiantly. "Chicago tells us the deal will get done soon, but who knows. That shit could drag on for an indefinite period.

"I say if they haven't completed their deal in say, three or four months the Colossus should be fair game for any of us."

"There'll be no war over this," Dominic Donato barked louder than the cacophony of voices that immediately had begun debating Gambino's suggestion.

"Six months seems fair," Donato grumbled out loud. "All right, here's the way it'll go down. If Chicago hasn't taken over, or at least have everything in place to take over the Colossus in six months, we'll have another sit down and decide who's next in line for a crack at it."

In the end, they voted 4 to 1 in favor of the six-month moratorium, with Mario the lone dissenter. He felt certain they'd wrap up the takeover quickly; still he wanted it on record he was opposed to any time limit. He was pissed, but concealed his anger, managing a weak smile when the others offered him congratulations. They were circling like vultures, hoping for a feeding frenzy, and he understood. He would have done the same.

An hour later the meeting was adjourned and the men left the room five minutes apart, to avoid arousing suspicion.

Mario fastened the top button of his overcoat as he stepped out the front door of the Sheraton Hopkins Airport Hotel into a cold blast of air. He had thought about staying and having dinner but he hated Cleveland. The weather was bad, the basketball team was horrible and the air was foul. The whole town was a slum. Tony Andreolli was in garbage, which was probably why the Ohio boss liked it. Andreolli and Cleveland were made for each other.

It was after 11 p.m. when his Continental Flight touched down at Midway. He would have preferred O'Hare because Midway added an extra ten minutes to his drive home. But there were no flights from Cleveland that fit his schedule, and tonight he didn't mind. He needed time to think about the events of the meeting.

He also had a stop to make.

Mario turned off at exit 63 and pulled into the parking lot of Molly's Roadside Diner. The closed sign was irrelevant. He parked in front of the empty phone booth, then reached in his glove compartment for a pre-paid phone card.

It was only 10:15 in Vegas so he knew where his man would be. He dialed the number from memory, the little long distance beeps and connection tones playing an odd musical melody in his ear.

The private line was answered on the second ring.

"I'm listening." The voice on the other end sounded cocky.

"Chicago here," he said, ignoring the attitude. "Sounds like you're in good spirits."

The man recognized Mario's voice immediately and turned serious.

"Just sitting around unwinding a bit. Must be important if you're calling so late," he said, anxious to know the reason for the call.

"What's important is what's going on at your end. Every so often I get a little nervous and I need to be reassured, so humor me. What's the climate like out there right now?

"Does it seem like the weather is beginning to clear or is it still a bit stormy?"

Mario did not like to talk in metaphors however he knew it was the safe thing to do, even from a supposedly secure pay phone.

One never knew what new devices the FBI might have up its sleeve. He randomly chose the pay phones he used, changed cell phones every few weeks and was careful about what he said when he did use a land phone.

"The weather seems to be clearing up nicely. In fact we may have blue skies a lot sooner than we expected."

"That's very encouraging." Mario felt the anxiety in his stomach easing a bit.

"We want to complete the transaction I talked to you about in the next sixty to ninety days. Any longer and we could run into some serious problems."

"That timing sounds right and I think you'll find a very anxious seller. The lady will be ready to do some business."

"Good. And I'm counting on you to guarantee there won't be any surprises or last minute difficulties."

"There won't be," the voice said quickly. "Remember, I have a lot at stake here too."

"I know you do," Mario answered. And he thanked God for greed. It was a wonderful motivator.

"I'll tell my people that we have your word things are on schedule and everything will go as planned. And I strongly advise you see to it that everything does," Mario said forcefully, and there was no mistaking the seriousness of his tone.

In Chicago, Mario Torino placed the phone back on the metal base, a contented smile on his face. It was going to be the biggest deal of his life.

In Las Vegas, Sonny Fremont's heart was still pounding, the way it did every time he spoke to Mario Torino. The beige telephone handset was still clinging to his damp palm. If this deal came off he'd finally be a casino owner instead of just another hired hand with his name in big letters on the marquee.

If it didn't, he didn't even want to think about it.

The Colossus was worth at least twenty million a year in skimming alone, and as much as $100 million a year could be laundered. Mario knew it could ensure his spot as head of the Chicago Family for as long as he lived.

Automatically, he dialed another number. It was answered on the first ring.

"Yes?"

"It's me," he said, knowing the listener had been expecting his call.

"The Vegas deal is progressing as planned. We should be ready to move on it in sixty days or less."

"Any problems in Cleveland?"

"Only what you predicted. Gambino led a move against us, and the board voted to give us six months to complete the Colossus purchase. Otherwise the property goes back on the table and will be up for grabs."

There was a short silence on the other end of the phone.

"Gambino isn't the only one, Mario. At least three of them would love to get their hooks in the Colossus. And no matter what they agreed to do, someone will make a move before the six months. It'll be up to us to move quickly and keep our plans private. We can't afford a mistake."

"I understand."

"Then make sure none occurs. The key will be your man in Vegas. You know I've never had good feelings about him."

Mario felt a sharp pang in his gut. His cousin was the one person in the world he didn't want to disappoint.

"Don't worry. I'll sit on him. He'll pull it off, and he'll do it right because he knows he won't get a second chance."

"I'll leave that to you."

"Caio."

The irony of it didn't escape Mario Torino. Sonny Fremont, a man who had once run out on him, was now the focal point of a business deal that could make or break him. Would he run out again?

Sonny Fremont was too focused on the Colossus to realize the tables had turned. He now had Mario by the balls.

He walked slowly across his living room in the dark, then up the stairs to his bedroom. He laid his monogrammed blue velvet robe on the end of the bed, then slipped his naked body under the covers next to Diana Forrester.

She awoke and turned to kiss him.

"You feel nice," she said sleepily.

"You do too," he said kissing her hair.

It had been a long time since he had spent two nights in a row with her, but it was easier now, thanks to the unfortunate accident that had cost Adam Forrester his life.

She turned on her side, the curve of her naked body barely visible in the dim light. He put his arm over her shoulder, letting his hand come to rest on her breast. Minutes later he was astride her, ramming his manhood into her soft pliable body and reveling in her passionate promises that she would never leave him and would do anything in the world for him.

He'd give her the chance.

"Oh God," she moaned as she came, the orgasm more intense and lasting longer than she expected. "It keeps getting better and better. Promise you'll never leave me."

"Not in a million years."

The sex had energized them and they were both wide-awake. Diana reached for a cigarette, lit it and let out a heavy sigh as she lay on her back atop two fluffy pillows.

"You still bummed about your meeting with Forrester's kid?"he asked, sensing something was bothering her.

"I guess I am, a little," she said, taking a deep drag on the Marlboro Light.

"The spoiled little bitch made it sound like I was some kind of gold digger. She has no idea how hard I worked to make the Colossus a success. I sweated over this place every bit as much as Adam Forrester. Maybe I'll just show her."

"What do you mean?"

He wanted to calm her down. He didn't need her flying off the handle or becoming distracted because of some stupid argument with Adam Forrester's daughter. There was too much at stake.

"What would you think if I kept it for a year or so? I can run it. I practically did when Adam was alive.

"And if I keep it, his spoiled brat daughter won't have room to talk. I'd make her eat her words." Diana was angry and her thoughts were pouring out.

Sonny's mind was racing.

Diana was definitely not stupid. Most people thought her looks were her main asset, but he knew better. She had a lot more street smarts than Forrester, plus she was shrewd and manipulative.

"I know I can run the hotel and I'm going to prove it. She'll see. Everyone will see. You believe in me, don't you Sonny?"

"Of course I do baby." There was more fear than conviction in his voice.

"Don't get weak on me Sonny."

She knew Sonny was a playboy who was always going to look out for number one. He'd do whatever she wanted. He'd better. If he didn't he was dispensable. She loved fucking him, but she wasn't in love with him.

"I'm not getting weak. I just don't want you to do something crazy because you're pissed off at Forrester's kid. Think things through before you act. And no matter what you decide I'll support you."

Hopefully she'd get over her anger and come to her senses in the next few days. He'd go slowly with her. It was just that he didn't know how much time he had.

Mario Torino was not a man you wanted to disappoint, and Sonny Fremont certainly didn't want to be the one to tell him that the weather in Las Vegas had just gotten cloudy. Very, very cloudy.

Chapter 7
Where There's A Will...

Three days in Vegas seemed more like three years to Tiffany, and she wanted out so badly it hurt.

Walter had tried his best to convince her to stay until late Thursday morning for the reading of the will but she had adamantly refused.

"I can't stay here another day," she said through swollen eyes. "I've had enough. I don't give a damn what Diana gets. I just don't care."

She did, however, agree to get a good night's sleep on Wednesday and move her reservation to an early morning departure on Thursday.

She refused to be there to watch Diana gloat. The way she figured it, she'd be somewhere over Denver about the time Diana Forrester was becoming one of Las Vegas' richest and most powerful women.

"You stay and handle the details," she had told Walter. "My father probably remembered me in his will, but I'll bet Diana approved the final draft."

Walter knew Tiffany was more than likely right. He had drawn Adam's original will, when his friend lived in Chicago, but following Susan's death and his subsequent marriage to Diana, it became more convenient for Forrester to re-draft a new document using a Nevada attorney.

They had arranged to meet in the Alpha Coffee shop at 6:45 a.m., a time they felt quite sure they wouldn't run into the widow Forrester. They had coffee, Walter made another feeble attempt to get her to stay, and she was out the front door of the Colossus by 7:15. The United flight was scheduled to depart at 8:15 but she was ticketed, and had only two small carry on bags.

Remembering how Diana had intruded on her plans for a private limo to the funeral home Tiffany decided to take a cab to the airport.

As she stepped outside the Strip entrance of the Colossus, the early morning sun was already warm and it felt good on her bare arms. She was wearing a dark blue cotton dress, with shiny gold buttons and gold trim. It had short sleeves and a v-shaped neckline, which she dressed up with a gold scarf.

She pulled her sunglasses from her purse and reluctantly admired the hotel's Greek themed main entrance. The rich, goldplated porte-cochere was held erect by white marble columns identical to those that supported the original Parthenon.

In front of the hotel was a scaled down replica of the city of Athens flanked by statues of a half dozen Greek gods, and a huge chariot drawn by six bigger than life marble horses. It had become the most popular stop for picture taking tourists in the past two years, outdistancing the Mirage's exploding volcano and the Paris Hotel's Eiffel Tower.

Tiffany motioned to the doorman for a taxi.

"It might take a minute or two ma'am," he said politely, "They're a little slow this time of morning." He looked at her bags and said, "airport?" already knowing the answer.

She glanced at her watch, then tried to concentrate on developing a list of priorities for the things she knew were waiting for her in Chicago. Her mind was 2,000 miles away, which is why it took a minute for her to realize someone was speaking to her.

"Good morning Miss Wayne, you're up awfully early."

The cheerful greeting was coming from the man she had met the night before at dinner. Tiffany smiled pleasantly as she tried to recall his name. He was dressed casually, in a blue and white jogging suit with the words "Fresno State" etched in white letters up the right leg of the pants.

"Brian Powers," he said sensing her lapse. "We met last night in the restaurant."

"Yes, I remember," she replied, hoping he hadn't noticed her forgetfulness. "I thought I heard Mr. Fitzgerald say you lived here?"

"I do," Brian answered, "but I came over for an early meeting with a friend who's headed back to New York this morning. We just finished."

"I'm on my way back to Chicago now," Tiffany said forcing a smile.

She hardly knew the man, yet she felt at ease with him. He wasn't trying to hit on her, and there was a sincerity about him that made her feel comfortable.

She thought for a split second about asking his opinion about her father's murder, but resisted the urge. It wasn't his business and there was probably little he could offer.

Move slowly,she thought. Operate on a need to know basis. And right now, no matter how nice Brian Powers appeared, he didn't need to know any more about her.

"Why are you leaving so soon?"

"Business calls," she replied. "Things seem to pile up whenever I'm away, despite the fact I have an excellent assistant. And I miss Chicago. Guess I'm not the desert type."

"Any minute for that cab ma'am," the doorman said apologetically. "And your car is up sir," he said nodding toward Brian.

Neither of them was quite sure what was said next, but three minutes later she was perched in the front seat of his Seville, headed for McCarran airport.

Other than asking what airline she was flying, neither of them said much until Tiffany kidded him about the phrase emblazoned on his T-shirt. It read, "Never try and teach a pig to sing. It wastes your time and annoys the pig."

"Cute saying," she laughed. "And so true."

Tiffany smiled.

"Need some air?" Brian asked, reaching for the air conditioner.

"No, I'm okay," Tiffany responded. "Hard to believe you guys need air conditioners at 7:30 in the morning. I can't imagine how people mange to survive in this heat."

Brian cast a peripheral glance at his dark-haired passenger. She wasn't your typical rich girl. She had no airs about her. She was witty, intelligent and impressed him by being real. For a minute it slipped his mind why she had come to Vegas.

She hadn't mentioned Adam Forrester so he stayed away from the subject. He also thought it strange he hadn't seen her at the cemetery. She didn't seem like the sort of woman who would skip her own father's funeral. There were a lot of questions he wanted to ask, but it wasn't the time nor place.

He also wondered how she got along with Diana Forrester.

Probably not too well. I can't see them going to the same dance.

If Adam Forrester's murder was part of the trouble T.J. Fitzgerald had run into, Brian hoped Tiffany wouldn't get dragged into the mess.

"Paris is certainly a beautiful hotel," she commented as they made their way down the Strip. "It seems quite charming." She had paid little attention to the dazzling hotel on her way in, but with the Eiffel Tower as its magnet, the French-themed property was an eye-catcher.

"It has a certain style," he replied. "And the restaurant at the top of the Eiffel Tower has a spectacular view. You'll have to see it if you get back out this way."

"Maybe I will some day," she said, not meaning it.

A few minutes later Brian pulled in front of the United terminal.

"You'll make it," Brian said checking the digital clock on the dash.

"No problem," Tiffany replied. "I have nothing to check so I'm going directly to the gate. And thanks again for the ride. I doubt if I would have made it if not for you. Maybe I can return the favor if ever you're in Chicago."

With a wave she was off, striding quickly past the skycaps before disappearing through the double wide automatic doors.

Brian watched her walk away then spent a full minute sitting idly behind the wheel of the Caddy, staring at the seat just vacated by Ms. Tiffany Wayne.

He didn't know if she was married, engaged or in love. No one who looks like that is unattached he thought, not wanting to set himself up for disappointment. But then again, a guy can dream...

The flight home went quickly, thanks to some gusty tail winds that pushed her arrival time ahead nearly twenty minutes. Both breakfast and a snack were served and unlike the trip out, Tiffany ate both hungrily despite having had a muffin and coffee with Walter at the hotel.

She was a bundle of nervous energy. She flipped through a couple of fashion magazines, read a couple chapters of a romance paperback and wondered if time could ever heal the hurt she felt inside. It wasn't until the final hour of the flight that she managed to drift off to sleep.

Val was at the gate when the DC10 touched down at O'Hare. After exchanging hugs there was an uneasy silence as Val tried to gauge Tiffany's mood.

"I'm okay," Tiffany said, looking at her friend as they rode the down escalator to the parking area. "Really, I am. I'm glad its over though. I was devastated by some of the things that happened in Vegas—things I'll tell you about later----but I'll get over them.

"And I'm anxious to get back to work. That may be the best cure for me. By the way, I'm also glad to see you," she said managing a weak smile.

The last comment put Valerie at ease and she took it as a cue to launch into a litany about everything that happened during Tiffany's absence.

"My goodness Val, I've only been gone a little over three days."

"I know," but it seems like a lot longer," Val said, continuing her rapid-fire recapitulation.

"The phone started ringing on Monday and it hasn't stopped. And almost every caller wanted to know where they could buy a dress from The Tiffany Collection."

"And all of this came from one little blurb in the fashion section?"

"That and your presence at the 'Friend's Ball'," Val raved. "Lucky you."

"Lucky us," Tiffany corrected. "Lucky us."

"Oh, and you had a call from Walter Thurston just before I left the office," she added. "He knew you hadn't arrived yet but he wanted you to call him as soon as you get a chance."

It was not a message she looked forward to returning.

She had regained a portion of her self-control on the flight and feared that hearing Walter give a blow-by-blow account of the will would bring back the numbing headache, which had only recently subsided.

Val had parked her Jetta in a nearby short term parking area, and since Tiffany had only carry on bags they were on their way out of O'Hare less than fifteen minutes after she had landed.

"This must be some sort of record," Tiffany joked.

"I think this is the fastest I've ever gotten in and out of this place," Val agreed.

"It's getting late so I think I'll just go home and get an early start at the office tomorrow," Tiffany said as soon as they were on the expressway.

"I had no intention of taking you to the office anyway. It's almost four o'clock, and with this traffic we'd be lucky to get there in an hour. Besides, I thought you'd want to call Walter from home."

Val brought her up to speed on their most pressing problems on the drive home, then insisted on helping her carry her things upstairs.

"I'll just stay a minute. I want to know everything's okay and you're all settled."

"You're worse than a mother hen," Tiffany teased, but she was grateful for her friend's concern.

It always felt good to be home, no matter where she'd been, and once inside the condo Tiffany felt strangely tranquilized. It took her a minute to realize Margaret had straightened the place and done the few dishes from Sunday. There were still clothes on her bed and a few Kleenex on the bathroom floor.

She laid her bags on the bed, stepped out of the black pumps that had been pinching her toes, and hit rewind on the answering machine. She quickly pressed the stop button.

She'd call Walter first. May as well get the unpleasant stuff out of the way first.

It was 2:15 in Las Vegas.

"Room 2104 please."

Walter picked up the phone almost before it rang.

"Hello, Walter Thurston here."

"Walter, its Tiffany."

"Hi honey. I was hoping it was you. How was the flight?"

"Fine, but I'm sure that's not why you called." She didn't want to be coddled. She preferred he come right out and tell her whatever sordid details he had to pass on. She knew it was the real reason for the call.

"You're right my dear, however I really don't have much new to tell you. The will wasn't read today. Your father's lawyer took ill with the flu and is expected to be out of commission today and tomorrow. His office reset the appointment for next Monday."

Tiffany's shoulders slumped. The last thing she wanted or needed was for the reading of the will to drag out for another week. She wanted it to be over so she could get on with her life.

She tried to be cordial.

"I'm sorry about the delay Walter. Maybe you should just come home. How important is it for you to be there anyway? Nothing's going to change."

"That may be Tiffany, but you need to be represented. It may be more convenient for me to stay the weekend rather than fly back to Chicago.

"I'm going to call Margaret to get her input. I may even have her fly out and spend a few days."

"That sounds like a great idea," she said, not feeling so guilty.

It was a good idea and he knew instantly that Margaret would love it. And it would be great for the two of them to spend a few days away from Chicago. There were no pressing cases in the office, and he rarely took time off. Now all he had to do was convince his wife to come.

"If she decides to come I'll let you know. I think she just might do it. Also, if I stay Friday, Saturday and Sunday it will give me a chance to get together with

Detective Sarabian." Walter's voice had descended into a deep baritone, something Tiffany noticed he did when he was trying to be serious.

She was relieved and confused. Relieved Walter was staying and confused about the feelings she was having about her father's death.

One minute she wanted to forget about it and close that chapter of her life, not caring who killed him or why, and in the next breath she was overcome by vindictiveness, wanting to extract a pound of flesh from his killer.

She wanted justice, but the only real justice would be bringing her father back, and that wasn't possible.

When she finished talking to Walter she pushed the play button on the recorder and listened to the messages. There were a couple hang-ups, a call from Val asking how the Friends of the Arts Ball had turned out, two from Roger Sanderson and one from Johnny Marciano.

They work fast, she thought, but I'm in no way ready to see anyone right now.

She listened to Johnny's message again.

"Hello Tiffany. I'm sorry you're not home. I was very pleased to meet you at the Ball and I was hoping you might agree to have lunch or dinner with me later this week so we can get better acquainted." His voice was strong and suave. He had polish, and the invitation was flattering.

Johnny's call intrigued her. She was also pleased she had interested Roger Sanderson enough to warrant two calls, but it wasn't the same thing. Now she had to decide what her next step would be with the Johnny man.

There might not be another step she muttered out loud, unless he calls back. I don't think I should call him back.

"Are you talking to me?" Val asked from inside the closet where she had begun to unpack and hang Tiffany's clothes.

For a moment Tiffany had forgotten Val was there.

"No, just mumbling to myself," Tiffany called back. "And Val, don't bother hanging those things. I'm going to send everything to the cleaners."

Johnny had not said he'd call back. She only hoped he would. She wondered if his call meant he'd dumped Ms. Cover Model, then reprimanded herself for being so vain. Of course he hadn't dropped her. He doesn't even know me yet.

"I'm hungry, do you want some pizza?" Val asked as she emerged from the closet.

"Sounds good."

"Why don't you finish unpacking while I run out to Arturo's and get the pizza."

They devoured an entire pepperoni pizza, along with bread sticks, salad and two cokes each, then exchanged high-pitched laughs as they surveyed the empty cartons in the living room.

Valerie didn't leave until after nine, and not until she managed to get Tiffany to tell her everything about what went on in Vegas, including her dramatic breakfast showdown with Diana. She also shared the highlights of the Friends of the Arts Ball and her phone message from Johnny Marciano.

"Thanks for staying, Val. You've saved me a lot of work."

"No problem," she said. They exchanged a hug and she was gone.

Tiffany appreciated the solitude. She drew a hot bubble bath and let herself sink slowly into the large round tub.

I'm living that old Calgon commercial she smiled, trying desperately to block out everything stabbing at her overworked senses.

She thought she heard the phone ring and regretted not remembering to bring the cordless into the bathroom. In the end she decided she was too comfortable, and too lazy to climb out to answer it, even if it had rung.

The "lover's tub" was one of the things she liked most about the condo, especially the Jacuzzi jets which were pumping a steady stream on her tired back and feet. She soaked for nearly half an hour then slowly dried off with her favorite towel, a deep blue bath sheet that swallowed her entire body.

She was beginning to feel alive again.

The red light on her recorder was flashing when she returned to her bedroom. *Damn. Someone had called.*

"Hi Tiffany, Johnny Marciano again. I guess you must be out of town. It's Thursday night around 10. If you're in town perhaps we can have lunch tomorrow. I'll try you at the office in the morning."

Well, he called back. I guess he is interested. That was a start.

Before she had time to fantasize about lunch the phone rang again.

It was Margaret Thurston.

"Hi honey, how are you?"

"Fine, and you?"

"I'm good. I'm glad you're back safely. I know it was a long tough trip. I've just spoken to Walter and he told me about the delay in the reading of the will.

"He feels it would be better if he stays in Vegas until its read, and suggested that I come there and join him. I said yes, of course. It's so seldom we get to spend any time alone anymore that I just couldn't pass up the opportunity."

Tiffany hadn't said a word since "fine".

"I think that would be nice," she agreed. "I hate to think of Walter being in Las Vegas by himself for the next four days. I know he'll be happy to have you there. Enjoy your trip and please ask him to call me after he speaks to the detective."

She wasn't sure if Walter had mentioned his discussions with Detective Sarabian to Margaret so she didn't elaborate.

"I'll remind him to call, dear. Are you sure you'll be okay?"

"Of course. I have tons of work piled up at the office and I need to get in there. I'll stay busy."

They spoke for another minute then Tiffany was alone again.

She was ready for bed, the hours she had spent staring at the muted TV in Vegas having exacted their toll. Her eyes were weary. She found an old bottle of Visine in the bathroom cabinet and used the last few drops before clicking on her electric blanket and sliding under the covers.

By 11:15 she was in a deep slumber.

The morning was unbelievably hectic. Val had not exaggerated about the calls or the growing interest in her creations. If they could turn the inquiries into orders it would keep them very busy.

Johnny Marciano called at 10 on the button. Unfortunately she was in a closed-door conference with a manufacturer's rep and had forgotten to instruct Betsy, the new receptionist, to interrupt her if he called. The standard rule of the office held that she was not to be disturbed in a closed-door meeting, except in an emergency.

He left a call back number, and Tiffany dialed it without hesitation, only to learn that Mr. Marciano had already left for lunch. Her turn to leave a message, and the game of big city phone tag was in full swing.

Except for the missed connection with Johnny the morning had been extremely productive. She had tentatively agreed to produce a line of clothing for the JC Penney stores, taken calls from two women who wanted original gowns, and gotten formal notification that she had been selected to represent the United States at a fashion show in Paris.

She had known about the selection for over a month but seeing her name on the engraved card and letter gave her a renewed sense of pride. Paris was where she would unveil "The Tiffany Collection".

The department store deal, which would focus on ensembles in the $50 to $150 range, would have to wait until Walter returned from Las Vegas. He had insisted from the beginning that she not sign anything until he had approved it.

On more than one occasion she had come close to making some financially disastrous commitments. Walter had saved her each time.

This time she was pretty sure the deal was solid because the store was nationally known and had upgraded its merchandise over the past couple years. However, an association with a chain, while guaranteeing some bottom line revenue, meant a lot of extra work.

The contract called for her to unveil a Fall line at a special showing in Chicago in May, just a month before the Paris show. It was a tall order because the clothes would be in totally different price ranges. "The Tiffany Collection" was for the society crowd, with prices in the $500 to $5000 bracket.

Preparing for two shows simultaneously would necessitate a major effort and require extra help. In order to make it happen she would put Val in charge of the

JC Penney project. She would personally design most of the selections but would also give her friend a chance to put her mark on a few of the pieces.

It would be a major career step, and she knew Valerie would be thrilled.

"Thought you might want a bite of something," Val said, depositing a roast beef sandwich on Tiffany's desk.

"You're a life saver," Tiffany gushed, wasting no time unwrapping the sandwich.

"What, no cokes?" Tiffany feigned mild shock.

"Presto", said the red-haired girl, producing two bright red Coca-Cola cans from a bag in her lap.

Between bites of their impromptu lunch Tiffany shared the details of the morning meetings, except for her plan to put Val in charge of the department store project. She didn't want to get her hopes up if Walter found some snag in the contract. Once Walter gave his okay she'd take Val out for a gourmet dinner and celebration.

It was three minutes until five when Johnny Marciano called back.

"This was it", he said in mock exasperation. "My last valiant attempt to lure you to dinner."

"Wasn't it enough that I returned your call?" she asked coyly.

"Well, I'll admit, that gave me the courage to call one last time," he said absently.

"Now that we've gotten that out of the way I'll break out my best lines. I trust four calls are enough to let you know that I was very impressed with you at the Ball."

"I'm beginning to get the idea." She didn't know what else to say.

"Before I go any further, or make a fool of myself, I suppose I should ask if you're married or involved." He hoped she was neither.

"And I might ask the same of you," said Tiffany, loving the repartee.

"Innocent on both counts," he offered. "Me too," Tiffany echoed.

"So far, so good," he continued.

"So how do you feel about having dinner with a man who's been pestering you with phone calls? And before you answer, I think you should know that the calls probably won't stop until you say yes."

"In that case when did you have in mind?"

"How about tonight?"

"Can't do it tonight," she demurred, and immediately wondered why she declined. She had no plans for the evening.

The truth was she was a little scared. Maybe she wasn't ready.

"So how about tomorrow?" he said persisting.

"That's do-able," she replied, feeling uplifted.

They arranged a time and closed the conversation without any further bi-play. So Johnny Marciano had come calling. Tiffany felt good, and the mood carried over throughout the evening. She was looking forward to Saturday evening.

On Saturday she shuffled through a mountain of paperwork she'd brought home, taking a break only long enough to talk to Walter who called to let her know that other than Margaret's arrival, all was quiet in Las Vegas.

"I spoke with Detective Sarabian," Walter started. "He said there were no new leads, however they're not through running all the fingerprints from the house." He did not share the news that the pathology report concluded that her father had died instantly.

Sarabian had also offered the opinion that Adam Forrester had been targeted.

"I just can't see some B&E guy wasting him for no reason," the detective had said. "It goes against everything I've seen in twenty years on the force.

"I'm not saying it doesn't happen,, but its very rare. Either somebody had a personal agenda or it had something to do with the Colossus."

Tiffany wondered if she had pushed herself into some sort of safe fantasy world because she hadn't given a thought to Vegas since returning home. Walter's call brought it all crashing back.

"I took Margaret to see the Sonny Fremont show at the Stardust," Walter said changing the subject. "I had to talk her into going, but she enjoyed it. He has a pretty good act."

"I'm glad she enjoyed it," Tiffany said sincerely.

"I also think she may be hooked on slots," Walter said, pretending to be alarmed.

"The first time she pulled the handle she won $100. She was very excited."

"You may have a hard time getting her back to Chicago," Tiffany kidded, realizing that they were both avoiding the reason he was there and what they had been through. "I'm glad you two are getting a chance to spend some special time together."

"I'll call you Monday after the will is read," he said, injecting a bit of seriousness. She gave him a brief rundown of the department store deal and he sounded enthused.

"Sounds like it could be a big break for you. I'll look it over as soon as I get back."

It was 8 o'clock when the intercom buzzed and Mike, the doorman announced a Mr. Johnny Marciano was in the lobby.

She greeted him at the door in a mid length skirt with a solid black sweater and a single strand of pearls.

"Mighty nice," he said admiringly, and she was pleased he liked it because she had agonized over the choice, having changed four times in the past hour.

They dined at "DiCicco's", an intimate Italian restaurant on the East Side, and Tiffany loved the food as well as the atmosphere. The restaurant wasn't ritzy, but it had charm. The little bottles of Chianti hanging from the ceiling added ambiance.

Johnny ordered a chilled bottle of Martini and Rossi and the bubbly Asti Spumante went right to her head.

They made mostly small talk, exchanging background information mixed with some childhood stories that each pretended embarrassment in sharing.

Johnny's hobby was dabbling in the stock market and he told her of his successes and failures, however his main business was sales. He was CEO of J&M Imports, a huge East Coast company that specialized in Italian imports.

"The market has been fabulous this year," he said modestly. "I don't know how high it will go, but with the economy strong and inflation down you have to believe in it."

She didn't tell him her father had made his fortune in the market, talking instead about college and how she got started in her own business. She also gave him some insight of her upcoming plans. And she did not mention the recent tragedy.

Better he not know about any of that right now, she thought. A need to know basis she reminded herself. Plus she didn't want to have him feeling sorry for her.

She begged off Johnny's invitation to go club hopping after dinner, laying the blame on the unfinished work waiting on her desk at home. He accepted her refusal graciously.

"Maybe next week," he said optimistically.

She was feeling a bit tipsy, and on the way home cracked the window slightly, enjoying the brisk Chicago night air. The strong smell of the leather upholstery in the Jaguar was intoxicating, as was the scent of his cologne.

There was no denying she was attracted to the man. She had known it from the moment she saw him at the party, and suspected she had let herself get a little drunk at the restaurant as a way of dulling the sexual sensations and fears dueling within her. It had been a long time since she had been with a man.

Johnny parked in the circular driveway in front of her building, an indication he did not expect to do more than walk her to the door.

"Thank you for a most pleasant evening," he said as they stood outside the entrance to the condos. He pulled her closer and kissed her gently.

Her body responded almost automatically and he kissed her more deeply. She felt herself melting.

"I hope you don't have any plans for tomorrow night, "he whispered, loosening his grip around her waist. Her head was spinning and when she didn't answer he took her silence for assent.

"Until tomorrow then," he said. "Same time."

She awoke to a knock on her door at 8 a.m.

It was Paul, the morning doorman.

"Delivery for you Miss Wayne," he said, placing a dark green vase loaded with long stemmed red roses in her hands. The card was simple.

"American Beauties for an American Beauty. Thanks for a beautiful evening.
-J.M."

It was the perfect way to start a day.

She also found the perfect way to end it.

After a slow, exquisite dinner they stopped at a couple of popular clubs for a nightcap and a few dances. They danced the way people used to. Cheek to cheek, their bodies pressed against one another, their eyes saying more than words ever could.

When Johnny suggested coffee at his place to top off the evening she readily submitted, and both of them knew what was going to happen.

And it did. Their lovemaking was passionate, tender and shattering. Johnny was an incredible lover and every way he touched her aroused her and made her want more. It was as if she was insatiable, and she wasn't ashamed. Her body was a pool of untapped sexuality and Johnny had somehow found it and released her every inhibition.

She heard bells, sirens and a gentle rain, which started about 2 a.m. and continued through the early morning hours. It was steady drizzle that tapped wonderfully against the window in Johnny Marciano's bedroom.

It was one of the most beautiful nights of her life and even though she had misgivings about sleeping with him so soon, she wasn't going to let guilt cast a pall over the moment. She slept peacefully on Johnny's right shoulder, her right leg draped over his body. Her entire being was content.

Johnny lay awake for what seemed like hours after Tiffany drifted off to sleep. He had made love to many women, taken pleasure from their bodies and given them ecstasy in every way he knew how, but he had always managed to keep his emotional distance.

He knew how to separate the pleasures of the flesh from real life, and how to give a woman what she needed and make her come back for more without making himself vulnerable. Johnny Marciano knew how to play the game.

Taking while giving the impression of giving had always been his forte.

With Tiffany he had felt something altogether different. He already knew Tiffany Wayne was not a woman to be taken lightly, and definitely not a one-night stand. She responded with a combination of innocence and sexuality unlike anything he had ever experienced.

Her smile was soft and trusting, and it said, "this is special. I hope you realize it..." and he did. Her body was lean and supple, her hunger all consuming. He wrapped his arm around her shoulder, breathed in the freshness of her hair and listened to the rhythm of her heartbeat as she slept.

She was smart, unpretentious and beautiful. She was independent, yet not hung up on women's lib. She was self-confident, not selfish. She was vibrant and exciting. She was dangerous.

Tiffany awoke around six, but he had already been up for an hour, fixing coffee and reading the paper.

It was Monday and he would have to drive her home before heading to his office.

"I can take a cab if you're in a hurry," she said, and every bone in her body hoped he wouldn't allow her to.

"Not a chance," he said. "I'm in no hurry to let you go."

Neither of them really knew what to say on the twenty-minute drive to her Lakeshore Drive condo, but both sensed a bond.

What they would do about it was the dilemma.

The feeling was idyllic, yet it did not take them by complete surprise. Each had sensed that it would be that way in bed. Their looks, their touches and their kisses all set the stage, and there were no awkward moments.

She came to him with no reservations, giving what came naturally and he did the same. It was more than either of them had ever given before.

"Last night was pretty special for me," he said when he walked her to the door. He looked into her emerald eyes and knew she felt the same.

She kissed him deeply, lustfully.

"I'm old enough to know something real when I find it Mr. Marciano. I'm also wise enough to know that a fire like the one we lit last night can sometimes burn out of control and scorch everything it touches."

Tiffany wasn't exactly sure what she meant. She was trying to let him know he had touched her soul and it was frightening, like walking down a dark alley. There was excitement and uncertainty.

It was the first time she had ever climaxed at the same time as her partner and it felt like her insides were pouring out and she had no control over her body.

"I felt my heart leap into your body," he whispered truthfully. "Our lovemaking was the most incredible sensation I have ever felt."

She wanted to believe him. Believe he shared the same feelings. She also wanted to tell him how incredibly out of character the whole thing was for her. She had never slept with a man on a second date. She had gone out with Jack almost a month before going to bed with him. Johnny Marciano would probably laugh if he were to learn she had had only three bed partners in her life.

"I have to go to New York this afternoon, "he said sheepishly, but I'll call you at the office from there if you like.

"I'd like", she said without hesitation.

"Deal."

She pecked him on the cheek and squeezed his hand tightly before slipping through the building's front entry door, which was held open by a tenant on his way out.

Tiffany hustled upstairs, showered, tossed the piles of loose papers she still hadn't read in her briefcase and headed for the office.

Johnny called later in the day, and they made plans to get together for a light dinner when he returned on Wednesday, provided he didn't return too late.

"If I get hung up in The City I'll call you," he promised, and he immediately felt trapped. He didn't like notifying someone, anyone of his comings and goings. He was accustomed to having his freedom, and even though he was the one who made the offer he was annoyed.

Tiffany felt so energized Val had to slow her down a couple of times.

"Whoa baby. I hope you brought some of those energy pills for the rest of us," Val laughed. They were in a meeting and Tiffany was in the middle of a sentence when she dropped everything to pick up an incoming call on the first ring.

"What's got you so wound up?" Val asked. Tiffany had not told her yet about her second date or the night with Johnny Marciano. She knew she would, but not yet.

I'm not sure where it's going. I can't tell her yet. And I certainly don't want her to know I slept with him so soon. What would she think? She knew what Val would think. Her friend wouldn't believe it. Not for a minute. It was so uncharacteristic of her.

She had arrived at the office at 9:05, had a second cup of coffee an hour earlier than usual and closeted herself in her office with Val to begin designing the new styles for the department store chain.

Betsy had instructions they were not to be disturbed unless it was Johnny Marciano or a major emergency.

At 2:40 the intercom buzzed.

"Is it Mr. Marciano," she asked, expecting it to be.

"No Tiffany, its Mr. Thurston on line three. I told him you said you weren't to be disturbed except for an emergency but he insisted."

She had gotten so engrossed in her work she had forgotten about Walter in Las Vegas, and she felt a warm glow when she realized the reason she had was Johnny Marciano. He had allowed her to momentarily put aside the sadness and hurt that had set up camp in her psyche.

"Tiffany!"

There was urgency and an air of alarm in Walter's voice.

"Yes Walter, I'm here." She had put the call on the speakerphone, giving her the freedom to move around the room and to write notes at her desk. Val already knew what was going on in Las Vegas so anything Walter had to report did not need to be private.

Ron Delpit

"Are you sitting down?"

"I am," she said prematurely, moving to the chair behind her desk as she listened.

"Are you OK, Walter? Is everything all right?" In that moment she feared the worst.

Perhaps something had happened to Margaret. Maybe he had a run in with Diana or her lawyers. Maybe he even had some unpleasant details about her dad's murder.

She shrugged her shoulders at Val with a "I have no idea what's going on" gesture.

"Tiffany, the lawyer has just finished reading the will and something unexpected has happened. I can't believe it myself."Walter Thurston was not an easy man to unnerve, but whatever had transpired in Las Vegas had done the trick. She had never heard him this way.

An eerie fear swept over her and she didn't know why.

He could hear the concern in her voice.

"I'm sorry Tiffany. I didn't mean to frighten you," he said, seeming to have regained his composure.

"Then tell me Walter. Don't pull any punches. Just get it over with."

There were tears in her eyes. She had a feeling what Walter was about to tell her was going to make her cry. And she was right.

"Your dad left you everything," he almost shouted into the phone. "Everything."

"What do you mean Walter? What exactly do you mean?"

"I mean he left you everything. His investments, his estate and the Colossus. It's all yours."

"And what about his wife? What about Diana?"

"He left her five million dollars. Five million dollars, the house they had here in Las Vegas and the clothes on her back."

She could tell Walter was still numbed by the news.

She didn't know what or if she was feeling. She was still stunned. It hadn't sunk in.

"This is the biggest shock of my life," the lawyer said into the speakerphone. "Diana, of course screamed loudly, threatening to challenge the will and sue for half of the entire estate."

"Can she do that?"

"She could but she'd be a fool. Adam was very careful about the way the will was worded.

Had he left everything to you without naming her she could probably contest the will and win, because Nevada laws protect spouses who are purposely omitted. But your father specifically said in the will that he was mindful Diana

100

was his wife, and that he was providing for her by leaving her a million dollars for every year they were married."

In Chicago, Tiffany slumped in her chair, tears coursing down her cheeks and confusion running rampant in her head. She and her father had made peace after all. It was the happiest moment of her life.

"Tiffany…"

She had forgotten Walter was still on the line.

"I'm not sure what should be done, or what I should do," she admitted. "I suppose you want me to come back to Las Vegas but I'd rather not."

"There are certain things you must be here to deal with, "Walter said sternly. "I could fax you some of the papers, but there are some things you need to handle in person. There are a lot of people out here depending on you. You now have 4700 new employees."

The thought overwhelmed her.

"I understand Walter. I'll be there. I'll arrange to fly out tomorrow morning. That will get me in by early afternoon. I'd appreciate it if you would try and have anything that requires my immediate attention lined up. I don't want to spend any more time out there than I have to."

"I'll start on it right away," Walter said.

In the five-bedroom penthouse high atop the Colossus, Diana Cord Forrester was trashing the entire suite, throwing lamps, breaking mirrors, ripping the paintings on the wall and cursing Adam Forrester.

At his ranch on the outskirts of Las Vegas, Sonny Fremont stood on the upper balcony, his strong hands locked in a death grip around the outer railing as he stared out into his huge yard. Suddenly he let out a deafening primal scream, picked up a heavy ceramic pot, complete with plant and soil and violently hurled it 30 feet down, smashing it on the roof of his Rolls Royce.

In Chicago, Mario Torino pounded his desk.

"This isn't possible," he yelled. "No fucking way this can happen." He took a .22 caliber pistol from his lower desk drawer and fired it at a framed picture on the wall.

Pieces of glass scattered all over the hallway. The photo of he and Sonny Fremont, smiling at each other in a happier time, was shattered in a thousand pieces.

"Is there anything else you want me to do before you get here Tiffany?"

"Only one, Walter."

"Just tell me and I'll get right on it."

"Tell the dragon queen to get herself and everything she owns out of my hotel. Diana Carter's no longer welcome at the Colossus, even as a guest. And if she gives you any trouble call security and have her removed.

"Tell her Adam Forrester's daughter is coming to town."

Chapter 8
A Rising Star

He had to admit that as far as his career was concerned things had gone just about the way Oscar had promised.

"Are you fucking kidding me? I'm filling in for Don Rickles! At the Sahara!" Sonny was thrilled.

He rewarded Oscar with a Rolex presidential and a box of cigars.

The agent seemed to have the Midas touch, arranging Sonny's first appearance in a Strip main room less than six months after he signed with Four Star Talent.

The Rickles gig was a last minute thing and there wasn't enough time to get his name on the marquee, but it didn't matter. He was there. Rickles had come down with what Vegas performers called Vegas throat forcing him to cancel the last three days of his engagement.

Sonny Fremont was an instant success, and after getting over their initial disappointment at not being able to see Rickles, audiences loved him.

And the appearances started to become more frequent. Three times in a six-week period Oscar booked him as a late sub for headliners who called in sick unexpectedly. He filled in for Paul Anka at the Riviera, for Tom Jones at the Flamingo and a full week at Caesars as a replacement for Diana Ross after the former Supreme developed a sudden case of bronchitis.

It wasn't until years later that Sonny discovered the headliners he had filled in for weren't legitimately sick. Oscar and Mario had somehow arranged for them to miss a night or two on short notice, sometimes offering kickbacks to their managers, other times calling in long overdue favors.

Hotel entertainment directors often went from the outhouse to the penthouse in a matter of minutes without realizing they were being played. First they'd get a call late in the afternoon informing them that the scheduled headliner had an emergency and had to cancel for the night. Then, by odd coincidence one of the next calls would be from Oscar Bento, just checking in to see if they'd given any thought to adding Sonny Fremont to the hotel's stable of stars.

Invariably the panicked entertainment booker would say he might be able to consider using Sonny on a more frequent basis if Oscar could help him out of a tight spot and have his client fill in for the suddenly stricken headliner.

"I'd consider it a personal favor, and a big one if you could get Sonny to work tonight, "said Ned Fisher, the entertainment chief at Bally's. Damn Tom Jones pulled out twenty minutes ago and we've got 900 reservations for the first show, 600 for the late."

"Just remember who saved your ass," Oscar would say, only half kidding. Bento, of course, kept close tabs of the booking agents he pulled out of the fire, planning to call in those markers when the time was right. In the meantime Sonny's legend was growing while others were fading.

Newton was still hot, Sammy and Jerry Lewis were drawing the older crowd, Sinatra didn't seem to care if he played Vegas at all, and Liza was less than dependable. Diana Ross was the leading female headliner even though most Strip entertainment buyers hated her guts. She was too arrogant, too demanding and too bitchy.

Sonny became a regular on the Strip after Oscar negotiated multiple non-exclusive deals allowing him to play any main showroom he could fit into his schedule. His popularity was reflected in his increased weekly salary. Less than a year after making the jump to the headliner rooms he was commanding $150,000 a week, playing as many as 32 weeks a year. A few big name stars were making more per week, but no one, with the exception of Newton was playing more weeks.

The $150,000 grossed out to almost five million a year. All of Sonny's monies were paid directly to Four Star Talent, which allowed Mario to launder four or five times that much. He didn't care, as long as he wasn't directly involved, and as long as he had enough cash to buy anything he wanted.

An old story making the rounds crossed Sonny's mind and he chuckled aloud.

It was about a professional athlete who had earned millions over the course of his his career, but somehow found himself filing for bankruptcy in front of a nasty tempered arbitrator.

"What did you do with all the money you earned, piss it away? "the bankruptcy referee challenged.

"No sir," the player drawled. "I figure I spent about 90% of it on gambling, loose women and expensive cars. The other 10% I guess I wasted."

Sonny's whims included antique cars, rare handguns and giving lavish gifts to his steady stream of one-night stands.

He had even gotten married somewhere in the 80s. Oscar referred to it as a temporary "brain freeze" or "crotch lapse".

"Either your brain temporarily froze or your dick forgot it could get satisfied without buying the store," he had reprimanded. He had fallen for a Hawaiian stewardess who gave him a blowjob in the back row of a 747 on the way back from Oahu.

"I'm not sure why I married her in the first place," he admitted to Oscar during the divorce hearing, but it didn't matter. The union lasted only eleven months and thanks to Oscar's insistence the girl had signed a pre-nup. He gave her $200,000 in cash and paid $25,000 a month for a year to make it go away.

One of the things Oscar had not been able to produce was a record deal, and the agent's failure to do so was an extremely sensitive area.

"I don't understand why you can't get some label to sign me," he said heatedly to Oscar who was visiting him in his dressing room. "Those fucking Hollywood jerks come to Vegas and see my show and they all want to come backstage and schmooze.

"The phony bastards. They know I can sing. They know the fans love me. I'm telling you I'll sell records if they give me a chance.

"Do your job and get me a deal."

"I've tried," Oscar said in a monotone. "We've paid for those guys to come here to see you. We've wined and dined them, and gotten them laid. You know that Sonny. Somewhere the plan gets killed in committee. I don't know why."

Oscar was stumped. He had talked to everyone he thought could establish a beachhead for Sonny. Neither of them wanted Mario to come in with a heavy hand, fearful that any strong-arm tactics would hinder rather than help Sonny's career.

"We'll get to them...somehow. Just be patient." Sonny was getting harder and harder to handle and Oscar knew if he didn't make a record deal or a major movie happen soon, problems were on the horizon. Success had gone to Sonny Fremont's head. He had to keep him under control.

In Vegas Sonny was a big shot, but nationally he had little credibility and was still derisively referred to as a "Vegas act".

And it wasn't entirely true that Sonny hadn't cracked the record business. A year earlier he had signed a deal with an outfit called Redbird Records, a small label that promised big results. Oscar had been against the deal from the outset because the company had no track record and a weak distribution network, but in the end he was forced to capitulate because he could not offer Sonny anything better.

The venture was a disaster. Lacking the funds to promote the record properly Sonny's "Casino Nights" was on and off the charts in a heartbeat, barely breaking into Billboard's Top 100 and never rising above #91.

Having a hit record obsessed him and he constantly reminded Oscar of his inability to come through. Being a Vegas star was no longer enough. Scoring with a hit record would bring him the credibility that being a marquee star in a Vegas showroom never could.

"Maybe what I need is a new manager?" he said boldly. "Someone who can get a recording studio to sign me. Or get me a movie."

Oscar had heard it all before. He didn't dare tell Sonny that maybe the chance had passed him by. Or that the record companies were more interested in "rap crap" than middle of the road singers. That would only enrage him.

"You've had more than your share of guest shots on TV," Oscar said defensively.

"And you'll get more. The record deal will happen when it happens."

Expecting Sonny to continue his ranting, Oscar settled in on the large sofa in Sonny's dressing room. He made it a habit to see as many of his client's shows as possible and usually came up from LA on Thursdays and stayed until Sunday morning.

"I'm thinking about getting married again", Sonny said loudly as he mixed himself a drink from behind the huge bar in the corner of the room.

Oscar was not the least bit ruffled by Sonny Fremont's announcement or by his temper. All the shouting in the world was not going to get him a record contract. Sonny was angry and was lashing out. Oscar had seen worse. Many times. Personally he didn't give a damn if Sonny got married, but Mario saw it as a potential problem. He didn't want some nosy spouse having a say in what Sonny did or didn't do, and if they got divorced, the woman's lawyers would demand to see all the financial records. Of course that could never happen.

"Who is she this week?" Oscar was sure Sonny had said it for shock value.

"Fuck you Oscar," Sonny screamed.

"A year ago you wanted to marry a black backup singer whose name neither of us remembers. Six months ago it was a Swedish masseuse and a month or so back it was that blonde lawyer from Cleveland. What was her name…Chloe, Chrissy, Candy?" Oscar tried to recall her name without success.

"Christy," Sonny intoned, not sure himself.

"Get serious Sonny. You like women too much to be with just one. You're having the time of your life, getting laid by the most beautiful women in the world and you don't have to marry them."

Sonny knew Oscar was right. He loved women. All of them. The way they looked, the way they smelled and most of all the way they would do anything he wanted just because he was a celebrity.

"Maybe I just need to get laid tonight," Sonny laughed, and the marriage talk was dropped from the conversation.

"But I still need a record, or a movie Oscar. Fuckin' do something. Make it happen."

An hour later Sonny Fremont was his charming self, entertaining Angela Duarte, an admiring fan from South America who had been seated at a table in the front row at the late show. He had invited her backstage and she readily accepted.

"You know I'm scheduled to do a concert in Bogota at the end of the month," Sonny smiled as he handed his guest a glass of wine.

"It's a great city," she replied. "It combines modern with old world South American culture. I think you'll enjoy it there, and I will be sure to come to your concert."

"I'd like that," Sonny said sincerely. "I'll arrange tickets for your family and friends if you like."

"That would be very nice," she said, impressed by his down to earth attitude.

Ron Delpit

The dressing room at Bally's had a large living room area with the wet bar, two sofas, two or three comfortable side chairs, a television and a sound system which was currently replaying his just concluded show. It also had a smaller private area where he got dressed and it opened to an adjoining suite complete with a Jacuzzi, king-sized bed and fireplace. The perfect retreat for a quickie with whatever lucky lady got the call to come back to the star's dressing room after the show.

At first Angela was surprised when he led her into the adjoining suite but she was also awed by Sonny's star power, and the chilled champagne at the side of the bed soon dulled her inhibitions.

In one movement he was on top of her, cupping her mouth to quiet her protestations. He massaged her breasts slowly, feeling her nipples harden and her breathing quicken. Her empty champagne glass slipped to the floor as Sonny continued to kiss her neck while unfastening her bra.

He kissed her rigid nipples, then sucked them gently. He moved deliberately down her body, his hand slipping expertly between her legs, parting them slightly as he fingered her dripping wetness.

Angela moaned. She could not help herself. She had never had anything like this happen to her before. She was 26, and had never in her life made love with a man she just met.

But this was Sonny Fremont. This was different.

In a moment her hips were rising and falling with the movement of his hand as he massaged her and she came powerfully. Her body, so tense and taut moments before, literally collapsed, like a suddenly punctured balloon.

Without pausing Sonny mounted her, straining to push his now rock hard penis as far as it could go, until she felt as if he were locked inside her body.

Angela was sobbing as she pulled him close, holding his buttocks as Sonny rhythmically pumped up and down, both of their bodies drenched with the sweat of their passion. She came again as she felt Sonny explode. It was the most incredible, and most sensual experience of her life.

They lay there in the dark for a minute or two, her body still shuddering, her mind still trying to make sense of what had just happened.

Sonny got up and headed for the bathroom. When he returned he was fully dressed, a blue and white silk scarf in his hand. She was still in bed with the covers drawn up around her neck.

"I thought you might like one of these as a souvenir." He was sitting on the edge of the huge bed speaking in a tone that said her he was finished with her. The scarf had his initials and logo in the corner.

The wonderful feelings she had just experienced raced out of her consciousness. Suddenly she felt cheap. And used. And stupid. He was finished with her. Tomorrow night he'd find a new babe. There'd be more champagne,

106

more fresh flowers and more soft music. And probably a souvenir scarf when he was done.

She couldn't allow him to treat her that way. Not Sonny Fremont. Not any man.

Angela Duarte's dark eyes flashed and Sonny never saw the palm of her right hand as it slapped hard against his face.

"You bastard. I won't let you use me and toss me aside like some toy," she said angrily. "Do you think being a celebrity gives you the right to do that?"

His face was stinging and the imprint of her open hand left a vivid mark. Maybe she wasn't just another groupie out for a star fuck.

"I'm sorry, "he said contritely. "I thought…I don't know what I thought, or what I was thinking." He was searching for the right words but they wouldn't come.

He realized he had grossly misjudged her.

"A lot of girls just want to be able to say they've slept with somebody famous," he said trying to defend himself. "I didn't know…"

He got her a robe from the bathroom and turned away while she slipped it on. She dressed in the bathroom then came out to face him. She was a beautiful woman, with dark skin and long black hair. Her black eyes looked even darker because her mascara had run.

"I'm really sorry Andrea. I wish you could understand."

"Understand what? That you can't even remember my name! That you're a user? That you jump into bed with whoever you can impress enough, then give them a scarf and say adios!"

"Can we just try and talk this out?"

"Why do we need to? You'll never see me again after tonight?"

"Maybe I'd like to," he said, not knowing if he meant it. "I am coming to your country, remember? If you'll give me a second chance we can have dinner."

"I don't think it would be wise for me to accept that invitation under these circumstances," Angela said. "I think you're just trying to soothe your own conscience."

They were standing in front of the fireplace.

"Would you at least consider seeing me in Colombia?"

"Here's my office number in Bogota," she said handing him a card.

"If you still feel you want to have dinner, call me a day or so before, and we'll talk about it. But don't feel obligated Mr. Sonny Fremont. Don't call me because you feel guilty." And with that she left the room and made her way downstairs to the casino and eventually to the hotel elevators. She wanted a shower even though she knew no amount of soap could wash away the shame she was feeling.

Sonny called as he had promised, two days before arriving in Bogota.

She was no longer angry at him, only at herself.

Still, she refused his dinner invitation.

"I'd rather not," she said. "I already have plans."

She did however accept his offer of front row seats and brought her parents as well as her sister to the concert. She did not go backstage, and she did not see Sonny Fremont during his visit to Colombia, nor did she ever see him again.

The concert, in an 18,000 seat outdoor arena was a sellout which pleased Oscar and served notice that Sonny was a star who could hold his own in the global market. He made no further attempt to contact Angela Duarte and a certain part of him was relieved she had turned down his offer.

After two standing ovations he returned to his dressing room to find a large package wrapped in a wide red bow. A huge white teddy bear dressed in a tuxedo and holding a microphone sat atop the box.

The card said, "Congratulations. You are an international star now. Have a safe trip home." It was not signed.

Inside the package was a breathtaking sculpture of a man and a woman holding hands. They were facing each other, looking intently into one another's eyes. The exquisite detail of the piece was incredible. The woman's figure was full and sensual, the hands and facial features so realistic they looked like miniature people. The entire sculpture was mounted on a wooden base with the artist's initials and the year carved into the side.

"That is a beautiful piece of art, and very expensive," exclaimed Jose Sulano, the Colombian promoter. It is by Hector Collazo, one of South America's greatest artists. None of his works sells for less than $10,000."

The statue stood almost three feet tall and Sonny planned on displaying it prominently in his Las Vegas living room.

In the eight years of his association with Four Star, Sonny had not seen Mario Torino more than two or three times, and never in those meetings had there ever been the slightest reference to their having met or been involved during Sonny's brief Hollywood career. For that he was thankful.

Torino, who seldom called Sonny directly, and never before at home, made a rare call the day after Sonny's return to Las Vegas, requesting a private meeting with Sonny the next day.

"How did you like my gift?" Mario said brusquely. "That guy is one of the best sculptors in the world."

The call itself surprised him and the fact Mario had never previously given him any type gift was even more confusing. Why the gift? Why was the card unsigned? What was it all about?

"It's very nice," Sonny stammered. "Thank you."

"Listen Sonny, I'll get into Vegas about four tomorrow and I need to see you."

Sonny did not ask why, and Mario gave no hint what the meeting would be about.

Whatever it was, he wanted it to be quiet and fast. He didn't want to be seen with Mario Torino.

"Where?"

"At your house. It'll be more private. I'll be there by five. Our business won't take long Sonny, but it is important. I have a flight back to Chicago at seven the same evening.

"And Sonny, make sure the house is empty. This is just between us."

Mario's pointed request piqued Sonny's curiosity. He hadn't done anything to cross Mario, but wondering kept him awake. It was nearly dawn when he finally faded off to sleep.

The Torino entourage arrived at his outside gate punctually at 5 o'clock.

Sonny greeted him at the door, having seen the limo pull into the driveway. Mario instructed the driver and his muscular associate to wait in the car.

"May I get you a drink?"

"Scotch. Neat." In his dark blue double-breasted suit Mario could easily have been mistaken for a banker or a Park Avenue attorney.

"This won't take long Sonny. I just came to visit the sculpture I had delivered to you in Colombia." Mario sipped his drink, then set it on a small table.

"It's right over here," Sonny said, motioning toward the huge living room. "You didn't think I'd shove it in some closet, did you?"

"It's beautiful, and I found the perfect spot for it."

Mario carefully lifted the statue, turning it over and studying it.

"It certainly is a work of art," he said, aware that Sonny was eyeing him curiously.

"I hope you haven't grown too attached to it."

Before Sonny could answer Mario took the statue in both hands and smashed it against the heavy stone fireplace, repeatedly banging it until the figures severed at the mid-section.

"What the hell are you doing?" Sonny screamed. "Are you crazy?"

There was no change in Mario's expression, and in a few seconds the outburst was over. Mario set the base of the statue on the floor, then reached inside and removed six tightly wrapped cellophane bags.

He looked at Sonny and smiled.

"Just business my friend. These little pouches are worth about $2 million each on the street, and who better to bring them back from South America than a celebrity with special customs clearance from the government.

"You even had a police escort to and from the airport.

"Now where's the teddy bear?"

Sonny was angry at being used. Physically, he towered over Mario, but he exercised restraint. He retrieved the bear, which he had positioned atop a grand piano on the other side of the room.

Ron Delpit

Mario ripped the stuffing from the bear and removed two more large packets of cocaine.

"I knew your VIP status would come in handy someday," he said sarcastically. And don't worry about your statue. I have another one exactly like it in the car, and another teddy bear as well."

Mario gulped down his scotch, then marched outside, ordering the burly limo driver to bring the items from the trunk. The man brought an identical sculpture and teddy bear, deposited them on the parquet floor in the foyer and returned to the car.

The cocaine packets Mario shoved into his briefcase.

"Nice doing business with you," he grinned. "Maybe we should visit more often."

Still stunned, Sonny watched the limo quietly draw away, pausing at the end of the driveway. He pressed the security button opening the heavy iron gate and the car disappeared into the late afternoon Vegas traffic.

He was furious, and frightened, but not crazy enough to challenge Mario. Besides, he loved the power, and over all they had been good to him. He was a star. A big star. And he was confident his day was coming. One day they'd need him more than he needed them.

But being their unsuspecting mule had one advantage. It gave him some leverage. Mario owed him something, and he intended to collect. Maybe a record deal would never happen, no matter how badly he wanted it. But a movie deal was still a possibility and he'd push Oscar more than ever before to make it happen.

They owed him.

Chapter 9
Hotel Business

Tiffany took little consolation from inheriting the major share of her father's holdings. Money had never been important to her.

She still felt emptiness in her gut whenever she thought about all that had happened. Both her parents being gone was something she had never anticipated. Death made other things seem so trivial.

The rush that had accompanied Walter's startling news was temporary, and late in the evening she welcomed the tranquility of her condo as a retreat to help collect her thoughts.

She really didn't want the Colossus, or to get involved in the business of owning a hotel thousands of miles from where she lived. And she sure as hell had no intention of moving to Las Vegas.

I'll ask Walter to handle getting the place sold. Or he can hire someone to do it. I don't care. Gambling is not my business. And she didn't want to be vindictive. She didn't hate Diana for marrying her father. How could she hate the woman for loving him?

She did hate her for ordering the casket closed. For that she could never forgive her. And that was also why she was happy her father did not leave the hotel to his wife. Diana didn't deserve it.

Tiffany's only satisfaction came from knowing her father had never taken her out of his heart.

Now it was time to figure out all this hotel business.

It was Monday, and Walter needed her in Vegas for most of the week.

She could leave Wednesday, spend the remainder of the week in Vegas and return to Chicago on the weekend. That would allow her to get some rest and get a fresh start on the work she needed to handle before the Paris show.

It was only 7:30 Pacific Time so she dialed the Colossus, and was mildly ashamed she knew the number without having to call directory assistance.

"Room 2104," she said as soon as the operator answered.

"The name of the guest?"

Thurston. Walter Thurston."

"Thank you, and have a lucky day."

Margaret answered and Tiffany was surprised, half expecting to hear Walter's deep voice.

"Margaret?"

"Yes dear," the older woman said, recognizing Tiffany's voice.

"How are you? Walter tells me you're enjoying your visit."

"I certainly am," Margaret replied, trying to gauge Tiffany's mood. "Would you like to talk to Walter? He's right here."

"Yes please. Just for a minute."

"Hi Walter," she said, hoping he would be agreeable to her travel plans. "I just wanted to check with you to see if the tentative schedule I've arranged is okay.

"I'll come to Vegas on Wednesday and stay until Sunday morning. Hopefully that will be enough time to have you fill me in on what I need to do and sign whatever documents are necessary."

Then softly, "I know I've been depending on you a lot, and asking you to go way beyond the call of duty," she said, "but I don't know what else to do.

"We both know I can't run that hotel and I don't want to. One thing I do want you do is put out some feelers for a potential buyer..."

He didn't answer right away and she didn't know if he was disappointed in her decision or if he was caught up in thought.

"I don't think selling would be wise right now," he said. "The Colossus is all over the headlines in the local papers, and word of a sale could damage the morale of the workers even more. Secondly, because of the tragic events surrounding the hotel at this point the most likely prospective buyers would be sharks looking for a bargain price. They'd try and prey on your vulnerability.

"It's also no secret you're not thrilled with the idea of taking over a Vegas casino."

He did not tell her that one columnist had wondered in print if she was a "Mafia Princess" or "Alice in Wonderland."

"How can they know my feelings Walter?" I haven't told anyone about my intentions with the Colossus. Other than you I mean. And I haven't spoken to anyone in the press. Have you?"

"Not a word," he said truthfully.

"Then...?"

"Diana," they said in unison.

"I have a hunch you're right," he said. "I'm sure she knows some local press people well enough to give them some ideas. Anyway, don't worry about it.

"And Wednesday will be fine," he said digressing to the original subject. "We can get a lot done by the end of the week.

One thing you'll have to do is file some formal background documents with the Gaming Commission so they can issue a temporary license."

She wanted to ask him to stay and take charge of the Colossus, at least until they could find a suitable buyer but she didn't dare. Not on the phone, and not after all he had done. She guessed both he and Margaret had probably had their fill of Las Vegas and were anxious to get back to Chicago. After all, Walter had a law practice to run.

Walter personally came to the airport to meet her, hoping to prepare her for the unfavorable and speculative stories he knew would upset her.

He had no chance to warn her.

They walked past a W.H.Smith newsstand and the banner newspaper headline caught her eye.

"FORRESTER A MOB HIT?"

"OmiGod Walter!! Did you see that headline?"

He had not only seen it, he was bracing himself for the next wave of indignation, which would certainly come as soon as she read the subhead, "Rumor Colossus Owner Had Ties to Organized Crime."

Tiffany rushed to the counter and bought both local papers. The Review Journal and Las Vegas Sun had similar stories and both were capitalizing on the sensationalism.

"What right do they have to print lies?" she said rhetorically.

She devoured the newspaper stories on the way to the hotel, reading paragraphs of each out loud. The articles were mostly circumstantial, their main point of contention centering on the fact no one really knew much about Adam Forrester's background. The writers also hinted there had been whispers from the beginning that Adam was really a front for the Chicago syndicate. Both cited the infamous "unnamed sources" as the key to their allegations.

"This is libel," Tiffany repeated for the fourth time as the white limo slowed to a halt in front of the Colossus.

The hotel looked different to her now.

When Tiffany had first heard about the Colossus, at the Oak Room, feelings of guilt as well as surges of excitement consumed her. Then came fond thoughts of the gigantic hotel and the planned fairytale reconciliation with her father. But those fantasies lasted only a few hours, until the phone call notifying her of the tragedy.

Days later, when she first set eyes on the 6,000 room palace she was sad, realizing she had been summoned there only for his funeral. She associated the hotel with her loss, and her confrontation with Diana only served to reinforce her distaste for the place.

Over the past two weeks she had been on an emotional elevator that had buckled her knees.

Inheriting the hotel had made her spirits soar, not for the material gain but for the link it established with her dad. A link even death could not break.

But now, with these hurtful headlines and the mess everything was in, Tiffany felt herself sinking. Despite its obvious aesthetic beauty, she feared the Colossus would turn into her own personal house of horrors. She couldn't let that happen. She was determined to make the Colossus her father's living legacy. Problem was, she wasn't sure she had the time or strength to do the job. For sure she couldn't do it without help. Lots of help.

Tiffany sized up the casino as she and Walter walked to the executive elevators. The lawyer had his familiar worn brown briefcase with the frayed leather straps and she thought again how much it looked like an old-time Pony Express mailbag.

Her attaché case, a shiny black leather bag that hung by a strap from her shoulder was almost exclusively stuffed with design patterns. The only exception being a report from the Las Vegas Convention and Visitors Authority offering a profile of the typical Vegas tourist. She had requested it through her secretary, and it had arrived via FedEx on the next afternoon.

The casino was busy, but not crowded.

"There must be two hundred people in here and it looks empty," she said to Walter. "When its crowded you forget how huge the area is."

Walter nodded.

They walked stride for stride to the elevators. She noticed a few heads turn as one employee or another pointed her out, but she didn't stop to talk. These weren't really her employees. She didn't know any of them. She didn't want to be responsible to them or for them.

Neither of them spoke until after they had walked through the thick, doublewide glass doors, past the executive office receptionist and were safely inside her father's office.

They had barely closed the door when Tiffany hesitantly slid into the leather chair behind the big mahogany desk and came face to face with a picture of herself and her father, taken a year or two after she had graduated. They were both smiling. The photo was in a worn silver frame and sat on the far right corner of Adam Forrester's desk.

Walter sat heavily in one of the handsome side chairs facing the desk.

She was still seething over the newspaper stories.

"Are you sure there's nothing we can do Walter?" She did not have to remind him to what she was referring.

"Can't we sue the bastards? Or force them to print a retraction?"

"We could, but we wouldn't win. Libel is a very tough case to prove."

"But they're lying. They're smearing him."

"I know," he said. "The truth will come out."

"And in the meantime we have to let them slam him in the press?"

"It'll die down," he said, not sure it would. "They're being very careful to use words like "alleged", "reputed" and quoting unnamed sources.

"Okay Walter," she said squeezing her eyes together to block the tears. "Let's get to it. What is it you need me to do?"

"I have some papers for you to sign with regard to the will," he said digging them out of his briefcase. He looked at Tiffany over the top rim of his glasses and could see her strong resemblance to Adam. Both had sleek, strong jawbones and penetrating eyes. Tiffany's nose was smaller, more like her mother's, but their mouths were shaped from the same mold.

She was comfortable in his chair.

"You'll need to fill these out to get a temporary gaming permit," he said, placing a stapled clump of papers on the desk.

"Is all that really necessary?" she asked, knowing the answer. "What if we sell the hotel in a week, or a month? It could happen."

"I know," he said, understanding, "but these you can't get around. The papers transfer the hotel stock, and officially put you in charge. The others are for the gaming Control Board and authorize them to begin a thorough background check on you, your business and your acquaintances. In exchange, they will grant you a temporary license good for six months."

She signed the documents and he filled her in on the general day to day activities of the casino, the problems and the revenue numbers. He generalized most of it, reluctant to fill her head with a mishmash of details she would probably never need.

They worked and talked for more than two hours before he suggested bringing T.J. Fitzgerald in for a report on some other areas.

"Walter, before Mr. Fitzgerald gets here, there's something I'd like to ask you."

He had dreaded this moment, but knew it would have to come. She had every right to ask, and no one had known her father better. He braced himself.

"Is it at all possible for you to stay and take charge of the hotel? Just until we can find someone to run it," she quickly added.

His muscles relaxed. He had expected her to ask about her father and the mob. He knew Adam had a wide range of business associates in Chicago and as a lawyer he was trained to be cautious. Overly cautious.

"Was my father in the Mafia, Walter?" The question was as unexpected as an earthquake. He stammered. Not because he doubted his own answer but because she had lulled him into relaxing his guard. It was a blind side blow.

He looked at her for a long moment.

"Absolutely not," he said strongly. "Don't let yourself get caught up in those newspaper articles. They're lies and all speculative. You know how the press is. They never let the facts get in the way of a good story."

"I want to know who killed him Walter. And why? That's more important than anything else."

She did not tell him about the nightmares. Or that she hadn't had a full night's sleep since the Ball.

"This whole thing is ridiculous," she shrieked, obviously flustered. "A reputable hotel owner is shot to death at his own home and no one knows anything. Where was Diana? Where was the maid or the help?"

"Diana was in Palm Springs. The police have already verified that."

"And the housekeepers?"

"Their day off. No changes there. It was their regular day."

He was trying to help her understand something he did not understand.

"What about the possibility that it was a robbery and the guy panicked?"

"The police are still investigating that angle," he said wishing he had something more to tell her. "They are working with Diana, taking an inventory of the house and valuables.

"That Detective Sarabian told me the floor safe in your father's den was open," the lawyer offered, "and they found broken paper straps that appear to have been wrapped around large amounts of money. We don't know how much."

"Then it was definitely a robbery?"

"Or someone wanted it to look like one," he said, echoing the detective's opinion.

"Why would anyone have to kill him Walter? Why would someone do that?"

"I don't know sweetheart. I just don't know."

"My father wouldn't have resisted if someone just wanted money. There had to be something else. I've got to know."

"Me too," he said, trying to get her mind back to the business at hand, "but first things first. I'm honored that you'd ask me to take charge of the Colossus," he said unsteadily, "but I don't think I'm qualified. I don't know the hotel business Tiffany. You need an experienced captain to take the helm of a ship this large. Otherwise people can get hurt."

He had to admit the thought of staying in Vegas for a couple months to get the Colossus ship shape had crossed his mind. It would be a challenge and he needed one. The Colossus was a project that could rejuvenate him.

"Can you at least do it until we can find someone?" she pleaded.

"I suppose I could do that, but I'd like to discuss it with Margaret before giving you a final answer. I don't think she'll mind," he added, giving her encouragement.

"We'll talk about it more later," he said rising to answer a knock at the door.

It was Fitzgerald. Walter had asked the secretary to locate him and have him come to Adam's office. He knew Tiffany wanted to get a better feel for the man, but had no inkling what else was on her mind.

"Hello T.J.," she said politely. "Please sit down.

"You're kind of the experienced hand here," she began. "You were with my dad from the time this hotel was built, so I guess you have more of a feel for what goes on around here than anyone else."

"I suppose," Fitzgerald said modestly, obviously wondering where Tiffany was headed.

"I've asked Walter to stay on and take charge of the hotel for a while. At least until we can find someone to run it permanently," she said, lining them up for her kill shot.

"And I intend to be around as often as possible." The statement surprised Walter.

"Not because I like Vegas, but the thing is, if I'm involved in a business I want it to be the best. Also, and this is my number one reason--- I want to use every resource at my disposal to find out who killed my father.

"Do you understand that? Any resource available, no matter what the price."

She gave both men a chance to digest her comments, and then picked up the pace.

"I'm sure you've seen the headlines and the trash stories," she continued.

"They're all bullshit. My father was no more in the Mafia than I am. Somebody killed him either because he was an enemy, or they wanted to buy this hotel and he wouldn't sell.

"Maybe in some twisted way Diana was even involved." She was sorry as soon as the words came out of he mouth. She didn't believe it and really didn't want to go there.

"I'm sorry," she said contritely. "That was unfair." Neither man had reacted but she felt it necessary to clear the air before either of them thought her a fool.

"How much help do you think we'll get from the police?" she said, directing her question to Fitzgerald. "I mean, do you think they'll give this case priority treatment?"

"They should," Fitzgerald said without hesitation. "After all your father was a key figure in this town. He was very high profile and the story is all over the papers."

"I know. I've seen the papers," she said sharply.

"A downtown hotel owner was killed by his girlfriend and her lover a couple years ago," Walter added, "and the cops were all over it. They stayed on it until they got a conviction."

"That was the Binion murder," Fitzgerald replied. "Teddy Binion. He was the son of Benny Binion, one of Vegas' pioneer's. There was no way that one could have been pushed to the back burner. The family has tremendous political clout so they kept the pressure on.

"It was real iffy whether that was a murder or suicide. Teddy was a wild man who was hooked on heavy drugs and on the road to self-destruction anyway."

"I really don't care about Teddy Binion," Tiffany interrupted. "This is about my father. And as far as I know, he wasn't on the road to self-destruction. He wasn't a drug addict and he didn't commit suicide.

"If either of you knows any different, please speak up."

Neither man spoke, so Tiffany continued.

"Maybe the best plan would be to start our own investigation, then feed the information to the media so they keep the pressure on the cops.

"What do you think T.J.?"

"T.J. Fitzgerald was pensive. His large hands were folded in his lap, and his lanky frame completely covered the desk chair opposite Walter.

A full thirty seconds passed before he spoke, and when he did it was in a strong, even tone and he did not mince words.

"The first thing I would do is talk to Brian Powers. There isn't much that goes on in Las Vegas he doesn't know about, and what he doesn't know he can usually find out. I think his advice on how to proceed would be our best bet. He could get us inside information. If we could convince him to help us I think we might have a chance," Fitzgerald concluded. "Brian knows both sides of the street."

"What exactly does that mean, Mr. Fitzgerald?" Tiffany asked curiously.

"It means he knows the cops as well as some of the bad guys," Fitzgerald answered.

"But I want you to understand Miss Wayne...

"Please call me Tiffany...

"Something about Brian. He won't pull any punches. He'll take you wherever the road may lead, and we all have to be prepared for that."

She gave him a hard look.

"I am prepared," she said harshly.

"I mean no disrespect, Tiffany. What I'm trying to say is, I don't think your dad had any links to the mob, but I couldn't be a hundred percent certain because I wasn't privy to every deal that came across his desk.

"Every now and then he'd announce a new arrangement for the hotel that I might question but that was your father. He took some strange chances and sometimes joined forces with some odd partners."

"Do you think some of those deals could've been Diana's doing?" Tiffany asked pointedly. "What if she made some deal that got them in trouble? Is that possible?

"She told us that she was very involved in every phase and level of the hotel's business?"

"She was," Fitzgerald answered without hesitation. "And yes, sometimes Diana did negotiate deals on behalf of the hotel. Nothing major to my knowledge, but I suppose it's possible something she was involved in could have turned sour. But that's a longshot."

"Thank you T.J. And to finish answering your earlier question, please understand that I am not afraid of what Brian Powers, the police or anyone else may uncover about my father.

"I know who and what he was, and I have no doubts. Everyone else can reserve judgment if they so choose. I am determined to take this as far as it goes. All I'm asking for is the truth."

They chatted for a few more minutes, then adjourned, but only after Fitzgerald agreed to talk to Brian Powers and feel him out.

"Don't tell him too much," Walter suggested. Let's just get him here and then we can talk. Tell him Tiffany and I are up to our kneecaps in alligators as we try and learn what it takes to run a hotel.

"Maybe you can hint that you've recommended bringing him on board as a special consultant," Tiffany added.

After Fitzgerald's departure Tiffany and Walter returned to the business of running the hotel and effecting a smooth transition.

The Colossus was her hotel now, and she wanted it to be a successful venture. Strong management seemed to be the key, and if Walter was going to run the place it would be important for him to meet and gain the respect of the other owners as well as the city's VIP infrastructure. She tucked that thought in the back of her mind and went back to the paperwork. It wouldn't be easy getting Walter to make social calls. There were a lot of hotels, and it would be awkward.

"We'll need a local attorney to handle your licensing application, and he'll have to handle mine too if I'm going to stay around here," Walter said thoughtfully.

"I'd have to be licensed as a key employee."

"Do you know anyone here?"

"Not off the top of my head, but my firm has done some business with some people here. I'll call back to Chicago and get some names."

"There are some papers here about a changeover in the Colossus insurance plan," she said looking up from the file. "Have you looked at these?"

He hadn't.

There was also a list of twenty-four local schools and charities requesting donations, a memo from the construction department regarding the proposed renaming of the Tiffany restaurant and a slew of overdue expense vouchers to be signed. It was after six by the time they were ready to call it a day and it didn't seem like they had made much of a dent in the paperwork.

"I can't believe we still have all of those to go through," she said pointing at a thick stack of papers in the in basket.

She had put on her light summer blazer and was ready to leave the office when the idea first entered her head.

"Sit down for another minute Walter. I have one more thing I want to run by you."

"I've been trying all day to think of a way you, or both of us could meet all the big shots in town. You know, the other owners and decision makers. I think it's vitally important they know who we are and vice-versa. I mean, I don't know if I'll have the hotel five months or five years.

"I want them to know that we intend to run this hotel as professionally as possible. If we can charm them, maybe they won't ignore us and treat us like outsiders."

"Sounds like a good idea. I just don't know how we'll do it. You're leaving Saturday and with the day to day running of this place I'm not going to have a lot of time to get out and meet people."

"Exactly. That's why I think we should do it in a more social atmosphere. I was thinking of a party. Not now of course, but when I come back from Paris. A VIP party unlike anything Vegas has ever seen."

"That might work," he said, warming to the idea. "I think the other owners as well as the city's high and mighty will be very eager to get a first hand look at you."

Over the years Walter had made some of his most important contacts at social gatherings in Chicago and he anticipated the same might hold true in Nevada. It would have to because he didn't play golf.

He knew Tiffany had no intention of ever moving to Nevada and if she was forced to run the casino from Chicago it would be helpful if some of Vegas' major players had a good feeling about her.

"How about June?"

"July might be better," he countered. "It would give us more time to prepare and give people a chance to handle graduations and get their own vacations out of the way."

Tiffany was becoming more enthusiastic.

"Then let's make it a Fourth of July bash. That might be kind of fun if we do it right." For the moment she had put the tragedy out of her head.

"Then its all set," she said. "You can get the ball rolling with the public relations department and whoever else needs to get involved. This is April, which means we've got two plus months to make it happen."

On Friday they plowed through the remaining workload and got a message from Fitzgerald informing them Brian was out of town.

"I left a message on his machine. He'll get back to me as soon as he gets it."

"Let Walter know as soon as he calls. I'll be gone but I'm sure the two of you can convince him to at least come in for a meeting. Once he's here, we can put together an open conference call."

On Sunday she returned to Chicago. She and Val didn't have a moment to themselves as a crush of last minute office details and instructions filled their day.

It was not until Tuesday, at O'Hare, as they were calling her Paris flight that she got a chance to call Walter and say goodbye. She had managed to call Johnny on Monday, and they had met for a quick glass of wine, but it was not convenient for him to come home with her. She would have felt awkward because Val had stayed the night so they could get each other up and share a cab to the airport.

She was also having second thoughts about the party, wondering if it was the right thing to do in view of the circumstances. In the end she decided it was.

"I'll be thinking about the party," she told Walter. "I want it to be very special. In fact I've jotted down a bunch of ideas for you, but I can't go into them now. They're calling our flight. I'll call you from Paris as soon as I get a chance.

"By the way, have you heard from the elusive Mr. Powers?"

"Nothing yet, but I'm sure he'll turn up soon." Walter was happy to hear the life in her voice. "You just take care of Paris and your show. We'll get things going on the party. We've already started putting together a guest list.

"One more thing Tiffany." She could detect the change in Walter's voice. It was his fatherly tone. "Please be careful. Take care of yourself."

"You almost sound like a worried…uh, parent." She was about to say father and caught herself.

Diana Forrester's name was conspicuously absent from the guest list, however she did have an indirect influence on the invitees. Walter had come across a VIP list the widow Forrester had left in a file drawer, and on it were the private numbers and addresses of some very powerful players.

He had to give the lady credit. She knew how to mix and get to the powers.

The Colossus party was going to come off, and he had a gut feeling it was going to be a smash. He knew in his heart that it would be eventful. He also knew that somehow, some way, Diana Forrester would crack the lineup and crash the party. He could hardly wait to see how she'd do it.

Chapter 10
The Silver Screen

"This could be it," Oscar said excitedly. He was waving a thick mailing envelope in Sonny's face.

"This could be the break that changes your life."

Sonny was in a lousy mood. He had just finished a grueling show and things hadn't gone smoothly. The stage mike was balky and in the middle of a romantic ballad the sound system malfunctioned, sending out a screech that had the audience covering its ears.

It wasn't a good night.

"What the hell is that?" He really didn't care and in recent weeks had made no secret of the fact he had become disenchanted with Oscar, Mario and Four Star Talent. They had served their purpose.

He was now one of the biggest stars on the Vegas Strip. He wanted a recording contract or a movie deal.

I'm not Tom Hanks or Mel Gibson but I'm not fucking chopped liver either. And why should they continue to get a percentage of everything I make whey they don't have to do anything anymore? He had been building up the courage to cut them loose for six months. And Diana Forrester had said she'd help him find some good lawyers. The kind of pricks who would stop at nothing to break the Four Star contract.

"This, my boy, is your future. It's what you've been waiting for. The script that will make you the biggest movie star of the new millennium."

Sonny wasn't enthused. He'd heard Oscar's song and dance before, and the only acting jobs he'd gotten were bit parts on television shows where he got to play a Las Vegas singer.

"So...? What makes this script different from the other hundred I've read over the past two years?"

"This one's different because the director thinks you're the man to play the lead. And the director is Sam Bradford. The Sam Bradford," Oscar added after a dramatic pause.

"And he wants me—Sonny Fremont to play the lead?"

"Damn right he does."

Sonny resisted to the temptation to get his hopes up. They'd been dashed before.

"You'd better not be fucking kidding me Oscar?"

The agent's serious stare told Sonny it was no joke.

"Is this the big project Bradford's been working on for two years? The sequel to "Casablanca"?

A cold wave shot through Sonny's body as Oscar slid the red covered script from the envelope. Was Oscar playing a cruel joke? Was it April Fool's Day?

His mood darkened.

"Don't bullshit me Oscar?"

"No bullshit Sonny. I've known Sam Bradford for a long time and I've convinced him you're the right man for the job. I suggest you start reading the script."

Oscar knew Sonny's patience was wearing thin, and that Four Star was in danger of losing him as a client despite the ironclad contract and Mario's obvious influence. The movie deal would get things back on solid ground.

"What's the catch?" Sonny rose to his full 6'1 height and eyed Oscar warily, not yet daring to believe what he was hearing.

"Well, there are still a few details to work out."

Sonny was hooked and he was beginning to buy into the fantasy.

"What kind of details?"

"Things like your salary and the shooting schedule. We'll have to rearrange your Vegas booking dates to get you free for six to eight weeks of shooting. I'm sure I can do that without much of a problem.

"Anyway, I have a meeting with Bradford in Hollywood day after tomorrow and we'll iron everything out."

Sam Bradford was the hottest director in Hollywood. His previous five movies had all grossed over $100 million and he had been rewarded with an Academy Award two years running, beating out Steven Speilberg and James Cameron. His genius was unquestioned, and he was being compared to the greats like Hitchcock, Huston and Peckinpaugh. Sam Bradford was the current toast of Hollywood.

Two days later Oscar Bento sat patiently in the tastefully furnished reception area of Sam Bradford's office on the Warner Brothers studio lot, a black leather briefcase at his feet.

"Mr. Bradford will see you now," the woman said without looking up. "It's the office at the end of the hall."

Oscar stood erect, gathered up his briefcase and strode down the hall. He was feeling extremely confident.

"Mr. Bento, I'm Sam Bradford. What can I do for you?"

The director was looking at him inquisitively, his boyish face open, his forehead slightly wrinkled.

"It's a pleasure to meet you, Mr. Bradford.

"Rather than fiddle around I'll tell you right off what you can do for me," Oscar said evenly. "You can announce to the world that you've decided to cast Sonny Fremont as the male lead in "Morocco Heat".

Bradford squinted at Oscar oddly.

"Excuse me?

"I really don't have time for jokes Mr. Bento. I'm extremely busy and I don't appreciate your wasting my time. Now if you don't mind…"

"But I do mind, Mr. Bradford", Oscar said holding his ground.

Sam Bradford was 36, with sandy blond hair and a wiry athletic build. His complexion was flawless, save for a small Robert Redford type mole on his left cheek, and in his short sleeve Polo shirt he looked more like a dentist or recently retired athlete than a budding Hollywood legend.

"I assure you this is no joke Mr. Bradford. Sonny Fremont is perfect for your picture."

"And you're a complete lunatic if you think I'm going to give the lead in the biggest film in thirty years to some Las Vegas cornball who's been panned by any critic who even noticed him in the bit parts he's had."

Sam Bradford was no longer amused by Oscar Bento.

"The original film was a classic. The remake will be a classic too. And I can guarantee you Sonny Fremont's name won't be anywhere in the credits."

The director's voice was getting louder as he rose from his chair.

Oscar didn't flinch and he wasn't the least bit unnerved by the director's shouting.

"Your boy isn't an actor, he's a ham, and this isn't television it's the big screen. I hate to have to be the one to break this to you but Sonny Fremont has no talent. He's a caricature."

"If you'll indulge me for one more minute I think we can get this worked out," Oscar said when Sam Bradford paused to catch his breath.

Oscar removed a manila folder from his case and slid it across the director's large oak desk. Sam leaned forward, pulling it closer, unclasping the metal clip as he opened it.

His face turned pale as he read the enclosed handwritten note.

On the other side of the desk Oscar Bento sat and waited.

"Seems like a fair exchange. A starring role for the no talent Vegas headliner and we wipe out your debt. In addition I'll see to it you get the negatives to those very interesting pictures."

Sam Bradford was not bothered by his gambling debt. A lot of industry executives gambled. He had suffered through an incredible run of bad luck and was stuck nearly half a million dollars. The bookies had been pushing him hard over the past few weeks and the more he pressed the worse his luck seemed to get.

He knew money was not the issue. In a week or two he'd have the money to cover his losses, and the thought of being physically manhandled by a couple of street thugs didn't frighten him nearly as much as the pictures he held in his hand.

When he looked at the black and white 5x7s he felt as if someone had suddenly cut off his air. He was unable to summon the strength to ask the little man in front of him how or where he had gotten them. Even worse, he knew it didn't matter.

Someone knew.

The pictures were of him and Boyd Matthews in what even a lenient film ratings commission would have classified as "X" rated positions.

Being gay in Hollywood was as common as bottled water and for most people it carried no stigma. Gay was in, but he was also quite sure the media and the world would have a field day with the news.

For God's sake, he was President of the newly formed "Morality in Motion Pictures" Association, and had been approached about running for State Senator.

That was what concerned him most. He was considering the jump to politics, and had even fantasized about being governor. Ronald Reagan had done it, so it wasn't impossible.

But what this bizarre little man in front of him was saying could destroy everything. It could and would ruin his life.

There was no doubt the pictures would hit the tabloids if Oscar made them available. They'd probably even be on the Internet. He'd be a laughingstock. Forget politics. He'd never be taken seriously as a director again. Pamela Anderson would have more credibility.

Not only would he no longer be Tinseltown's Golden Boy, he'd be branded a hypocrite. Sexual indiscretions had driven Roman Polanski out of Hollywood and virtually ruined his career as a director.

Six months with a shrink had helped Sam sort out his sexual preferences, and he was now sure he wasn't gay. His involvement with Boyd Matthews was a fling born out of curiosity. His only regret was the hurt he had caused Boyd.

Being exposed now would send out the wrong message and only serve to complicate matters.

He thought of his sister, and his mother. What would they think? Seeing those pictures would destroy them. He could never let them see.

He was holding his career in his hands. He had no choice.

The media went wild when the studio announced the leading man, and half the male stars in Hollywood fired their agents. Harrison Ford had expressed interest in the role, so had Michael Douglas, Denzell Washington, Russell Crowe, Ben Affleck and a dozen others. But Sonny Fremont got it.

Sam Bradford and Warner Brothers were relieved to discover that the sheer boldness of the decision was, in itself, worth a few million dollars in free publicity. Sonny's picture made the cover of almost every entertainment magazine in the country.

Entertainment Tonight and Access Hollywood did features. People, Us, Life, George, Cosmo and Entertainment Weekly all had splashy stories and varied opinions about why Sam Bradford had tapped Sonny Fremont to be the star of "Morocco Heat".

Some called the choice brilliant; others saw it as a daring way to bring new blood to the screen. Still others were not so kind, lambasting it as a sham and a disgrace to the memory of Bogie.

"I appreciate your being willing to take a chance on me in such an important picture," Sonny said to Sam when they met for the first time two weeks later at a Los Angeles press conference.

The flashbulbs were popping and Sam looked at him hard, trying to read Sonny's eyes but there was nothing in the singer's demeanor to indicate he knew the circumstances that led to him being given the lead role. Sam didn't buy the innocent routine for a minute. No one could be that naïve, or that stupid.

He was convinced Sonny knew.

He had to know, and he had to be mixed up with the mob. Why else would they be doing him a favor?

"Let's hope it turns out for the best," Sam muttered through clenched teeth as the photographers begged for one more shot. "It's a hell of a script. It doesn't need an Olivier. It would be a hit with King Kong or Hulk Hogan in the lead," Sam added, enjoying the hollow opportunity to zing Sonny.

It hardly qualified as revenge.

Sam's cryptic barbs confused Sonny. He couldn't understand why the director was so distant. In public Bradford was civil, even polite, but away from the cameras Sam ignored him.

Maybe he's just uptight with all the pressure. Or maybe he's just a high strung guy who's second guessing himself about giving me the lead. He dismissed the thought when he remembered Oscar telling him how Sam had specifically asked for him. I didn't even go after the part. What the hell! These Hollywood people are just plain fucking nuts.

The shooting schedule called for five weeks on location in Georgia and three additional weeks of interiors on a sound stage in Burbank.

Oscar rearranged Sonny's Vegas schedule to get him ten free weeks just in case the filming ran behind schedule.

His Las Vegas stage shows, despite being physically taxing twice a night, did not prepare Sonny Fremont for the long difficult filming hours, nor for the humidity of Atlanta.

"I can't believe we start shooting at five o'clock in the morning," he complained. "I have to get up at 3:30 and be in make-up by 4:15. On top of that the humidity is ridiculous. I don't know if it's worth all the trouble..."

"It's worth it," Oscar said strongly. "Eight or nine weeks out of your life and you'll be a hero forever. Stop acting like a prima donna. We had to pull a lot of strings to get you this part and you better damn well see it through."

Getting Sonny the movie role had given Oscar the upper hand again.

"By the way, how are you and Sam Bradford getting along?"

"Okay, I guess. We really don't talk much, and when we do it's strictly business. It's pretty fucking strange, Oscar. Sometimes I feel he resents me and doesn't give a damn if I'm here or not."

Oscar had been concerned that Bradford might try and run Sonny off the picture or, worse yet, confront Sonny about how he had come to get the starring role. He was pleased the director had used sound judgment and avoided the subject.

Maybe Sam Bradford would make a good politician after all.

Sonny's contract called for a minimal salary against a couple points in the picture which might mean as much as $10 million if the movie hit it big at the box-office. Mario would be very happy if the film did that kind of business because it meant laundering at least three times whatever amount Sonny brought in.

Sam Bradford was trying hard to like Sonny Fremont, perhaps because he realized they were stuck together. For better or worse. He wanted to believe Sonny didn't know what Oscar had done to get him the part, but it didn't wash. Sonny had to know. Maybe he'd even seen the pictures.

The thought of Sonny looking at the pictures made Sam Bradford feel inferior. He couldn't look Sonny in the eye, and tried to avoid direct contact unless it was absolutely necessary.

Aside from a little whining about the hours, Sonny had not caused any problems on the set. He took direction well and was willing to work, unlike some actors Sam had directed.

Still, Sam's worst fears were realized. Sonny Fremont was simply too inexperienced and too methodical for such a key role. Sam had to admit the man tried, but he always got the feeling Sonny was reading from cue cards.

A series of torrential summer thunderstorms cost the production four straight days in the third week and it made everyone a bit edgy.

In his trailer Sam Bradford sat alone, consoling himself with a bottle of Chivas and a healthy supply of ice. The last person in the world he expected to join him was Sonny Fremont.

"Mind if I share one with you? "Sonny asked as he shook the rain from his jacket and stepped into the director's trailer.

He caught Sam by surprise.

"I suppose not. Pull up a chair."

"I thought this might be a good chance for us to talk about the picture a little," Sonny said. "We don't get much chance to swap ideas when we're working."

Sam Bradford knew it wasn't a good time. Not when he was a sip or two away from being plastered, and not after he had seen the rushes from the past two days of shooting. He was afraid he might come unraveled, and vent his hostilities on Sonny.

"Not much to talk about," Sam lied. "We've still got a long way to go."

"Yeah, but I heard you saw the rushes and I wondered what you thought. I mean, how do I look? Think I'll make them forget Bogie?"

Sonny Fremont had meant it as a joke, but in his drunken state Sam didn't pick up on the humor. He only heard Sonny Fremont comparing himself to Humphrey Bogart and he came unglued.

On another day they might have shared a laugh about it, and Sam Bradford replayed the details in his head a thousand times later on, but it was too late. On this day he snapped. Perhaps it was the combination of the liquor and the rain. It didn't matter. He lost control.

He started thinking about the hours he had spent in the screening room earlier in the day, poring over the dailies of the first two weeks shooting.

And every time he looked at the rushes he was more convinced.

Sonny Fremont did not come across very well on the silver screen. The man had movie star looks, carried himself well and seemed to deliver his lines decently but there was something missing. Some spark. Some magic. The big stars all had it. Pacino, Hoffman, Hanks, Streep. They all had the kind of intangible charisma to justify giving them the lead in a major big budget film. And even those stars had to watch their step. Two or three flops in a row and studios would be whispering that they were "cold." No one would be willing to risk $100 million.

Ask Eddie Murphy or Stallone.

Sam thought Sonny's problem was that he had not yet learned to caress a camera the way he had learned to work a live audience. You had to virtually make love to the camera. It caught everything, and it was unforgiving.

Whatever it was, Sam was positive Sonny did not fit as the leading man and it was eating at him. He had compromised his professionalism and it was tearing at his insides.

He took another sip of the scotch.

"The truth is Sonny, I don't like what I'm seeing. It's just not working." Sam was in deep now and he felt as if a dam had broken.

"What do you mean it's not working?" Sonny asked, fearing the answer.

Sam took another long sip of the Chivas, this time directly from the bottle.

"More exactly I mean you're not working Sonny. The problem is you. You aren't coming across the way I hoped. If we continue, everyone who sees it will ridicule all of us. You, me and the picture. Instead of a classic, we'll be a joke."

Sonny couldn't believe what he was hearing. His ego flared and he became defensive.

"How can that be? You handpicked me for this role. You've won Academy Awards. How could you be so wrong? Or maybe you're a little too drunk to talk about it now."

Sonny was grasping. His head was reeling. He didn't know what to think. Or do. The rain was hammering the trailer's roof and it sounded like a machine gun in his head.

"I'm not too drunk," Sam said sharply. There was a slight slur to his words. At that moment an earsplitting clap of thunder shook the trailer windows and the relentless southern storm beat down harder, sounding like a waterfall as it cascaded down the sides of Sam's silvery shelter.

"If you feel I'm not good enough why don't you just fire me and get yourself another leading man," Sonny challenged. "I'm sure there are a hundred guys who'd jump at the chance."

"You can bet there are," Sam said quickly. I'd like to fire you. More than you'll ever know, but I don't think your band of Goomba friends would like it very much. In fact I know they wouldn't. And as much as I want to I can't. One picture, even one as historic as this one is not worth my career."

"What the hell are you talking about?" Sonny screamed over the pelting rain.

"You really don't know, do you? You big dumb Okie. You have no clue what's going on. How could you be so stupid?

"You're not an actor. You never will be. Think carefully about your career. Have you ever done anything significant enough to deserve a part like this? The answer is no," Sam said before Sonny could reply.

"I had no choice but to give you the lead. Your pal Oscar and his gang have me by the balls and they blackmailed me. Your starring role was the ransom."

"You're a lying bastard," was the best Sonny could do.

"We'll probably muddle through and make the picture but I don't ever want you to think you earned the part, or that I would ever have given you a second thought if they hadn't twisted my arm."

Sonny had a flashback to the day Mario tried to intimidate him into doing porno films.

Sam was still rambling.

"And maybe, if there is any justice, one day the whole world will find out how and why you got this role.

"But you'd better hope that never happens, because if it does, your career even in Vegas will be finished. If you do manage to get booked you'll get billing somewhere between the 99c buffet and the free shrimp cocktail."

Sonny opened his mouth but no words came out.

The liquor was bolstering Sam Bradford's courage and the insults kept coming. His inhibitions were gone. He had no master plan for what he was saying. He only knew he had to say it. To get it out. For his own peace of mind.

"I'm trying to think of a way to beat you, all of you," he said snidely. "In fact, I may have just thought of a way to stick it to you and all your strongarm buddies who think they can push their way into this business."

Sam pushed himself to his feet. His eyes were bloodshot.

Ron Delpit

"I'm not going to finish this picture," he said defiantly. "Not with you anyway. And I'm going to get away with it because I've come up a plan to protect myself.

"I'm going to write a letter exposing you and all your lowlife pals. I'm going to reveal who you are and what you are. And Sonny, I know the names, all the names. And if anything happens to me that letter will be made public. It'll destroy you and them in one swoop. If they get me it'll cost them.

"Do you get it Sonny Boy?"

The "Sonny Boy "jolted Sonny Fremont out of his lethargy. He saw his career disappearing before his eyes. Like an enraged animal he leapt at the director.

"You sonofabitch. I'll kill you. No fucking way are you going to pull the plug on me." He was much stronger than the director and easily pinned Sam to the wall of the trailer.

"Go ahead, you stupid bastard, kill me." The stale smell of Sam Bradford's liquored breath punctuated Sonny's nostrils.

Sonny pushed Bradford away, knocking him over a chair into a cheap floor lamp.

"You don't have the balls to expose anybody," Sonny screamed. "This picture means too much to you. Your career is on the line too." He wasn't sure if what he was saying was true. He was babbling, searching for something to hold on to.

And even while he was saying it, somewhere deep within Sonny Fremont knew Sam Bradford was telling the truth. He had never wanted him for his leading man. Oscar or Mario had somehow forced or blackmailed the director into giving him the part.

Knowing it made him feel empty, and angry at the world.

Sam, a bruise forming under his left eye, sat sprawled in a corner. He did not reply. He was also no longer drunk. Sonny Fremont's hands around his throat had sobered him quickly.

A script lay on the table near the door. Sonny picked it up and threw the red-jacketed pages at Sam as he bolted out the trailer door into the rain.

"We'll make this picture, whether you like it or not, and I'll be the star," Sonny said heatedly. "And if you try to fuck up my life or my career, I won't need any help from my friends, I'll kill you myself. Remember that."

Sonny left the trailer door wide open and the pelting rain ricocheted into the room. Lightning lit up the Georgia sky.

Sam Bradford knew he had two important things to do. First he had a letter to write. Second he had to destroy the film.

Calling on reserve energies he sat at his laptop and put down his thoughts. His head was exploding, and his body ached. He covered everything his could think of, even admitting his brief affair with Boyd Matthews and his gambling

130

addiction. And he named names. Oscar's, Sonny's, Mario's and the Los Angeles bookies. To be sure his allegations would be taken seriously, he included dates, figures and code names.

He spent the next few hours on the phone, calling friends and friends of friends. Anyone he could think of who placed bets through the same ring of bookies. He called pals in Chicago and LA, picking their brains and adding the names of their contacts to his ever growing list.

None of them suspected that they were helping him amass a dossier on mob capos and underbosses.

He worked through the night, gathering his last information from Ted Cox, a former college pal who was a field agent for the FBI in Washington. It was eight a.m. when he reached Cox at his home in Virginia.

Cox, who specialized in organized crime for the bureau, was already intrigued by the film industry and Sam had once relied on Ted's expertise while filming a political thriller. Sam preyed on that interest, spinning a story about the possibility of making his next film a Mafia drama.

"Something like the Godfather, eh Sam? Well, whatever you do, don't use my name. Unless you're prepared to come up with a million dollar consultants fee so I can retire."

"That won't be necessary, Ted. This is supposed to be a fictional story. The information is for reference only. To give it a touch of reality," he laughed." And we'll be sure to protect the not so innocent."

"Be careful Sam. These guys play for keeps. I've had my nose in mob crap since we got out of college. They play rough."

"I imagine they do," he said, now fully aware that he had Ted's attention. And for an hour they swapped stories, Ted trying to impress him with some Mafia horror stories, he dropping names that were supposedly in the screenplay's rough draft.

Unknowingly Ted Cox filled in some missing pieces.

"I'll call you if I need a consultant on the movie," Sam teased as they hung up.

"Do that," Ted said. "I'm sure I'd like Hollywood better than Washington."

And so it went. Overnight he had gathered enough names and information to be dangerous.

His prodding was gentle, his questions casual and Sam was surprised that some of his industry friends were willing to tell him some of the things they did. In the end he had the names and the pecking order of the mob's Los Angeles and Chicago players. He also came to understand how the system worked and who was pulling the strings.

He knew the day would come when he would need the information.

When he finished, Sam Bradford had six full pages, not enough to put them out of business, but enough to put some of the people he named in jail. Or worse.

Worse would be to give them high visibility. That would upset their peers and lead them to be taken care of by their own kind. That would be fitting justice.

It had taken him hours but he had it all down. He pulled the envelope Oscar had given him out of the old metal file, took another long look at the pictures of himself and Boyd, then stuffed it all into a large mailing envelope along with the printout of his incriminating letter.

He addressed it to his sister, Laura Powers. On the outside he wrote in bold print, "Personal. Open Only In Case of Emergency".

Sam Bradford reached for his rain slicker and caught a glimpse of himself in a tiny mirror above the coat rack. A small mouse had formed above his right eye and there was a trace of dried blood in the corner of his mouth.

He grabbed a cap and his car keys, not wanting to waste another minute before getting the package in the mail.

In the car he changed his mind.

Laura doesn't deserve this. She doesn't know anything about the affair with Boyd. She wouldn't understand. And she might get worried and open the package even if nothing happened to me. He also feared the letter might put her in danger.

For a second he thought about sending the package to Laura's ex, Brian Powers, but vetoed the idea. Brian was too inquisitive. He would open the mailer immediately and go for the jugular. In this situation Brian's determination would be a hindrance. Sam only wanted insurance. He had no interest in stirring up the bad guys if it wasn't necessary.

He searched his memory. It would have to be someone he trusted completely.

Boyd. I'll send it to Boyd. He's angry but it doesn't matter. He'll understand.

In the months immediately after severing their ties, Sam had written to Boyd regularly, sending the letters by Federal Express to ensure they were hand delivered. Boyd had never responded.

Over the past six months he had sent only one or two letters, always trying to explain why he had broken their tryst. It didn't matter that Boyd didn't answer. The letters were his personal therapy. He wrote to cleanse his own conscience.

He wanted them to remain friends.

The road was covered with standing water and the wipers did little to improve his visibility. Sam was undaunted. He drove the twenty-two miles into Atlanta and personally handed the package to a clerk at the Peachtree Avenue Federal Express office. The $15 fee was a bargain. Boyd would have the package by 10 a.m. the next morning and he detailed specific instructions to turn the letter over to the LA Times or the police if something unusual happened to him. He was sure Boyd would do it.

"He was serious, Oscar. He's lost his mind. He was drunk. He's going to ruin us all." Sonny Fremont was screaming into the phone.

"Mario's behind this isn't he. The fuckin' asshole."

"Calm down Sonny." Oscar Bento's pulse was on triple-time. If the deal blew up it would all be his fault. He'd get the blame. He was the one who sold Mario on the scheme.

Torino had never been hot on the idea of making Sonny a movie star, but this latest development could have repercussions far beyond Sonny failing. It might affect Mario's position and threaten the plans for the Colossus.

He knew Mario would not let that happen.

"Like you said, he was probably drunk," Oscar continued.

"Yeah, well why did it have to be like this in the first place? Why didn't you tell me?"

"Would it have made any difference?" Oscar asked dryly. "Listen Sonny, just sit tight. Let me call Sam. Maybe I can reason with him. In the meantime, don't do anything stupid. Let me handle this."

A thousand ideas flashed through Oscar's head. He'd call Sam first. Maybe he was over his tantrum, and when he was sober Sam Bradford was a rational man. He'd cut him some kind of deal if he had to. The last thing he wanted was get Mario involved. It would be much better if he could take care of things himself. He couldn't let the picture fall through. There was too much riding on it.

He let the phone in Sam Bradford's trailer ring at least 20 times, then hung up and re-dialed. No answer. He knew the director kept a room at the Hyatt in downtown Atlanta but there was no answer there either. He left a cryptic message with the operator instructing Sam to call back as soon as he got in.

"Tell him it's extremely urgent," he told the operator.

Oscar waited by the phone for half an hour, then tried both numbers again. The operator said Sam had not picked up the first message. He left two more.

He waited another forty-five minutes then called Mario.

The rain didn't let up, so Sam spent the day in Atlanta. By late afternoon he was rested and sober enough to drive back to the location. He would view the rushes once more before enacting the final phase of his plan.

He sat alone in the darkness of the screening room, staring again at the rushes.

He did not move for 40 minutes, the images dancing hauntingly in front of him on the 20x30 screen. Finally the screen went dark.

"That's it Mr. Bradford," said the projectionist.

"Thanks Rique," he called up to the man in the booth. "That'll be all for today. By the way, is that the master?"

"Yes sir. It's due to be shipped to LA in the morning."

"Okay, leave it in the booth. I may want to run it once more. I'll leave it on the machine so you can ship it out tomorrow."

"Whatever you say Mr. B. And if you're sure you won't be needing me anymore I'll be going."

"That's fine Rique. See you tomorrow. Have a good evening."

Sam Bradford sat mesmerized for another ten minutes then rose and walked slowly into the projection room. He removed the master reel from the projector's sprocket and put it in one of the empty silver film cans lying on the floor in the back of the makeshift booth.

The rain had eased a bit.

He tucked the silver canister under his right arm, plopped into his jeep and pointed it toward Atlanta again. He wasn't sure of the time but he knew it was very late. The air was damp and there were no signs of life around the complex. The rainstorm had driven the actors inside, and he knew most of them were asleep, anticipating a 5 a.m. call if the weather broke.

As he approached the main road back to the city he caught sight of the lone security guard who patrolled the remote location.

The man waved his flashlight as he recognized the familiar jeep, and Sam waved back. They did not speak.

Forty minutes later he was standing in his room at the Hyatt in Atlanta.

The red message light was flashing.

"A Mr. Bento has called three times," the operator said. "He said it was urgent you get in touch with him immediately. And a Mr. Torino called. He said you have his number and he'll be expecting your call."

"Do me a favor and save those messages," he said to the girl. "I'll come by and pick them up later."

"I may not be here," Mr. Bradford. "I'm off in twenty minutes. I'll put the message slips in my drawer and you can ask the supervisor to get them."

"Thanks..."

"Candi," she said filling in the blank for him.

"Thanks Candi."

He didn't even consider calling Oscar Bento. His first call was to Delta, booking a flight back to Los Angeles. His next was to his sister and he was taken aback when a man answered, then recognized his ex-brother in law's voice.

"Hi Brian, it's Sam. What are you doing in Los Angeles?"

He really didn't have to ask. Brian and Laura had been divorced for almost five years but had remained good friends. He had a hunch they still slept together on occasion and maybe even still loved each other. The only thing they really agreed on was the fact they could not live together.

Brian's lifestyle was fast and furious. Sam saw him as a bit selfish with his time, but he was generous and always willing to help someone in need. He also lived on the edge and the edge made Laura nervous so they agreed to disagree.

"Is Laura there?"

"Hang on," Brian said as he called to her. He and Sam had always gotten along despite having diverse opinions on a wide range of subjects including Bill Clinton, freedom of speech and the casting of Sonny Fremont.

"How's it going in Atlanta?" Brian asked.

"Better you don't ask," Sam answered, forcing a low laugh.

"The shooting's been chaotic, and the weather's horrible. We've had some torrential downpours. I think it must be monsoon season down here."

"Well one day you'll have to tell me the truth about how you picked a scumball like Sonny Fremont to star in your picture," Brian said sarcastically. "That's a story I want to hear."

Laura picked up the extension and Brian hung up the downstairs receiver.

"What a nice surprise," she said warmly.

"How's it going sis? And hello from beneath the sea in Atlantis?"

"I've heard about the weather down there. Are you okay? Are you still able to shoot or have you had to stop?'

"The rain has forced us to shut down for a day or two, "he said not wanting to answer questions. "Listen Laura, I need a favor. I have to come back to Los Angeles tonight for some personal business and I wondered if you could pick me up at LAX?"

"What, no studio limo?" she teased.

"No limo," he said without explanation. "This was a spur of the minute thing and it was too short of a notice to get the studio car. But I can call a private limo company if you can't make it."

"Don't be silly," she said sensing how important it was to her brother. "I'll be there."

"What time do you get in?"

"I'm scheduled to arrive at 11:42 your time, on Delta," he said glancing at the note pad on the nightstand.

"Must be awfully important business if you're flying at night," she said, snooping a little. "I know how you hate to fly at night."

"This couldn't be avoided," he said abruptly. "I'll tell you about it when I get there."

"Shall I bring Brian along?"

"I'd rather if you didn't. I'd like to talk to you alone. We can share it with Brian when we get home."

"Sounds serious," she said, hoping he wouldn't notice the worry creeping in. "Are you in some kind of trouble?"

"Not really." He was trying to sound convincing. He didn't want her to stress about it the remainder of the evening. "Don't worry Laura. It's nothing we can't handle. Just be there, please."

"I'll be there."

"Okay. See you in a few hours."

Sam's next call was to Mario Torino and it was not a pleasant conversation.

"You've lost your fucking mind Sam. You can't kill an entire picture, especially one with a $100 million dollar budget. You'll ruin your career. The studio and the investors will crucify you."

He tried to reason.

"I don't think so Mario. I don't like being blackmailed. Movie making is an art and you're trying to force me to work with an inferior product."

"But you've gone this far. Fremont has gotten you lots of publicity. People won't care. Just make a great picture. You'll win another Academy Award."

There was no way Mario would understand.

"Can't do it Mario. I just can't do it. Fremont's out."

"I can't let you do that," Mario said, and his voice was hard. "You don't want people to know about your little boyfriend do you? And I don't think you want those sexy little pictures spread all over the tabloids or have copies sent to every studio in Hollywood so they can use them for copy room pinups."

"I guess we have a standoff then," Sam snarled. "I know enough about you and your people to cause you lots of problems. I know names, places and dates and they're all in a letter I've sent to someone I trust. If anything happens to me it will disastrous for you too."

He paused to catch his breath, standing now, next to the bed in his suite.

"I've decided I can't sell myself out. I'd be selling out the business I love. Somewhere people have to draw the line. Sonny Fremont is my line."

There was a temporary silence on the other end. It was the calm before the storm. Sam knew Mario's wrath was not far behind.

"Your plan sounds simple enough but this is the real world Sam. You'll piss off a lot of people if you go public. People who don't give a shit about your ethics or the picture business. The kind of people who wouldn't betray you for a million bucks but who'd kill you for nothing if you embarrassed them. Do you get my drift Sam? Maybe you ought to think about this some more..."

"I've already done my thinking Mario. Now it's your turn. Do you want to lose some face having Sonny Fremont canned from the picture or do you want to risk public disclosure of you and your whole slimy organization..."

Sensing that Mario was weighing his comments, Sam continued.

"I've already mailed the letter Mario, and I sent the blackmail photos along with it. I admitted everything but I also pointed the finger at you.

"I hope you'll do the right thing and walk away. Sonny Fremont isn't worth it. You have to know that letter is my insurance policy."

Still holding the phone Sam used his right leg to nudge the metal trashcan by the desk over to the bed. With his free hand he snapped the master film out of the round silver case and dropped it into the empty receptacle. He tossed the sports section of the Atlanta Constitution into the can and moved the basket into the center of the room.

He put a match to the newspaper and moved away to avoid being seared by the rush of heat.

"Too bad you're not here to see this Mario. I've just burned our picture. The master copy is turning to ashes as we speak."

"I hope, for your sake, you're joking."

"I'm not kidding. And tomorrow you'll know it for a fact. I'm going to hold an afternoon press conference in Los Angeles to announce that Sonny Fremont has been forced to withdraw from the picture for personal health reasons.

"I'll pretend to be sufficiently shocked and saddened, and explain that we'll have to recast the part and start over from scratch."

"Are you crazy?" Mario was screaming now, and Sam ignored him.

"It'll be up to you to work something out with Fremont so he can save face Mario. I don't care what he says.

"My answers about Sonny will be very vague. I'll be contrite and disappointed and say all the right things. I'll tell the media that it would be best if they got the exact details from Sonny. I'm sure you can come up with some believable story. You're probably good at that sort of thing."

"No one can do this to me," Mario raged. "No one. Someone's going to pay."

Mario dialed Oscar and ordered him to work out a statement with Sonny in the event Sam wasn't bluffing. Then he called his cousin. He'd know what to do. He always did.

"If Bradford has burned the film we cannot let him go unpunished, "his cousin advised. "And the only way you can save Fremont is to stop the press conference."

No wavering. No wasted discussion of why or if. Just solutions based on what had to be done. The bottom line.

"But you should also think carefully about Sam's letter and who he might have sent it to. It has the potential to be very damaging if in fact he has gotten names, or if someone on the inside cooperated with him."

Mario was listening intently.

"I don't think he would have mailed it to the police or to his lawyer. If it does exist, and my guess is it does, he probably mailed it to his sister. To my knowledge Sam Bradford doesn't have any other relatives."

Mario knew if the Sonny Fremont situation hit the papers it would bring unwanted publicity and possibly compromise his position as head of the Chicago family. More importantly, it might in some way affect the Colossus deal, and that was something he couldn't risk.

"Are you still there?"

"Yes, sorry. I was just thinking," Mario apologized.

"Check the plane schedules out of Atlanta. Find out what flights are going to LA tonight. Call and say you're Sam Bradford and you've forgotten which flight you're booked on. Say your secretary booked it and you've misplaced her memo. That way you'll know exactly what flight he's on and you can make the appropriate arrangements."

He scored with his first call.

"Yes, Mr. Bradford. My pleasure. Your reservation is confirmed for Flight #466 to Los Angeles, leaving Atlanta at 10:15 p.m. this evening, arriving LA International at 11:42 p.m. Will you need a Hertz Rent-a-Car in Los Angeles?"

"No that won't be necessary," Mario said, amused at how easy it had been to get Sam Bradford's schedule. The airlines were security crazy and protective of their passenger lists but, anyone with a little moxie could find out whatever they needed to know.

It was 9:35 p.m.

There was no way he could get a flight from Chicago in time to intercept the director's Delta flight to Los Angeles. He'd have to improvise.

Ordinarily, Laura Powers would have waited at the curb for her brother to come out of the terminal but something told her to park and meet him at the gate. He had aroused her curiosity and her intuition told her whatever he was involved in was more serious than he wanted her to know.

She was waiting at the gate when he deplaned, taking his garment bag and slinging it over her shoulder. Her brother carried his half-filled flight bag in his right hand.

"Any other luggage?"

"Nope. Just this."

"I'm right outside," she said, trying to be patient.

They walked side by side down the corridor in silence. Sam was never very talkative, but on this night he was particularly listless and pre-occupied.

Sam Bradford settled into the passenger seat of his sister's red Mustang and looked out at the lights of Los Angeles. When they were younger it had all been so simple.

Maybe it's best to let him start, she thought. Let him get comfortable.

"I was surprised when Brian answered the phone," Sam said, breaking the silence.

"He had to come to LA for business and just stopped to say hello," she explained. "He's going back tomorrow."

"I hope he didn't mind my asking that you come alone."

"He thought it was a bit odd, but he didn't make a fuss. He said he had some notes to write and was going to call home and check his messages."

Laura navigated the sports car expertly through the light traffic on Sepulveda Boulevard, turning onto the 405 San Diego freeway headed north.

She couldn't contain herself any longer.

"Okay Sam, what's going on?" she blurted. "You're wound tighter than a snare drum."

He did not keep her in suspense.

"I'm going to kill the picture, Laura. The general public will be told that Sonny Fremont pulled out for health reasons. The real reason is personal. He's just not right for the part and never was."

"Then why in hell did you give him the lead? You had your pick of every leading man in Hollywood. I don't understand."

They were twenty-five miles from her home in Woodland Hills, a small affluent little bedroom community at the far end of the San Fernando Valley.

His voice cracked as he began to speak.

"This may be difficult for you to understand," he began. "I can only hope you'll try," he said in a barely audible voice. "In the end it wasn't only a decision about talent.

"I was blackmailed into giving Sonny Fremont the lead."

"What do you mean blackmailed? And by whom?"

She was impatient, wishing he could tell her everything in one sentence.

"Be patient Laura. I'll tell you everything. I only hope you'll forgive me."

"Forgive you for what?"

She was all ears as her brother bared his soul. They had not spoken so intimately since they were children. His gambling problem didn't surprise her, even though she was stunned by the amount of his debt. She knew he and Brian had often discussed games and pointspreads and on occasion made a killing. She hated it when they lost because they'd get moody and let it affect everything in their lives.

Laura tried not to act shocked when Sam told her about his homosexual affair with Boyd Matthews. Sam had been married for two years when he was in his early 20s and had dated some top Hollywood starlets. She asked few questions and tried not to judge him. She just listened, occasionally wondering if there was another way out.

Sam had decided to tell her everything, even explaining why he chose to mail the letter to Boyd instead of her.

"I didn't want to put you in danger," he said. "I don't think these people will try and retaliate but I didn't want to take that chance."

"Thank you, but I'm a big girl. I could have handled it."

He smiled in the dark. She was as feisty and independent as ever.

"I didn't even think I could be this honest," he admitted. "I didn't think I could admit all of this to you. I've been such a fool. Now it doesn't matter."

"Of course it still matters, you big dope. I kind of like the idea of having a senator, or better yet a governor as a big brother," she smiled. "I could live with that."

She cast a sideways glance at her brother, a soft, understanding look on her face. His face was drawn, his eyes sad, yet in an odd sort of way he seemed relieved.

It was after midnight and only a few scattered cars and trucks dotted the freeway and Laura was glad she didn't have to concentrate on driving. She felt compassion for Sam, wanting at that moment to hold him close and tell him everything was going to be all right.

And she knew it would be.

She did not notice the dark blue pickup coming up dangerously fast on the right shoulder. The driver of the truck pulled alongside, and then deliberately turned his wheel to the left, smashing into the passenger side of Laura's car, sending it spinning into the path of an oncoming semi.

Unable to stop, the big rig crushed the sports car, collapsing its roof and trapping its two passengers inside. Ambulances and paramedics were on the scene in a matter of minutes.

Sam Bradford died instantly. Laura Powers was not as lucky. She lapsed into a coma, lasted through the night on life support systems at Centinela Hospital and succumbed at 7:12 a.m. without ever regaining consciousness. Brian Powers was at her bedside, holding her hand.

At 2 p.m. the same day Sonny Fremont called a press conference in Atlanta. His announcement was brief.

"Ladies and Gentlemen. We are all saddened by the tragic accident in Los Angeles last night, which claimed the life of my good friend, Sam Bradford, and his sister. I will be forever grateful to Sam for having the courage, and the faith in my ability to give me the biggest part of my life. However, Sam's loss will mean an indefinite delay in the shooting schedule, and although it disappoints me greatly, I must announce that I am formally withdrawing from the picture. in the shooting schedule, I will be forced to withdraw from the picture.

"I apologize to the studio and to all the people who were looking forward to seeing me in "Morocco Heat", however my schedule will not allow me to spend another two to three months away from live performances.

"Sam Bradford was not only a great director but a man I admired and respected. I am sure he will be deeply missed by everyone in the entertainment business."

In Santa Monica, Boyd Matthews opened his apartment mailbox to find another correspondence from Sam Bradford. It had come Federal Express but so had most of the others. His first thought was to toss it in the row of waste cans next to the mailboxes, but he didn't.

He carried the cardboard envelope up to his apartment and flipped it in the shoe box with the dozen or so other unopened letters from Sam. He knew they were all the same. Asking his understanding and begging his forgiveness. Sam telling him that even though he really loved him, they could never be together again.

Boyd resented the fact Sam had never come to grips with his sexuality. More than that, he was angry that Sam refused to meet him face to face. He truly believed that if they met they could talk their way through it. Sam would come back to him.

Sam had a very difficult time accepting being gay, and insisted what they shared was more a curious fling. Boyd believed Sam was simply in denial.

After the breakup Sam had cut him off completely, ignoring his calls, and not returning his messages. He'd read Sam's first two or three letters, then simply took to storing them in the old Adidas tennis shoe box. Maybe one day he would read them.

If he didn't open them he could always fantasize that he and Sam would one day be lovers again.

That was his dream. It was his sole reason for living.

He didn't want to open a letter that might tell him otherwise.

Boyd Matthews was the Art Director for a stylish LA Magazine. It wasn't hard work, and it filled the hours. If the editors had been more visionary, the job would have been perfect.

He poured a glass of white wine, slipped off his shoes and fell back in a big easy chair. He'd read the paper, grab a shower and maybe order in some Italian food.

He never got past the front page headline.

"Director Sam Bradford and Sister Killed in Freeway Crash". He was aghast.

It couldn't be true. There had to be some mistake. But there was a picture of Sam, and a caption identifying him. It was true.

Now there was no chance. He had nothing to live for.

Fifteen minutes later Boyd Matthews hanged himself.

Chapter 11
Looking For Answers

Brian called from Los Angeles and listened to the three messages T.J. Fitzgerald had left on his recorder, but he was in no mood to return the calls. His initial shock had given way to confusion and anger at the tragedy that had claimed the lives of his ex-wife and former brother-in-law.

Laura. Sam. Adam Forrester. All dead, and for what?

They were good people in a fucked up world. They deserved better. Much better.

He knew Fitzgerald wanted an update on Forrester. To see if he had any more information. He didn't.

And right now he had his own assortment of pressing and depressing things to handle, like making arrangements for the double funeral of Sam Bradford and Laura Powers.

Nothing about the "accident" set well with him. And every few minutes he replayed the details of that night. Was he making too much of the little things? Was he reading between the lines when nothing was written there?

Brian thought back to the short conversation he'd had with Sam before summoning Laura to the phone.

Nothing really unusual. Normal chit-chat, although Sam did seem to be a bit anxious to speak to Laura.

Laura said Sam sounded worried, or had she said troubled? Then she said Sam had requested she come to the airport alone? Certainly Sam coming home in the middle of the night, during a shoot meant something. He hated to fly at night. His heart wanted to let it go as an accident so he could feel closure. The antennae in his psyche said not yet.

When he did get a minute to return Fitzgerald's call, the Colossus' Security Chief was out of the office. He did not leave Laura's number in California.

"Please tell Mr. Fitzgerald I'm out of town on personal business," he told the secretary. "I'll be back in Las Vegas in a few days and I'll call him as soon as I get in."

The Forrester situation could wait.

The California Highway Patrol questioned the driver of the big rig and released him, ruling the crash an unavoidable accident. The truck driver claimed Laura's Mustang had swerved directly into his path and the skid marks substantiated his account. The man also said he thought he had seen a dark blue pickup on the outside shoulder but couldn't swear to it.

The passenger side of Laura's car had been smashed and paint chips imbedded in the right fender supported the contention there was another vehicle involved and that it was dark blue in color. No one else had seen the pickup and the driver had not stopped.

The investigating officer explained that even though Laura's car had apparently been bumped and inadvertently forced into the speeding semi, there was not enough evidence to suggest foul play. In other words, the accident wasn't going to get the kind of fine tooth comb attention as the crash that killed Princess Diana. No one was going to launch an all out search for a mysterious blue pickup.

"I'm sorry to say it really appears to have been an accident, Mr.Powers. Nothing here really suggests foul play."

"But what about the dent, and the blue paint?"

"I'm not saying your sister's car wasn't bumped," the patrolman replied. "I'm only saying that isn't enough reason to believe it was done intentionally. Or with malice of forethought.

"These things happen," the patrolman apologized. "My best guess is the other driver was probably scared. Or maybe a kid with no insurance. That's usually why they don't stop. Without more of a description or a license plate number we have very little to go on.

"I'm sure you know how quickly traffic moves along this freeway Mr. Powers. This happened in a matter of seconds. And when accidents happen at night, it's usually more difficult to re-create the actual event. And, even if someone saw the other car, there's little chance they got a plate number.

"But we will follow up."

He was no help.

"We'll make routine checks of the city body shops to see if a vehicle matching that description comes in for repairs to its left front," he said half-heartedly.

Brian nodded but was not satisfied.

He knew Laura didn't have any enemies. At least not people who would go out of their way to kill her. He wasn't so sure of Sam's circle of friends. So that's where he had to direct his energies.

Nothing else made sense. If it was anything but an accident, it had to be because of something Sam was involved in. He had brought it on.

What could Sam have been involved in that would make someone want to kill him?

Drugs? Doubtful.

Something to do with gambling? A definite maybe.

A jealous rival? Possibly. But in Hollywood they whispered about you behind your back. They didn't kill you. They rumored you to death.

All of that sounded possible, even logical, but it made no sense. Each one of those theories had one major flaw. No one knew that Sam was coming back to LA. At least no one in LA knew. He had told Laura his coming was totally unplanned.

That was bothersome too.

Sam Bradford was one of the most methodical people Brian knew. He didn't make spur of the moment decisions.

Lots of questions, all of them with multiple choice answers. And Brian knew the answers could only be found in Atlanta. Someone there had to know something. It was worth a shot.

But first he had to deal with the funerals.

All of Hollywood turned out for Sam, and the eulogies were heartfelt. A small group of Laura's friends were also in attendance. Following their wishes, he had them both cremated.

He was restless, with a stomachful of pent up emotions following the services, so he booked a 9 p.m. flight to Atlanta, checked into the Hyatt and hoped someone there would be able to help. He didn't know what he was hoping to find but figured he'd snoop around for a couple days and see what turned up.

He had come because he had to. The funeral had been an emotional downer and he figured a change of scenery might help clear his senses.

Most of the film and production crew had already packed up and cleared out of Georgia. The few who remained were still numbed by Sam's death, and no one could offer any personal insight about the director or any problems.

Hotel bellmen and front desk clerks didn't remember Sam, which seemed reasonable because he had spent most nights in his trailer, on location, finding it more convenient than commuting from Atlanta every day.

Bob Mason, the film's Public Relations liaison, had little new information.

"Everyone is still in shock," he said when Brian met him in the hotel bar. It was happy hour and they both filled mini-plates with meatballs and some unidentifiable little goodies wrapped in bacon.

"This is without a doubt the strangest picture I've ever been associated with," Mason volunteered. "It was strange from the beginning."

"How so?

"Well, first of all it's a sequel. That's not the unusual part. I mean most sequels are done within a year or two. In this case the original was made sixty years ago. Even Godfather III only had a lapse of a dozen years and it still lost a lot of its power.

"Then, instead of using an established star, Sam chooses an unknown bit player in Sonny Fremont, which was bizarre for a number of reasons. Some critics started calling "Morocco Heat" a freak show, others referred to it as "Morocco Heap".

"I will admit though, Sonny Fremont's name did get us a ton of exposure.

"The topper comes when the producer, who's supposed to be in Atlanta filming, leaves without telling anyone and winds up getting killed in a car accident in Los Angeles.

"Toss in the fact no one can find the master copy of the film and you have a case Angela Lansbury couldn't solve in a two-hour episode. Of course it's all a moot point now."

Sam's leaving on the q.t. was no surprise, the missing film was.

"Who was responsible for the film?"

"The projectionist, but he has no idea where it is. The last time he saw it was the day Sam was killed. Sam asked him to run it in the early evening and when the guy left to go home Sam was still in the projection room. The film was still in the booth."

Is the projection guy still around?" Brian asked, holding little hope.

"He was this morning," Mason said softly. "Name's Martinez. Enrique Martinez. They call him Rique. He said he was going to head back to LA this evening or early tomorrow morning, depending on when he could get a flight."

"Martinez was in 1703," Mason called out as Brian walked away.

"Thanks."

He stopped at the first house phone and crossed his fingers.

Martinez answered on the second ring.

Brian identified himself as Sam's brother-in-law and asked the projectionist if he could spare a few minutes.

"Come on up if you want to," Martinez offered. "But I've already told the cops everything I know. I'm going back to LA tonight, but my plane doesn't leave for three hours."

Rique Martinez was a slender Hispanic, in his early 30s, with curly black hair and small John Lennon-like spectacles. In less than two minutes Brian could sense that Martinez was someone Sam trusted, and he was equally sure the man had a great admiration for Sam.

Martinez related what had gone on in the projection room the last time he had seen Sam. He made it clear that when he left Sam Bradford had remained in the screening area and that the master copy of the film was still in the projector.

Brian felt Martinez knew more, or more probably, suspected more.

"I gather you knew Sam pretty well," Brian said leadingly. "Obviously he liked you, and respected your work."

"I think he did," said Martinez. "We worked together on three other pictures."

"Knowing Sam like you did, could you sense his moods at all?"

"Well, most of the time I could tell if he was satisfied with what he saw on the screen, but Sam Bradford was a genius. He had a vision few other directors could match. He could see things other directors missed. That's what made him so great."

"What was he seeing with this picture Rique? Could you tell if he was pleased, or at least satisfied? And why did he ask for a second screening when he had just seen it the day before?"

"Whoa. One thing at a time," Martinez protested, holding up his hands.

"Truthfully, I don't think he was happy with the rushes but don't quote me on that. I don't want to be speaking out of turn."

"I understand," Brian said obligingly.

"Look," Martinez said lowering his voice as if he feared someone might be eavesdropping. Brian could sense his reluctance to continue.

"It's okay. Anything you noticed. Anything at all might help. Sam's moods off handed comments, the general attitude of the cast..."

Martinez had taken a seat on the bed. He was dressed in jeans and tennis shoes, hunched over with his head in his hands.

"I don't want to start no rumors, "he said slowly, "but Sam was my friend. He gave me a chance a few years ago and I think what happened to him is a shame. People are already saying he was blowing it on this picture and that's not true."

"What is true?" Brian pushed.

"What's true is Sam was disgusted with Sonny Fremont. He couldn't stand the guy. On screen Fremont was a stiff. Every time Sam watched the rushes he was in agony, and Fremont was acting like a primadonna. Like he was some box office sensation. He treated the crew like garbage.

"I remember a picture about five years ago, I think it was the second one worked on for Sam. Yeah, it was called "Restless Heart". Sam had a similar problem. The guy playing the lead just didn't come across on film. The picture would have been a disaster."

"And what happened?"

"Sam talked the studio into replacing the lead even though the man was a triple A star. The studio and the actor's agent concocted a story about him being sick and no one ever knew the difference. I heard the guy got a $2 million dollar buyout.

"Are you saying Sam wanted to, or was going to replace Sonny Fremont?" Brian's juices were flowing.

"I'm not saying nothing," Martinez said defensively. "I don't know anything for sure. That kind of stuff is out of my league."

"I will tell you this though," he said moving closer, "and if you tell anyone said it, I'll swear you're a liar. Sam did say, 'I wish I could get rid of that sonofabitch, but he's got me by the balls. My hands are tied. And the last time he came in to see the film he'd been drinking. A lot.

"And that was very unusual because Sam seldom drank, especially on a shoot."

"Do you have any idea what happened to the film?"

"None," Martinez answered almost before Brian had finished the sentence.

"Let me put it this way," Brian said, trying to re-phrase and get some help.

"Give me your best guess as to what happened to it."

"My best guess! Sam hid it. I bet no one ever finds it. Unless he took it with him to LA. Did they check his baggage and his car?"

"Yeah. It wasn't in either."

"Then I'm sure he hid it or maybe even destroyed it." Martinez raised his eyebrows.

"One last question," Brian said, rising from the chair next to the bed.

"Why would Sam go to LA so suddenly? It was a question he had also asked Bob Mason, and neither man had an answer.

Brian thanked Martinez for his time and honesty and wished him luck.

He still had doodly squat.

If everything the cameraman told him was accurate, and he had no reason to think otherwise, the best he could figure was that Sam had decided to return to LA to discuss dumping Sonny with the studio bosses. It presented some interesting possibilities, all of them wild, most of them crazy and none of them criminal.

Another day in Atlanta turned up no new information.

He called Delta and made a reservation for Vegas. He had to go home sometime, even if he didn't want to.

He spent the next few hours sprawled across the queen-sized bed, dozing on and off, trying to make sense of the facts, hunches and opinions he had gathered.

When he awoke he tossed his things in a duffel bag and headed downstairs. At the front desk he asked Nancy, the night clerk, about Sam. She was a student at the University of Georgia majoring in communications.

"I knew who he was, "she said. "I think everyone did, but I never actually spoke to him."

"Did anyone around here get to know him at all?

"I don't think so," she said, her brown ponytail bobbing. "I think the only people he ever talked to regularly were the hotel operators. He always had lots of messages, probably because he only picked them up on weekends."

Five minutes later Brian was in the hotel's message center, face to face with a blonde with "Candi" on her name-tag and seduction written all over her forehead. She had wild hair, gel frozen in half a dozen directions and a "come fuck me smile" that almost made him forget why he was there.

He explained that he was not with the police and quickly re-hashed the story of the accident. Candi remembered talking to Sam the night he left, and if Brian's hunch was right, the homewrecker in training he was staring at, might have been the last person in Atlanta to actually speak to Sam.

Candi couldn't remember anything unusual about her conversation with Sam, recalling only that he had a stack of messages.

Brian prodded her for another minute or two, wondering how God could possibly assemble anything more perfect, thanked her and ducked out of the small phone room.

He was halfway down the hall when she called after him.

"I do remember one thing a little weird," she said as she moved closer. "He asked me to save his messages. Said he was going to come down and pick them up, but he never did. I think I still have them in the drawer." She was near enough for him to smell her perfume.

"We don't usually save them, but I did. I think they're still there." She was in her late 20s with tits that stood up and said touch me, and eyes that said take me upstairs and then out of this town. He was hurt and depressed, not dead.

"Here they are," she said handing Brian a stack of pink message sheets that she pulled from the center drawer of her little desk.

He took the message memos, which were paper-clipped together, and stuffed them in his jacket pocket. He kissed Candi on the cheek, telling her how much he appreciated her extra effort and she returned his kiss much too eagerly. It would have been so easy.

On the flight back Brian slowly looked through the message slips.

He recognized Oscar Bento's name.

Must have been something pretty important for the guy to call Sam four times. He wondered which of them had placed the first call.

There was urgency to the messages, each more cryptic than the last.

From the message notes Brian created a possible storyline. Sam had probably told Sonny he wanted to replace him on the picture. Sonny then called his agent, and the agent was trying desperately to reach Sam to iron things out.

That worked, but it spelled shouting at each other and threatening lawsuits. Certainly that scenario didn't suggest or call for anything as serious as murder.

Maybe he was paddling up the wrong river.

Brian had no idea who Mario Torino was. His message said he would be expecting Sam's call, and he left no number. Probably someone from the studio.

Nothing in the notes gave a hint as to what had happened to the film.

For his own satisfaction he wanted to know, but he had a feeling no one would ever learn the real story. It did piss him off that people were forming the impression that good old Sonny Fremont was coming out the big loser.

The public was actually feeling sorry for the jerk, with magazines portraying him as the man the fates had cheated out of the biggest break in his life.

Brian had already locked horns with Sonny Fremont in Vegas. Sonny liked throwing his weight around, and once had stiffed a couple drug dealers, then ratted them out to the cops.

And Sonny was not above making a play for another man's woman, always using money and his celebrity status to get what he wanted.

But Sonny Fremont portraying himself as the grieving friend and hard luck leading man was no crime, even if it was a blatant lie.

The trip to Atlanta had not really turned up anything startling or underhanded. He didn't have much more than when he left Los Angeles.

He skipped the inflight dinner and began programming himself to accept what had happened. Laura and Sam were dead and it was nobody's fault. Their deaths had apparently been an accident. And he was still nauseated to think of Sonny Fremont playing the victim. If the opportunity ever presented itself he'd let Sonny know he didn't buy the humble act.

He wanted Sonny to know that he hadn't conned everyone. Brian was convinced Sam was ready to dump Sonny. He couldn't prove it, but it didn't matter. He just wanted to make the asshole squirm.

His mood darkened as the lights of the McCarran runway drew closer. The bright beam from the top of the Luxor stood out in the black night sky, as did the unique form of the Stratosphere Tower.

Las Vegas' neon skyline was welcoming him home, but on this night it burned a little less brightly. There was no joy in his heart.

Chapter 12
Joining The Team

Brian had arrived after midnight, but as usual he was up early on Friday, his sleep interrupted by a series of earsplitting thunderclaps accompanying the driving rainstorm that had moved in during the early morning hours.

He looked up from the morning paper just as a vicious wind deposited a tree branch in the shallow end of his pool.

A young singer named Alliyah had been killed in a plane crash...Adam Forrester's death and questions about the Colossus still dominated the news, and a sudden change of climate had blown in an April cold front.

The mellow sound of Chris Isaak's "Baja Sessions" CD was playing just loud enough to be heard over the rain and wind. It was a lazy type morning. He had programmed Rod Stewart, Fats Domino and The Backstreet Boys on the CD jukebox that peeked out from the far corner of the room. It was one of the things he insisted on keeping in the divorce.

Take the money, take the furniture. Leave the jukebox, the sports memorabilia and the celebrity pictures.

He was busy thinking of nothing when the shrill ring of the phone commanded his attention. It was 8:20 a.m.

"Welcome home stranger. Hope I'm not waking you up." It was T.J. Fitzgerald.

"I've been up for an hour Fitz. Sorry I haven't been in touch, but I had a personal family tragedy to deal with, and it kind of knocked the wind out me."

"Are you okay? Anything I can do?" Fitzgerald sounded sincere.

"Not right now," Brian answered, not knowing what else to say. There really wasn't anything T.J. could do, but he thought it a good idea to fill him in on Sam and Laura just so he'd have an idea of what he was going through. And why the Adam Forrester case wouldn't be the only thing on his mind.

"My god Brian. I'm truly sorry. That's a shame. I read about Sam Bradford in the paper, but I had no idea he was your ex-brother-in-law.

"Hey, if you want to take some time for yourself, and back off getting involved in the Forrester thing, just say the word. I'll explain it to Walter and Tiffany. They'll understand."

"Nah. That won't be necessary. It might be best if I threw myself into the Forrester case. God knows I can use something to keep me busy, and keep me from going crazy."

"Well, if you change your mind..."

"Thanks Fitz. But for now let's give it a shot."

"Whatever you say,Brian."

"Okay. Might as well take it from the top. Anything new from your end, Fitz? Have things quieted down at the hotel?"

"A bit," he lied. "We're moving on because we have to move on. What else can we do?"

Brian understood perfectly. It was also what he knew he had to do.

"That's about all any of us can do," he said, wishing he could have come up with something more meaningful.

"Nothing suspicious has happened with chips or credit for almost a week now, "Fitzgerald confided. "I've been monitoring the transaction sheet every day. Maybe they've moved on?"

"Maybe. And maybe they've just backed off because of Forrester. It could be coincidence, but no matter which it is, you have to stay alert," Brian warned. "As far as either of us knows, you are the only other person who knows about the scam."

"Other than you, you mean?"

"Right." And Brian realized that both of them could possibly be in danger. Or worse yet, targets, if someone considered them a threat.

They had not had a serious conversation since their meeting at the Colossus, mainly due to all the commotion surrounding the murder, and the fact Brian had been out of town.

"Listen Brian, I called because Tiffany Wayne and her lawyer, the guy you met at dinner, want to get together with you."

"Why?"

"Well, first of all, I should tell you that even though it hasn't been announced publicly yet, Tiffany Wayne is the new owner and president of the Colossus.

"What?" Brian let out a low whistle. "I thought the wife was getting it all."

"So did she, and the rest of us. Everyone thought Adam Forrester would leave Diana everything. No one even considered his daughter."

"Well, kiss my ass," Brian blurted. "That's kind of an upset, isn't it? Just goes to show, blood's always thicker than most any other liquid. How will her taking over affect you?"

"I don't have a clue," Fitzgerald replied. "But anyway, she and Walter would like a sit down. Okay by you?"

"C'mon Fitz. You're on the inside. What's it all about?"

"I'd rather let them tell you," Fitzgerald said, dodging the issue.

"And I'd rather hear it from you," Brian said quickly, leaving the ball in Fitzgerald's court.

Fitzgerald respected Brian too much to be coy.

"Brian, do me a favor and keep this between us, okay?"

"Deal."

"They want to make a proposal to you," Fitzgerald said without hesitation. "I don't know exactly how they'll phrase it, but when the smoke clears they're going to make a pitch for you to work as a special consultant for the Colossus."

"Consulting on what?"

"Adam Forrester's murder. Or more precisely, the progress the authorities are making in their investigation. I'd prefer to let Walter and Tiffany fill in the blanks from here."

For a second Brian was speechless. Life was so strange. At least his was. Sometimes it was worth living just to see what tomorrow had in mind. Perhaps that's why he wanted, "Every day was an Adventure", etched on his own tombstone.

"I'm not sure I'm ready to start another project right now," Brian said candidly.

"And you know how I feel about working for hotels. I don't punch clocks, keep office hours, wear ties, want to go to meetings or have to play by anyone else's rules."

"I already know that stuff," Fitzgerald laughed. "Tell them that and maybe the meeting will be over in a hurry."

"Aw hell, Fitz. You know what I mean. I just hate corporations with all their bullshit politics. Everything has to go through committee."

"Do me a favor and just hear them out. You can always say no. Won't make no nevermind to me. Especially with what you're going through. See how it feels."

"I suppose there's no harm in that."

"Good. How about 11 this morning?"

"How about noon?" Brian laughed. "May as well break them in right."

"See you then."

A secretary showed him into Walter Thurston's office. It was 12:10.

Punctuality was not one of his strong suits. He either tried to cram too many things into too tiny a window or something came up at the last minute to delay him. He had to admit though, ten minutes was about the earliest he'd ever been late.

Thurston knew nothing of the tragedy that had recently visited Brian's life and Brian felt no need to mention it. He had also asked T.J. to keep it confidential, and it appeared he had.

Tiffany was nowhere in sight when Walter began their meeting.

"Aren't we going to wait for Miss Wayne?" he asked.

"I'm sorry, but Tiffany had to return to Chicago. She and I have discussed this matter at length," he said, "and we are in complete agreement.

"By now I'm sure you know that Miss Wayne has inherited the Colossus, "he said slowly, "and we are currently in the process of assembling some key management personnel.

"We'd both like to have you to join us as a special consultant."

"To do what?"

"We have a very specific project in mind to begin, but I'm sure with your expertise you'll be a fine asset to the Colossus in the long run."

Thurston was skating. Brian knew he hadn't laid all of his cards on the table yet.

"I don't know Mr. Thurston," he said cautiously. He didn't want to reject the offer out of hand and offend the man. "I've worked on my own and been my own boss for so long I'm not sure I can fit in. Or want to."

"I can appreciate that Brian, and thank you for your candor. Here's the deal in a nutshell," he said as if he were sharing a pentagon secret.

"The special project is Adam Forrester's murder. Tiffany and I are not convinced the police are doing everything they can, and we don't want Adam's murder to fall through the cracks or get put on the back burner.

"I guess I'm saying we want to hire you to do your own investigation. To find out if there is any other information on the street and to follow it wherever it may lead."

Brian thought about the request.

They really didn't need him to be part of management, and that was a good thing because he didn't want to be. And having a project to consume the hours, to keep his mind off Sam and Laura would help.

The prospect of seeing Tiffany Wayne again was also a plus. She seemed so young. And vulnerable.

She won't be young very long if she starts running this place Brian thought. Vegas was a town that could eat you up and spit you out like an olive pit if you weren't ready for it. And few people were.

"The idea of having you join the Colossus team was as much Tiffany's as mine and T.J.'s." Walter Thurston said openly. "If you're sufficiently interested we'll get her on the phone."

"I'm interested," Brian said, surprising himself, "but only as an independent agent. You can find a way to put me on a kind of retainer that makes me eligible for company health insurance, give me an office and a secretary.

"I'll report only to you or Ms. Wayne and I'll make my own hours."

"Done. Anything else?" Thurston was not taking no for an answer.

"A few, but they're really only important to me. I want the health insurance to be a lifetime deal, even after our association ends, and I want that in writing. And most important, I'll need complete cooperation from you, Ms. Wayne and the Colossus on the investigation. Furthermore I want you to know in advance that I'll follow all leads, no matter where they go. You and Ms. Wayne need to be prepared for that."

"We are," he said without hesitation. "We both want to know the truth. I just want you to keep me informed every step of the way, If you get something from the street, or from your cop friends, I want you to share it with me first. I don't like to read about things I should already know in the morning paper. Can you live with that?"

"I think so," Brian said thoughtfully. "I don't see that being a problem."

They agreed on an initial retainer of $50,000, then put in a call to Tiffany.

"I'm very happy you're going to be with us Brian. I'm confident you can help get to the bottom of what happened to my father."

The only things Brian knew about the case so far were that Forrester had been offed and that the lead detective handling the investigation was one of his old softball buddies.

"I know the detective in charge," Brian said, not yet ready to reveal how well he knew the homicide cop.

"I've worked with him before, and we've known each other a long time. Don Sarabian is a good cop, and an honest one," he said coming down a little hard on the "honest".

"That's the way he came across when I spoke to him on the phone," Tiffany agreed. "But I also got the impression that any major decisions in this case will be made by the Chief of Police. And he didn't sound as friendly."

"Marksbury's all right," Brian said, trying to be reassuring. "But I'll bet he's up to his ass in alligators on this thing right now. He's probably getting heavy breathing from the Mayor and a bunch of nervous politicians."

"Let me be honest with you, Brian. Both Detective Sarabian and Chief Marksbury told me quite bluntly that they'll be passing on any information regarding the case to Diana Forrester, my father's wife. They suggested I call her for updates, and that just isn't going to happen.

"He was my father. I don't want to go through Diana to find out what's going on. Can you understand that?"

"I hear you loud and clear, and I agree with you," he said. He could tell from her tone that she and Diana weren't a threat to be roommates anytime soon.

Brian thought about how similar their situations were. Both of them had recently lost a loved one, and they were both trying their best to survive. Trying to get on with their lives despite the pain. He imagined she was hurting. He knew he was.

Tiffany wasn't going to return to Vegas for a week or more, and then only for a day before heading for Paris. His new boss did, however, promise to spend a fair amount of time at the Colossus when she returned from Europe.

He retreated to his new office while Walter got back to the day-to-day business of running the huge hotel.

It was going to be interesting.

Brian had always thought of Las Vegas as a place basically safe from big city crime, but that was changing. Los Angeles street gangs and drug suppliers had begun to infiltrate the city, finding it close enough to LA, San Francisco and Phoenix and far enough from police departments experienced in gang control.

Las Vegas was a city that made its own rules and didn't give a damn what the rest of the country thought.

The mayor, a colorful character named Oscar Goodman, was once one of the best criminal defense attorney's in the country. And he specialized in representing high profile mob figures.

Brian loved Goodman and thought he was great for the city. His Honor said what he thought, didn't engage in political double-speak and had enough money of his own to resist being anyone's puppet. Besides, with all the real life criminals and made guys he had gotten acquitted, who was going to fuck with him? With those credentials he'd probably make a great governor too.

As per his request, and Walter's internal memo, Brian was given carte blanche at the Colossus. No door was closed to him.

"Once a week we'll have a conference call with Tiffany about the general state of affairs around the hotel," Walter informed him, "but most decisions will be made right here. And I'll ask for your input. I really think you'll be able to steer me in the right direction when I have a dilemma."

The rest of the briefing was routine. Walter asked if any of his street sources had heard any rumors about the possible sale of the Colossus.

"No one's mentioned it yet," he said.

"There was a lot of pressure on Adam to sell this place according to my information, "Walter said solemnly, "so I figure there'll be talk and maybe some inquiries about it as soon as the publicity dies down."

Walter was standing next to Adam Forrester's huge desk. His dark brown suit was set off by a maroon tie and matching pocket-handkerchief. The entire ensemble spelled lawyer.

"There is one other thing you should be aware of Walter," Brian said as Walter parked himself in the high-backed desk chair. "If Adam Forrester was murdered because he wouldn't sell the hotel, whoever did it still wants this place. Don't forget that. Sooner or later they'll make a move, so let me know if anyone, anyone at all inquires about buying the Colossus. Even if they just ask informally. You never know what information will turn out to mean something."

"I'll let you know if anyone comes forward," Walter agreed.

Later he introduced Brian to Eddie Pinto, the hotel's entertainment director, who proceeded to complain about low showroom counts.

"Maybe you just need some new blood in the showroom," Brian said, only half-kidding. "I'd like to see Bryan Adams or Sara McLaughlin."

"Almost sounds like you've been talking to Oscar Bento, Pinto laughed.

"He thinks we need some new talent too. However Sonny Fremont is the only name on Oscar's very short list.

"Now that Sonny's not tied up making a movie Oscar makes it a daily habit to call and try to convince me to book Sonny. I must be on his speed dial. He thinks Sonny's the answer to all our problems."

"Is he?"

155

"I doubt it," Pinto said without rancor. "He might improve the show count, but Sonny brings a whole new set of problems." Eddie Pinto didn't elaborate and Brian let the remark slide, but he filed it for future reference.

Oscar Bento's name kept bouncing around in his head. He didn't know Bento, but felt like he should. He'd love to ask him why he was calling Sam Bradford and if he'd talked to Sam the night he died. Small world.

For personal reasons he didn't want the Colossus to book Sonny, but it wouldn't hurt to have Pinto arrange a lunch with Oscar. Sort of an exploratory meeting. Then he could drop by their table, be introduced and he'd take a shot.

If Oscar wanted Sonny in the Colossus as badly as Pinto indicated, he'd jump at the lunch idea. In the meantime he'd check out the word on the street, call Detective Sarabian at home and say hello to some old friends up and down the Strip.

It took him 15 minutes to get to downtown Vegas and another ten minutes to locate the man he was looking for.

"What's up, Suspect?" he said grinning at the gangly, unshaven black man sipping coffee in the sports book at the Horseshoe Club.

"As I live and breathe," the man replied letting out a low whistle. "Mr. P., man about town. How's it hanging Player?"

"Not too good right now," Brian said as he embraced his friend. "Been dealing with some heavy stuff."

"Know what you mean Mr. P. I know what you mean."

They had been friends for fifteen years, yet the only name Brian had ever known the man by was "Suspect." He had long since gotten over feeling self-conscious about calling him by the alias.

The friend who had introduced them insisted "Suspect" acquired his nickname because whenever there was a police sweep in the downtown area "Suspect" was always the first guy in the wagon.

"Seems he looks like everyone else, and he's the perfect guy to stand in a lineup," the pal had explained." So we just got to calling him Suspect. If a 7-11's robbed, or a purse gets snatched downtown and the culprit is black, you can bet the cops are gonna' come looking for Suspect.

"Thing is, no one can ever remember him doing anything other than having been picked up for being publicly drunk and taking a leak in a city parking lot years ago."

For all the teasing, Suspect was a very good-natured human being. And he was like wallpaper. People seldom noticed him and he was everywhere. Few things went down on the streets of Vegas that Suspect didn't have a line on.

He had provided key information on a number of other occasions and Brian was hoping he could do the same again.

When they were seated in the coffee shop, Brian told Suspect what his friend already knew. He was searching for information.

"Ain't none of my business, but why you want to know about that?"
There was no point in telling Suspect anything but the truth.
"Colossus hired me to see what I can dig up."
"Could be some ugly shit," Suspect said as he took a deep drag on his
cigarette.
"Wasn't no accident and it wasn't nobody local."
Brian started to ask how Suspect knew, but he didn't care. How the man got
his information had always been his secret. He had his ways. And Brian never
tested their own unspoken agreement.
He'd pay Suspect for the tips, not reveal his name to anyone, and never,
under any circumstances expect him to testify in court. It was up to Brian to take
the information and run with it. Once Suspect gave it to him the black man was
out of it.
"I need a little more than that," he said blankly.
"Ain't got no more than that now. See me Sunday. Same place. After all the
games are over." Suspect got up and walked toward the Horseshoe gaming area.
He never looked back.
It was blind trust.
It had to be.
Brian had no phone number for the man and didn't know where he lived.
The rest of the week Brian stayed busy, catching up on news with sources
during the day and hanging out in virtual anonymity at local nightspots in the late
evening.
The street was silent.
"I heard the Colossus has been losing money ever since the owner got killed.
that true?" asked a cocktail waitress at the MGM's very loud Studio 54.
It wasn't until the end of the week, in the cocktail lounge at the Mirage that
Brian came across a nugget he could keep, and he didn't have to ask any
questions to get it.
"I guess the biggest loser is Forrester's old lady," said a dark-haired man in a
navy blue suit. He was sitting at a table a few feet behind Brian. "She thought she
was going to get fat and get it all. I'll bet she was surprised."
"I heard she threw a fit and trashed the penthouse when she found out
Forrester cut her out of the will," the second man added. Brian pegged them as
off duty floor men or pit bosses having a pop before going home. He thought he
recognized one of them from Caesars.
Their voices were low and he had to concentrate hard to hear their
conversation.
"Is she still banging Sonny Fremont?" It was the blue suit talking.
"No idea."
The second man put down his drink. "It'll be interesting to see if he's still got
the hots for her now that she's odd man out."

Diana and Sonny Fremont.

It was an ace Brian wanted to save for the right moment, along with the stuff Suspect had given him.

He also knew he couldn't accept the Sonny-Diana tryst as gospel on the word of two jimokes in a bar. He'd need more meat. It did however, sound plausible.

Sonny probably figured he'd juice his way into the Colossus showroom through Diana and she no doubt got off on the idea of screwing a celebrity. Maybe it was worth mentioning to Sarabian.

Don Sarabian was one of Brian's true friends. He was a rock solid guy who stood up for his principles and his friends, no matter what the consequences. Departmental politics didn't intimidate him, which is why Brian knew if there was any funny business going on in the Forrester case, Sarabian wasn't part of it.

If the detective had anything Brian was confident he'd share it. They had an implied trust for each other forged over twenty years of exchanging favors and covering each other's ass.

His first meeting with Sarabian produced little.

"What's the big news in town these days other than the Colossus owner getting wasted?"

"Not much pal. There's always the nickel and dime crap and like I told you on the phone, they've dumped another murder in my lap. Some lounge singer got himself dead. Looks like a dope deal gone south to me." Sarabian was sipping an iced tea. His hair had thinned since Brian had seen him last, but otherwise he was still heavy, and as out of shape as when they had played softball together years before.

"The Forrester murder is still a high priority ticket but you know how these things go," he said. "Every day that passes the trail gets a little colder. Seems like no one downtown really gives a rat's ass.

"That's the way it's always been in this town…As long as they kill their own and leave the public alone…"

Brian was mildly surprised by his friend's reference but played it off.

"I didn't know the guy," Brian said openly, "but from what I've heard didn't get the impression he was connected."

"Me neither," the big cop answered as he turned his droopy face to look Brian squarely in the eyes.

"Thing is, it seems like the boys in headquarters think he was. I haven't gotten any pressure yet but my sixth sense tells me any day now they're going to tell me to stick this one in the deep-freeze. And if they do you won't hear anymore about it unless it makes "Unsolved Mysteries.""

"One more thing. You say you never met Forrester, but I did," Sarabian said.

"He did me a favor about a year ago. I was stuck trying to arrange entertainment for some police fundraiser and I called his office to see if I could talk the Colossus into letting us use one of their lounge singers at a discount price. Forrester was nice enough to arrange it and picked up the tab. A week or so later I stopped in to thank him in person and he struck me as being an all right guy. That was my only contact with him."

Sarabian was a pretty good judge of character. In his line of work he had to be, but one quickie meeting with Adam Forrester wasn't enough to make a determination.

"Was it a robbery or was somebody just trying to make it look that way?"

He knew he was asking Sarabian to divulge information that was probably confidential.

"Well...," and the pregnant pause told him the detective was choosing his words carefully.

"Personally, I don't see it as a random hit. It could be, but I don't think so. The security system was disarmed which indicates it was someone with some smarts. He was robbed though, and we think they took a pretty good sum out of the safe. Maybe as much as a quarter mil in bills of various denominations.

"At first we found no sign of a break in, but some new evidence indicates somebody was there uninvited. This is how I figure it. Forrester was home alone, maybe in his study, or maybe watching TV in his bedroom.

"Perp comes in and waves a gun at him. Forrester thinks the guy's there to rob him. He's a smart guy so he probably figures if he cooperates the guy will take what he wants and go away.

"Forrester probably never figured the guy was there for him. After all, B&E guys seldom strike unless they're pretty sure no one's home. They don't want a confrontation or to hurt anybody, and usually they're not armed.

"We call it a "hot prowl" when they're ballsy enough to go in when people are sleeping. Most "hot prowls" are junkies too impatient to care if anyone's home. They're just looking for something they can carry and hock. Money, jewelry, some small appliances.

"But this guy has a different motive. He came with the intention of killing Forrester. The guy had to be masked, otherwise Forrester would have known what was up right away. He would have suspected the guy was there for a hit. The mask would have made him think burglary.

"Anyhow, I figure the bad guy told Forrester he wanted money and Forrester led him to the den where he had the floor safe. He got down on his knees and opened the safe, then the guy blasted him. And here's something nobody knows yet, so keep a lid on it. Okay."

Brian nodded.

"It doesn't shape up as a typical mob hit, and that's what's so confusing," Sarabian said in exasperation. "Those guys leave their signature. A .22 slug behind the ear is their calling card. Forensics says the gun that killed Forrester was a .38. And another thing. The blow to Forrester's head came after he was dead. Somebody wanted to make it look like there was a struggle.

Ron Delpit

"So here's the long and short of it. If it was a mob hit they didn't want it to look like one. It wasn't a message murder. It was an intentional homicide, not an accident. And the robbery appears to have been a coverup, although making off with that much jack is a nice bonus."

Maybe it wasn't a bonus," Brian offered.

"What if whoever ordered the hit knew about the cash, and told the shooter that would be his payoff."

"That's a good theory," the detective agreed. "The shooter would probably have iced Forrester for fifty-grand, but this way he hits the lottery and scores a quarter mil. Makes sense."

"And if it goes down as a homicide during a robbery there's no heat on whatever family called the shot. Good thinking ace."

"How are the wife and kid?" Brian asked, changing the subject.

"Kid's great. Wife and I are no longer on the same team. She asked for and got her unconditional release about eight months ago. She traded me for a player to be named later.

"What about you? Still hot for your ex or is there a new player?"

Brian looked away.

"Laura and her brother were both killed in a traffic accident last week in Los Angeles," he confided.

"I'm sorry man. I know she meant a lot to you. She was a good lady."

"Thanks," he said. "They were both good people."

Sarabian had earned his shield four years earlier but still looked out of place in the civilian dress of a detective always having a shirttail flapping or a coat and tie combination that was a little hard on the eyes. Even at an imposing 6'2, 270 he was one of the few guys who definitely looked better in blue.

Brian slipped in a few more questions about the Colossus, about Diana Forrester and the power on the street in Vegas.

"Gino Petraglia is the new man on the street," Sarabian offered. "He's tied to Kansas City and he's a mean motherfucker. He's got his fingers in a lot of things, but in the end he's only a puppet He takes his orders from the home office.

"As for the Forrester woman, I hear she gets around." He didn't explain.

"Be careful with this stuff," the cop cautioned. "And let me know if you come across anything unusual. It might match up with something I've heard."

"Will do boss," Brian said, jokingly saluting the big cop.

"What's the girl like, anyway?" Sarabian asked, taking his turn on offense.

"You mean Forrester's daughter?"

"Yeah. I spoke to her on the phone for a minute or two but that doesn't help me get a real feel for her. Not the same as knowing her."

"Her name is Tiffany Wayne. Took her mother's maiden name after an argument with her father a few years back, and she doesn't have a clue what

160

Vegas is all about," Brian said without flinching. "She strikes me as legit though, if that's what you're asking."

"That's what I'm asking. How about the lawyer, Thurston? Is he on the up and up?"

"Far as I can tell he is," and Brian wondered if the detective knew something he wasn't saying. Sarabian didn't ask questions without having a reason.

Brian had worked with Walter very closely over the past two weeks and was convinced the Chicago lawyer was one of the good guys. But he'd been wrong before.

The one thing about Walter Thurston that didn't add up was his complete unwillingness to offer his opinion about Adam Forrester's murder. He was okay handling facts, and information Brian delivered, but never seemed willing to inject his own theories.

Sarabian guzzled his second Coors and waved off an offer from a waitress who offered a third.

"Don't have time," he croaked, looking at his watch.

In the parking lot he shot Brian a hard look.

"Stay cool pal. And watch your step."

"I will," Brian promised as he watched the detective turn out of the parking lot onto Sunset Road.

The sky was a brilliant canvas of colors streaked in the orange-red of the sunset, with puffs of gray, purple and blue hovering over the neon lit city. Its natural beauty begged a question.

If Vegas was the epitome of decadence and Los Angeles the City of Angels how come God painted his masterpieces in the desert sky and gave LA a throat full of smog? Some questions just never got answered.

The Strip and the Colossus were ten minutes away and the short commute allowed Brian a chance to piece together what he had learned from Sarabian with his own research. Questions raced in his head like greyhounds furiously chasing after a metal rabbit.

Was Forrester in any way involved with the mob? Did he know Diana was screwing around? If he did that would explain him shortchanging her in the will and dumping everything in Tiffany's lap. If someone had been pressuring him to sell the hotel, was he killed with the idea Diana would inherit it and sell? And exactly how did Diana and Sonny fit in? Diana was hot and Sonny was Sonny, but a roll in the hay was a long way from conspiracy to commit murder. And what about Walter? How exactly did he figure in the big picture?

He needed to chill and let his subconscious work. He needed to relax.

It was Friday night and the town was jumping. He veered into the parking lot of a gas station mini-mart across from the Luxor and dug a scrap of paper out of his wallet. Jeri, an auburn haired twenty-one dealer from the Stardust answered on the third ring and they made hurried plans for a light dinner, a little music and whatever else might suit their fancy.

He wasn't sure what time he took Jeri home, but he was fairly certain they were both smiling when she said goodbye. She had an insatiable appetite and took him places a travel agent couldn't, none of which required a boarding pass. Before he clicked off the light next to his bed he tucked her number safely back in his wallet.

It was a little before nine when Brian's eyes caught their first glimpse of daylight, and as usual he was instantly awake. Adam Forrester's funeral still dominated the news so he moved on to the sports section.

Next up was a hot shower. It was the place he held his one on one reality check every morning. The place where he planned out his day and reminded himself of priority tasks. He stepped out feeling alert and revitalized.

He was still drying off when the phone rang.

It was Walter.

"Sorry to disturb you so early on a Saturday," he apologized. "Tiffany sent a fax to the office sometime last night asking if the three of us could have a conference call meeting this morning."

"What time?"

Brian hoped Walter didn't want him there in the next ten minutes. He wanted to finish reading the paper and relax a bit longer. It had been a long night and Jeri's perfume was still in the air.

"She's supposed to call at eleven our time," he said. "It'll be evening in Paris."

"I'll be there.

Uncharacteristically, he was on time. He was in jeans and a lightweight Cal Berkeley Law School T-shirt. Walter had on slacks and a sport coat, no tie. A sure sign it was Saturday.

Tiffany's call came in at 11:03.

"Hi Brian," she said after acknowledging Walter. "And I'd like to both thank you and officially welcome you to the Colossus team. We're very happy to have you working with us."

"Thanks. I only hope I can be of some help."

Walter had a half dozen things to discuss with her, from culinary union demands and her gaming application to her preference in wine for the party.

The Gaming Control Board had granted her a sixty-day emergency license but they still required a thorough background check.

"That shouldn't take very long," Walter advised. "There's not much background for them to check on you. Besides, from what Brian tells me, they're mainly trying to determine if you have any connections to organized crime. You should be safe in that area."

"I should pass with flying colors," Tiffany chuckled.

"They made Sinatra sweat and eventually turned him down," Brian added, ot wanting her to think it was a walk in the park. "They asked him about people e hadn't seen since fifth grade."

Brian also knew the commission would take into consideration the hotel's ,000 employees and the fact Tiffany was already the legal owner. That was a ice one-two punch, and no appointed ruling body wanted to be responsible for utting that many workers on the street. It would be political suicide.

When it was his turn Brian shared some of the information Detective arabian had given him. He told her the detective had promised to do everything n his power to keep the case as a priority item.

"He also thinks there is a significant amount of money missing from your ither's safe. After talking to the caretaker and the maid, Detective Sarabian ainks there was definitely a robbery but he thinks it was an afterthought. He elieves whoever killed your father went to his home with that in mind."

"Have they found the gun, Brian?"

"No. And results from the fingerprint lab aren't back yet."

Brian then addressed them both...

"Do either of you know if there were any problems in your father's iarriage?"

"I hadn't spoken to my father in five years," Tiffany admitted. "All I know is vhat Diana told me when we met her. She said they were very much in love and iat my father had never been happier.

"Why do you ask Brian? Do you have reason to believe the marriage was in ouble?"

"No particular reason yet," he fibbed. "I've just heard some bits and pieces iat make me wonder. When I get something concrete I'll let you know."

"Thanks Brian. Good work. Now Walter, what about the party?"

"Things are moving along, and I'm going to go over the guest list with Brian rhen we get off the phone. You just take care of Paris and your show. Knock m dead."

"I'm going to try. The weather here is a bit depressing but the food is great nd the city is wonderful. I'll call again in a couple of days and give you an pdate."

Walter followed Brian's suggestion, making the intimate details of the July ourth bash available to only a handful of top-level executives. The Colossus' ice-president of public relations and marketing was briefed in a closed-door ieeting, and instructed to keep the party and guest list confidential.

"Have we missed anybody important?" Walter asked as Brian scanned the ugh draft of the guest list.

"Not that I can think of," Brian responded. "How the heck did you get addi's private number? Only a handful of people know who he is."

"And I must confess I'm not one of them," said Walter, raising his eyebrows in a way that clearly meant he wanted Brian to help fill-in the blanks.

"He's the son of a billionaire Middle East arms dealer. I think his father was involved in the Iran-Contra arms scandal in the late 80s. Shortly after that story surfaced the old man's plane mysteriously went down on a short flight in bad weather. They found it smashed against a mountain in Nepal a couple days later. No survivors.

"The kid inherited everything." Brian was trying to make the story as brief as possible.

"Anyway, in the last two years, Mohammed here has sort of taken Vegas by storm. He's been the silent money behind at least three hotel deals that I know about, including the Aladdin. He's replaced junk bond and IPO financing. The way I hear it he's lent twenty, thirty and as much as fifty million without batting one of his very thick eyelashes. In exchange for a piece of the action of course."

Walter was fascinated by the story and impressed that Brian had the inside scoop.

"What about the Gaming Commission and the Gaming Control Board? How has Sheik Mohammed gotten around the licensing regulations?"

"The loans are made through a Saudi bank the Sheik owns and all the i's are dotted and t's crossed before any money changes hands. The clincher is, there's never anything in writing about Mohammed getting a piece of the casino action."

The arrangement awakened the lawyer in Walter.

"Seems like he's taking quite a chance if the hotel goes belly up or chooses not to honor the deal."

"Not likely pardner," Brian grinned. Walter still had a lot to learn about the unwritten laws of the old west.

"The Sheik is not only rich, he's shrewd.

"Mohammed protects himself by having the borrowers sign two sets of loan documents. The original set is for the Gaming Commission and meets their standards. The second set is identical to the first, except for an ironclad clause that allows the bank to call the entire loan due in seventy-two hours and foreclose on the property within fifteen days if a payment is missed. And there is a rider that states the second set of documents supersedes and nullifies the first.

"Mohammed gets the legitimate loan payment plus a very substantial sum under the table every month. If you miss either of those two payments he fills in the date and brings the mountain down on you."

"Nice deal." And Walter meant it. The contract was both clever and binding. The Sheik had apparently taken a few pages from the Huey Long School of business. When Long ruled Louisiana politics in the thirties he demanded a signed letter of resignation before he would appoint anyone to a state office. The only thing blank on the letter was the date.

Brian didn't have much more input on the guest list except for turning thumbs down on a couple of mid-level executives from rival casinos and a few bimbos who made good set decoration but had little else to offer. Enough of them would slip through anyway.

"It'll be quite a coup if Sheik Mohammed does show up," Brian said as he left Walter's office. "He keeps a very low profile and doesn't go to many parties. If he comes you know your event is a hit, and he'll attract the rest of Vegas' rich and famous. They'll come just to see him."

The message light on his phone was blinking when he got home.

"Brian, its Sarabian. Call me at home as soon as you get in." His tone sounded official.

"Sarabian here."

"Don, its Brian."

"Meet me in 15 minutes at Sunset Park," the detective ordered. "By the basketball courts. I don't want to talk on the phone."

He got there in 10 and Sarabian was already waiting.

"Did you know the Forrester broad was banging Sonny Fremont?"

"I'd heard some talk, but I wasn't positive," Brian said a bit intimidated.

"Well it's a fact. It's also a fact that there are some heavyweight names coming down the pike on this one. Chicago names."

"Where's all this new information coming from?" Brian asked.

"Feds popped a guy on a racketeering charge in Cleveland and he's trying to sell them a deal. Said he had inside information on a lot of shit going down in Vegas. They've passed some of it on to see if it's worth a deal."

"And he mentioned Sonny Fremont and Diana Forrester? That sounds like a stretch."

"I thought so too, and by itself that info doesn't mean shit. But he says he knows who was behind the Forrester hit? He's willing to give it up if they let him walk."

"Will they?"

"I'm not sure. He could be lying. He's a small time weasel trying to save his own neck. He did throw out some news that might mean something though, to show good faith he said."

"What's that?"

"He said the broad who inherited the hotel was next on the list?"

"What list?"

The detective looked at him in mock disbelief.

"Do I have to spell this out for you," he said without a smile, and he could see the light come on in Brian's head.

"Did he mean Diana…or Forrester's daughter?" Brian's breath was coming faster, his voice tense and excited.

"He didn't say. The Feds don't think he knows. They think he might just be blowing smoke.

"I've already assigned someone to keep an eye on Diana Forrester. Where's Forrester's daughter?"

"Paris."

"France?"

"France."

"Fuck."

They looked at each helplessly.

Tiffany Wayne didn't like Vegas, and she didn't believe in luck, but both Brian and Sarabian knew if the snitch was telling the truth, luck was all she had going for her at the moment. It might be the only thing that could save her life.

Chapter 14
Favors

By his own mother's definition Carlo Monetti had always been something of a problem child.

Even his birth had not been without complications. Doris Monetti had been in hard labor fourteen hours with no drugs and she still had not fully dilated.

It was 8 p.m. and the young doctor attending her had promised to look in on her again at 8:30. She doubted she could last that long. The beads of perspiration on her forehead were sliding down the sides of her temples and her bedclothes were soaked.

The contractions were coming every three minutes and each one hit with the force of a hammer slamming into her stomach, causing her to lose her breath and beg for God's mercy. A worn string of white rosary beads was clutched in her right hand and each time the pain came she squeezed the beads so tightly the small metal cross bit into her palm, leaving an impression in her tender skin.

She was a slight woman, weighing barely a hundred pounds, with coarse brown hair and a smooth round face with gentle wrinkles that made her seem older than twenty-six.

"I'm getting a little concerned about you Mrs. Monetti. I think if we don't see some movement in the next half an hour we might have to do a Caesarean section."

She had been biting her lip to keep from crying out, and she could feel the warmth of a drop of blood in her mouth. She had not heard the doctor enter the room but the sound of his voice caused her to look up through the tears.

"Thank you doctor," she said weakly. "That would be fine."

Neither of her two older children had come with so much difficulty. They too had been born at St. Rita's Hospital in Palermo. The hospital was only three miles from her house and whenever she passed it she was filled with good feelings because her children had brought her so much joy.

At 9:47 p.m. Doctor Antonio Brunelli wheeled her into the operating room, and eleven minutes later announced the birth of her second son.

"It's a good thing we did the Caesarean," he said when she regained consciousness.

"Your baby was in danger. Somehow he had turned and the umbilical cord had become wrapped around his neck. If we hadn't taken him when we did he could have suffocated. But don't worry. He's fine. And I know his lungs are in excellent condition because he came out screaming.

It was fitting that Carlo Monetti should come out with such fanfare because in the next few years he made a lot of noise. He was a precocious, extremely hyperactive child.

167

Carlo was unlike other children, especially his siblings. He was, in many ways, more like an adult. Children's games did not interest him, and Doris Monetti could not deny that Carlo was shrewd; but he was also sneaky and often unnecessarily cruel.

Her husband noticed it too, and had often counseled the boy about the virtues of honesty and compassion. Tomas Monetti was a good man but clearly over-matched when it came to arguments with his son. Carlo grew into an adept con artist, one quite good at getting others to do his bidding.

It concerned Tomas that his son was obsessed with money, and he soon learned that the boy would stop at nothing to get what he wanted. Carlo had incredible charisma and the extraordinary ability to make people do what he asked of them.

Unfortunately, he also had a temper. Most children got angry and exploded. They'd cry or fight back. They'd yell or pout, but Carlo used a totally different tact.

When he got angry, or someone hurt him he would keep it bottled inside and pretend he wasn't bothered. But hours or days later he would retaliate, when his foe least expected it. And he was so clever his opponent would oftentimes not realize it was Carlo secretly getting his revenge in the form of a pound of flesh.

A schoolmate who beat him out of a starting spot on the soccer team had the brakes fail on his motorbike some two weeks later, resulting in an accident that broke his leg so severely he was forced to use a cane.

By the time he was eleven, Carlo had been in trouble a dozen times and the local policia knew him by his first name. At fifteen he began running with a group of village thugs and he was out of control at home. Yet, unlike many of his friends Carlo did not quit school. For that small favor Tomas and Doris were grateful.

Carlo was a brilliant and gifted student. Learning came easily and he was one of the top students in his school. Like most Italian students he was required to take a second language and he mastered French in less than a year. He pleaded with his father to hire a tutor to teach him English, which he began to speak with a heavy accent.

As he got older, there was even some talk of Carlo pursuing a law degree, but he was too impatient, and nothing came of it.

He was a contradiction.

On one hand a scholar, on the other a young tough, and it was the latter reputation that spread like wildfire across the countryside. He had disassociated himself from the street hoodlums, deciding they had little imagination, were too openly violent and much too stupid. He did however find a use for them.

He arranged for them to terrorize vulnerable storeowners, vendors and certain wealthy families, then he would come to the aid of the shopkeeper or injured party, thereby earning their gratitude and trust.

168

Soon they were offering him generous amounts of money to keep a watchful eye on their businesses and homes. They respected him, and when he savagely beat one of the young hooligans for harassing a butcher, he did it in full view of the townspeople. After that, they also feared him.

By his nineteenth birthday he was making more money than his father. He had also fallen in lust with his tutor, a homely looking but shapely village girl who had never been married and was only too eager to please the fast-rising Carlo.

It didn't matter that she was four years older and stood almost a full head taller. She knew how to please him and was smart enough to know that he would not tolerate her meddling in his business.

Despite his parents protestations, he married Melina Pellegrino, learning only after the wedding that she was already three months pregnant with his child.

Over the next few years Carlo expanded his "security and protection" business, adding legitimate import/export purchases and sales and some minor drug dealings to his portfolio. Money was plentiful and he and Melina lived well. They had a three-year old son, Carlo Jr., and an infant daughter, Rosa, named in honor of his sister.

It was a Saturday night, and as was his custom, Carlo got decked out in his finest suit, gassed up his Fiat and prepared to make his rounds. On his way home he would stop and see Andrea, his mistress of the month. He loved his wife but he also had an insatiable sexual appetite and found it hard to be satisfied by just one woman.

There were times Melina was tired, or on her period, or nights when he did not make it home. Wherever he was, he wanted a woman. He needed sex the way most people needed food.

He needed it daily, sometimes twice a day, and it didn't really matter who satisfied his desires. Except for Melina, his partners were nameless, faceless and interchangeable. He treated them well, often buying them expensive trinkets but he had no loyalty to his many women.

He checked his watch. It was almost one in the morning. He could make it to Andrea's and spend an hour or so and still be home by three. Melina wouldn't expect him before then, especially on a Saturday, which was his busiest night.

There was little traffic and he made it to Andrea's neighborhood in less than ten minutes. As he turned onto Via La Pone a long black car swerved in his path and came to a complete stop. Carlo slammed on his brakes to avoid ramming the other car. Immediately he reached for the pistol he kept under his seat.

He looked in his rear view mirror and saw an identical black sedan behind him and three heavily armed men making their way toward him.

He didn't know what he had done, but he did know he stood no chance in a shoot out. There were too many of them, and they were all armed and dangerous.

Carlo Monetti sat very still and waited. The men from the rear vehicle fanned out and stood guard, their shotguns poised.

Three men in dark suits stepped out of the lead car and approached him.

"Please get out of the car," said the tallest one.

Carlo did so without question.

"You are Carlo Monetti?" the man said rhetorically, eyeing Carlo warily.

"I am."

"You have made a very grave mistake my friend," he said, still not sounding threatening.

"One of your people has done harm to one of Don Alberto Fanzi's uncles and the Don is very displeased."

"My people?"

"One of your young thugs. And please, do not insult us by lying. The hoodlum has already admitted being in your employ. In fact, it was he who told us where we might find you tonight."

Carlo swallowed hard. He was afraid to say anything that might provoke his captors. If Don Fanzi had wanted him dead he would already be a memory. He also knew that the goons surrounding him could justify killing him if he did anything to incite them.

"What do you want of me?" he asked.

"Come with us where we can talk more privately," said a squat muscled man with blue veins outlining his bulbous nose. "Don Fanzi requests your presence."

He went passively, finding himself in the back seat of the black sedan wedged between two large men who smelled of tobacco and garlic. When the car turned sharply he was tossed against the larger of the men and felt the hard butt of the pistol in his inside pocket.

They drove for nearly twenty minutes, no one speaking. Occasionally the sound of the window being rolled down as someone threw a cigarette into the night broke the silence. The car turned into a back alley and glided to a stop in front of a warehouse where a dim yellowed bulb on a brown, rust tarnished chain hung over a narrow door.

Carlo felt a cold shiver as he was pulled from the car. He knew they were going to kill him. He hoped they would do it quickly and not torture him.

Don Alberto Fanzi was one of the most feared Mafioso in all of Italy, and Carlo had been careful to stay out of his path, until now. How had he gotten careless?

Fanzi's organization was widespread and controlled most of the drugs in Sicily. There were rumors The Don had most of the police and politicians on his payroll, and was powerful enough to have anyone he wished elected to office.

The Don owned brothels and taverns, controlled gambling in the southern part of Sicily and pretty much had things his own way. Politicians who cooperated were protected and re-elected. Those who opposed him soon found themselves embroiled in scandals, trying to explain newspaper headlines linking them to drugs, bribes and prostitutes.

Don Fanzi was more popular than the Pope, perhaps because he was responsible for more everyday miracles, or because he didn't care whether his subjects used birth control or not. Furthermore, it was a safe bet that in the course of a year more people kissed Don Fanzi's ring than the Pope's.

Carlo had seen Fanzi a number of times but had never been personally introduced. Apparently that was about to change.

The warehouse was cold and quiet. Two cars were parked inside and he knew immediately that the tan Rolls belonged to Don Fanzi.

"Sit down." There was no anger in Don Fanzi's voice. With his eyes The Don motioned for the gorillas to back away, out of earshot.

"I know who you are and what you do Carlo Monetti. I have watched you closely over the past few years, and my friends wonder why I have allowed you to exist."

That Don Fanzi knew who he was surprised Carlo. That he was not dead yet told him Don Fanzi had more than revenge on his mind.

The Don was a small man, slender as a reed, with tiny, almost delicate fingers. He was impeccably dressed in a black suit, white shirt, print tie with a diamond stickpin and two-tone shoes. In his left hand was a small black pearl cigarette holder.

He certainly did not look very menacing, but Carlo knew better.

"I have not bothered with you because up to now you have not interfered in my business," he began. "In a way you reminded me of myself when I was younger. You're not just a common street thug. You are very clever. Violent only when you have to be, and with a soft spot for the weak. And you have a special charm.

"I suppose I just wanted to see how far you could go, or how far you dared go."

Carlo made no attempt to interrupt The Don.

"I knew it would be just a matter of time until you did something to cross me. A couple of your young hoodlums tried to strong-arm my wife's uncle earlier tonight and when he resisted they beat him. He died two hours ago.

"Fortunately for you, I didn't like the man or you would be dead too. However, in deference to my wife, I am forced to exact some measure of revenge."

"I am truly sorry Don Fanzi, and I swear to you I will take swift revenge on whoever did this. On whoever harmed your relative and caused you grief."

He was willing to do anything to appease the Don.

"That won't be necessary," Don Fanzi said quickly. "That has already been done."

171

The Don stopped to remove what was left of his cigarette from the holder, replacing it immediately with a fresh one he fished out of a new pack in the inside pocket of his cashmere overcoat.

"However, if you wish to spare the lives of your wife and children, and your parents, it will be necessary for you to do something for me to atone for the disrespect you have shown to my family."

"Anything, Don Fanzi. Anything." Carlo knew he was bargaining for his life.

The Don looked at him with steely eyes. Eyes that pierced his skin and said nothing. Eyes that seared through him, looking for a reason to distrust.

"There is a matter in Palermo I want you to take care of," Fanzi said in a hushed tone. "It will be very dangerous, but if you handle this for me I will consider your debt repaid."

Carlo did not have to speak. The Don knew what he was thinking. What he wanted to ask.

"Because my people are too well known," he said, answering Carlo's unasked question. "They could never succeed. It would have to be a stranger."

"And after it is done, I will arrange for you to leave the country. There would be no way you could stay. It would never be safe."

"My family?"

The Don looked at the concrete floor.

"It would be too burdensome for you to take your wife or your children. I know this is a heavy price, but once you have done this you will have my blessing, and wherever you go I will see that you are looked after."

"If I live you mean..." His eyes locked on Don Fanzi, and neither of them looked away for a long moment. They both knew that his punishment, while severe, was simply one of the hazards to be expected in their chosen line of work. Sooner or later everyone's luck ran out.

Carlo understood he was being hired as an assassin, and in lieu of payment his family would be allowed to live. His own life was being spared for the moment, but there was little chance he would survive his mission.

Don Ferdinand Domingo was his target. Domingo was Don Fanzi's most hated rival and the most ruthless drug lord in all of Italy. He was also one of the most protected. Eliminating Don Domingo would give Don Fanzi free reign throughout the entire country.

On his own Fanzi could not move against Don Domingo, because to do so would set off a bloody gang war.

Carlo pondered the big picture. The first problem was going to be getting to Don Domingo. He was almost never alone. The second difficulty would be escaping Domingo's bodyguards who would surely attempt to avenge the death of their leader. The third might be eluding Fanzi's men because Don Fanzi would be eager to eliminate any one or anything that connected him to the assassination.

And it would appear to be an act of support if his men were the ones who killed Don Domingo's murderer.

Whether he lived or died depended on two things, his own cunning and Don Fanzi's honor.

One of Fanzi's capos gave him information concerning Don Domingo's schedule and suggestions about when the Don might be the most vulnerable.

Following his meeting with Don Fanzi, Carlo was returned to his car. His first inclination was to run. To flee Italy. However there was no sense in running. He would have to complete the assignment or die trying.

Carlo realized he would need help, so he turned to his most trusted friend. Peter Delpini was a man without fear, and someone who would not be intimidated by the magnitude of the task.

"It would be best to do this as quickly as possible," Peter whispered as he took a drag on his cigarette. "Today is Sunday. According to your information Don Domingo always attends mass at 10:30. Inside the church he will be alone, without his bodyguards. He is too respectful to take them inside."

Carlo thought for a second about the sacrilege of committing a murder in a church, then he thought about the hypocrisy of a murderer like Don Domingo being in church in the first place. In an odd way it was the perfect place for him to die.

It was already 5 a.m. They had only five hours to get everything in place.

"First we must stop at St. Rose's," said Peter. "It's only a few blocks from here. My cousin, Father Dumante, is away. I will get two of his cassocks."

The rest of the plan unfolded as if they had prepared for months. Wearing the cassocks and collars they had "borrowed" from Father Dumante's closet, Carlo and Peter slipped virtually unnoticed inside the huge wooden door at the side entrance to St. Augustine's Cathedral in Palermo.

They appeared to be just two more young priests, there to join in celebrating the end of the 10:30 service.

Within seconds after entering Carlo spotted Don Domingo, on the aisle about two thirds of the way to the back of the huge church. He was kneeling, with head bowed, and it appeared he was with his wife and two other elderly women. Don Fanzi's capo had said Don Domingo usually attended mass with his two sisters.

Carlo and Peter sat three rows behind the Don, to his far left so they could keep an eye on him without drawing attention. When it came time for the communion service the women at his side rose, slid out of the pew and made their way to the altar.

It was the perfect opportunity. He was alone.

Swiftly and silently the two men moved to the center aisle and walked directly up to the Don, who was seated, leaning against the back of the pew. Carlo leaned over as if to ask him a question, pulled the 9mm glouck from under his cassock and fired three quick shots. The sound of the organ and the silencer muffled the shots so thoroughly no one even turned to look.

Don Domingo slumped lifelessly in the pew, his eyes wide open, his reign as a Mafioso kingpin halted in the most unlikely surroundings. The priestly impostors did not linger or look to the sides as they strode meaningfully toward the carved double doors at the rear of the church, their hearts pounding and their knees weak. Outside, they kept their heads bent and their eyes averted as they passed within ten feet of Don Domingo's waiting bodyguards.

A feeling of exhilaration swept over Carlo as he started the engine of his car, which they had parked nearly three blocks away on a seldom-used side street. The first half of the test of fire was behind him.

He had not been home, and he had not contacted Melina since the night before. She would be mildly concerned, but it was not unusual for him to be gone for a full day without calling.

His instructions were to meet Don Fanzi's lieutenant at a small tavern near the docks at eight o'clock. The man was to give him papers and documents he would need to gain passage aboard a cargo ship set to depart at 9 p.m.

Peter had insisted on coming, to serve as a backup if Don Fanzi's men tried to do him harm, but Carlo refused to put his friend in jeopardy.

"If Don Fanzi goes back on his word, I want you to be able to tell my wife and family what happened to me," he said. "This time I must go alone."

Carlo kept out of sight the rest of the day, and when darkness fell, he made his way to the tavern.

A voice in the dark spoke to him.

"Don Fanzi is extremely pleased. You are an exceptionally clever and resourceful young man, and for what you've done the Don is very grateful."

The man put his fingers to his lips when Carlo attempted to speak.

"You will not be harmed, "the burly man said in Italian. "I have the papers you need, and when you arrive at your destination there will be people there to help you. Don Fanzi's influence is far and wide. There are many people in America who owe him favors."

It was the first mention of where he was going.

Word of Don Domingo's sudden death in the Cathedral spread like a virus throughout the countryside and Carlo heard a number of villagers discussing it in the pub. There were conflicting reports about just how the famous Don had died.

One story claimed the Don had died of a massive heart attack during the Sunday mass. A second suggested the Don had committed suicide, and a third, even more bizarre tale said Don Domingo had been murdered by one of the parish priests.

"Personally I believe the hypocrite took communion and died of shock," an old woman muttered.

"Certainly no priest would kill him," said another. "He was too big a contributor."

From the table talk Carlo deduced that no one at the church had actually heard a shot, or seen the murder, but that did not stop Don Domingo's son from having his father's bodyguards executed in full view of a hundred witnesses.

Carlo understood young Don Domingo's reasoning. If the bodyguards were in on the coup, they had to be done away with. And if they weren't part of the conspiracy they deserved to be punished for not doing their job.

"Pier 14 in half an hour," the bearded man whispered, making sure no one else heard his instructions.

"The ship is the *Freda Luna* and it is bound for Alaska. From there you can make your way into the United States when the time is right."

"My wife?"

The older man shook his head.

"Take your new name and make a life for yourself. Wash your hands of all this."

The man handed him a small paper sack with some papers and $5,000 in American currency.

"Ask for Victor when you get to the gangway. He will be expecting you. And hurry. Time is growing short."

Carlo Monetti watched the man turn and disappear into the darkness before he started to move in the opposite direction, toward the docks. As he approached Pier 14 he stopped under a street lamp to examine the papers and learn his new identity. He read his new name and repeated it a dozen times before reaching the *Freda Luna.*

"Who goes there?" the musty looking sailor at the bottom of the gangway asked when he reached the walkway.

"Gianni," Carlo replied. "I am looking for Victor."

"I am Victor," a deep voice from the boat bellowed. "Welcome aboard."

Chapter 15
One Car West

Rita Matthews did not remember much about her five-day journey from Grand Rapids, Michigan to Los Angeles.

The trip was only four hours by plane, but she was afraid to fly, and besides she hoped the long stretches of open highway would give her time to try and sort out the tragedy that had suddenly visited her life. Maybe to look for signs she should have seen. Signs that her boy was in trouble. The police had not mentioned drugs, which was no surprise, because she was sure Boyd had never used them.

So what then? If not drugs, or a random bullet, which everyone knew could happen at any moment in LA or New York, what could have gone so wrong? What could have made her only son take his own life?

The guilt gnawed at her.

There had been no time to think before leaving Michigan. The call from the Los Angeles police had stunned her even though she had always feared something terrible would happen if Boyd moved to Los Angeles. She'd had a bad feeling about if from the moment he left Michigan.

As soon as she hung up the phone she began packing. She would go and take care of her son's body. There was no one else.

Methodically she tossed clothes in a well-preserved JC Penney suitcase, packed toiletries in an overnight case and carefully placed them in her trunk.

She was not an experienced highway driver and had only a general idea of the roads she would need to take so she armed herself with maps, flares and an emergency road kit from a neighborhood service station.

And somehow she made it.

The sun was just beginning to peek over the San Bernadino Mountains as she approached the Los Angeles County line, her small bony hands clutched tightly to the hard vinyl steering wheel, her seat belt firmly around her shoulders.

She had driven cross-country in a trance, operating on some kind of automatic pilot. Now the snarl of traffic and the testiness of the early morning commuters on the LA freeways were jarring Rita Matthews to alertness.

"I can't believe people actually drive in this every day," she said out loud. "This would make me crazy."

She had taken only scant notice of the hundreds of highway signs, roadside diners and gas stations as she wound through eight states. She had stopped at AAA recommended motels on each of the four nights, parking her 1987 Oldsmobile just outside her room whenever possible. She wasn't sure why it was important to park there since the car held nothing of value except her clothes, but it made her feel more secure.

Perhaps she did it because it was the only thing she had left connecting her to her son. He had sent her $4000 to help buy it.

She and Boyd had not been close the past eight or nine years, not since the day he had admitted being gay. Following a hurtful and emotional argument Boyd had packed his things and headed for Hollywood.

At the time she had not been terribly sorry to see him go. A psychologist had assured her that her reaction was normal, and that in time she would learn to deal with it. He was wrong.

Over the past year Boyd Matthews had phoned regularly, and their once strained relationship, while not all hugs and kisses, was at least civil.

Now she had come cross country to pick up the left behind pieces of his life. To clean out his apartment and perhaps cleanse her own soul of the bitterness she had harbored for so many years.

The building manager unlocked Boyd's apartment, and for the first time since being notified of his death, she felt a touch of sadness.

"This is it ma'am, "the man said, as he opened the door and stepped into the small living room. He was thankful someone had come to clean the place out.

"I appreciate your coming to take care of his things. I really didn't know what to do with them."

"I've never had anyone commit, uh, die in one of the apartments before."

Rita Matthews looked back at Gus Cavel through cold eyes.

She was a practical woman and had come prepared, bringing seven or eight cardboard boxes in various sizes. They were unassembled, but she had brought masking tape and twine.

"I'll pack the personal things in these boxes," she told the manager. "If you help me carry them to the car I'll leave the sofa and other furniture. You can sell them and keep the money."

Gus readily agreed. He would not be able to rent the apartment for at least two weeks anyway, and the woman hadn't mentioned the $200 security deposit Boyd Matthews was entitled to have refunded. He would make out quite nicely on this deal.

"Just yell when you're ready and I'll haul the stuff down," Gus said. He was in his fifties, with a barrel chest and a flat mid-section that came from working out.

"Is that your blue Olds down by the trash bins?"

"That's mine," she said blandly, deciding it was a senseless question considering hers was probably the only car in the visitors' area with Michigan plates.

She was surprised at how easily she was able to detach herself from the reality of the job at hand, deluding herself into imagining that Boyd was away on a trip and that she was packing up his apartment for a move back home.

She worked in the kitchen first, carefully wrapping about a dozen different sized glasses and the few dishes in the cupboard. There were dirty plates in the dishwasher along with some unclean silverware. She poured a small mound of Cascade into the Kitchenaid and turned the machine to the energy saver cycle, the hum of the motor a welcome intrusion on the silence in the room.

Boyd did not have a lot of personal belongings other than his clothes, which she decided to donate to the Salvation Army or the local Goodwill.

The police had already given her his ring, a silver chain with a small cross, and his watch.

In the bedroom she found a photo album and for a long while she sat on the bed staring at it, afraid to open it. She held it on her lap and for the first time felt Boyd's presence in the room.

Rita hesitated opening the album, then slowly began turning the pages of her son's life. As the faded photographs of Boyd's childhood flashed before her eyes she grew melancholy. Nearly twenty minutes passed as she watched Boyd grow up again in pictures.

The knock at the door startled her.

"Got any boxes ready to go down?"

"There are a couple in the living room and two in the kitchen," she said, hoping the apartment manager would not notice how little she had actually accomplished.

"I'll get these to the car and check back with you in about forty-five minutes," he said, sounding as if he really wanted to help. "I'll need your keys to open the trunk."

"The keys are on the kitchen counter. The round one will open the trunk."

She put away the photo album stripped the bed and boxed up the bedding. In the bedroom closet she found his tennis racquet, skis, a Monopoly game and assorted sports equipment.

In the far corner of the closet, on the floor behind a pair of worn ice skates she found an old Adidas shoe box full of what appeared to be personal papers.

She saw Boyd's passport, an envelope with a negative HIV test result, his birth certificate and a stack of unopened letters.

She withdrew one of the letters from the box.

"Boyd Matthews, 1655 N. Roman Street, Apt. 228, North Hollywood, Ca."

It looked important, even official, but it had never been opened. It was postmarked seven months earlier. If it was junk mail why hadn't he thrown it away?

She lifted another envelope from the box. It was obvious from the handwriting the letters were from the same person. The second envelope had an even earlier postmark, and neither had a return address.

A third envelope caught her eye. It was a FedEx letter dated only a week ago, and sent the day before Boyd had died. She turned it over in her hand, examining it more closely and debating whether she should open it.

The writing was identical to the others, however the name "S. Bradford" was scrawled in the section set aside for the sender's name. The return address was the Hyatt Regency, Atlanta, Georgia."

She did not hear Gus come into the bedroom.

"I've got those boxes packed away in your trunk," he said. "It's getting a little crowded so we'll have to put some things on the back seat."

She felt guilty going through Boyd's personal mail.

"I won't be much longer. I'm not going to take the clothes. I'd appreciate it if you could call one of the local thrift shops. Most of his things seem to be in good condition. I'm sure they'll be able to make use of them."

Casually she laid the letters back in the shoebox, tied it neatly with a piece of twine and returned to her busywork.

An hour later Gus Cavel hauled the last of the boxes to Rita Matthews' car, then gave her directions to the freeway and wished her a safe trip.

"If you leave now you'll miss the afternoon traffic," he said helpfully. "The rush starts about 4 o'clock." It was two-twenty.

She had made arrangements for Boyd's funeral before leaving Michigan, and the Los Angeles mortuary had assured her everything would be handled. She had wired them the money, having taken it out of her savings, and her son's body had been shipped back to Grand Rapids.

As promised, she left the big pieces of furniture, and Gus figured he could sell them for about $500, even to one of the tightfisted wholesalers.

Rita Matthews hadn't spoken much but Gus pegged her as a very troubled lady.

"Your son was a nice guy and a good tenant," he told her. "Never caused any trouble and always paid his rent on time.

"We didn't talk about personal stuff much. And like I told the police, he didn't seem depressed or nuthin'. His mood had changed a little in the past year though. He started keeping to himself more. Seemed like he had something on his mind. He wasn't as happy as when he first moved in here."

"Thank you for trying to be his friend," she replied, not knowing what else to say.

It was close to 3:30 when she hit Anaheim, with Disneyland's Matterhorn visible out the driver's side window. She was Eastbound, headed home.

On the floor behind the driver's seat was Boyd's box of letters. She had decided to leave them be. Maybe one day she could read them, but not now. She didn't need any more pain. Besides, if Boyd didn't think they were important enough to open, why should she bother?

It was nearly dark when the traffic began to thin and the lights of Los Angeles were far removed from her thoughts. She needed a bathroom and something to eat.

A Wendy's at the next off ramp served both her needs. She ate slowly, relishing the break from the glare of headlights and the endless stream of merging freeways.

Her back ached.

The black coffee aroused her senses. She picked up a newspaper left on an adjacent table and flipped through it absently, reading only the headlines. She put it back on the table, picked up her tray and cup and was headed for the trash bin when the headline caught her eye.

Police End Investigation In Bradford Car Crash.

The name sounded familiar. She thought about it for a second then retrieved the paper. She put it under her arm and stuffed it into the storage pocket behind the passenger seat.

The return trip seemed to go much more quickly, even though it again took her four days. This time her load seemed lighter.

Her next-door neighbors, Sharon and Angelo Dombrowski, came bounding out of their house as soon as they saw her car pull in the driveway.

Sharon, like Rita, was a supervisor with Michigan Bell Telephone. They had known each other twenty-six years and been neighbors for twenty.

"You just get in the house and relax a bit," Sharon scolded when Rita attempted to begin unloading some of the boxes.

"Angelo will unpack those things and have everything shipshape in a flash. You come on in and tell me about the trip. I'm so happy you're back safe and sound."

True to Sharon's prediction Angelo had everything unpacked and the Olds cleaned out in less than an hour.

"I've got most all of it stacked in one corner of the garage," he reported. "It's all to the side so you won't have any trouble getting in and out. I put a few things on the overhead shelf, but it's all secure. Nothing will come crashing down on you."

"Thanks Angelo. I really appreciate your help. I don't think I could have handled seeing those things right now. It's been like a bad dream. I'm thankful it's over and I'm home again."

It was two weeks before she began to sense that the tragic nightmare might not be finished.

While cleaning out her car she discovered the yellowed Los Angeles Times newspaper with the story about Sam Bradford.

Was it the same S. Bradford who had written to Boyd?

According to the article the well-known director and his sister had been killed in a car accident the night before Boyd committed suicide.

Was it a coincidence?

Rita Matthews didn't understand, and she wasn't sure she wanted to.

Boyd's death had definitely been a suicide. The police and the Los Angeles County Coroner's Department had no doubt about that, so what difference would it make if Bradford had written the letters. Obviously Boyd didn't want to hear from the man.

On Saturday she was rummaging through the garage when she came across the shoebox with the letters, again. She held the box to her bosom.

She wasn't ready. She didn't want to start hurting all over again. She had done so well for the past few days, the pain creeping in only when she let herself realize her son wasn't merely away on a long vacation. Rita Matthews returned the box to the shelf and closed the garage.

Soon. Soon she would have to open the box. She knew that.

As days passed her curiosity was getting the better of her, and at night, when she lay awake in bed, she often wondered just what the connection was between Boyd and Sam Bradford. Were they friends? Were they lovers? And was it any of her business?

Her mind imagined all sorts of things.

None of them as explosive as the truth.

Chapter 16
Paris

Valerie could hardly contain her excitement.

"I love it," she blurted almost as soon as the plane touched down at Charle DeGaulle airport.

"I love the hustle, the confusion and the everything. I even love the smell."

Neither of them had ever been to Europe, so even the smallest experience were new and unusual. Even the heightened security and long customs delays di not dampen their enthusiasm.

Val's red hair was limp from the humidity but she was captivated by the Cit of Lights even before exploring it. They had traveled first class, on Air France and Valerie had spent much of the time reading brochures about Paris and it colorful history.

By the time they deplaned she had a notebook full of ideas about places t see, restaurants and side tours they could take if time allowed.

Tiffany's legs were wobbly from sitting for so many hours and her neck wa a little stiff, yet inside she was every bit as excited.

Paris was everything it was supposed to be. Old, enchanting, historic and th natives were more fond of American dollars than Americans.

Friends had warned them about the rudeness of Parisian cab drivers and th general uncleanliness of the city so they were prepared to look past the surfac problems, embrace the country and enjoy their time abroad.

And for two entire days following their landing they behaved more lik wide-eyed schoolgirls than businesswomen. It was as if they tried to inges everything Paris had to offer in one breathtaking gulp.

By the third day they had already visited the Eiffel Tower and marveled a the Arc de Triomphe.

They had also had a brief meeting with Marcel Campeau, head of th International Fashion Design Group that had conceived the show. Within minute they became aware of the amount of preparation that still remained, and wer forced to put their planned side trips to the Grand Palais and Opera on hold.

"You have been informed I trust, that the committee voted unanimously t dedicate the show to the memory of Gianni Versace," Campeau declared in hi best English. "His death was a terrible tragedy. He will certainly be missed."

They both agreed.

"He was brilliant, and extremely charming," Tiffany responded. "I met hir in New York and he was very encouraging to me."

Following their meeting with Campeau they stopped for an espresso at sidewalk café.

"I don't know if we'll have another spare minute," Valerie said when sh looked over the Show's agenda. My God Tiffany, there's just so much to do."

"I know. I thought we had a pretty good handle on things before we left Chicago, but I guess not. But don't panic. We can get it all done and still have time for fun."

"I hope you're right boss."

They were staying at the Lutetia Concorde, a traditional hotel on the Boulevard Raspail on the left bank. It was near Montparnasse in the heart of St. Germain. The hotel was upscale and expensive and they loved it.

Fortunately the Lutetia, with its elegant Louis XIV furnishings, was only a few minutes from the site of the mart, and following their meeting with Campeau, they opted to walk the eight blocks back to the hotel. The journey was not only scenic, it gave them a chance to discuss their plans for the show.

It was to be a multi-national show featuring new designers from Italy, France, England, Australia, Spain and Germany. Tiffany was the lone representative from the United States, a fact that both flattered and frightened her.

On paper it seemed as if their every waking minute would be spent interviewing prospective models, meeting foreign press correspondents and attending the blitz of cocktail parties.

Only once in the first five days did she have time to call Walter, but that one call was a "doozy". It was odd she should refer to her brainstorm as a "doozy" because for the longest time she had no idea of the word's origin. It was one of her Uncle Gene's favorite expressions and he explained that the term was derived from the sporty "Deusenberg" roadster, one of the flashiest and most innovative cars of the 1930s.

The Colossus Party was only two months away and Tiffany had a bizarre inspiration to bounce off Walter and Brian. She knew they would be surprised she was calling again since it had been less than a week since their conference call.

"How are things on the Paris design front?" Brian was sitting at the corner of Walter's desk, trying to speak clearly over the speakerphone's static.

"So far so good," she said excitedly, "but I didn't call to discuss Paris. I've come up with an idea that I think might really add something special to the Colossus Party."

Walter was pleased to hear that she was thinking about the hotel.

"I'm not sure it can be done in time for the party, but if it can, I'd like to see you guys make it happen." The static cleared and Tiffany sounded crisp and close.

"Well, come on young lady, don't keep us in suspense."

"You've both convinced me that this will be THE party of the year, so I thought we'd give it a special touch so people will remember it for a long time."

"I suppose you're about to tell us you want this to be more than just another sock-hop in the gym," Brian kidded.

"You bet," Tiffany said seriously, her delicate voice reverberating off the walls of the executive office. "But just in case it gets boring maybe you can bring some old records and something to spike the punch," she laughed.

It was good to hear her in a lighthearted mood.

"What's the weather going to be like the night of the party?"

"Hot," they answered in stereo.

"No one needs a weatherman to predict the weather in Vegas in July," Brian laughed. "It's usually about 110, even at night. But it won't matter since the party's going to be inside."

"You're not thinking of moving it outdoors, are you?" Walter asked timidly, suddenly wondering if she intended a last minute switch.

"No Walter, but you're on the right track."

"Whatever it is already sounds interesting," Brian joined in.

"It's probably going to be a beautiful summer evening and if they're stuck inside our guests are going to miss it. I thought about moving the whole thing poolside, but that would allow too many uninvited people to snoop on the whole thing."

"Guess you can't have it all Miss Wayne," Brian said formally. He knew Tiffany still had not dropped her bombshell.

"Okay, here goes," she said, taking a deep breath.

"And before either of you starts telling me how much this corny little idea will cost, I want you to find out if it can be done in time for the party. Put cost aside for a minute.

"I want a sliding glass roof installed in the Acropolis Ballroom. The same type roof they use at some sports stadiums. That way guests can enjoy the moonlight and the stars and still be inside and private."

Before either of them could comment she addressed her next question to Brian.

"Does any other hotel have anything like that?"

"Not to my knowledge Tiffany. That's some little brainstorm," he said, duly impressed.

"It's also a very tall order," Walter said solemnly. "I'm not even sure it's possible. And even if it is, I rather doubt something like that could be ready in such a short time.

"Don't be a spoilsport Walter, "Tiffany said pleadingly. "Las Vegas is a twenty-four hour town. If we hire the right construction company and they get enough men on it, it can be done. What do you think Brian?"

"Construction companies here are very competitive," Brian said into the speakerphone. "They'd try and rebuild Rome in six weeks if someone was willing to pay the price. I'm sure we can find one who can meet the deadline. Personally, I think it's definitely doable."

"There you go Walter. Words of wisdom from a man who knows the town."

A minute or two later the conversation was over. Brian and Walter sat staring at each other.

"She sure sounded enthused."

"She did at that," Walter agreed. "Do you really think it can be done Brian?"

"I wouldn't bet against it, Walter. Give me a day or so to get in touch with some friends in the construction business and I'll let you know."

Despite the enormity of the project Walter, realized it was an incredible idea and one that would allow the Colossus to maintain its status as Nevada's leading hotel property. Even the Bellagio, with its authentic Italian décor and Martha Stewart decorated conservatory area and the new Paris Hotel had nothing to compare to Tiffany's roof idea.

Three days later, following Brian's successful meeting with architect Dom Cambeiro, they were able to inform Tiffany that the roof could be built, and on time.

"My friend guaranteed me it would be done by July 1st," Brian beamed.

Walter purposely neglected telling Tiffany that he had personally contributed an additional dimension to her idea. He wanted it to be a surprise.

The sliding roof over the Acropolis Ballroom would be made of reinforced stained glass, giving it a Sistine Chapel look when closed while still allowing the moonlight and sunlight to filter in.

Walter had also overcome his initial shock at the project's hefty six million dollar price-tag. He reasoned if it was done right, and was as spectacular as the architect predicted, the price would soon be forgotten.

The roof issue resolved, Tiffany turned her full attentions back to the business at hand. She had enough on her mind in Paris. Any other Colossus business could wait until her return to the states.

Johnny had called twice, and both times she was out. His message said he'd call back at midnight Paris time and she was there waiting.

"I figured midnight would be a good time to catch you," he said cheerfully.

"How's Paris treating America's most beautiful designer?"

She was happy to hear his voice, and in a way sorry to be away from him. Her body longed to feel his touch and the passions he aroused. It was the first time she had thought about sex in a week.

Valerie was in the bathroom, getting ready for bed so Tiffany made the most of her temporary privacy.

"I miss you," she said simply. "The only way the trip could be better is if you were here," and she could almost feel him through the phone.

The last time they were together was fresh in her memory. Before either of them could say good morning he was on top of her and she buried her face in the softness of his dark brown chest hair. She could feel herself panting and she welcomed him with open arms, passionately smothering him in kisses. They were tender, they were savage, ravishing each other repeatedly more times than she could count.

"Hey, are you still there?" The phone was pressed against her ear, and whatever he had been saying, she had not heard.

"Yes, I'm here," she said loosening her grip on the receiver. "I'm sorry. I was just daydreaming about the last time we were together." She wondered if it had been as memorable for him. Was it ever for a man?

Their conversation was mostly just idle banter. How was the hotel? Had they had time to do any sightseeing? Were there any last minute problems with the show?

Fine. Some. The show was more work than she had imagined and basically they had encountered no major problems.

"I'm glad everything's going smoothly. I hope you're giving your full concentration to your show. Try not to even think about anything else."

She knew he meant the Colossus. Ever since he had learned about her connection with the hotel he had dropped subtle hints that he thought she should let someone else handle it.

"Hotels, especially Las Vegas hotels, are not a business for women," he had said. "Besides, how are we going to spend any time together if you live in Las Vegas?"

"I wouldn't live there in a million years," she had assured him, not appreciating his chauvinistic view. She knew his macho thinking was more a conditioned response than a studied philosophy. Still, she didn't want him thinking that because she was a woman she couldn't handle a large company, even if it was a hotel.

In a flash she brought her rambling thoughts to a halt. She had better things to do, and Johnny was still on the other end of the phone.

"The hotel is the farthest thing from my mind," she said as Val emerged from the bathroom, "Walter can handle everything. All I know is we're working our little tails off and I wish you were here."

"Me too," Johnny said softly.

Tiffany could feel herself blushing, self-conscious about the erotic mental trip from which she had just returned. Hoping Val wouldn't notice, she turned toward the wall and said goodbye, almost inaudibly.

"I guess I know who that was," Val smiled. Her partner had one of the hotel's fluffy white towels wrapped around her wet hair. She already had on her pink nightgown and woolly gym socks. She was dressed for comfort.

"Johnny sends his best. He said he wished he was here."

Val was glad he wasn't. She knew Tiffany had fallen hard and Johnny had never done anything to cause her to dislike him, but she had an odd feeling about him. In truth she had to confess it was pure jealously, because whenever he was around her time with Tiffany was cut short.

The informational packet they had received from Marcel Campeau contained printed list of agencies that supplied runway models, and Val immediately got usy making the necessary calls.

The Tiffany Collection would only require ten models, but the show was just ix days off and they had little time to be choosy. Many of the top girls had been ontracted months in advance or were committed to European designers who had iside connections.

"Try and arrange for the models to come here to the hotel," Tiffany uggested as Val dialed the first number. "It will be informal, and we'll get a feel or the girl and be able to explain the image we're trying to create."

"Do you think we'll need a translator?"

"I don't think so. Most of them speak enough English to communicate. 'hey'd better, or it will be chaos backstage at the show."

Valerie continued dialing and Tiffany made for the door, whispering a "wish 1e luck" as she headed for the lobby to do an interview with Liz Mallon, an .merican correspondent for Women's Wear Daily and the Chicago Tribune.

Mallon was based in Paris and was interviewing Tiffany for an in-depth rofile piece scheduled to run in both publications.

Tiffany knew the value of publicity and decided it wouldn't hurt to have ome additional exposure in the Tribune's Sunday Style Section, especially since 1e story would carry a Paris dateline.

On the phone Liz Mallon sounded friendly and Tiffany's first impression of er was favorable. Tiffany guessed her to be in her late thirties or early forties.

The writer was seated in the lobby, looking a bit ill at ease in a traditional 'rench wingback chair. She had positioned herself directly across from the ntiquated elevators so he could spot Tiffany as she alit.

Liz recognized Tiffany and extended her hand as an introduction.

"Hi. I'm Liz Mallon."

"Is it that obvious I'm an American tourist?" Tiffany laughed.

"Not really," Liz smiled. "I recognize you from your picture in the Fashion ihow press guide."

Liz liked Tiffany immediately. She seemed different from most of the full of hemselves designers she routinely interviewed. Tiffany Wayne didn't appear to ee spoiled, and she certainly didn't come off as prissy or some kind of rrimadonna.

It was easy to write nice things about people who were nice. Tiffany was »pen and cooperative, answering even the few tough questions honestly without vausing to think about how the quotes would look in print.

One day she'll need a public relations department Liz thought, and someone o teach her how to be less candid. I'm not going to take advantage of her but she night not be as lucky with the next journalist.

They strolled along the wide, relaxing paths of the Tuleries Gardens then along the Rue de Palais, stopping to enjoy a croissant and juice in an outdoor café.

Liz Mallon was dressed casually in olive green pants with a beige blouse open at the neck and a sweater tied collegiate style around her neck. Tiffany wore a sleeveless powder blue summer dress with white sandals and matching purse.

The interview concluded in the hour time frame Liz had requested but neither of them wanted it to end. They were oddly attracted to each other and felt strong kinship that made them want the conversation to continue.

They talked about their childhoods, which had been remarkably similar and were amazed to discover that both had attended the same Chicago elementary school, albeit at different times. And despite Liz Mallon's professional demeanor Tiffany could feel a sense of loneliness in the thirty-eight year old writer.

And Liz' reportorial instincts told her that despite all her worldly success Tiffany Wayne had a mountain of pain somewhere deep inside.

Later, they sat on a park bench, and Liz shared a tragic moment from her own life, telling Tiffany of her mother's death from alcoholism. She also confided that the real reason she'd left the states was to put distance between herself and a failed love affair.

Tiffany could feel Liz' pain, and she could feel tears in her own eyes as she revealed her own mother's suicide. She did not discuss her father's recent murder and it was the first time she had talked to anyone but Val about her mother. And while it stirred up the hurt, it felt good to confide in someone who could understand.

She did not have to ask Liz to keep that part of their conversation out of the story. She instinctively knew those intra-personal insights would never appear in print.

Tiffany was also sure Val and Liz would like each other, and they did. For the remainder of the week they were like the Three Musketeers. Inseparable and into everything they could be whenever their workload permitted.

Liz had been a big help on that front too, putting them in contact with the head of one of the agencies that had told Val they had no available models. With Liz' help they recruited some of Paris' most sought after models and the writer also showed them how to bypass much of the red tape which often slowed designers operating in a foreign city.

Liz Mallon was tall, almost 5'10, with lifeless brown hair that hung near her shoulders, framing her long angular face in a haunting Victorian style. She had not bothered much with her personal appearance since leaving Chicago.

She had always been self-conscious about her height and long arms, often slouching and rounding her shoulders to appear shorter. She wore little make-up and made it a habit to wear loose, non-revealing clothes. She was always more relaxed in pants, sweats and jeans. She owned only one evening gown and dragged it out whenever she was forced to attend a formal party.

With Liz' help the show came off beautifully, and *The Tiffany Collection* earned high praise from the international press as well as rival designers.

Val and Liz joined forces to persuade Tiffany to spend an extra day or two in Paris instead of going home as originally scheduled.

It wasn't a hard sell.

On one of the off days they rented a car and traveled to Nice and Monte Carlo. On another they soaked up the sun of the French Riviera, teasing Liz who refused to join the natives and go topless.

Neither Val or Tiffany was brazen enough to walk around uncovered but both unstrapped the top half of their newly purchased bikinis as they lay face down on beach towels. And when they didn't see any men around they turned over, allowing themselves the luxury of an all over tan. That would be something to talk about at home.

Liz used her press influence to reserve a table at Maxim's on their last night, and they celebrated in style. It was Saturday and all three were in a festive mood. The pressures, pleasures and excitement of the ten days in Paris were ending and it would be the last night they would spend together.

Tiffany and Val were scheduled to leave for Chicago early the next morning.

They drank two full bottles of wine, interrupted by frequent toasts, the most touching being Valerie's poignant observation about good friends. And something about how neither miles nor time could dim true friendship. They agreed unanimously and promised to keep in touch.

Each of them genuinely intended to honor the commitment, especially Tiffany, who had formed special bond with Liz. She had not yet seen the article, but knew it would be insightful, and probably touch areas no one had ever explored.

After dinner they strolled back to the hotel, happily chatting and making plans as they covered the two-mile stretch. The air was warm and the lights of Paris were as brilliant as a meteor shower on a starless night.

They walked along the Champs d'Elysee, past the Eiffel Tower and along the banks of the Seine, babbling about everything from the backstage chaos at the fashion show to their planned reunion in Chicago or Paris.

It was after 2 a.m. and the streets were quiet with only an occasional car scooting past. They walked three abreast, next to the river, with Valerie on the inside, Liz in the middle and Tiffany nearest the road.

None of them heard, nor paid attention to the small black Citroen as it raced up behind them. Liz was the first to turn as the vehicle neared and she shrieked as she watched the driver veer directly at them. The car catapulted the small curb onto the bank of the river and was bearing down on them.

Instinctively she pushed Valerie hard in the back, hurtling her to the ground near the river, then used her strength to yank Tiffany away from the road, throwing the three of them into a heap as the car swerved back onto the deserted road and kept going.

Slowly the three women picked themselves up, thankful they weren't injured. Tiffany had broken a heel and Val had a small bruise on the side of her now muddied face.

"Damned maniac," Valerie screamed at the long gone driver.

Tiffany was more poised.

"I guess he had a little more to drink than we did," she said trying to keep the mood light. "And you guys think American drivers are bad?"

"Why didn't he stop to see if we were okay?" Valerie asked absently.

The street was silent and for a moment they embraced, holding each other tightly. Their collective thoughts were of the near accident, the fragility of life and how near they had come to seeing their new friendship disintegrate before ever really starting.

Liz brushed off the front of her jacket and looked long and hard down the empty road. She was positive the incident was not an accident. She had looked directly at the driver a split second before and she knew he was not out of control. She also knew he had not intended to kill them. So what was the purpose?

The only one of them really at risk was Tiffany. She had been closest to the road and to the car. She and Valerie would only have been in serious danger had the driver actually been drunk or out of control.

Liz did not want to worry her friends. She would check it out on her own.

In the morning, Valerie and Tiffany were packed and ready when Liz Mallon arrived to take them to the airport. She had insisted on giving them a ride, and both girls were happy to see their friend one last time before leaving Paris.

It was a triumphant return to Chicago for the "new darlings of American design" as one story said, and any thought of the mishap in Paris was quickly forgotten in the rush of their frenetic schedule.

But Liz Mallon had not forgotten. The reporter in her wouldn't let it go.

Tom Felton wasn't in the Chicago Tribune office when she first called and she was out when he returned her call. It was sometimes difficult making connections because of the time difference, but Liz was determined to keep trying. She'd catch him at home.

Chicago was seven hours behind France so she waited until 6 a.m. to call again. It was 11 p.m. and Tom was watching the local news.

"To what do I owe the honor Mademoiselle Mallon," Tom said jestfully. For her sake he was trying to keep the conversation on an informal and unemotional basis.

It had been hard for her to call and they both knew it. There was so much history.

He was the reason she had left Chicago. When their relationship hit the rocks she had come apart, and felt a major change of scenery might be the best solution. Two years had passed, and she still harbored a sense of failure, but now she needed his help.

Felton was a senior editor at the Tribune and one of the most respected journalists in the city. He had come up through the ranks, starting as a beat reporter and advancing to the highly visible post of reporting on organized crime in Chicago. He was rewarded with a Pulitzer for a six-part series that had fingered more than 25 mobsters, resulting in six of them getting prison time. None had stayed in very long but his investigative work earned him respect from his peers and the coveted Editor's post. Now he mostly kept his finger on the pulse of everything political.

"Tiffany Wayne," Liz said just tossing the name in the ring. "Does the name mean anything to you?"

"Up and coming fashion designer," he replied. "You profiled her in Sunday's features section. Seems like a nice girl with everything going for her."

"That's the way I see it too," Liz said thoughtfully, "which is exactly why I'm wondering why someone would want to kill her. Or frighten her half to death."

In the next few minutes Liz explained what had happened and her suspicion that the near miss was not an accident.

"I'd like you to do me a favor and check her out," Liz asked. "See if you can find a reason why anyone would want to harm her. She's a nice kid and I like her, but I get the feeling there's a huge black cloud hanging over her head and she has no clue it's there. I don't want to see her get hurt."

"Give me a little time and I'll get back to you with all the news and views fit or unfit for print."

There was still a tension between them. Distance had not changed that.

"Thanks Tom," she said awkwardly. She purposely didn't ask how he was. She didn't want to get into it, and she was glad he didn't ask about her. They both still cared.

"Get back to me as soon as you can."

It was four days before he called and she immediately sensed something disturbing in his voice even though he tried to keep his tone very even.

He was friendlier now and it made the situation easier.

"You know of course that this will cost you dinner next time you're in Chicago," he began. He was only half teasing, and neither of them knew if it would be a good idea, but at least the suggestion was out there. Liz was relieved Tom had made the first move.

"Sounds fair to me," she answered quickly. "Did you come up with anything interesting?"

"How well do you know your Miss Wayne? he asked.

Tom's voice was low and his attitude turned serious. Tom Felton never joked when he was discussing business.

Liz was silent, fearful even. Did Tiffany have some deep dark secret?

"Just met her but I thought I had a pretty good idea of who she was during the time I spent with her," Liz said defensively. "I don't know. You tell me."

"Seems Tiffany Wayne is a lot more than she seems," Tom began. She's bright, clean cut, graduated from a top school and has no bad habits from what I can tell. She's divorced and has no kids." It sounded like he was reading from a crib sheet.

"So far she sounds pretty normal," Liz prodded. "She told me that she lost her father recently, and that her mother committed suicide a few years ago."

"Both of those things are true," Tom confirmed. "She should also have mentioned rich, as in obscenely wealthy," Tom added. "As in just inherited a possible billion dollar fortune along with Las Vegas casino called The Colossus. And by the way, her father didn't just die. He was murdered. Just a few weeks ago, and as of yesterday Las Vegas police had made no arrests."

Liz was speechless.

Tiffany had not mentioned the casino, nor how her father had died, and those weren't the kind of things one just overlooked. Maybe she had read the girl all wrong.

"Okay. Give me between the lines," she said into the phone.

"My sources think her father could have been a mob hit."

Tom Felton didn't let Liz' silence interrupt his thoughts.

"It's hard to break into Vegas without making some concessions or stepping on some toes Lizzie." *He had not called her that in a long time.* "The casino business is like politics. Along the way you have to make choices, and sometimes you make deals with the devil."

"Are you saying Forrester was a hood, or some sort of made guy?"

"I'm not saying anything yet. It's too early to draw conclusions. But let's not be naïve. It's possible he was the 'clean shirt' that someone needed to get licensed and that the bad guys were the money. I don't know. Those type arrangements are made all the time."

"Then eventually Mr. Clean Shirt becomes expendable. Am I understanding this correctly?"

"You are," he said. "Remember, a lot of people wanted his casino and most of them aren't the type you'd invite to the opera, if you know what I mean."

"Do you think Tiffany knows about any of this?" she asked.

"Do you?"

"Truthfully I don't think so, unless she's the greatest actress this side of Meryl Streep. I spent days with the woman…if she's a mobster's daughter I'm the Queen of England."

"Maybe she's just naive, and I don't know yet whether she is or not, but if she is, your designer friend could be in for a very rough ride because the cast of characters in this movie know how to play hardball."

Liz could sense that Tom was withholding something, maybe because he wasn't positive of the facts yet, but it didn't matter. She'd have to find out on her own what Tiffany knew, and then pump Tom to fill in the blanks.

"I'll check further and get back to you when I have more." Tom didn't know Tiffany and had no opinion yet. To him she was only a name and a picture in a file. The information he had passed on to Liz was a compilation of stuff he'd gotten from the society editor, the business editor and the man now in charge of the organized crime watch.

Liz thought of a hundred reasons to call Tiffany, from just wanting to chat, to asking if she had read the piece in the paper. Every reason seemed contrived, and she was sure Tiffany would see them for what they were, pretenses to pry into her private life and it would upset their new friendship.

It bothered her that Tiffany had not mentioned the murder or the casino. She had to find out why the young designer had been so evasive.

Her reason to call surfaced a few days later, when an engraved card appeared her mailbox:

Liz,

Paris could not possibly have been so wonderful without you. I consider you special friend and so does Val. Please write or call when you can. Both of us look forward to seeing you whenever you return "home" to Chicago. You'll stay my place of course. And many thanks for all the kind words in your article. My friends are all impressed. So am I.

                                                           Love,
                                                           Tiffany

S. If you can take your vacation in early July I'm throwing a party at the Colossus Hotel in Las Vegas. I promise it will be fun and it will be even better if you're there. Please try."

Liz studied the note. It gave her the perfect opening. She had to learn more about Tiffany's friends and find out who would want to hurt her and why. And being there in person meant she could give Tom some firsthand information.

Getting the time off wouldn't be a problem. In two years she had never taken vacation, being satisfied to steal an extra day here and there whenever the job took her to interesting parts of Europe. It made for a nice perk.

She waited until the following Friday to call, and was surprised to get Tiffany instead of her answering machine.

"Wow. I didn't think there was much chance you'd be home on a Friday evening," she gushed. "I was very happy to get your note and to know that you still remember who I am."

Tiffany recognized Liz' husky voice with the first words.

"Did you think I'd forget the famous writer I met in Paris," she teased. "Are you here in Chicago?"

"Not yet my dear, but I expect I'll be there before too long."

"That's great. I'm really glad you called Liz. I've thought about you a lot since getting home." They rambled on about nothing for a couple minutes before Liz confirmed that she'd do everything she could to make arrangements to attend the Colossus party.

"By the way, why didn't you tell me you owned the Colossus?" Liz asked hoping to get a reaction. When Tiffany didn't take the bait she pressed a little harder.

"That's not the sort of thing a girl forgets you know?"

"I'm sorry I didn't bring it up," Tiffany apologized, "but I wanted to try and keep my fashion career separate from the casino thing. Besides, it's not like I bought the place. I inherited it and I will probably be selling it as soon as my lawyer finds a suitable buyer. I hope you're not upset. I didn't mean for it to be a big secret."

"No big deal," Liz said backing down. "I was just surprised when my editor asked why I hadn't mentioned it in the article. Anyway, I hope this means I'll get a good rate on my room."

"I'll talk to the boss," Tiffany teased. "You never know Ms. Mallon, I might even be able to pull enough strings to get you a room with a view of something other than the parking lot."

Liz laughed.

"Please try and do that." Liz seized the opportunity to inject a serious note in the conversation.

"Tiff, please be careful. Las Vegas can be a very tough town."

"Stop being a mother hen," she scolded. "That sounds an awful lot like the advice I got from a certain man right here in Chicago. You haven't by chance been talking to Johnny Marciano, have you?

"Anyway, I'm not running the hotel by myself. As I said, my lawyer, Walter Thurston is temporarily in charge of everything and I trust him with my life."

Liz hoped it wouldn't come to that but she had some ominous feelings.

"Just be careful," she ordered.

"I will, and thanks for caring."

"See you at the party," Liz said hanging up.

Late that night, as she lay in bed with Johnny, she related the conversation.

"She seemed so worried. It seems she's convinced someone's out to get me and take the Colossus. Wasn't one murder enough? I just can't understand why the hotel's so damned important."

"Money darling. Nothing but money. It's always about money."

"Do you think Liz knows something she's not telling me?"

"I doubt it," Johnny said sleepily.

Initially he had been surprised, perhaps even dumbfounded to discover that the Tiffany Wayne he was seeing was the Forrester heir he was reading about in the papers.

The first news accounts were just stories, with no pictures, so he didn't make the association. Almost every story in the Tribune, Sun-Times and USA Today focused more on Adam Forrester's murder than his prodigal daughter.

"Why didn't you tell me what was going on?" he had said angrily after seeing her picture in the paper. "If we're so close how could you not confide in me?"

"At the time it wasn't important," she said. "When we first met I wasn't speaking to my father. He was virtually out of my life. I hadn't talked to him in five years. He was killed the night of the Friends Ball. You and I hadn't even spoken yet, or gone out. Then things happened so fast. Maybe I was trying to bury it all inside.

"I know I didn't want it to interfere with what we had started. Then when the whole thing happened with the will everything got crazy. I certainly didn't expect for him to leave me the damn hotel." She was sobbing.

She came very near saying, "and that was all before I fell in love with you" but didn't, and the moment passed.

Johnny held her close but she started talking again before he could speak.

"My father's lawyer and best friend, Walter Thurston has been kind enough to help me and take charge of things. He's been wonderful, and in the end I'm sure he'll give me sound advice as to the right time to sell the hotel, and to whom. I didn't want to bother you with any of this. I know you have enough things on your mind."

The truth was she thought Johnny had put it all together as soon as it happened, and when he didn't mention it, she assumed he wanted to stay out of it completely.

"We know something has to be done," she continued. "Walter's got a law practice here in Chicago and I have a life to live."

"I'm really sorry about your father." It was the first thing he was able to squeeze into the conversation.

"Thank you."

She was determined not to let the Colossus come between them, which was another reason she downplayed her involvement.

Still, an uneasiness had developed, and it had crept in to their comfort zone. He had never come right out and suggested she sell the Colossus, but he didn't have to. It was obvious he didn't want her to have anything to do with it, and he was always a bit edgy when she discussed hotel business.

They continued living, loving and doing the things they ordinarily did but both of them realized something had changed.

Twice she had told him harmless little lies about phone calls, pretending they were design business when in fact she had been talking to Walter about something to do with the Colossus. It was a no-win situation for him. Maybe for both of them.

Reluctantly, Johnny had agreed to attend the Colossus party.

"I'll come, but just as a favor to you," he acquiesced. "The truth is I really don't like Vegas."

She couldn't blame him for that, but she found his excuse incongruous considering she had phoned his office on two occasions in the past six weeks and been informed he was in Atlantic City for the day.

When she asked him about it he sloughed it off, saying he had gone on business. The explanation seemed contrived, and she wondered if he might be seeing someone else. Perhaps Jennifer again?

Anyway, with the Paris show over, and the new line completed she could concentrate on the party. There was no doubt she was looking forward to it, especially since learning that Liz Mallon would be coming.

They didn't sleep well and neither was disappointed when Johnny was called to his office to handle some overdue paperwork.

"I'll check with you later to see how you're feeling."

"Okay. I'll be here. I'm going to take a hot bath, read and catch up on some rest." Their kiss and subsequent hug were more patronizing than genuine.

She unplugged the phone, drew a bath, and then soaked long and luxuriously in the steaming water, trying unsuccessfully to shut out the world. Her most pressing concern was locating the soap that was hiding somewhere under a million white bubbles.

By ten she had read the paper, done some laundry, dusted and washed her hair. It was truly going to be a lazy day.

She was curled up on the sofa watching a "Frasier" rerun when the intercom buzzed.

It was George the doorman.

"Miss Wayne?"

"Yes George."

"A Federal Express just arrived for you. Shall I bring it up?"

It was from Walter. Probably more papers to sign. She laid the unopened package on the dining room table determined not to open it until Monday, or at east sometime Sunday. She didn't want any business, especially any Colossus business to interfere with her Saturday.

She managed to ignore it the rest of the day.

Johnny called at six thirty to see if she wanted dinner.

"I'm going to pass if you don't mind," she said, hoping he wouldn't be angry. "I have a slight headache and I don't feel like going out. I think I'll turn in early."

He didn't protest.

"Sleep well sweetheart. I'll call you in the morning."

She lay in bed and watched part of the Cubs game while reading.

It was a little after 10 o'clock when the game ended. Sammy Sosa had hit two homers and the Cubs predictably lost anyway. She had been a Cubs fan since she was a little girl, having gone to games at Wrigley Field regularly with her dad.

Tiffany went into the kitchen to fix some tea and the familiar blue and orange FedEx logo seemed to beckon. It wasn't very thick, and while she waited for the water to boil she picked it up and read the information label.

Walter had addressed it himself. He didn't do that very often. When the labels were typed the contents were normally business documents he had entrusted to a secretary.

She was about to open the envelope when the whistle of the teapot intervened. She set the package back on the table and prepared the tea.

Her curiosity subsided and she made her way back to bed, tea in hand.

Half an hour later she was up, seated at the kitchen table ripping the perforated cardboard strip off the Federal Express letter.

There was a short handwritten note from Walter.

"Tiffany,

I know this is going to come as something of a surprise, but enclosed is a personal letter to you, from your father. His lawyer retrieved it yesterday from a private safe deposit box your dad kept at a local Nevada State Bank. The rent came due on the box and someone called the Colossus executive offices to see if we still wanted to maintain the box. The only other things in the box were a few old coins, his army discharge papers and a picture of your mother.

I hope there is nothing upsetting in the letter. It was sealed so I did not think it appropriate for me to open it. I think he wanted it to be for your eyes only. Call if you need me."

Love,
Walter

Her hands were shaking.

She turned the letter over a dozen times, her eyes boring in on the inscription.

It was addressed to "My Daughter, Tiffany Forrester", with "Personal" and "Confidential" in bold block letters on both the front and back. In addition to sealing it, he had put small strips of scotch tape to secure it shut.

Tiffany propped the envelope against a vase on the table and eyed it as if it were a visitor from another galaxy. What could he be telling her from the grave? It was eerie.

She procrastinated, finding every reason to delay, then rummaged slowly through her small desk in search of a letter opener.

Finally she unsealed the package.

"My Darling Tiffany,

If you are reading this it is because I am gone. You are probably wondering why I left you the Colossus and the bulk of my estate. I want you to know I never stopped loving you and I am deeply sorry for the hurt I caused you. I carry the burden of your mother's death to my grave and hope that someday you can forgive me for something for which I never forgave myself.

The tone of the letter was somber but Tiffany was not saddened. It soothed her to know her father had regrets about having left her mother, and even though he did not say so, she could feel he never stopped loving either of them.

She continued reading.

"I know having to deal with the Colossus is going to put a tremendous strain on you, and many people will speculate as to why I didn't leave it to Diana who already knows a great deal about the casino business.

I believe Diana loved me, but I also know she was having an affair. I don't know with whom.

"I'm sure you have enlisted Walter's help and I urge you to rely on him implicitly. My death was no accident, and if I had to make a guess I'd bet it was set-up by someone from New York or Chicago. They probably figured I'd leave everything to Diana and they'd strongarm her into selling.

But none of that is important now. Do not let it cloud your judgement. Diana no doubt realizes by the terms of my will that I discovered her indiscretion. Keeping the hotel from her is probably the greatest punishment she could ever suffer for her betrayal.

I'd like to see you maintain control of the Colossus until a reputable buyer surfaces. Tiffany, I am not sure who masterminded this coup. Something in my gut tells me it is someone who knows me well. Someone I'd never expect or suspect, so be very careful who you trust.

I'm sure you'll do the right thing, and with your flair for fashion, you'll be able to put your own special mark on the Colossus. I'd like that.

I'll always love you.

Daddy

Now she was trembling. Her father had known he was in danger. She felt scared, and vengeful. The emotions that had overwhelmed her the night she learned of his murder swept over her again, only this time she did not cry.

He was wrong about one thing though. Taking the Colossus from Diana was not punishment enough. She deserved more pain for taking her father away and then betraying him. And she wanted to know who Diana's lover was. He should pay too.

A million possibilities flooded her brain.

How much did Diana know? Did she and her lover have anything to do with her father's murder? **Murder**...the word came so easily to her now. It had six letters but every time she uttered it she felt dirty, as if she had just spat out a four-letter street vulgarity. Saying it made her feel strangely violated.

She and her dad were on the same side again and it felt good. Now more than ever she would do everything in her power to find out who killed him.

And she would operate with one simple by-law...*Trust No One.*

Chapter 17
Body of Evidence

It was a bright Saturday in June, and the humidity was as much a part of the day as the warm Michigan sun.

Rita Matthews had awakened early, as usual. She seldom stayed up very late but even on the rare occasions she did her body clock seemed to tap her on the shoulder about 6:30 a.m. She hadn't used an alarm in over 15 years.

She was going to the annual telephone company picnic, along with Ruth and Angelo, and she was in the garage looking for her old picnic basket.

The basket, wrapped in heavy plastic to discourage spiders and other insect from taking up residence was at the far end of her late husband's old workbench. Above the basket, on a ply board shelf was the box with Boyd's letters. She had thought of them often during the month following his death, but had managed to push them out of her thoughts for the past few weeks.

Now she was face to face with them again. She remembered how close she had come to opening them that one afternoon when she held the box to her bosom.

It was only 8:15, and they weren't due to leave for the picnic until ten. There was time. But was she finally ready?

She stretched her five-foot three-inch frame and extended both arms. She pulled the box with her fingertips and it tumbled off the shelf, raising wisps of dust as it slipped through her hands, landing on the counter.

She untied the soft twine that circled the box and stood there for what seemed like an eternity staring at the assorted envelopes.

There was light from the side door through which she had entered the garage and a steady stream of sunlight from the little window directly above the workbench.

She picked up the most recent letter, the one postmarked the day before Boyd had died, then put it back. Reading that one first might be confusing. She would start with the earliest letter to get a better understanding of the sequence of events.

It was dated almost a year before the final letter.

She pulled a note from the already open envelope.

Dear Boyd,

I know you are hurt. I am too. Words can never express how sorry I am. I don't expect you to understand but it has to be this way. I cannot see you again.

Our friendship will always be something I cherish.

Sam

Is that what it was all about, a quarrel between Boyd and an ex-lover? So Mr. Hollywood director was gay too. Who cares? Weren't they all like that out there?

She slid the letter back in the envelope, wondering if it was necessary to open the others.

The next one was postmarked a month after the first. It was very similar and had also been opened.

Boyd,

I received your note. Thanks for being thoughtful enough to put it on my car instead of sending it to the office. Much of my mail here is opened before I ever see it.

I suppose more than anything else I'm confused by my feelings for you. I care about you and very much enjoyed your company, but I am convinced I am not gay. I went through a very difficult period, and I reached out. You were there, and I appreciate it.

But it is meaningless for you to wait for me. Things will never be like they were.

Be strong enough to put your feelings for me aside. Please move on with your life.

Sam

How ironic. Move on with your life.

Rita wanted to blame Sam Bradford for her son's death but couldn't. Boyd had obviously read the letter and knew Sam had no intention of renewing their affair. She hated that word. The letter was dated five months before Boyd's "accident". She couldn't blame Sam's letter. It had to have been something else.

There was no reason to read the others. She left the box on the counter, grabbed the picnic basket and went back into the house.

In the kitchen she cried as she packed the basket. She disapproved of her son's lifestyle but felt sorry he could not have the love he had ached for.

The picnic was pleasant, the weather perfect and she, Ruth and Angelo were among the last to leave. She had enjoyed the outing, especially the folk/blues music of a group called the Subterraneans.

They played mostly original songs written by the lead singer, a seemingly laid back little man with a scraggly beard and a well-worn black beret. The picnic provided a pleasant diversion from Boyd, Sam Bradford and the letters.

A hot shower and a cup of warm milk were the highlights of the remainder of her evening. By eleven she was sound asleep.

It was 2:30 a.m. when she awoke. Her throat was dry and she felt coldness in her bones despite the down comforter covering her shoulders. She had experienced a rare nightmare. She could not recall having one since she was a little girl, when she had dreamed her parents were killed in a car accident.

Rita Matthews turned on the bedside lamp, pulled herself up to a sitting position and sat perched on the side of the bed, her legs dangling, her feet barely touching the floor. She was trying to remember her dream but couldn't bring it back.

Moments before it had been so real. Real enough to jolt her awake. She pushed her left arm through the sleeve of her robe, stepped into her slippers and made her way to the kitchen. She felt a little disoriented, unaccustomed to being awake in the middle of the night.

A little more hot milk. She turned the knob to medium high and was watching the milk heat when it came back to her. The letters. She wanted to read the last one. Maybe it could explain what had thrown Boyd into a state of desperation and caused him to go over the edge. Maybe she could blame Sam Bradford after all.

Rita Matthews stared out the kitchen window into the darkness, her gaze focused on the garage. In the morning she would retrieve the box and read the final note. Then, and only then would she be able to rest.

Before the milk finished boiling she knew she could not wait. She turned the flame off and dashed out into the night.

She felt like a teenager on a dare as she walked briskly toward the garage, a dim uncovered 75-watt bulb lighting the side-door entrance. She had never realized how weak the bulb was, and in the blackness of night it seemed more like a candle.

The box was where she had left it, and there was no hesitation in her stride as she made her way around the Oldsmobile to the workbench.

In one motion she scooped up the box, put it under her arm and turned to retrace her steps. Her heart was racing as she walked the dozen or so yards back to the house. The cool night air had no affect on her. Rita Matthews was sweating profusely.

She gently set the box on the cherry wood dining table that was covered by an off-white, hand crocheted tablecloth that had originally belonged to her mother.

The strong smell of dried milk emanated from the kitchen and sent an unpleasant odor through the small house. She'd need to air it out in the morning. It didn't matter about the milk. She no longer needed anything to help her sleep. She didn't want to go back to bed. Not yet anyway.

Her runaway emotions told her to grab the envelope, rip it open and be done with it. Instead she picked it up slowly and cautiously slid her finger across the top, opening it neatly.

It was not what she expected.

It was not another plea from Sam Bradford for forgiveness, nor some rambling personal love letter.

As she read it she shivered. Its contents were colder than the night air and more frightening than her worst nightmare.

"Dear Boyd,

This is a very tense and troubling time for me. By sending this information to you I may be asking you to become involved in things that I no longer have the right to ask, but there is no one else I can trust.

Please understand, the information contained in this letter is literally my life insurance policy. I am hoping it can somehow protect me from some very dangerous people who are so angry over what I am about to do with this movie that they may try and kill me.

I am being blackmailed and I am fighting back. Boyd, I do not mean to sound dramatic, but if something strange should happen to me you must come forward and get this letter to the right people."

Rita Matthews didn't want to read any more. What was she getting herself into? Boyd was dead, as was Sam Bradford, so there was no reason to get in deeper.

But she couldn't help herself and her eyes flew back to the page, hungry to read the typed words.

In the next paragraphs Sam explained the blackmail, and how he had been forced to use Sonny Fremont in "Morocco Heat" and how Oscar Bento had somehow gotten his hands on sex pictures of the two of them.

"I don't know where he got them Boyd. Do you?"

Boyd would never be able to answer.

There was more.

"I didn't send this letter to my sister for two reasons. First, it would have been too obvious since Laura is my closest relative. Secondly, no matter how much I'd swear her to secrecy if she felt I was in danger she'd tell her ex-husband, Brian Powers. He's a private consultant in Las Vegas, and he'd jump into this with both feet.

I don't want what happened between us to wind up in some sleazy tabloid.

I've done some snooping on my own, contacted some friends in Chicago and have kept a journal detailing the threats and visits these thugs have made. And now I think I have a lot more information than they realize.

Maybe not enough to convict them, but enough to make their names public, and for them that would be almost as bad.

You've heard me mention Mario Torino. He is the most visible, and it appears he is the new boss of Chicago, but my sources tell me the real power is his cousin. Unfortunately I don't know his cousin's identity but I may have a lead on him.

Once, when Mario and a bodyguard came to my office to shake me down he had to make an outside call. He didn't want to use the office phone so he picked up what he thought was his pal's cell phone. What he didn't know is the phone was mine. It was identical to his friend's.

The other man was busy pouring a drink and didn't notice the mistake.

Later I tried to retrieve the number from my caller list but could only make out part of the number. The prefix is 312. The partial number is 543-16?? If it becomes necessary you can have the cops try and get the last two digits.

I also believe they murdered or ordered the murder of some Vegas casino guy named Forrester.

Torino tossed a newspaper on my desk with a story about Forrester.

He said, "It's a shame what happened to that guy. Murdered like that. And the cops have no clues. What a tragedy." His meaning was clear.

A week or so later Torino asked me for a favor. He wanted me to give a friend of his a few minutes. Said the guy needed advice for a client. I figured what the hell. Maybe if I did it they'd back off a little. His friend was a schlocky little agent named Oscar Bento.

Oscar offered to forgive the half million I owed and also give me the actual negatives in exchange for me casting Sonny Fremont as the lead in Morocco Heat.

I agreed, of course, but now that I'm reneging on that deal I don't know what they'll do.

The mention of murder made Rita's face go white. Sam and Boyd were no longer in danger but whoever had Sam's letter was definitely at risk.

She was safe as long as no one knew she had it.

The next three pages were full of names, dates and places Rita Matthews had never heard before and she imagined all the evil things they had probably done. Just seeing the names made her feel threatened.

She didn't need a detective to know that Boyd's death wasn't suspicious. The mob hadn't killed him. If they had they would have taken the box of letters.

There was no getting around it. Boyd had committed suicide and she had to live with it. But why? He hadn't even opened Sam's last letter. If he had, he certainly wouldn't have taken his own life. He would have been encouraged that Sam was reaching out to him.

I'm not going to do anything, she reasoned. Nothing I can do will bring my son back to life. And I don't want to have these people coming after me.

A week passed before she changed her mind.

I have to do it. For Boyd. Boyd would have wanted to help Sam. This way he can do it from the grave. And I can help.

She reread the final letter again, searching for a name. Someone to call. Someone who could help.

Like a startled alley cat, it jumped out at her.

Brian Powers. Sam Bradford's brother-in-law. The letter said he was a consultant in Las Vegas. He'd know what to do.

Contacting him proved to be anything but easy.

She started by calling Warner Bros., Sam Bradford's former studio. In enty plus years with the phone company Rita Matthews had learned a few cks about getting information.

She asked to speak to Sam Bradford's former secretary. Her name was Traci d she had been transferred to film distribution.

"Foreign film distribution. This is Traci." The voice was smooth.

"My name is Jill Parker," she said sweetly. "Lisa in public relations thought u might be able to help me..." She had called the PR department a few nutes before and been referred to a Lisa who was out for the afternoon.

"What can I do for you Miss Parker?" The woman was more inclined to give r the information she needed because of their mutual "friend" Lisa.

"Well, years ago Sam Bradford and I went to school together and I just cently learned of his passing. I would like to send a sympathy card to the mily and it's my understanding someone named Brian Powers handled the rangements." She was guessing.

"Do you have any idea how I can reach Mr. Powers?"

"I really don't," Traci said quickly. "I believe he was Mr. Bradford's former other-in-law, but I don't have a number or address for him."

Rita was not discouraged.

"Maybe I'll just send it to the funeral home,' she offered. "I'm sure they'll rward it to Mr. Powers."

"That might be the best idea," said the secretary, happy to be done with the ll.

But Rita wasn't.

"Was that Forest Lawn?" she asked, sounding familiar with the name she eard on television anytime a Hollywood celebrity died.

"Yes Forest Lawn, in Burbank."

"Thanks. I'll send it there. You've been a big help."

A minute later she had gotten the number from information and was dialing e mortuary.

"Forest Lawn," a woman's voice answered.

"Hello," she said softly. "Could you tell me the name of your funeral irector?"

"That would be Mr. Peterson. Would you like to speak to him?"

"Yes please."

The man's tone was reserved, his baritone voice a mere whisper, as if he ere talking in church. Rita decided to maintain her alias.

"My name is Jill Parker," she began.

"And how may I be of service Miss Parker?"

"I'm a life-long friend of Laura Powers"...she waited to see if the man ecognized Laura's name.

"I see..."

"Well, after the funeral I realized I still had some personal things of hers tha I believe her family might appreciate having returned. I thought her ex-husban might like to have them."

The man had not interrupted so she plunged ahead.

"I started looking for Mr.Powers' number and I can't find it anywhere. W seem to have lost touch. And I'm afraid to send the things to Laura's old addres for fear they might be lost.

"Mr. Bradford's secretary, Traci, at Warner Brothers suggested I call you t get Brian's number or address." She made it sound as if he should give her th information without hesitation. Her voice was self-assured and she knew her so assertiveness left little room for argument. Polite but confident.

"I don't know Miss Parker," the Funeral Director said slowly. "I'm not sure can give you Mr. Powers' number, even if I have it."

She didn't respond, and Rita knew whomever spoke next was the perso guaranteed to concede. She'd learned that in a paperback called, "How t Negotiate Anything and Win."

Seconds passed.

"I suppose I could give you his address," said the deep voice, giving i "After all, you're only sending him something in the mail. Is that right?" He wa trying to justify his decision.

"That's right Mr. Peterson. Just a package in the mail. The address will b enough. You're very kind."

Even with Brian's address and her phone company contacts it took three cal before a Las Vegas Sprint supervisor came through with Brian Powers' unliste number.

"Hi. This is Brian. I'm not in right now but if you leave your name an number I'll return your call as soon as I get in."

Rita was about to hang up, then heard the last part of the message.

"If this is an emergency you can reach me through the executive offices c the Colossus Hotel."

Jackpot.

Chapter 18
Appointment in Chicago

Reaching Brian Powers still turned out to be quite a challenge.

He was in a meeting when she first tried, and was "off property" when she called back.

"Do you know if he's going to be back today?"

"I'm not sure," the operator replied. "Mr. Powers doesn't keep regular office hours. He's really not in the hotel very often."

Rita was unsure about leaving a message. Leaving her name and number might not be enough to get him to return her call, and she had already told the receptionist the call was personal.

"Mr. Powers does pick up his messages every few hours," the operator said trying to be helpful.

"Thank you. No message. I'll just call back." She was about to hang up when the operator spoke.

"Miss, it really might be better to leave your name and number. I'm sure Mr. Powers will return your call if you leave your number."

She wondered whether she should leave her real name or the pseudonym she was using to protect her identity. She decided to remain consistent.

"Please tell him Ms. Jill Parker from Michigan is trying to get in touch with him and that it's urgent he return my call." She left her name and number, then added, "tell him this is a personal call regarding Sam Bradford." She hoped the mention of his ex-brother in law's name would at least get Brian's attention.

Brian sat back in his chair staring at the pink memo, not knowing whether to crumple it into a ball and bounce it into his trash can or call back and spend part of the afternoon rehashing painful memories.

Why would a woman in Grand Rapids Michigan know anything about Sam Bradford, and how had she tracked him down at the Colossus?

He was quite sure he didn't know her? He'd never even heard her name. Maybe she was a friend of Sam's or Laura's. Probably not Laura's or the woman would have mentioned her instead of Sam.

Twice he picked up the phone to return her call, both times hanging up before he finished dialing the number.

I've got to think this through. I need to be prepared for whatever's coming. For whatever Jill Parker has to throw at me. His mind played out a number of different possibilities.

...Jill Parker was a bimbo who had an affair with Sam. Maybe she'd claim she had a child and wanted child support, or worse yet, a piece of his estate.

...Perhaps she was just a friend wanting to express her condolences.

Then his imagination went into overdrive.

...Maybe Jill Parker was a witness to the accident, or even better maybe she was the one driving the blue pickup and wanted to confess. Maybe, maybe, maybe...

He tried her number.

No answer.

He'd try again tomorrow. It would give him more time to think of other possibilities.

He'd call in the afternoon since Michigan was on Eastern Time, three hours ahead. If Jill Parker worked days he'd catch her in the evening.

Brian could feel the anxiety building.

It was 4:30 the next afternoon before he had an opportunity to try again. His day had been spent dealing with the real estate company handling the sale of Laura's house, and a representative from Mutual of Omaha who had to verify a thousand details before authorizing payment on Sam's life insurance policy. By the time he had a spare minute most of the day had slipped by.

The phone was answered on the third ring.

"Hello."

"Miss Parker? Miss Jill Parker?" Rita almost blew her cover, hesitating for a moment to slip back into the Jill Parker role.

"Yes, this is Jill Parker," she said casually, recapturing the personna. "Who's calling?" She already knew.

"My name is Brian Powers. I'm returning your call about Sam Bradford."

"He was your brother in law wasn't he?" Rita asked, wanting to be sure she had the right Brian Powers.

"Yes he was, Brian said losing patience. "Did you know him?"

He was anxious to put it together. It was a key question and her answer would tell him right away whether the lady was a source or a sorceress. He hoped she was the former.

"No, I didn't now Mr. Bradford," Jill answered honestly. She wanted to add more but thought it might be better to take things slowly.

Brian's spirits fell, then just as quickly lifted again as he theorized that she could have witnessed or been part of the accident and still not know Sam. But if that was true why hadn't she called the Highway Patrol?

"Do you know anything about his death Miss Parker?" Brian's tone was hopeful, but there was stress in his voice.

"Not first hand," she said, feeling pressured.

Brian's mood was changing. He had no patience for games, and who was this woman anyway. He forced himself to be polite a little longer, opting to give Ms. Jill Parker the benefit of the doubt.

"I am in possession of some information, a letter actually, that I think you might want to have, "Jill Parker continued. "I believe it will tell you a lot about your brother-in-law's death.

Great. A fucking extortionist.

Brian jumped to what seemed like an obvious conclusion.

"How did you get this letter, and how much do you want for it?" His tone was sarcastic and angry.

Rita sensed Brian's growing hostility. She wanted to calm him down, and hoped she could give him the information without revealing the true link between her son and Sam Bradford.

"You don't understand, "she said a little flustered. "I'm not trying to sell you information. My son Boyd and your brother in law were friends. Special friends."

Rita knew she was being evasive.

"That's fine Miss Parker, and I appreciate your interest. But my brother-in-law and my ex-wife were killed in an auto accident on the San Diego freeway. They have already been buried and this is not an easy time for me.

"Unless you were a witness, or know someone who was a witness to the accident I'm afraid you can't be much help. I thank you for your interest though."

Brian was no longer paying attention. His intercom was buzzing and the second line was blinking with someone on hold.

"My son and your brother in law were lovers," Rita blurted before Brian could hang up. "I think the information I have could also prove that Sam Bradford's death may not have been an accident."

"Sam and your son lovers! Bullshit." If the thought hadn't been so ridiculous he might have been amused. He should have seen the scam coming. For a moment she almost had him. He had started to believe her, but now he knew if he let the conversation go any further she was going to put the squeeze on him for money. It was a con.

"Peddle your story to someone else," he said rudely. "I'm not interested. But remember this lady. I'll sue your ass from here to Michigan and back if you try and smear Sam's name or make any attempt to extort money from his family or friends."

He slammed the phone down so hard it bounced out of the cradle and disconnected the call holding on line two.

It had been a lousy day. He'd lost a three-team parlay when the horse-shit Dodger bullpen blew a three-run ninth inning lead in Atlanta, locked his keys in his car and forgotten to pick up his dry cleaning on the way in. Now his hopes of learning something new about Sam and Laura had been dashed by a nut case broad from Michigan who had nothing to say and obviously got a kick out of jerking him around.

Forget the bad day. It hadn't been a good month or a good year. The more you complain the longer God makes you live. What a thought for the day.

The call had been from Tiffany.

He rang her back.

209

"Any complaints from the troops about the absentee WASP Princess?" At least she was in good spirits. He had told her about some employee grumblings.

Brian wasn't in the mood for frivolity, even from Tiffany, so he faked it. If women could fake orgasms so convincingly the least he could do was pretend he was cheerful. What a world. It was days like this that made him miss being his own boss. He hated to "make nice" when he wanted to say what was on his mind.

"Haven't heard anything about the servants storming the castle today," he answered. "What's up?"

She noticed his abruptness and ignored it. Even Brian was entitled to have an off day.

"Walter filled me in on the progress of the roof and it sounds great. But there are some other things I'd like to discuss with you. Some personal things, if you're not too busy."

That caught him off guard.

"Fire away."

"Not on the phone," she said flatly.

"I'd like you to come to Chicago if you can, just for a day or two". It wasn't exactly an offer he could refuse. "My schedule won't permit me to get to Vegas now and Walter has to be there to run the hotel."

"Must be pretty important if you want me to come east," he said, hoping to get a clue.

"It is," she answered, giving him no idea. "Try and get a flight tomorrow or Wednesday and let me know when you're arriving. You can take a cab to the Executive House on Wacker Drive. I'll book a room for you and we can meet there for dinner later in the evening."

It was definitely official business. It also meant he'd have to call Stardust Jeri the wonder girl and cancel their plans to see "O" at the Bellagio. It was one of the most talked about shows in town and always sold out, even though tickets were $100 plus tax.

Did you already talk to Walter about my coming to Chicago?" he asked, knowing that she had. He wondered if she ever spoke to him about anything without briefing the lawyer first.

The whole Chicago trip sounded suspicious to him.

"I mentioned to Walter that I'd like you to come to Chicago to discuss some very important personal matters," she said. "He also has some papers that he needs me to sign. Would you mind bringing them?"

"Of course not," but he knew the papers were not the main reason she wanted him to come to Chicago.

He could not get a fix on the situation. The thought of being a carrier pigeon pissed him off. Errand Boy was not part of his job description.

The day wasn't ending any better than it began.

"I'll make the arrangements as soon as we hang up," he said diplomatically.

He hung up, then, stormed out of his office looking for Walter.

"He and Mrs. Thurston had dinner reservations," the secretary told him. "They left about half an hour ago. I can reach him at the restaurant if it's an emergency."

Brian turned, and without a word pushed his way through the double-wide glass doors of the executive offices and headed for the casino where he found a comfortable booth in the Nike Bar.

He sat for the better part of an hour, sipping a VO and ginger ale and stilling. When he had sufficiently mellowed he stopped by the gift shop, bought a USA Today and went home.

"I have no idea what it is," Walter said when they faced off in the morning. "It's got to be more than just these documents. Heck, we could have handled them by mail.

"Tiffany did ask if I could spare you for a day or two," he said, making Brian even more curious. "I've racked my brain trying to think what it could be."

Brian was a little less uptight after learning that Tiffany hadn't told Walter why she needed him in Chicago.

"She sounded calm," Brian mumbled. "Maybe she wants to discuss her licensing in more detail and wants more input from me." Brian was reaching and he knew it.

"Could be," Walter countered. "Why don't you plan on going Wednesday? That way you could stay a day or two if necessary and still be back by the weekend."

"You know Walter, it may have nothing to do with the licensing," he said after giving the situation more thought. "Tiffany may want to talk about the July party. It just occurred to me she might want some advice about hosting a Vegas party and she may have been a little embarrassed about asking in front of you. This could be her way."

That idea played. Walter bought it, and Brian said a prayer. He even made himself believe it.

Tuesday was off to a better start than Monday.

It couldn't be anything but the party. Tiffany had never looked at him romantically, much to his chagrin, and if it were Colossus business she would have dealt with Walter. He was convinced.

Brian booked a 9:30 a.m. United flight on Wednesday which would put him in Chicago in mid-afternoon. That would give him time to get to the hotel and relax before meeting Tiffany.

The convenient in-flight airfone prompted him to call Tiffany's office forty minutes into the flight.

"Miss Wayne is out of the office this afternoon. May I take a message?" Brian had hoped to speak to Tiffany but left his flight information with Tiffany's secretary even though he was taking a cab to the hotel.

"I should be at the Executive House by 5 o'clock," he added.

The flight went smoothly, but Chicago traffic was a bitch and by the time th Checker cab crisscrossed through the maze of rush hour commuters Tiffany ha already called the hotel.

"Sorry I missed your call this afternoon. I'm going home to change. I'll b there by seven. I'll leave the choice of restaurants to you. There are a couple c good ones in the hotel."

Tiffany arrived promptly at seven.

Dinner was relatively uneventful. Brian had veal Marsala, while Tiffan ordered baked chicken. Their conversation was shallow, ranging from th excitement of her Paris trip to Brian's genuine satisfaction with his associatic with the Colossus.

"I could never live out there," Tiffany said bluntly. "Somehow Las Vega doesn't seem real. It's like a make-believe place. You go there to escape, the after your fantasy is over you return to reality and the real world. Plus there's th heat, the gambling, the whole atmosphere. It's just not for me."

His mind bolted ahead. Was she trying to tell him she had already decided t sell the hotel?

Of course not. That would have been something she shared with Walter fir and Walter would have told him. Or would he?

Perhaps the decision had been made and Walter wanted to make it seem lik her idea. Maybe Detective Sarabian's pointed questions about Walter weren just speculative.

If anyone could influence Tiffany's judgment and decisions it would b Walter.

Dinner was finished and they were sipping cappuccino laced with amarett He wanted to invite her to his room so they could continue the conversation in more comfortable atmosphere but didn't want her to get the wrong idea.

Her delicate voice broke through his thoughts.

"Have you learned anything more about my father's murder?" The questio was direct, her voice gentle.

He looked at her, studying her eyes.

She sensed his reluctance.

"Brian, you can talk to me. Level with me. I'm a big girl."

Was this why she had summoned him to Chicago? To grill him about he father's murder one on one?

He decided to be as straightforward as he could.

"No one is quite sure of anything yet," he started.

"Except that my father was killed, wasted or whatever the curre euphemism they use in Las Vegas these days. We all know that. What else hav the police got? What have you found out?" Her tone was more demanding.

Tiffany was listening intently.

"You're not going to like this Tiffany, but the police are pretty well convinced it was a mob hit."

"And what exactly does that mean?"

"It means they think your father may have somehow been involved with the mob. Or maybe he just pissed off someone in the mob. If there was some sort of disagreement what happened makes sense, because that's the way those people handle their business."

He laid it out without sugarcoating, hoping she could deal with it. He told her about Sarabian's suspicion that the killer or killers had tried to make it look like a robbery and that it appeared her father had cooperated thinking he would be spared.

"And according to Sarabian, there's some political infighting in the department about the case. While you may be getting polite "this remains a top priority" reports from the chief, the truth is, if they don't get some new clues soon, the case is going on the back burner."

"I see. So what you're telling me is that if bad guys kill other bad guys the cops just sort of look the other way."

He looked away. Neither of them spoke for nearly a minute. He used the time to sign the check and leave a tip.

"Would you mind if we went upstairs and continued this conversation in your room?" she asked, choosing the option Brian least expected.

They rode the elevator in silence.

He sat in the large burnt-orange armchair opposite the sofa. Tiffany seemed quite comfortable on the sofa. Dressed in a black jump suit that zipped to the waist, black heels and an over-sized silver bracelet she looked like a milk shake tasted, soft and creamy and something you could hate yourself for in the morning.

"I've got to take these off," she said removing her shoes. "I hope you don't mind. I've been in heels all day."

He didn't mind, because it meant she was at ease. Maybe letting her guard down a little. If she did he hoped to learn more about her and who she really was.

Tiffany refused to accept any suggestion that her father was involved in the mob, but admitted she had no proof to the contrary.

"I guess you think I'm being pretty naïve," she said, "but despite the fact my father and I haven't been close for the past five years you shouldn't overlook the fact I've known the man my entire life. I know what he was like. He did not have a secret life. My dad was a man of character. People don't change all that much."

Brian wanted to tell her that people did change all that much, especially when they were in a business like gambling, but he didn't.

Gambling, like politics, changed people because it forced them to make compromises, beg favors and sometimes get into bed with partners they despised all in the name of success and the almighty buck.

213

Hotel VP's and executive hosts rubbed elbows and broke bread with bookies, embezzlers, morally corrupt heirs and drug dealers with big time credit lines every day, but they wouldn't invite them to their homes. Money was the great equalizer.

There were a thousand reasons Adam Forrester could have gotten messed up with the mob, and Brian knew some of them made perfect sense. He could also have gotten sucked in without knowing who he was dealing with.

The mob controlled most union pension and retirement funds and hotels had found them an easy target for loans. The downside was the mob would get its foot in the door and eventually start making demands.

On paper the loan was clean, the percentage rate fair and the terms favorable. It was like applying for a loan. You were so happy to be approved you didn't bother to read the fine print until you got home. By then it was too late.

Loans, construction problems and union workers were all areas where Adam Forrester could have taken a wrong turn. Or he could have been a consenting adult and gotten into bed willingly. Brian wasn't sure.

Tiffany liked Brian, even finding herself somewhat attracted to him. And she felt like she could trust him. To a degree. At least she could trust him enough to confide the real reason she asked him to come to Chicago.

It was an intimacy and a bombshell he didn't see coming. He wasn't accustomed to being so unprepared. Most people were very predictable.

"I'm sure there were a lot of things going on in my father's life that we'll never know about," she began. "But he wrote me a letter which he left in a safe deposit box. It wasn't discovered until last week. Walter sent it to me unopened." She emphasized the "unopened".

"In it he talks about the possibility of being killed by people who wanted to take over the Colossus. I'm sure you'll be able to make more sense of it than I can.

"He also said he was fairly sure Diana was having an affair, "and before Brian could ask, Tiffany added, "but he didn't know with whom. Only that he thought it was with some celebrity."

All the pieces fit, still Brian didn't feel the time was right to out Sonny Fremont. However the letter to Tiffany upgraded the conversation he heard in the Lagoon Bar from possible to highly probable.

He would tread lightly.

"I've heard the same rumor about Diana," he said a bit tenuously.

Tiffany pounced on his admittance, taking hold of it like a puppy with a favorite slipper.

"And who is the other party?"

"Look Tiffany, what I've heard is only hearsay. It came from two goofballs in a bar and I don't know yet if they were guessing or really knew something."

So..."

"My guess is they could be right, but..."

"Okay. If you want to play cat and mouse we can do that," she said, trying not to be adversarial.

"Let's play two questions."

She wasn't giving up.

"First question. Who's the rumored celebrity?"

Brain wet his lips. No sense playing games. He trusted her too, and she'd probably find out soon enough anyway. If he wanted her complete trust he'd have to tell her what he knew.

"Sonny Fremont."

Tiffany showed no anger or outrage. It was clear she wasn't very familiar with Fremont.

"Isn't he sort of Mr. Las Vegas?"

"That's Sonny," he said sarcastically. "He's kind of Las Vegas' answer to Will Rogers. Only in Sonny's case he never met a skirt he didn't like."

"I read something about him recently, in some entertainment magazine. Something about him getting a bad break because a movie he was doing was canceled. They said he stood to lose millions but the money was secondary to what the movie would have meant to his career."

"That's true," Brian confirmed. He didn't want to get into that story any deeper until he knew more.

"Okay, second question."

"Fire away."

"Do you believe the Sonny-Diana thing?"

Brian did not want to say yes just because he disliked Sonny. He wanted to be objective.

"Yes."

His honesty had a calming effect on her, and they began talking. Sharing and feeling instead of interrogating. They questioned each other about growing up, about likes and dislikes and fears. She felt as much at ease with him as she had with Liz Mallon in Paris.

She told him about Liz. She also told him about Johnny.

"At first everything was so good. It was like a dream. He was kind, gentle, caring, and we never argued.

"Now it seems we argue about silly little things all the time. I think maybe it's just the stress of everything going on, from the hotel to my father's death.

"Three months ago I was so positive it was the real thing. Now I don't know. We seem to be building walls and putting distance between us."

Brian had feelings for her and he could not deny them. He didn't know she was involved, and he could understand her sadness and confusion over her troubled relationship. But the selfish, romantic side of him could not feel sorry for her. He had been stupid not to anticipate she might be in a relationship. She

215

had never mentioned it but she had no reason to. They had never spoken on a personal level before.

Later Tiffany spoke of her mother's suicide and the grief she felt when she learned of her father's death. Walter had explained that she was torn up inside, and doing her best to weather the storm, but the lawyer had not told him about the brutal timing of the incidents.

Not how Tiffany had learned of the murder on the same night she had decided to forgive Adam and make amends with him. In Vegas lingo that was a bad beat, like having four kings lose to four aces.

He told her about Sam and Laura and she was genuinely saddened.

"I'm so sorry," she said. "I had no idea. Walter never mentioned it. Neither did T.J."

"That's because I haven't told them."

She was the first person with whom he had shared his grief.

They talked for another hour, until one of them noticed it was almost midnight.

"This has been special," he said, reaching across the glass coffee table to take her hand.

"For me too," she smiled, not moving her hand. "I wasn't sure how you were going to react to my asking you to come to Chicago, and to be honest, I needed to see you face to face and talk to you to know whether I could trust you. I needed to sit across from you to decide."

She squeezed his hand, then withdrew hers and leaned over to get her purse.

"Did you reach a decision?"

"Here's the letter from my father," she said answering his question. "Even Walter hasn't seen it."

"He read it quickly, but carefully, then read it again.

Adam Forrester knew what was happening. He was worried, but not afraid.

Brian also came to one other important conclusion.

Adam Forrester was not "in". Just "in" the way.

Tiffany stood and braced herself on the couch while she slipped on her shoes. Brian put the letter back in the envelope and handed it to her.

She looked at him, waiting for a comment.

"Your dad wasn't in the mob Tiffany. His letter proves that. However, I don't think there's much doubt the mob killed him. They wanted the Colossus. Your father refused to sell to them so they did away with him, figuring he'd leave it to Diana and she'd sell.

"He left it to you hoping you wouldn't sell to the wrong people. With Walter advising you I'm sure that won't happen." He stopped abruptly. His eyes were focused on the floor.

"What else Brian?" She could tell he was upset.

"The what else is the danger you could be in," he said, looking deeply into
e two little pools of green that were her eyes.

"These guys have no conscience. They won't let anyone stand in their way."

"I don't think they're ready to do that now," she said defiantly. "They
ven't even approached us with an offer I can refuse." She smiled and moved
ward him.

He hugged her.

Their lips met and she made no motion to pull away. When she finally
cked away she said nothing.

She opened the door to the suite and stood in the doorway, seeking refuge
om the emotions running wildly through her body. She was partially in the hall
hen she spoke and she did so from the heart.

"Thank you Brian. For being a friend. For being honest and for believing in
y father. When you get back to Las Vegas please do what you can with the
formation from the letter. Tell your detective friend about it. It may make a
fference."

He nodded.

"Do you want me to share the information with Walter?"

"I'll leave that to you."

He wanted to ask her about Walter, but didn't. Did she have any doubts
out him? How could she be sure he couldn't be bought? He wanted to know
ny Walter was so closed about Adam's murder? Walter was the man in control
w. On paper Tiffany owned everything but she would do whatever Walter
ggested.

He felt guilty even thinking Walter could be involved, but it was his nature.
spect everyone and you won't be surprised. Kind of a "kill them all and let
d sort them out" approach.

Tiffany turned and moved toward the elevator, mindful that Brian was still
tching her. She pressed the down button and waited anxiously for the car to
ive. Part of her wanted to turn and run back to him.

He stood in the doorway, hoping she'd suddenly pivot and come back. She
d not, and in a minute she was gone.

Brian slept restfully despite having a great number of things on his mind.
ffany, Adam Forrester, Laura and Sam, the Colossus, Detective Sarabian, the
ss, the mob, Diana Forrester, Sonny Fremont, Jill Parker and more of Tiffany
ayne.

He awoke around seven, rested, but with carloads of nervous energy. There
s something he had to do but he couldn't remember what it was. His flight
sn't until 11:40.

In the shower he let the hot spray ricochet off his face and body, hoping it
uld clear his head and help him recall whatever task had escaped his memory.

Finally, it came to him. It was not something he was forgetting. It was an inevitable he was avoiding. It was something he had been thinking about for days, consciously and subconsciously.

He dried his hair, slipped into the hotel's soft terry cloth robe and headed for the living room. He retrieved his leather address book and picked up the phone.

Stretching the phone to the coffee table he opened the address book and fished a crumpled memo stuffed in the pocket of the inside cover.

He studied it for a moment then dialed the number.

She answered on the first ring.

"Miss Parker. This is Brian Powers...I think there are some things we should talk about..."

They started slowly, literally sparring with each other, each choosing their words as if they were selecting weapons for a duel.

Brian believed Jill Parker had something, but what? And he still wasn't buying the nonsense of Sam and her son.

"Listen Ms. Parker, I don't mean to be disrespectful but you must understand the story you've told me about your son and Sam Bradford comes as a total shock. I am still trying to make sense of it."

What he really wanted to say was, "what the fuck are you talking about?"

"But even if it were true, it wouldn't explain Sam's death. Unless you have a lot more information than you're telling me."

Rita Matthews stammered.

"Well...maybe I do have some," she admitted, "but only because of the letter and stuff. I didn't know who Sam Bradford was until recently, and it was quite a coincidence that I found out."

She hardly sounded like an extortionist. Brian imagined her being frail. Meek even. And his perception of her made it even harder to understand how she could be of help. Or know anything at all.

"You said you have information that might prove it was more than an accident. Does Sam say in the letter that that he was afraid of being killed? Brian was zeroing in.

"Does he mention any names?"

"He said he was using the letter as sort of an insurance policy," she said trying to summarize.

Brian wanted a name. Any name. If she gave him a name he could recognize her story would seem more real. Maybe then he could start to believe in the timid little woman.

"Can you read the letter to me over the phone?" he asked

She declined and her reluctance turned Brian's hopes to skepticism again.

"I'd rather not do that," she said. I think you can understand why?"

He couldn't.

"Besides, if you saw it for yourself, in Sam's own handwriting you'd understand."

What she meant was he'd be more apt to believe, and she was right of course.

"Okay," he reasoned, "but try and understand my position. A woman I've never heard of calls me out of the blue, three months after my brother in law and ex-wife are killed and claims she has a letter that could prove it wasn't an accident.

"To complicate things even more, she also claims Sam Bradford and her son were lovers, which you must admit Miss Parker, sounds like it could be the basis for some sort of blackmail."

"But..."

"Just a minute," Brian said firmly.

"Furthermore, the woman is from Michigan, the accident happened in California and she doesn't know either of the people who were killed. Are you with me so far Ms. Parker?"

"Yes, but..."

"Ms. Parker, I really want to believe you because I've had an extremely hard time convincing myself that this was just an accident. But at the same time I don't want to rehash this and raise false hopes. I have reconciled myself with their deaths. I have an uneasy peace inside of me. In other words I need something more before I open myself up again. Can you understand that?"

"Yes. I understand, but I don't know what you want me to do."

"I need you to give me a name. Maybe someone Sam mentioned in the letter. If you can do that I'll at least know this isn't a scam or a cruel hoax."

There was pleading in his voice.

Rita Matthews knew it was a test. She had to think.

"Mario Torino," she replied.

Brian did not make an immediate connection.

He repeated the name. He thought he'd heard it before but couldn't remember the circumstances.

"Anyone else?"

Silence again.

Rita was scanning the letter.

"Someone named Oscar...Oscar Bento," she added, half-whispering.

"Sonny Fremont's agent!" Brian was almost shouting.

It took him the better part of the next hour to re-arrange his schedule so he could go from Chicago to Michigan and then to Vegas.

Jill Parker had agreed to meet him.

There were no direct flights to Grand Rapids. Nearest thing was East Lansing, home of the Michigan State Spartans.

He used most of the ninety-minute flight reading and dictating into his hand held tape recorder. He tried desperately to keep an open mind and not anticipate his rendezvous with the mystery lady from Michigan, but couldn't help it.

Jill Parker had agreed to meet him in the Flite Deck restaurant at the East Lansing Airport.

She was nervous about meeting Brian. The whole thing was mushrooming. She had always kept to herself. Meeting Brian Powers was in direct contrast to her "don't make waves" lifestyle, but she felt compelled to do it. For Boyd.

As she drove from Grand Rapids to the East Lansing airport she had second thoughts. Her stomach was upset and her palms were moist.

Was Brian Powers really one of the good guys? What if he secretly worked for the mob and was meeting her just to get the letter? He could kill her.

She realized her imagination was working overtime, but she also knew the world had gone mad. People killed for no reason. Out of anger, lunacy, for a few bucks or for a thrill. Parents killed their children, children killed their parents. People blew up buildings to protest perceived injustices, the government incited things like Waco and the term "going postal" had slipped into the American mainstream.

It didn't used to be this way she thought. Now a mother drives her car in the river killing two beautiful children. And she does it because the man she thinks she loves doesn't want her children.

A man injects his child with the HIV virus so he won't have to pay child support. And a Hitler like dictator in Serbia kills, mutilates and attempts to eradicate an entire race of people in what he calls ethnic cleansing. Rita Matthews did not understand it all but she knew the world had gone mad.

She would have to see just where Brian Powers fit in.

She exited at the last ramp before the airport turn-off, spotted a corner minimall and pulled in. She stepped into a self-service copy center and made a copy of Sam's letter, then put the original in her trunk. It wasn't much of a safety precaution but it was something.

After she met Brian, and talked to him for a bit she'd decide how much she could trust him. If she was convinced he was on the level she'd give him the letter. He didn't know her car, so if something did happen, her Oldsmobile would eventually be found in the parking lot and the police would discover the original copy of the letter in the trunk.

On the outside of the envelope in her trunk she had written a personal little note,

"Meeting Brian Powers from the Colossus Hotel (Las Vegas) in Flite Deck Restaurant at East Lansing Michigan", along with the date and time. It was her insurance policy.

As she turned into the airport parking lot Rita mouthed a silent prayer, hoping that Brian was sincere and that she was doing the right thing. More than anything else, she wanted out of the whole mess.

It was 11:25 by the time she reached the entrance to the restaurant. Brian's flight was due at noon, which gave her enough time to panic and leave, or wait for the booth facing the arched doorway so she could see him come in.

She chose the latter, ordered a medium coffee and waited for a man in his early 40s wearing a U Conn sweatshirt and matching cap. Brian figured the outfit would make him easy to recognize, and he was right.

Jill Parker had given him a fairly good description of herself, although she was shorter than he expected, and a little older than she sounded on the phone.

He spotted her and walked directly to the booth.

"Hi. I'm Brian Powers," he said standing over her as he extended his hand. He wanted to be positive she was the right person before he sat down.

Rita Matthews shook Brian's hand.

"Jill Parker," she said.

"It wasn't easy getting a flight in here this morning," he said, trying to break the tension.

"I'm sure it wasn't, especially on short notice," she said nervously.

Rita Matthews managed a weak smile, and Brian could see her red, tired eyes studying his every move. He looked back at her sympathetically, eyeing her just as warily through the wine-colored rims of her hexagonal shaped glasses. She had been crying, and the puffs under her eyes told him she hadn't been getting much sleep either. Her hands said early fifties, although it was hard to tell because she was tired and wore little if any make-up.

Brian laid his briefcase on the vinyl booth seat, ordered a root beer and waited for the waitress to leave.

The high-ceilinged restaurant had begun to empty out within minutes after Brian arrived, and it was obvious the restaurant was more of a waiting lounge than a dining spot.

The booths on either side of them were unoccupied so they were able to speak without fear of being overheard.

"As you might imagine I have a million questions Miss Parker. Everything from who your son was, to how you got the letter and how you came to contact me." Brian was doing a mental sound check of his tone, not wanting to sound patronizing or accusatory.

Rita Matthews wasn't sure where she should begin.

"The funeral home gave me your address," she started. "I know a few people in the phone company and they helped me get your unlisted home number."

"And when you called my house the message on my answering machine said you could contact me at the Colossus in case of an emergency."

"Right. Listen Mr. Powers. It's like I was telling you on the phone. I don't want to be in the middle of all this. I wish I'd never read those letters. But I did and I can't undo that. I just want to be done with it."

Brian sat up straight. She'd said letters, as in plural.

"Why don't you just start at the beginning Miss Parker? Take your time and try and remember everything you can even if you don't think it's important.

"There are a lot of people and a lot of lives involved and I want to be sure we get all the facts straight. We're talking about real people, innocent people being murdered." Brian didn't want to frighten her but he wanted her to understand that it was not a game.

She took a handkerchief from her purse and dabbed at her eyes.

Over the next hour Rita Matthews replayed the past three months, including her drive to Los Angeles, her discovery of the letters in Boyd's apartment and her happenstance finding of the Los Angeles Times newspaper with the story about Sam Bradford.

Brian sat riveted to his seat. It was a fascinating story and he tried not to let his jaw fall slack, even though he was awed by the tale Jill Parker was weaving.

She talked and he listened, occasionally interrupting to ask a question or to clarify something he didn't comprehend.

Finally she was done, but he still didn't fully understand, and she knew it was time.

"Here's the letter," she said, pulling it from the depths of her purse.

He could see it was a copy.

"I made a copy because I wasn't sure I could trust you, "she said openly, feeling now that she could.

Nothing in her story could have prepared him for what he read.

He knew Sam's signature. The "S" was incredibly distinctive. There was no mistake Sam had addressed the letter and signed it.

And there, in black and white was Sam telling Boyd Matthews that he loved him. And trying to explain the pictures of them together.

Brian was dumbstruck. For a moment he couldn't read on. He paused. His eyes blinked wildly at the words on the page in front of him.

Basically Sam's letter was self-explanatory but in the end it had not been the insurance policy the director had hoped would save his life.

The next paragraphs answered Brian's quandary about the whereabouts of the film. It detailed Sam's dissatisfaction with the early rushes of "Morocco Heat" and singled out Sonny Fremont's poor performance as the main reason. Sam admitted burning the master copy, and said he was going to Los Angeles to formally announce cancellation of the project.

"At least that explains what happened to the only copy of the film," Brian said aloud as he continued reading.

So Oscar Bento had blackmailed Sam into giving Sonny Fremont the lead.

Another mystery solved.

Bento and Torino were in up to their necks.

Brian's brain was on overload, juggling multiple thoughts while he read. The tter might be enough reason to have the police re-open the accident vestigation but there were still no witnesses and no real proof that it was ything but a freak crash.

Furthermore, according to the tone of the letter, Sam did not expect anything happen before his news conference. He appeared confident he'd be able to get me safely and make the announcement.

How did they get to him? It was obvious Sam had made hasty plans and a st minute decision to fly to Los Angeles. There was no way they could have own.

He also knew that if Sam had any doubts about his safety that night he would ver have had Laura pick him up. He adored his sister and was extremely otective of her.

The mob couldn't have done it. They could not have known where everyone as going to be and acted so quickly, so the idea of it really being an accident emed more and more probable. Somehow they must have found out. Maybe d Sam followed.

He thought of Tiffany, and how, with this strange twist of events, their lives d become even more intertwined.

Three months ago they had never heard of each other, and neither of them as grieving. At that time they had no reason to fear for their own lives or to be ncerned about organized crime or its operatives.

Now, Tiffany's father was dead and there was irrefutable evidence that it was syndicate hit. And Sam, And Laura. In death, they too were all eerily linked to dam Forrester. Even though the three of them had never met there was more an an outside chance they had all been killed by the same people.

He shuddered.

Wasn't life a kick in the ass? They wanted Sam and got Laura as a bonus. e just happened to be in the way.

Brian knew he was getting ahead of himself again.

Mob assassins were professionals. As a rule they didn't kill innocent people cidentally. Laura's death was probably part of the plan. In case she had been e one to receive Sam's letter.

He wondered again if they would have killed him too had he been in the car. was an easy question to answer.

It had been an incredible twenty-four hours.

His spur of the moment trip to Chicago and meeting with Tiffany. His traction to her. Adam Forrester's letter, and his premonition of being murdered. w Jill Parker, and Sam's letter from the grave.

There was nothing similar about their deaths. One was very straightforwar and looked exactly like it was. A mob hit. The other appeared to be an accider and Brian knew no police department anywhere would ever think to link th crimes together. The murders had happened weeks apart, in different cities, unde different circumstances and the victims did not know each other.

And even considering all he had read, and suspected, the possibility sti existed that Mario Torino had been bluffing when he tried to intimidate Sam b showing him the LA Times story about Adam Forrester.

There were at least five major crime families and any or all of them coul have wanted the Colossus. There was no proof it was Chicago.

Brian slumped back against the booth, exhausted.

"What's wrong?"

Jill Parker was confused. She knew the letter had surprised Brian but she ha hoped the letter would be the "hard evidence" he needed to "make somebod responsible" as he had said on the phone.

"Why don't you just turn the letter over to the police and let them handle it?"

Brian didn't answer, and Rita Matthews wasn't sure if he was ignoring her c had not heard the question. He seemed a long way away.

And he was.

In Vegas people were gambling as usual. Visitors were streaming into th new Venetian, to Mandalay Bay and the Bellagio, fascinated by the lights and th hype, unaware and unmoved by the misfortunes of others.

There was no justice.

Assholes had money, idiots had jobs and nine-year olds ran corporation Rap singers were multi-millionaires and legitimate crooners couldn't get on th radio or the charts with a court order. Average ballplayers made millions, fin print was the rule rather than the exception and scams were everywhere.

Law-abiding people feared for their lives, social security was in seriou trouble, politicians padded their own pockets and "heavy paper" as the kic called it was the determining factor in most battles.

The morning paper carried a story with a Vegas dateline claiming Phyll McGuire of the singing McGuire sisters had reached a plea agreement in battery case. She had been charged with assaulting an officer and resisting arre in a minor dispute.

The Vegas DA's office agreed to dismiss the case provided she donate $5,000 to the department's retirement fund. She was represented by the son of former Clark County sheriff and did not even appear in court. "Heavy Paper".

"Mr. Powers...."

Rita's voice snapped Brian back to the present.

"I'm not ready to turn the letter over to the police right now," he picked u "Not quite yet."

He had some ideas about how the letter could be used. There had to be a way to get to Mario Torino. He was way above Oscar Bento on the totem pole.

Brian wondered if Sonny Fremont might be the Achilles Heel.

"Okay for me to keep this stuff Ms. Parker?" He was holding a copy of the letter and the disgusting 5x5 photos in front of the woman across from him. She nodded.

He would call a meeting. This time Tiffany would have to come to Las Vegas. He wanted Walter and Sarabian there too.

"Mr. Powers!"

He looked up at Jill Parker.

"There's something else I think you should know."

He couldn't imagine what else this thin, homely looking woman could still have to unveil.

He wasn't sure he could take any more.

"My name isn't Jill Parker. It's Rita Matthews. At first I was afraid for you to know my name."

The deep worry lines on her face explained why she was telling him. They both understood.

"If anything should happen to me…"

He stopped her. They stood at the same time, and Brian gave Rita Matthews a gentle hug that said, 'You're safe, don't worry', and wished he believed it. He hoped she didn't notice that his hands were trembling like dishes in a china cabinet during an earthquake.

He couldn't make it to Vegas until late evening. There were no direct flights from East Lansing to Nevada. He had to take a commuter shuttle to Detroit, then connect to an American flight that made a stop-over in Dallas.

On the way to the commuter gate he paused in front of the bank of telephones. He passed on calling Walter, Tiffany or both. He had to digest it all first. The letter and pictures were in his briefcase that he was clutching as if it were a lifeline. And in many ways it was.

No hasty decisions. He'd re-read it all on the plane and let it sink in.

One thing he was sure about. He would demand that Walter and Tiffany allow him to choose the entertainment for the party.

Talk about a short list. There was only one name on it.

Sonny Fremont was the only name Brian considered.

Ron Delpit

Chapter 19
Homeward Bound

Arranging time off from the Parisian bureau was not a problem for Liz Mallon.

Deciding if she was strong enough to see Tom Felton was another story altogether.

The thing was, she wanted to see Tiffany Wayne. She wanted to check her out. Go to her party and find out what she was all about.

Had she totally misjudged the woman? Was she a conniving manipulative little rich girl, or was she as unaffected and genuine as the woman she had profiled in her Tribune article.

She was still convinced Tom had more information than he had shared on the phone.

Her feelings for Felton would also be a big part of the trip. Was she over him? Did she still need him? Was she going to crumble when she saw him?

Liz Mallon didn't know any of those answers.

She also didn't have a clue how Tom would react. It had been two years since she had licked her wounds and crawled off to Paris after their breakup. And it had been more than a year since he had been dumped by her replacement.

Liz promised herself to keep things in perspective and not let anything get in the way of her mission, which was to determine if Tiffany Wayne was a diamond in the rough or a cubic zirconia princess. She was also determined to get as much information as she could from Tom, and persuade him to use his editorial pull and former Organized Crime Task Force sources to create a dossier on Tiffany.

She had been careful not to say exactly how long she'd be gone to the Paris Bureau Chief, managing to finagle an "open-ended" vacation to compensate for the accrued time she had built up over the past two years. She did agree not to be gone more than a month.

"I'll be back by July 15," she promised. It was already near the end of June so there wouldn't be much down time during her visit.

The plan was to spend two or three days in Chicago, visiting with old friends and assembling every scrap of information she could on Tiffany, her friends and the Colossus. Maybe she'd even hang out with Tiffany and her boyfriend, Johnny Marciano.

That would mean asking fewer questions and letting her eyes and ears do most of the investigating. After Chicago she'd head for Vegas and The Colossus Fourth of July gala.

Mark Brown, a friend who had recently retired from Reuters had happily agreed to fill-in during Liz' hiatus because it meant additional paychecks as well as a few extra weeks in Paris.

226

Brown was a hard news guy and Liz had worked with him on numerous occasions. He had been stationed in Paris for more than a decade and had adopted almost all the Parisian vices, including a penchant for coffee and cigarettes, a laid back style, wine with every meal and a mistress. None of which kept him from being an excellent reporter.

In view of the fact she was paying her own way, Liz had searched for the lowest available fare, securing a seat on a TWA flight direct to Chicago. A friend at the airline had managed to get her upgraded to first class and she was extremely grateful.

Tom was not at O'Hare to meet her, which came as no great surprise. He had offered but she had politely backed him off, claiming she'd probably be exhausted and badly in need of some sleep.

She would have been happy to see him at the gate if she could have been sure he was coming because he wanted to, instead of out of some sense of obligation.

In the end she spent $28 for a cab to the Palmer House, a quiet well-respected hotel within walking distance of the Trib. The hotel's proximity to the paper was a bonus. She had arranged to stay there because the manager was an acquaintance who put her in for next to nothing.

She had no trouble sleeping, lapsing into a coma-like state before midnight. By morning she had shaken off most of the effects of the time change, and after a breakfast of coffee and croissants she headed for the Tribune office.

Tom had not come in yet so after a round of hellos to old pals in the newsroom and a quick conference with the Sunday Features Editor, she headed for the morgue.

She wanted to read over the background material on Tiffany, but more importantly she wanted to read every available story and quote on Adam Forrester.

Liz was disappointed to find the newspaper's archives had little more than Tom had told her over the phone. He had also faxed copies of the articles so there was little more for her to do.

"Hi there. How was the flight?"

The voice was friendly, even more so than on the phone, and Liz turned away from the Adam Forrester file to see Tom Felton in the doorway. He had a round, open face and had lost more hair since she had last seen him. He had also lost a few pounds and looked healthier because of it.

"Flight was great," she said remembering the pampering she had received in first class. "I was really whipped last night but I think getting a good night's sleep helped me beat the jet lag blues," she smiled.

"You look great," he said meaning it. "Looks like you've found a way to keep in shape despite living in a city where there's bakery on every corner," and immediately she was glad she had chosen the brightly colored gold blouse with the navy trim. The dark blue skirt always made her look slimmer and she was pleased by his compliment.

"You don't look so bad yourself," she replied. "I guess being an executive agrees with you. The hours are certainly better," she said glancing at the clock on the far wall.

"Hey. It isn't everyday I come in at ten o'clock," he teased. "It just so happens I was here pretty late last night, checking out some new information on your mysterious Ms. Tiffany Wayne."

"Anything interesting?" She was dying to know.

"A few things we can discuss over that dinner I promised you," he said, "and also a few blanks I hope you can fill-in."

The rest of the day passed quickly, Liz getting a little bleary-eyed from staring at the micro-fiche, reading and re-reading stories about Adam Forrester and how he had made his fortune as an investment wheeler-dealer during his years in Chicago.

She found nothing linking Forrester to mobsters or anything else illegal.

On a hunch she called up the file on Walter Thurston. After all, if he was Tiffany's advisor, and the man now running the Colossus, it might serve her well to know his background.

Walter's name appeared in numerous stories including a long feature piece from the early eighties when he was elected president of the Chicago Trial Lawyers Association. Another was a well-written profile piece from 1990 and it mentioned Thurston as a possible senatorial candidate. A subsequent story told of Thurston declining the nomination.

Liz read everything twice, and when she finished she still felt there was more to the man than she could pull from the stories.

She wondered if she was looking too hard. Trying to make something out of nothing.

"What's the scoop on Walter Thurston?"

Her question caught Tom by surprise. He was busy editing something on the computer and had not noticed her slip into his office.

"Solid guy. Great criminal lawyer. If you're looking for a good guy gone bad you'd better look somewhere else. Walter Thurston is as clean as they come.

"Almost ran for the senate in '90. Party would have given him the nomination if he'd said the word, and I think he would have won, but in the end he declined."

"Why?"

"Personal reasons. He said he wanted to start winding down, maybe spend more time with his family."

"Or maybe he just didn't want the scrutiny that goes with being a political candidate?" She knew she was digging.

"Anything's possible I suppose, but I wouldn't bet on it." Tom was leaning ick in his chair, thoughtfully re-examining the Adam Forrester-Walter Thurston nnection.

"Just how does Thurston figure in your designer girl's script?" he asked. What are you thinking? What are you looking for?"

"I don't know?" Liz was exasperated. "Anything. I just know there's mething upside down in the picture and it isn't Tiffany. Besides, she's a new ayer. Whatever's going on, and I'm convinced something is going on, has been motion for a while."

"Thurston has no previous connection to Las Vegas as far as I can tell," Tom plied.

"Other than Adam Forrester, the owner of Vegas' biggest hotel. They were st friends since they were kids."

"Okay. That's something to think about, but it doesn't mean anything."

"Tiffany also told me that during the years she and her father didn't speak urston kept in contact with Adam. He was their middle-man."

"So..."

"So, it figures Thurston had advance knowledge of the will. About Adam iving everything to Tiffany instead of the new wife. That's the kind of thing rrester might have discussed with him since they had remained close."

"That could work." Tom was playing out possible conclusions in his head. ut for that to be part of the equation Thurston would have to be in on the rder of his best friend..."

"And then use his influence to get Tiffany to sell," Liz intruded, finishing m's sentence. She was still attracted to him. She could feel herself losing ntrol and she paused to reel in her emotions.

"What, we've never heard of people knocking off their best friends or siness partners? Get real. It's done all the time, and for a lot less than what's at ke here." Liz didn't know what had turned her loose on Walter Thurston but more she rambled, the more plausible it seemed for the lawyer to be the chpin.

Tom Felton was stunned by what he was hearing, partially because he had ver, not for a second, ever considered Walter Thurston to be one of the bad ys. He was also impressed by Liz' newfound tenacity.

She had certainly brought a fresh viewpoint to the scene.

"One more thing," she said, looking every bit as if a lightbulb had just one f in her head.

"Walter Thurston is a criminal lawyer. Maybe the top defense attorney in icago. Who's to say he didn't get in bed with one of his sleazy clients and me in the back door?

"I'd never thought about that," Tom confessed. "Let's try and sort this out night," he said before she could get revved up again.

Ron Delpit

"Sorry," she apologized. "I know you have work to do. Over dinner then." She waved and was gone.

There were still a few files she wanted to check, and she also wanted to call the Associated Press bureau in Las Vegas and have them fax copies of the clips about Adam Forrester's murder and the disclosure of his will. Maybe she'd tripped over something.

She hadn't called Tiffany yet, deciding she'd wait and see what came out of her dinner conversation with Tom. And she wanted to wait until she'd studied the articles from Vegas.

The material from Vegas didn't arrive until late in the afternoon, preventing her from scanning it before returning to the Palmer House. However one particular piece did draw her attention.

It was by a columnist for the Las Vegas Review-Journal, and the headline declared: "A Colossal Mistake By The Mob". The writer didn't have any hard facts but he theorized that whatever mob family engineered the "hit" on Adam Forrester had not counted on the owner leaving his estranged daughter in control of the hotel.

"This new turn of events could cause an all out war for control of Las Vegas' biggest casino," the writer hypothesized. "It appears somebody put all their eggs in one basket and wound up with an omelet."

Tom arrived promptly at seven, ringing her from a house phone in the lobby.

"I'll be right down," she said cheerfully and took one last approving gander at herself in the mirror on the bathroom door. She had a small evening bag on her shoulder and the manila file folder clutched tightly in her left hand.

They made small talk before dinner avoiding mention of their dissolved relationship as well as the Tiffany Wayne situation. They talked about his promotion, how Chicago had changed, and her experiences in Paris.

Tom Felton was still attracted to Liz, and silently questioned whether he had made a mistake by ending their involvement. She was bright, fairly attractive and sexually much more explosive and responsive than she appeared. In bed she was anything but a conservative, although it had taken a long while for her to trust him enough to let herself go.

Did he want to rekindle the flame? He wasn't sure, and he didn't know he'd get the opportunity to try.

They shared chateaubriand after enjoying an appetizer of sautéed mushrooms followed by an expertly tossed Caesar salad.

After dinner there was an awkward silence. They had already ordered coffee and neither knew what to say.

Tom wrapped his hand around hers, giving it a gentle squeeze.

"I've missed you Liz. It's been a long time."

He didn't have a chance to apologize, or say anything that would have let her know if he was sorry they parted, because the waiter returned with their coffee, spoiling the moment.

When the server departed the mood changed.

"Is that the file on Thurston?" he asked, motioning to the folder on the cushion beneath her purse.

"No. It's stuff the AP in Vegas faxed to me. Stories about Forrester and his will."

"Anything funky?"

"I'm not sure yet. I only scanned it although a local columnist took some pot shots at the mob, suggesting there could be an all out war for control of the Colossus."

"If that columnist's hunch is correct it really muddies the waters."

"What do you mean?"

"I mean it opens up the possibilities. If there was an agreement between the families that the Colossus was up for grabs, any of the five major families could be responsible for Forrester's death. It means you could be way off base chasing Walter Thurston.

"Some loose cannon from The New York, Kansas City or Cleveland groups is much more likely to have pulled the trigger."

They finished with snifters of brandy, Tom offering a soft "welcome home" toast. Their eyes locked and each wondered what the other was thinking.

It seemed quite natural to ask Tom up after dinner. He had not yet looked over the articles in the file, and she wanted to see if he could pick up any subtleties she might have missed.

However, what happened later was not planned and neither resisted.

It had been a long time since Liz Mallon had felt a man's hands roam hungrily over her body and even longer since she had enjoyed it so guiltlessly. Perhaps some of the sexual freedoms of France had worn off on her.

They hardly spoke during their lovemaking, content to let their bodies express the passions, hostilities and questions that were locked inside. It was a breakthrough for her.

When Tom made the first move she did not play hard to get. If it turned out that the night was just a reunion of old lovers getting it on one last time then so be it. She wasn't looking around any corners. Tonight she was living the moment.

And it was quite a moment.

He kissed her neck and pressed his body against her and the familiar scent of him filled her senses again. When he first touched her, explored her, it was as if she had never been touched. The desire was so new, the pleasure so complete.

When he first touched her she moaned. She wanted to scream. She didn't want him to stop.

And when she touched him there was magic. It felt good to hold him again, to feel him grow harder. She wanted to devour him but teased him until he whimpered. Within minutes he was pleading to be inside her but she pretended not to hear. She was fully engrossed and enjoying what she was doing. The most exciting part was realizing that she was getting totally aroused giving him pleasure.

Her body rose to meet his and when he entered her it was as if he filled a huge void in both her body and her life. Tears soaked her face, streaking her mascara, but they did not slow her furious assault on his body.

It was blissful, and both of them became lost in the passion. Strangely, it was better than it had ever been before, and it was because both took what they needed, without fear, and in doing so each gave more than they had ever given.

Spent, they lay still for long minutes.

"I'm sorry," he said, almost inaudibly. It was a concession she had not expected and it brought an inner contentment. She knew it no longer mattered whether they reconciled their relationship. It had come full cycle and she could now close the book without harboring the hurt.

Tom stayed the night, awoke before her, and ordered room service, all before 8 a.m.

He was ready to talk to her about Tiffany Wayne.

She showered and joined him at the small round breakfast table, pouring a cup of coffee as he spoke.

"I think you know there are things I didn't tell you on the phone," he began.

She nodded.

"I think we agree that Adam Forrester was a mob job. Which family ordered it is unknown. According to a one of my reliable sources in Cleveland, no one expected Tiffany in the picture. Everyone figured the new boss would be Forrester's wife, an ex-Chicago looker named Diana.

"This is where it gets tricky, and it all makes sense if your theory is right and Thurston is involved.

"He would be the only guy on the inside who knew that Tiffany was going to get all the toys. And his control of Tiffany would be the key. No one else would have knocked off Forrester if they'd known he was leaving everything to his daughter.

"That would be too much trouble. Bring them too much visibility. They wouldn't want to hit her because she's not in the loop. And a second murder might bring the FBI and the Organized Crime boys down real hard.

"That brings us back to Chicago."

"Sounds like they were pretty sure they could get the hotel from the wife," Liz said quizzically. "That could mean she's in on it somehow."

"Maybe. And that's an angle we'll continue to work on, but you can be anyone interested in the Colossus is trying to get a reading on Tiffany."

"She's already told me she's not sure what she's going to do with the Colossus. I think she's leaning toward selling. For God's sake Tom, she's a dress designer and her business is in Chicago. She doesn't know a damn thing about running a Las Vegas casino.

"Which might be exactly what Thurston was counting on…if he's the Judas," he finished.

Tom was fumbling unsuccessfully with the strawberry jam packet. She deftly located the little tab and peeled it back, giving him access to the contents.

"I can never seem to get those things open," he laughed.

"They're like airline peanuts," she giggled. "I have this theory that some company made a couple thousand of those mini-peanut packages way back in the '0s and the airlines have been using the same ones over and over again because no one can get the damn things open." Tom smiled, then returned to their conversation.

"Look Liz. This is dangerous stuff. Personally I think she should sell the place and get back to making dresses, but it's not my place to tell her that."

"Which brings us right back to Walter Thurston doesn't it?"

"I guess so," Felton answered, crunching into his now strawberry toast.

"Thurston's the guy advising her and probably the only one she'll listen to or trust.

"There could be an up side to that," he added.

Liz looked at him blankly.

"In a way, scary as it seems, he's also her protection. If the syndicate feels confident in Thurston's influence over her, and he handles the deal, she's safe. In a twisted sort of way he's her savior."

"That's pretty fucking sick," she said hotly, shocking him with her language. "To Tiffany he's a father figure. Her protector. And all the while he's playing her."

"Don't get all worked up. I admit all of this stacks up logically, but we could be all wrong. Thurston is in the perfect position, but it could all be a coincidence.

"And there's one other hitch I haven't told you about yet," he said heavily.

"Which is?"

"Which is, according to an informant who I have to believe knows the score, there's a time limit on this whole takeover."

"A time limit? What do you mean?"

"Supposedly the five major crime family bosses took a vote about the Colossus, and I don't know if this was before or after Forrester was hit. According to my man the Chicago family was given first crack at the Colossus. If they weren't able to gain control of the hotel in six months the place was to go up for grabs. Then the battle begins and there will be no holds barred. Control might go to the most cunning family but it could also go to the most ruthless."

"Jesus Christ. Tiffany could be in the middle of some old style gangland war. It's already been four months. There isn't much time."

"Have you talked to her since you're in town?"

"Not yet. I plan on calling her today. I'd like you to meet her. Maybe dinner?" She felt funny making the offer. She did not want him to think she was taking for granted that they were an item again."

"It might be better if you got together with her first," he said, and she could tell from his tone that he took no offense to her previous remark.

"I'll do some more digging on Thurston, and see if I can come up with some other names. Someone should know." He rose from the table.

"I've got to get to the office. Why don't you call Tiffany. Try to spend some time with her and pick her brain a little."

"Exactly what I had in mind, sir."

He kissed her before leaving but made no comment on their night.

"Call me if you come up with anything."

"You too," she said.

Tiffany was thrilled to hear from Liz.

"Does this mean what I think it does?" Tiffany said excitedly. "You sound so close. Are you here? In Chicago?"

"In the flesh. Figured I'd do a little visiting in the Windy City then head out west. I hear there's going to be a big party in Vegas in a few days."

"That's wonderful. But let's not wait until then to get together. What are you doing tonight?"

"I'm at your service my dear." Liz was pleased Tiffany had taken the initiative. It meant her instincts were probably correct. Ms. Wayne had nothing to hide.

"Great. Johnny and I were going to have dinner around eight, but he had to cancel. I was bummed, but now I don't have to eat alone.

"This will be perfect. We'll have plenty of time to catch up. Tell me where you're staying and I'll pick you up. And maybe, if you're lucky, I'll forgive you for not calling to let me know you were coming. Remember, you were supposed to stay with me."

"It all happened so fast I really didn't have time to alert anyone," Liz said in a mock defensive tone. "I'll tell you all about it this evening."

Tiffany arrived promptly at 7:30 and the women exchanged smiles and hugs.

"I hope you're hungry. Johnny made arrangements at his favorite Italian restaurant and I guarantee you'll enjoy the food."

"I'm sorry Johnny couldn't make it," Liz said, with mixed feelings. She wanted to meet Tiffany's prince charming but also wanted to be able to talk to her friend candidly, and privately.

"How are things going with you two?"

"Right now, not bad," Tiffany said openly. "I want it to work and I believe does too so we'll see."

Outwardly Tiffany appeared in good spirits, a detail for which Liz was ateful. It was obvious she had no idea how much danger was swirling around r.

At dinner Liz resisted the urge to grill Tiffany about her plans for the lossus, choosing to refer to the hotel indirectly.

"And how is the Baroness Hilton of the design business managing with her -coastal kingdoms?"

"Walter and I are going to discuss it after the party," she said. "As far as lling it or keeping it, I think I'm leaning toward holding on to it for a while. aybe even a year or two. Who knows? But I'll leave the final decision up to alter.

Liz could feel the color drain from her face. She wanted to ask ten questions once.

"What made you change your mind?" she blurted, "and does Walter have any ea you want to keep the Colossus?" Both questions came out in the same ntence.

"A personal letter to me from my father was discovered in a safe deposit box Las Vegas. It was forwarded to me, unopened, last week.

"He was afraid if he left the hotel to Diana she'd sell it immediately. He ved the Colossus and didn't want that.

"In view of how my dad felt, and that he died for his principles, I don't think would be right to sell it now. It would mean he died for no reason.

"My father even had a premonition he'd be killed. He said so in the letter. He o said he'd been pressured by mob front men to sell the hotel and that he had fused." Tiffany skipped telling her about Diana's affair.

Everything Tiffany was saying tied in with what she and Tom had pieced gether.

"And what does Walter say about all of this?"

"Nothing yet. I haven't told him what was in the letter. I want to do that in rson, but I'll rely heavily on Walter's judgement when it comes to selling and 10 to sell to. Once we get the party behind us Walter and I will sit down and k more seriously about the future."

"I'm sure he'll give you solid advice," Liz said vacantly.

"Have you thought about who would run the Colossus if you maintain ntrol?"

"I wish it could be Walter," she said innocently. "But I know he has to get ck to Chicago, to his law practice. If I do keep the hotel I'm certain Walter will oose a worthy successor to run the place.

"Walter said he had a few people in mind, but he hasn't mentioned any mes yet."

"I'm sure he has some ideas," Liz said dryly.

That was the last they talked about the Colossus.

The party was less than a week away.

"I'm going to go to Vegas on the first," Tiffany said. "It would be great you could come then too. I need to be there early in case there are any last minut details that need my attention."

"I've already booked a flight for Friday morning, the third, "Liz said. "And if you don't mind, I want to invite a guest."

Tiffany smiled, a wide happy grin.

"Judging by your red cheeks I'm willing to bet it's a man."

"Bright girl," Liz said, still blushing. "Tom Felton and I have renewed ou friendship and I'd like to ask him to be my escort."

"Why is it I don't think you'll be needing two rooms," Tiffany teased. Sh was delighted Liz was seeing Tom again. In Paris Liz had shared her feeling about Tom, admitting that she still hurt over their separation. Obviously th reunion had been pleasant.

"And you'll both get a chance to meet Johnny," Tiffany continued. "He going to fly in on Friday night."

It was almost midnight when Liz Mallon slipped off her dress and ploppe into bed at the Palmer House. She still knew Tom Felton's home number b heart.

He answered sleepily.

"Pack your bags," she said without identifying herself. "We're going to party in Las Vegas next weekend."

"What's going on?" he said, shaking himself awake.

"Tiffany plans on keeping the hotel, Walter Thurston is the man calling th shots and I have a strong feeling all hell is about to break loose."

Chapter 20
Crisis in the Desert

By the time he arrived in Vegas Brian's memos had memos.

He had made notes on envelopes, cocktail napkins and the back of business cards in addition to using up both sides of the ninety-minute tape in his cassette recorder. And he still had questions.

Were Laura and Sam's deaths really an accident? Did Mario Torino order the hit on Adam Forrester? Was Sonny Fremont in on the takeover? Was Diana? Did either of them realize Adam knew they were playing footsy? Who would step up for the Chicago boys and make the first offer to buy the hotel? Who really killed JFK, how good would Mickey Mantle have been if he had healthy knees and why did anyone think Sara Bernhardt was funny?

The last couple of questions told Brian he was badly in need of sleep. When he got tired, his thoughts tended to run together in a wild, kaleidoscopic stream of consciousness.

One thing the four-hour flight from Detroit had done was dampen his enthusiasm. Initially he was so pumped up after his meeting with Jill Parker/Rita Matthews he couldn't wait to share the details with Walter and Tiffany.

He wanted to slam the door on the mob. Pin Adam's murder on Mario Torino, expose the Chicago syndicate and ride off into the sunset with Tiffany.

Then, somewhere over Missouri reality jumped in and bit him on the ass. He realized he had nothing, and presenting the information he had to Walter and Tiffany would be premature. Besides, Tiffany had been through enough hell. It would be foolish to get her all worked up until everything was in place.

He knew Sarabian would say the same thing.

Even the letter to Boyd Matthews wasn't conclusive. It pointed fingers, but in truth it was no more than what Sam said it was. A couple of pages that detailed his being blackmailed, exposed some members of the Chicago syndicate, gave him a forum to confess he was gay and destroyed Sonny Fremont's career.

All he had on Torino was his veiled reference to Adam Forrester. A smart defense attorney would say his client was only using it as a threat to collect his money. Much like an insensitive parent might threaten a child with the boogey man.

Making the letters public would cause more damage to Sam in the grave than would to Torino in the flesh. Sam's memory would be the only thing tarnished.

He needed more.

It was Tuesday. The Colossus party was only four days away which meant he didn't have much time to try and tie things together.

Arrangements had already been finalized for Sonny Fremont to provide the entertainment at the party. Oscar Bento had eagerly accepted the hotel's offer to make Sonny the feature entertainment at the party, especially since Fremont had maintained a low profile since his setback in "Morocco Heat".

Oscar saw the party gig as an opportunity to showcase Sonny and possibly get a long-term deal with the Colossus. Adam Forrester's hotel was one of the few Strip properties that had never booked Sonny Fremont in its showroom. Now he would get the chance.

He couldn't use his cell phone on the plane, so Brian kept the Airfone busy.

His next call was to Sarabian. He gave the detective the partial phone number Sam had listed in his letter.

"Hi hoss. If the connection sounds a bit funny it's because I'm on board a flight home, probably 40,000 feet in the air somewhere over Colorado."

"What's up?" Sarabian asked. "I didn't even know you were gone. Did you come up with something?"

"Maybe. Too much to go into on the phone right now. But there is one thing you can possibly help with. It could clear up a lot of questions."

"What've you got?"

"A source gave me a partial phone number and I think it might be important. I was wondering if you could somehow check it out and see if it means anything."

"Gimme what you have."

"It's 312-543-16 blank blank."

"That shouldn't be too hard to check," Sarabian said as he repeated the number.

"I'll get somebody right on it.

"But what does it mean? Whose number do you think it is? What are you looking for?" The detective was suddenly full of questions.

"Possibly the key man behind all the dirt," Brian said in a low voice so the passengers around him wouldn't hear. "I think the number could lead us to the real head of the Chicago mob. The man who ordered the hit on Adam Forrester."

He didn't want to complicate matters by going into detail about Sam and Boyd.

"Are you okay?"

"Getting' there," Brian answered. "I'm beginning to get a lot clearer picture of what went on and why all of this happened. I've chased down some leads and come across some stuff that I think you'll want to run with."

"Call me when you get in and we'll sit down." Sarabian's sixth sense was working overtime. Brian would have made a good detective. He was definitely smart enough to know a good lead from a pile of hearsay. "In the meantime I'll run the possible numbers and see if anything familiar shakes loose."

"Thanks." Brian hung up, and stared mindlessly out the window at the low, jagged mountains. Was he getting closer to solving it all or was he merely flapping his wings?

His next call was to Walter.

"I'll be arriving within an hour," he told the lawyer, "but I wanted to update you on my trip."

"Is everything okay with Tiffany?"

"She's okay," he said absently, not wanting to go into detail. "But there's some new information regarding Adam's murder that might turn into something. A lot has happened in the past couple days, Walter. A lot of interesting and bizarre connections."

"I'm anxious to hear what you've found out," Walter replied. "I'll have a Colossus limo at McCarran to meet you.

Walter Thurston wanted to ask Brian for more, but was wise enough to understand than an open air to ground conversation had no assurance of privacy.

Brian hoped Walter wouldn't be disturbed that Tiffany had chosen to show him Adam's letter first. He was confident the lawyer would understand once he explained it was only because Tiffany felt he had enough on his mind running the Colossus, and that she wanted Brian to take her father's suspicions directly to the police.

The seat belt sign illuminated unexpectedly as the 747 dipped sharply, causing several passengers an uneasy moment. Since the World Trade Center attacks, no one flew without some degree of trepidation.

Just as quickly the captain's baritone voice filled the intercom.

"Nothing to be alarmed about folks. We ran into a little turbulence caused by the heat inversion layer. We'll be through it in a minute and you'll be free to move about the cabin again."

The ride was a little bumpy the rest of the way but Brian was too lost in thought for it to bother him.

Some people gasped and others giggled when the stewardess announced the Las Vegas temperature as 109, but they hadn't seen anything yet. By August the mercury would routinely hit 115, forcing tourists off the blistering streets into the air-conditioned casinos.

The pavement turned into a furnace with heat vapors rising off the sidewalks and pedestrians gasping for a breath of air. They'd flock into the casinos not caring if they won or lost. Anything to cool off.

Vegas. Even Mother Nature was a shill for the house.

The Colossus limo was curbside, as promised, and Brian settled back in the upholstered seat. He took another look at his notes trying to decide where to begin when he sat down with Walter.

It was lunchtime, and the Colossus' executive offices were nearly empty. Eric "Big E" Eisenberg, the hotel's top casino host, was finishing up a phone call and Brian waved to him as he made his way to Walter's office.

Walter was sitting behind the large oak desk, nervously fidgeting with a letter opener.

"Brian. Glad to have you back home. How was the flight?"

"A little bumpy, but not too bad. It's just getting harder and harder for me to sit in one place for four or five hours."

"I know what you mean. Incidentally, Detective Sarabian called and said something important came up and he won't be available this afternoon. He said he'd get in touch with you as soon as he could."

Brian was disappointed Sarabian couldn't make the meeting. He wanted the cop to hear everything fresh and get his immediate reaction.

"I'll call his beeper when we're done and arrange to meet him later," Brian said.

The small talk was over.

"What did you find out?" Walter asked while motioning for Brian to close the office door. "And why did you have to go to Michigan?"

"One thing at a time," he answered. Brian wanted to be sure he covered everything that had happened with Tiffany before moving on to Rita Matthews.

"The first shocker was Tiffany," he said. "We could never have guessed what that was all about."

Walter didn't interrupt.

"She opened the letter you sent her. The one from Adam."

"I'm surprised she didn't call to tell me about it," Walter said, and there was confusion in his tone. "Was there something in it that upset her?"

"Plenty," Brian said coldly. "This entire thing is incredible, and the story keeps unfolding. There are so many twists, and yet everything is somehow tied together."

Unable to focus his thoughts Brian unleashed a barrage of sentences that left Walter's jaw agape.

"No doubt anymore about Adam being a mob hit. It definitely wasn't a robbery. His letter to Tiffany says he was being pressured to sell the hotel and didn't know who to trust. He said in the letter that he had a strong hunch he was going to be killed. He also said he knew Diana was having an affair although he didn't know with whom.

"I now know who she was sleeping with, which we'll get to later. And that's the reason he left the hotel to Tiffany."

"That clears up one point," Walter said stiffly. "And frankly, I'm not surprised about Diana even though I don't know much about the woman. How did Tiffany take that news?"

"I couldn't tell. She had already read the letter, probably more than once by the time I met with her, so I have no way of knowing how she reacted when she first learned about it. My guess is she wasn't surprised.

"When we talked she was almost all business." There was no reason to tell Walter about his feelings for Tiffany or their kiss. And there really wasn't much to tell.

"Did Adam's letter say anything about who he thought might be trying to kill m?"

"Not exactly. He thought either New York or Chicago hoods. And it figures," rian said angrily. "They're the two biggest crime families and with a hotel like e Colossus they could launder a hundred million a year and probably skim other twenty or thirty million without drawing any attention from the Feds or e Gaming Control Board. The Colossus is a very important property to these ys. It means a lot of power."

"I can see now why owning the hotel is so critical," Walter said pensively.

"In his letter Adam also suggested that Tiffany hold on to the hotel for a hile," Brian added. "Unless, of course, she was in danger."

"I'm not so sure that's a good idea. I believe things are already a bit too hot ound here."

Walter's response set off a silent alarm in Brian's head.

Why would the lawyer agree so quickly? There had been no threats, no offers d no problems. I know he's thinking of Tiffany but I've got to convince him to ld fast. Selling now would be playing right into their hands. It occurred to rian that maybe Walter was scared too. That had to be it. That plus maybe he anted to get back to Chicago instead of being in the middle of some gangland keover in the Southern Nevada desert.

Walter was the consummate professional but Brian could tell the attorney as mildly disturbed that he was being fed information secondhand. He decided try and soothe the older man's wounded pride.

"You know Walter, in the beginning I couldn't understand why Tiffany ked me to come to Chicago instead of discussing all of this with you. Then it wned on me.

"She thought she needed to prove that she trusted me. Tiffany believed I'd y harder if I knew I had her unquestioned trust. After all, you and she have own each other. I'm kind of the outsider and new kid on the block."

"Makes sense," Walter said, sounding more appeased.

"But still, unless there's something you're not telling me, all we have to go a are Adam's suspicions. Nothing concrete. Nothing to tie it all together."

"You're sounding an awful lot like a defense attorney," Brian laughed. "But ere is more."

Walter's thick silver eyebrows arched and his big, brown-spotted ears came attention.

"It has to do with my detour through Michigan and a woman named Jill arker," he started. "I'm not sure you're going to believe this Walter. I'm not re I believe it myself." Something inside told him it was not time to reveal Jill arker's real name.

Walter's eyes widened and he silently nodded, encouraging Brian to go on.

"The day before you called and asked me to come to work at the Colossus I had gone to the double-funeral of my ex-wife and her brother. They were killed in an auto accident in Los Angeles, and their deaths literally turned my life upside down.

"I thought coming to the Colossus might help me to get my mind off the accident and be good therapy at the same time. I wanted the work to keep me busy. Too busy to think."

Brian didn't want to drag the whole thing out, but he wanted to be sure Walter had enough background to fully assess the situation.

For the next forty-five minutes he talked almost non-stop, filling Walter in on his meeting with Rita Matthews, the letters from Sam to Boyd, the pictures and how Rita came to discover them.

The lawyer leaned back in his chair and listened, much as he would have in court to a prosecutor addressing the jury. He did not interrupt, object or disturb Brian with questions, choosing instead to jot notes on a scratch pad.

When he finished, Brian laid Sam Bradford's final letter on Walter's desk, then slumped back against the cool back of the small black leather love seat, waiting for the inevitable questions.

It seemed like five minutes before Walter spoke, and when he did, he stood, pencil in hand, with his glasses perched atop his head.

It was his turn to address the jury. To question, cajole, convince and coddle. To try and prove or disprove whatever evidence or opinion had come before.

And Walter Thurston was truly a master of his craft.

"I don't need to tell you how startling and incredible this information is," he said calmly.

Walter's insides were churning, but Columbia Law School had taught him to control his emotions, to keep them in check regardless of the excitement running through his veins. Savor. Don't pounce. This was a moment that tested those lessons.

"Adam's letter was prophetic," he continued, "however we can only deal with it as conjecture."

"But..."

Walter raised his hand, quieting Brian's attempt to interject.

"What I mean is, nothing you've told me about his letter gives us any hard evidence. There's not enough to make a case, even though we both know Adam was right. In court I'd ask for an immediate dismissal. And I'd get it.

"The other material, the pictures and Sam's letter to Boyd Matthews, is a very different ball game. It gives us names and dates, but again, it is only a starting point. And none of it would be admissible in a court of law. Remember Sam's letter is typed. We can verify his signature but not his accusations. And that's all they are—accusations. No witnesses, no murder weapon, no fingerprints and no motive since whoever killed him did not inherit the hotel."

"Are you telling me that neither of these letters help solve these murders? Brian was agitated. He was practically screaming at Walter out of frustration.

"To the contrary Brian. Look at them as breadcrumbs, or arrows pointing us n the right direction. Without these clues we're coal miners groping around in a lark tunnel. Now we have a light."

They both started to speak at the same time.

The lawyer deferred to Brian.

"Go ahead."

"The way I see it, Bento and Torino are the key players. These are the guys ve need to watch."

"They were both mentioned in Sam's letter," said Walter, "but what's their connection to Adam other than Torino allegedly making reference to a newspaper clipping about the murder. That's not a crime."

"Bento is Sonny Fremont's agent," said Brian.

"Still not a crime," Walter countered.

"True," Brian agreed, and he relished the opportunity to drop his own nuclear nugget. "We both know that Sonny was the reason Sam ditched the picture, but what you don't know counselor is that Fremont is also the mystery guy who's been watering the widow Forrester's garden."

Walter was aghast.

"How sure are you of that?"

"If you mean have I actually seen them doing it, the answer is no. Do I think my sources are reliable? A definite yes."

Walter was trying desperately to be dispassionate, taking the conservative approach, playing the devil's advocate.

"Their affair is only relevant if they were somehow involved in Adam's murder," he said, sounding more like a lawyer than Brian liked. "We have to consider that it is possible their affair was forged purely out of lust."

"That would be naïve of us," Brian countered. "The way I see it Fremont could have had two reasons for hooking up with Diana. Lust, as you suggest, and which I doubt, or he had inside information that Adam was going to be out of the picture soon and he wanted to be in a position to pick up the pieces."

"There are still other possibilities," Walter said methodically.

Brian looked at the lawyer, waiting for what he knew would be a list of logical alternatives he had not considered.

"Fremont could have been sleeping with Diana to try and better his chances of getting a contract to play the Colossus."

"Possible but probably not necessary since our entertainment department tells me we were already close to making a deal to add Sonny to our roster of headliners," said Brian.

Walter was undeterred.

"Maybe Fremont had some dirt on Diana and was blackmailing her."

For the next few minutes they verbalized every option they could imagine.

"The most dangerous alternative of all would be that one of them or both o them were in on the murder in some way," said Walter. "Either they did it fo their own gain, which would make them both stupid and vulnerable, or they were pawns for the mob."

"Either way their plans were ruined when Tiffany emerged as the new owner," said Brian.

"Which brings me back to why I think it's a good idea for her to dump this place," Walter said. "I don't want her in any danger. And her father wouldn' want her in harm's way. I can guarantee that.

"What I still don't understand though is why you insisted on hiring Sonny Fremont as the main headliner for The Colossus party?"

"Because it will be easier to talk to him on our turf," Brian explained. "We won't have to go chasing him down and arouse his suspicions. The fact we approached him, as if nothing was wrong, could cause him to drop his guard a bit."

"It might work," said Walter wrinkling his brow.

"You know Brian, with all the information you've gathered it would seem the rest would be easy, but it won't be. I'm afraid it will be up to us to force the issue."

"I know that Walter. But if we get lucky it could have a domino effect Sonny and Oscar seem to be the weakest links. If we could get one of them to trip over their own feet some other heads could roll."

"These people aren't stupid," said Walter. "Don't you ever forget that Brian Don't underestimate them. If something doesn't smell right they'll cut their losses, cover their tracks and steam roll anyone in the way."

Brian knew the party wasn't the kind of function at which Sarabian would be comfortable but he wanted him there anyway.

"Do you think we should call Tiffany and let her know what's going on?"

"No." Walter's voice was stern. "I don't want her to become paranoid o think there's some sort of conspiracy. Anyway, she's due here tomorrow. That will be soon enough to share these things with her.

"By the way Brian, it's my understanding Tiffany knows nothing about the Jill Parker material. Am I right?"

"Right. I didn't meet Jill until after I left Chicago, and I haven't spoken to Tiffany since."

"Very well. Let's get on with what we have to do here."

Almost all of the RSVP's had been returned, and as Brian had expected, the cream of Las Vegas' social circle would be attending.

The most impressive confirmation came from Sheik Mohammed Gaddi. His appearance guaranteed that the Colossus party would not only be the most pectacular gala of the new millennium, but of international significance. Brian vas impressed.

It was after 10 p.m. before Brian met up with Detective Sarabian but it was vorth the wait.

He told the big detective about his meeting with Tiffany, and Adam's letter, hen showed Sarabian a copy of Sam's letter to Boyd.

"Holy shit buddy. You've come loaded with some high-powered mmunition. And since you're giving me what you've got, I've got some goodies or you too."

Quid pro quo.

"As to who was dogging Forrester, you can forget the New York mob. It was efinitely Chicago and your pal Torino. They have first dibs on the Colossus and ley only have six months to get it. After that it's open season."

That information jibbed with what Brian already knew.

"We've also confirmed that the shooter was out of town muscle. Probably ut of Cleveland or Detroit. No murder weapon yet but forensics thinks they may ave one partial print that could mean something. More on that later.

"We both know Fremont was poking Diana which could be a coincidence or n indication they knew what was going down and were planning on playing ouse in the open as soon as she became a rich widow."

"What do you think?"

"I think Chicago has to make a move soon," Sarabian said. "And I don't see lem trying to take out Tiffany, if that's what you mean. At least not until ley've made a serious bid to buy the joint.

"Torino is a major player, maybe the highest we can go in the Chicago amily. But he's slippery. He's been into a thousand things and his name has ome up a lot but never a conviction. He's as teflon as Gotti. Unless Bento or omeone who has first hand info rolls, Torino will skate.

"And as far as re-opening the investigation into Laura and Sam's accident ased on Sam Bradford's letter, forget about it. Without a confession or an eye /itness there'll never be enough evidence. We'll have to be content trying to put lem away for Forrester."

"What about Fremont and Diana?" Brian repeated. The detective still had not ffered an opinion about the level of their involvement.

"I don't think they'd trust Diana," he said flatly. "These guys don't like oing business with women. Never have. Never will."

"Fremont?"

"Possible. Maybe even probable since they had him by the balls after the lovie deal. My best guess is they intended to use him as a clean shirt to buy the otel from Diana after they did Forrester. Like Allen Glick at the Stardust back in le late 70's and that guy at the Tropicana…"

"Deil Gustafson?"

"Yeah, the financial genius from Minnesota. He was a piece of work. All these little number crunchers that suddenly find themselves in a position of power. You'd think they'd be smart enough to realize they're only patsies, but they never catch on 'til it's too late."

Brian wanted a conclusion.

"I want your honest opinion Don. Based on your expertise, did Sonny or Diana set Forrester up?"

"Can't tell," he said quickly. "If I had to guess I'd say Diana didn't know anything about the hit. But I'd bet my ass she suspected it. She's not some stupid broad. But based on my dealings with these low life scum I'd have to rule her out. They just don't trust skirts.

"Sonny's a different piece of shit. He could've known beforehand but it doesn't matter. He knows now, which makes him an accessory after the fact. What's more, if the only reason he was playing hide the salami with Forrester's old lady was to be in position to console the grieving widow and take the hotel off her hands, he's outlived his usefulness. He could be the weak link."

"You'll get a chance to see the Sonny man up close and personal Saturday night," Brian chuckled.

"Why's that?"

"Because we've hired him to entertain at the Colossus Hotel's Summer Welcoming Party and you're on the invited guest list."

"Thanks a lot asshole," Sarabian said sarcastically. "You know how I hate to put on a monkey suit."

"I know big fella, but this will give you a perfect chance to keep an eye on all the key players and maybe say a few choice words to Fremont. Maybe rattle his cage a little."

Brian made a move to leave and Sarabian grabbed his arm.

"One more thing pal. That number you gave me. The one you only had part of…"

"Yeah…"

"Our numbers guys checked it out. Ran all the possible sequences. There were exactly one hundred possible combinations in the Chicago area. I looked at the names of the people on the other end of those numbers. Only one of them rang a bell, and it's the reason I removed myself from the meeting with you and Thurston earlier today."

"What do you mean?" Brian asked, taking the bait.

"I wanted to share the information about the telephone number with you privately, before discussing the results with Mr. Thurston."

"And why would that be?"

"Because the number that makes the most sense dials into Walter Thurston's law firm."

Brian Powers almost wet his pants. What the hell was that all about? There d to be some mistake. He tried to conceal his amazement, but Sarabian picked ● on it in a second.

"Don't go jumping to conclusions," he warned. "Things aren't always what ey seem. First of all, because the number fits doesn't mean it's the one that was aled from Sam's cell phone. It's just one of the possibilities. Might just be a ●incidence."

Right. And Liberace wasn't gay. He just liked sequins and feather boas.

"C'mon Brian. You said you thought Thurston was on the level. Nothing else ●out him turns up sour. Don't jump to conclusions, but keep him on a short ısh. At least for now." He was relieved he hadn't given Walter Rita Matthews' al name.

Brian took the long way home, winding down the Strip, past the Luxor, andalay Bay and the Four Seasons. He needed to think.

Walter Thurston. A new country heard from. Could it be?

A sign on a vacant building just past the Signature Air Terminal for private anes proclaimed, "Jesus is Coming".

Brian grinned.

If He's coming for the Fourth of July, He'd better have a reservation.

Tiffany arrived on schedule, at noon Wednesday and was met at McCarran ● Walter and a Colossus limo. Brian had not been invited to be part of the ●lcoming committee.

"Obviously the desert agrees with you," Tiffany said as she hugged Walter. "You're looking very fit, maybe even lost a few pounds as well."

Walter accepted the compliment graciously.

"It's good to see you Tiffany," he said once the limo was moving. "I've ıssed you."

"I've missed you too Walter. Talking on the phone isn't quite the same as ing here."

"Everything is on schedule for Saturday," Walter announced proudly, guring it was his turn to beat Tiffany to the punch.

"Even the roof?"

"Yes, even the roof. And I must admit that your little brainstorm is not only autiful but also a work of art that will probably get worldwide publicity. You ve already put your personal imprimatur on the Colossus."

Tiffany was pleased.

"I can hardly wait to see it," she said excitedly. "And what about the guest t? Are Las Vegas' rich and powerful coming?"

"They certainly are, including the governor and some billionaire Sheik whom ian claims has more money than half the countries in the world."

"Geez. I won't know whether to thank him or ask him to buy the place," she ıghed.

247

Neither of them was ready for the heavy discussion they both knew was inevitable.

"I'm surprised Brian didn't come along." She had expected him, even hoped that if only a one-man greeting party met her it might be Brian. She was confused about her feelings for him.

"He was out of the office when we left the hotel," Walter explained. "I believe he had some last minute details to handle with T.J. We'll all get together later."

"The sooner the better," she said.

The limo crawled past the MGM, and grid locked traffic brought it to complete stop in front of the defunct All-Star café.

"Isn't that the place Andre Agassi owned?" she asked.

"I believe so," Walter answered. At least he did own it. I'm not sure if he still does. He and Steffi Graf live in Vegas you know?"

"No, I didn't know," Tiffany admitted. "Did you invite them to the party?"

"I'm not sure, but if we didn't we can have an invitation hand delivered today."

They were moving again, and a couple minutes later the stretch black Cadillac eased to a smooth stop in front of the hotel and a Colossus doorman helped Tiffany out of the low back seat.

"Welcome home Miss Wayne," he said cheerfully.

"Thank You. It's good to be back." The doorman calling her by name put her a little off balance. She wasn't sure she was glad to be back, and the Colossus certainly wasn't home.

"Walter, I'd like to freshen up then get right to work. Say half an hour. I want to get a general briefing on Colossus business, and then have a look at the party guest list. I'd like to go over the names with Brian to see if there are any key people who haven't responded. When we're finished with our meeting I'd also like a run-through test of the sliding roof."

"Yes ma'am," he said with a smile. "Brian's got his cell phone and expecting my call. We'll be in the executive offices whenever you're ready."

Tiffany followed the bellman across the casino to the elevators. She had requested a room in which she could entertain, in the event she wanted to invite Liz and Tom for a private get together.

She wasn't disappointed.

"Here we are Ms. Wayne, The Athena Suite," the bellman announced as he animatedly opened one of the solid oak double doors to the massive 4,000 square foot penthouse.

"This is the best suite in the hotel. President Bush stayed in it when he visited Las Vegas. So did Princess Diana and that Microsoft guy, Bill Gates."

"Thanks Cappy," she said, reading his name tag. "I'm sure this will be perfect."

The white carpeting was at least an inch thick and there were three fireplaces, including one in the bathroom which she thought was a good idea. The fireplace in the master bedroom was across from the bed and slightly elevated. The third was nestled in the corner of the monstrous living room opposite the large marble Jacuzzi. Paintings by Renoir and Monet adorned the walls.

Outside the huge double-paned glass window was a breathtaking view of Las Vegas and the neon wonderland known as The Strip.

In the bathroom were his and her showers, the "his" doubling as a sauna. A heart-shaped tub with therapy jets, a bidet and an incredible twenty-foot onyx counter added to the splendor. The fixtures were a combination of black marble and 24-karat gold.

It was a bit over the top but Tiffany was duly impressed.

The rest of the suite was equally spectacular. She knew Johnny would love the room. He had promised to make the party even though he would not arrive in Las Vegas until 11:50 Friday night.

She gave the bellman $20 and hoped he hadn't noticed how awed she was. After all, she owned the joint.

She unpacked, took a quick steamy shower, changed into some loose fitting pants set off by a lightweight cardigan and headed for the executive offices.

Brian and Walter were already there.

"Sorry, I didn't make it to the airport," were the words she heard, but the warmth in Brian's eyes said so much more.

"I've changed my mind," she said impulsively. "Before we get started on business I'd like to go down and take a look at the new toy. Is that all right with you guys?"

"Let's do it," Brian said as he stood up. "Every time I see it I'm amazed."

"Okay with me," Walter echoed.

"The rich and famous are buzzing over this party," Brian said once they were in the elevator. He wanted to tell her how much he had looked forward to seeing her, but thought better of it. He was as confused as she was about what had happened in Chicago.

The elevator lurched gently as it came to a halt, opening its gilded doors to a recessed foyer containing some priceless Greek sculpture. There were no gaming tables in the immediate line of sight, a fact Tiffany found greatly relaxing.

Walter led the way as the trio walked across the spacious casino and past the front lobby into the convention and ballroom area. The Acropolis Ballroom was at the far end of the corridor.

As they arrived at the 14-foot high entry doors, Walter paused.

"Close your eyes Tiffany. I want this to be a complete surprise."

She complied willingly.

"I feel like a little girl on her birthday, waiting for someone to wheel a bicycle into the room," she said happily.

Ron Delpit

"You can open your eyes now," Walter told her.

She did not immediately look at the ceiling. Instead, her eyes slowly rolled around the entire room, drinking in its full grandeur. Tiffany could feel an enormous strength in the room, as if it were alive.

Her eyes climbed the sidewall, working their way to the ceiling. When finally they focused on the unbelievable "moon-roof" she was flabbergasted.

Walter's improvisation of the stained glass had taken the roof from the spectacular to the work of art category.

"My God, Walter...Oh my God."

Tiffany kept repeating the words.

"Beautiful can't even come close to describing it," she exclaimed.

"Wait until you see it in operation." Walter was beaming like a child on Christmas morning. He put his arm around Tiffany and led her to the far right corner of the room.

"Here's the switch," he said pointing to the wall. "Turn the key and see what you've created."

She hesitated for an instant then turned the silver key to the on position, all the while keeping her eyes transfixed on the ceiling.

Magically and majestically the roof began to part in the middle, sliding back to reveal a hot sun burning in a cloudless blue summer sky. The movement of the roof was nearly silent, the murmur of the hydraulic engines barely audible to the naked ear.

Tiffany was speechless.

"It's fantastic," she gushed. "I've never seen anything like it."

"Neither has anyone else," Brian ad libbed.

She stood and gazed at the sky for long minutes, her mind filled with visions of everything from her trip to Paris and Liz Mallon to Johnny, Brian and the ugly business of her father's murder, which was the one nightmare that wouldn't go away.

The nightmares were still haunting her and she had considered seeing a shrink. It wasn't something she wanted to discuss—with anyone.

Sarabian was waiting in the outer foyer as they returned to the executive offices.

He and Tiffany had never met, and she was surprised to see him.

"I thought it might be a good idea for Detective Sarabian to join us," Brian said after making the introductions. "Just so we can all get on the same page. I think he has some information he wants to share."

Sarabian was pretty much as she had pictured him when they spoke on the phone, and she liked the big detective on sight. He did not come on like a know it all, or try and patronize her.

Still, Tiffany decided she should be the one to set the tone for the meeting. Unless she made it perfectly clear from the beginning that she wanted to know

250

verything, the three men would probably tell her only what they felt she should now, or what they felt she could handle.

"I'm glad the party is shaping up like we hoped it would," she said when hey were all seated. "But the party and everything surrounding it are all econdary to seeing to it that my father's murderer is brought to justice. That is till my main priority.

"It's the reason I asked Brian to come to Chicago. I suppose the roof fulfills ny dad's wish that I leave my own mark on the Colossus, so all that's left is to ind out who killed him so this whole horrible dream can be put to rest."

But would that be enough to make her nightmares end?

The men looked at each other for a sign. Neither had expected her to come n so strong.

Walter spoke first.

"Perhaps it will be best if we all lay our cards on the table," he said. "Brian as shared the contents of your father's letter with both me and detective arabian.

"And?" Tiffany turned her gaze toward Sarabian.

"And, thanks to one of Brian's street informants, a fellow called "Suspect", ve're working on some crucial information.

Somehow, Suspect had come through with the street name of a shooter from ersey known as "Bounty". He never revealed his sources, so Brian had no way f knowing how the mysterious black man had come up with it.

But it didn't matter. Suspect's tip was the key. The police had uncovered a artial fingerprint at the crime scene, but came up empty when they ran it hrough police and FBI files.

The fingerprint revelation was a bombshell.

"Is that true?" Walter asked.

"Yeah, but it took Suspect getting the nickname and a rough physical escription to keep things on track, "Sarabian explained.

"Why, when you had a fingerprint?" Tiffany asked. "Wouldn't the FBI, the IA or somebody be able to match it eventually?"

"Not in this case," Sarabian continued. "This man, "Bounty", has never been rrested. He's been a primary suspect in a number of high profile murder cases ll over the world over the past several years, but he's managed to avoid rosecution. Therefore his fingerprints aren't on file and there are no known ugshots of him."

It was Brian's turn to pitch in.

"He's just an outside hired gun. He works for the highest bidder. Sarabian aid he wouldn't be surprised if he worked for the government or CIA at one me.

"The Jersey police know his whereabouts and are keeping him under 24-hour urveillance, "Brian said, hoping Tiffany would be satisfied.

251

"We're not ready for them to pick him up yet, "Sarabian cautioned. "When it's time. For now they'll just watch him and not let him leave the city. If he tries to leave they'll be forced to detain him. Once we get them the print they'll try and get a match."

"Are you sure it's his print?" Walter asked skeptically.

"Not yet," Sarabian answered cautiously. "And we can't pick him up until we're sure. The first thing we have to do is eliminate the possibility that it belonged to any of the help, or some friend of your dad's. We know it doesn't belong to Adam or Diana Forrester."

"How soon will they know?" Tiffany asked anxiously.

"It'll take a few days, maybe even a week," Sarabian said cautiously. "The FBI lab is working on it, but there's no guarantee. It's a longshot, but it's all we have right now."

"The police can now confirm what your father suspected in his letter," Walter observed. "They have no doubt it was a mob hit and part of a planned takeover of the Colossus."

"But they still don't know if it was gang people from Chicago or New York, do they?" Tiffany was looking at Brian for an answer.

"I think that's still undecided," Walter said.

"Not anymore," Sarabian said convincingly. "We have positive evidence it was the Chicago syndicate."

"How can you be sure?" Walter, Tiffany and Brian asked in unison.

"We picked up an informant," Sarabian explained. "And he's provided us with information that has checked out."

"Well they may have counted on buying the hotel from Diana, but that's not the case any more," Tiffany said defiantly. "And what about Diana? Is she still free and clear? Did they absolutely rule her out as a suspect?"

"Yes," Brian said somewhat apologetically. "Her alibi has been verified."

"What was she doing, screwing Sonny Fremont?" Tiffany knew her frustration was the reason for her crudeness but she felt no need to apologize.

The three men ignored Tiffany's emotional response.

"There's a chance both Sonny and Diana could be accomplices," Sarabian said, trying to give her something to hope for. "They could both be prosecuted if they had any advance knowledge of the murder."

Brian then proceeded to enlighten Tiffany about his meeting with Rita Matthews and the possibility the three murders were connected.

Tiffany's body became rigid and her stare hardened. Her face went pale and for a moment Brian thought she was going to faint.

"How can this be happening?" The question was rhetorical but Brian could see a look of helplessness in her eyes. She was trying to be so strong but she was also close to collapse. To giving up. She would have to find some inner strength. He knew she couldn't take many more jolts.

Her tough exterior was fading.

"How can these animals still be on the street if the police know who they e? They've killed at least three people we know about." Her words were hard t her voice was lifeless. "What the hell is the matter with our legal system?"

"It worries too much about the rights of the criminal and not enough about e victims," Brian answered. He was trying to console her.

"We only need one of the smaller fish to roll over," Brian said trying to inject me hope into the conversation. Detective Sarabian believes he may be able to are Sonny or Diana, or maybe even Oscar Bento into cooperating. He might en offer them immunity in exchange for their testimony."

"Why let them off the hook?" Tiffany said heatedly.

"Because we're virtually positive none of them actually committed any of the urders," Sarabian responded, "and because we may not be able to build a strong ough case against the people who did without help."

Sarabian had only suggested the idea of immunity. Brian knew it had to be eared with a lot of prosecution types and he also knew the chance of getting ne of the little people to roll was a million to one.

But what the hell. This was Vegas, the fantasyland where longshots came in very day of the week.

"We've already put some rumors out on the street that we think will get back Sonny and Oscar pretty quickly," Sarabian added. "That might spook them a tle."

"And you are coming to the party, aren't you Detective?"

"Wouldn't miss it," Sarabian answered. "It should be mighty interesting. nd, if you guys don't need me any more, I must get out of here. I have a eeting in a few minutes."

"I think that about covers it," Walter said, taking charge.

"Then I'll show myself out."

"Thanks for coming," Tiffany added as Sarabian headed out. "See you aturday."

"See ya."

"I'm going to have a very tough time dealing with Sonny Fremont as the main entertainment." Tiffany remarked after Sarabian had departed. "I'm not ure I'll be able to even look at him, knowing what he and Diana did to my ather."

"You'll have no contact at all with him," Brian said calmly. "He'll be on tage. You'll be busy with the guests, and I'll see to it he never gets near you. I romise you that."

Brian's promise seemed to soothe Tiffany for the moment.

"Before we leave the subject of the guest list, I'd like to have some special ames added," Tiffany said softly.

"Fire away," said Brian, pad in hand.

"Valerie Reston, Liz Mallon, her escort Tom Felton and Johnny Marciano."

"Johnny's coming?" Walter seemed surprised.

"He's arriving late Friday night," Tiffany said blankly.

Brian was suddenly blue, but he shouldn't have been surprised. He had n reason to think Tiffany wouldn't invite her boyfriend. He wondered how he react when he met Johnny Marciano?

"We'll also need to arrange rooms for Valerie and Liz, and keep one on hol for Tom Felton. I don't know if he and Liz are planning to stay together."

"Felton...isn't he the investigative reporter for the Chicago Tribune?" Walt inquired.

"I think he does work at the Trib," Tiffany replied, "but I'm not sure what h does. I thought Liz told me he was an editor."

"If I'm not mistaken Felton was once the Tribune's Organized Crim reporter," Walter said out loud, more to himself than anyone else.

"And Liz Mallon is the reporter you met in Paris?"

"Yes Walter. We've become very good friends."

Brian jotted down the names, and the fact she made no mention of a room fo Johnny Marciano did not escape him. He circled Felton's name on his pad. If th guy was familiar with the players in the Chicago syndicate he might prove to be valuable contact.

This was going to be the party to end all parties.

The only way we could have more fireworks would be to invite Bill an Hillary and seat them at a table with Monica Lewinsky and Kenneth Starr. An wouldn't that be a kick. Brian laughed at his own foolish thoughts. What was th big deal with the politicians anyway? Clinton was the unibanger, Starr was backstabbing hired gun and Lewinsky was a tramp who raked in $5 mil for a fe blow jobs and a tell all book. Hillary was the only one he couldn't get a hand on. Did she just want to be the First Lady and not care about her sex craze husband or was she that forgiving and understanding?

Had to be the First Lady thing Brian decided. No woman was th understanding.

For the next fifteen minutes they went over minor party details, wrapping u when Tiffany gave final approval to the menu and the trumpeted red carp introductions that would be given to all arriving guests.

When they adjourned Brian took care of the room requests then popped ou to get a haircut and a little touch-up color to cover the isolated gray strands I was blaming on stress.

Walter called Margaret to make dinner plans and Tiffany uncharacteristicall opted to take a lazy walk through the hotel.

The evening entertainment was just beginning and she paused briefly at th back of the Corfu Lounge to enjoy the mellow voice of a young singer name Denise Clemente.

Despite her flashy costume, Clemente had an easy manner and a nice voice. 'he girl appeared to be enjoying her job, even though there were only a handful f people in the lounge, and Tiffany wondered how many performers actually ked what they did.

Tiffany felt a touch of sadness when the singer did "Help me Make it hrough the Night". It had been one of her dad's favorites.

She looked in on a couple of the hotel restaurants, then walked past the long ail of show-goers waiting in the evening reservation line to see Paul Anka. iffany had seen his show in Chicago and was impressed the way the performer ave everything of himself on stage, and by the sheer volume of hits the man had ritten over the years.

For the next hour she roamed through every part of the Colossus, observing verything from the action at the craps tables to a high stakes blackjack player at reserved table playing six spots at $5000 per hand.

In the baccarat pit she watched an Oriental gambler lose $400,000 in ten iinutes without ever changing expression.

It was easy to understand how the soft lights, fast action and enticing green bles could seduce the customers. She even found herself feeling the excitement.

Without thinking she swerved into the Alpha coffee shop. She didn't know if was light or dark outside but her stomach told her she had skipped dinner. The aitress had no idea who she was, and seated her in a no smoking booth toward ie rear.

It was the same room where she had first met Diana, and that was not a leasant recollection. She had a salad, fries and iced tea and was in and out in venty minutes.

It was after ten when she got back to her room and the message light was ashing.

She dialed the automated message center and pushed the playback button.

"Hi boss. I'll be arriving at 11:40 Friday morning on United flight #2342. ee you then." Valerie's high-pitched voice was unmistakable and Tiffany was ad she had insisted on her assistant being part of the celebration.

The second message was from Johnny.

"Tried paging you a couple times, obviously without success. I imagine ou're very busy. I miss you. I think I've managed to clear my schedule for the eekend. Don't worry, I'll be there."

The third message was from Liz.

"Hello Cinderella. This is your fairy godmother. I'll be in Vegas mid- orning Saturday afternoon, with Tom in tow. And as much as I'm afraid to say , I think we'll only need one room. And that scares the shit out of me. But c'est vie. See you soon."

A wry smile played on Tiffany's tired face.

Liz Mallon was something special.

Thursday literally flew by.

Brian spent most of the day wrestling with what he considered his biggest problem...

What to make of Walter Thurston? Was he friend or foe? Could he be trusted?

A mistake would be disastrous.

He had asked Sarabian to hold off on discussing the phone number issue with Walter, and he himself had not confronted or questioned the lawyer about the call and it was eating away at him.

He went over it again in his head.

Sarabian said the police cryptographers had compiled a list of all the possible phone numbers that could have been dialed from Sam's cell phone the day Mario Torino visited him in Hollywood.

There were a hundred possible numbers. Walter Thurston's law firm was one of the possibilities. It was the only one that made sense. Walter's was the only phone number that fit in with the case. Brian was positive it was not a coincidence. What other explanation could there be?

If Torino was calling Walter it meant the lawyer was somehow tied in with the Chicago mob. As their consigliore? Or was he possibly being paid to choose the Torino group as the Colossus' buyers?

He couldn't just come out and accuse Walter. He'd have to keep his ears open. Hope the attorney said or did something to erase any doubts, one way or the other. He'd have to wait.

Val's United flight touched down almost half an hour late and Tiffany spent the rest of the afternoon showing her associate the wonders of the Colossus.

Valerie Reston loved every second of it. She had never seen so much money or so much decadence. And best of all, she was part of it. At least for the weekend.

"This is like being the Queen of Wonderland," Val said between bites of veal parmesan.

"There's a lot of energy and excitement here. Probably more than there is in the real world back in Chicago," Valerie chirped. "If it were me, I'm not sure I could give all of this up. Not if I was the boss."

Tom Felton and a slightly apprehensive Liz Mallon arrived Saturday morning at 11:20. A last minute hotel meeting kept Tiffany from greeting her friend at the airport.

A uniformed Colossus chauffeur, waving a placard that read, "Liz Mallon Paris" met them in the baggage claim area and offered apologies from Tiffany.

Liz had spent much of the flight picking Tom's brain, and he had been responsive, sharing what he remembered from his days on the organized crime beat as well as filling her in on new information he had picked up from informants in the past two days.

Nothing Tom said changed Liz' opinion. She remained convinced that Walter Thurston was the man behind the plot to take over the Colossus.

"He knew Adam. I'm willing to bet he knew about the will and he was one of the only people in the world to know where Tiffany was in Paris," she said trying to make a case.

"I'm still not completely sold," Tom resisted. "There's someone in Vegas I'd like to talk to. An old friend who used to keep his finger on the pulse of the underworld. Also, I have a hunch this big party might throw some new light on the whole thing."

"Why?" Liz asked. "I doubt if anyone would try and harm Tiffany in public, or even show up at an event like this. Remember, this is a very exclusive, invitation only affair."

Tom gave her a disappointed look.

"Don't you start being naïve," he warned. "I'm not much of a gambler but I'd be willing to wager that whoever is after the Colossus will show up at the party. I don't mean goons. I mean the people behind the plot, if there is one."

It irked Liz that Tom still had doubts about whether there really was a conspiracy.

"How will we know who they are?"

"We won't," Tom said dejectedly. "In all likelihood we won't."

Saturday arrived before Johnny Marciano did.

He had been unable to make the Friday night flight but had called Tiffany to assure her he would be there in time for the party and could stay until Monday.

Brian's tux was hanging neatly in the closet when he returned to his room at four o'clock. He wasn't sure if he should thank housekeeping or the bell desk for getting it done on short notice but he owed one of them a nice tip.

He'd met Val, taken an immediate liking to Tom and Liz and heard that Johnny Marciano was not due in until 4:45, a little more than an hour before the festivities were set to begin.

Cocktails were scheduled from six to seven, with dinner from seven to eight-thirty followed by the Sonny Fremont show and dancing in the Acropolis ballroom. That's when Tiffany would do the honors and open the roof.

Brian sensed there was more to Tom and Liz being there than met the eye. Neither of the reporters seemed like the party type, nor did they seem to have any special affinity for Las Vegas.

He would explore it further over cocktails. Someone had mentioned that Felton was a former organized crime reporter. Another coincidence? He didn't think so.

Once is an accident. Twice is a coincidence. Three times is a pattern.

By 5:30 limos were stacked outside the Colossus front entrance like planes in a holding pattern over JFK.

The crowd marveled over the ice carvings and the wide assortment of food, however the biggest hit of the early evening were the two gypsy fortune-tellers hired to amuse the guests. They had tables set up in colorful mini-tents in opposite corners of the room and there was an eager throng waiting in front of each.

And why not, Brian reasoned? The future was good business. In fact there were more than a few guys in the sports book who would be willing to sell their souls for a peek at tomorrow's scores and results.

In true royal fashion, guests were announced by the sounding of six trumpeters, standing three abreast on either side of a long red carpet.

An emcee announced each of the arriving parties. After being presented the guests proceeded down the red carpet to a receiving line where Tiffany stood waiting to extend personal greetings.

Tina Robertson, the most competent and outgoing member of the Colossus public relations staff, stood just inches from Tiffany's shoulder, whispering bits of pertinent information about each guest before they covered the thirty or so feet of the walkway.

By the time the new arrivals reached the end of the carpet Tiffany knew all she needed to know to make her greeting seem customized and personal.

Nevada's governor, two state senators, Barron Hilton and the chairmen of the board of Bally's and Caesars Palace filtered through the line. So did former Mirage owners Steve and Elaine Wynn, who were about to unveil plans for their newest hotel venture on the grounds of the former Desert Inn. And the dashing Maloof Brothers, owners of the Sacramento Kings and the new Palms Hotel were in attendance with their significant others.

The president of Circus Circus Enterprises, then two Japanese hotel owners whose names Brian couldn't pronounce, and financier Kirk Kerkorian who rarely made public appearances followed them.

Tiffany's eyes sparkled and her heartbeat quickened when she saw Johnny Marciano, looking elegant and handsome in a white tuxedo, make his way down the runway.

"You know I wouldn't have missed this," he whispered as he kissed her cheek. She squeezed his hand tightly and exhaled deeply. The evening was going to be okay despite her trepidation.

Bruce Willis, in town filming a movie, came in solo while Antonio Banderas and wife Melanie Griffith, both looking tan and trim, helped add some glitter.

A smiling Tiffany greeted two former astronauts and CBS broadcast legend Walter Cronkite, all in Vegas for a NASA convention.

Valerie Reston, in a stunning low cut gown, was having the time of her life enjoying the attention being lavished on her by some of Las Vegas' most eligible bachelors.

Tiffany was pleased to see that Liz, Brian and Tom had apparently taken to ch other, huddling in a corner engaged in what seemed like a serious nversation.

With all the commotion, the next entry caught Tiffany totally unaware. And :e a swift kick in the stomach, it took her breath away.

She had turned her head for a moment to chat with a guest, and when her ze returned to the front entrance, the trumpets were again blaring.

The announcement heralded the arrival of Sheik Mohammed Gaddi of Saudi :abia.

He was a strikingly handsome man, tall and dark with heavy eyebrows and own eyes so intense Tiffany imagined they could pierce steel.

There was a presence about him that commanded and demanded attention.

His right arm hung stiffly at his side. On his left arm was Diana Forrester, :aring a smile more luminous than the sparkling diamond tiara that sat mfortably atop her well-coiffed red mane.

Most of the guests were too busy mixing to notice the impending conflict. 1ose who did trained their eyes on the battleground as the Sheik and Diana ade their way down the carpeted runway to Tiffany.

It was all she could do to keep her heart in her chest.

"Sheik Gaddi. I'm so glad you could come," Tiffany said, extending her oved hand.

"I'm happy to be here Miss Wayne, but I must admit, if it weren't for Mrs. :rrester's persistence, I might not have come," he said without a hint of malice.

"That's right," Diana gloated. "I insisted we should come."

Brian was fifty feet away with an unobstructed view of the developing head-. collision and alerted Walter to the unfolding drama. The lawyer moved across : room with catlike quickness, and in seconds was standing only two feet hind Tiffany, out of the line of fire, but ready to step in if an unpleasant scene >se.

"I told the Sheik that anyone who is anyone would be here tonight," Diana id mockingly, and the luster of her red locks shone brilliantly against the ivory lite of her designer gown.

Tiffany recognized the dress. It was her design, from the new Tiffany >llection that had been unveiled in Paris. It was a one of a kind, specially signed for the show and cost $5,000.

How did she get the goddammed dress? Valerie told her it had been sold a •ek ago, but to a woman in Chicago.

Diana's diamond and ruby neckpiece was another item you weren't likely to d in the corner drugstore, and Tiffany knew it wasn't costume jewelry.

"You're certainly right about that Diana," she answered out of earshot of the eik. "We had a very elite guest list, but you know how it is. No matter how

careful you are, a few has beens and hangers on seem to slip through. You kno
what I mean, don't you?"

Walter stepped in to introduce himself to the Sheik, and Tiffany seized th
chance to fire a parting round at Diana without anyone else eavesdropping.

"I suppose parties, like politics, makes for some strange bedfellows," Tiffar
said cynically. She was looking directly into Diana's cold eyes and squeezing h
hand hard.

She then leaned her head toward Diana's face, as if to brush cheeks, an
whispered in her ear.

"I mean, how else could one explain Sonny Fremont and his favorite who
showing up at the same party," she said in her most innocent voice.

Launching her own verbal attack helped soothe her jangled nerves, but
wasn't a cure-all.

The opening of the roof was anti-climactic after her confrontation with Dia
Forrester.

The Dragon Lady had trumped her again, and Tiffany was as mad as she
ever been in her life.

Chapter 21
Trust No One

Tiffany was determined not to let Diana Forrester's party crashing escapade ut her in a funk.

Outwardly she was handling it calmly, her pretense so perfect only her losest friends could have suspected the delicate tightrope her emotions were alking.

The party was turning out to be the gala spectacular everyone had predicted, nd the unveiling of the roof had left the crowd in awe. But only for a moment.

After fully grasping the beauty and technology of it, the assembled guests roke into a polite applause that gave way to a thundering ovation.

It was a hit.

And none of the invited elite were the least bit aware of the mini-dramas nfolding all over the room.

Liz and Tom had moved into a semi-circle with Brian, Detective Sarabian ad Oscar Bento's ear, and in a far corner Walter and Johnny were face to face in hat appeared to be an intense conversation.

Tiffany wished she could listen in, and hoped Walter was not sharing any of e hotel problems, or her personal difficulties with Johnny. She had purposely voided telling Johnny about some of the problems, fearing it would put more of strain on their relationship.

The music was energetic, and Sonny Fremont was on a roll. It was his kind f crowd, and he was playing to them as only he could. The audience and dancers ere shouting song requests and he was fulfilling them almost before they could nish mouthing the full title.

He was at his best, and he had to give Oscar credit. Despite all the shit, Oscar ad managed to get him the juiciest Vegas gig of the year. He was finally in the olossus, and with a performance like this, all the top hotel owners would be egging him to headline their hotels.

Tiffany and Brian glanced at the stage at the same moment, as Sonny faltered n the lyrics of the next song. He had spotted Diana Forrester, snuggled mfortably in the arms of Sheik Gaddi. She had her head on the billionaire's oulder, defiantly glaring at Sonny with a twisted smile on her lips.

Sonny was shaken.

The bitch had found a way to get in...

The singer regained his composure and picked up the tune, but he was finitely flustered. He hoped Diana showing up with the Sheik didn't mean she asn't interested in him anymore. He still had plans for her. She could still be eful.

Diana had called him the moment she learned he was going to be the main adliner and begged him to take her as his guest.

261

on Delpit

At first he had hemmed and hawed, then put her off, saying it wasn't a good idea for them to be linked together. Not yet anyway. In truth, Oscar had advised against it, not wanting to do anything that would antagonize the new Colossus management, and queer a possible long-term showroom deal.

"I don't give a crap about them," Diana had fumed. "I want to go to that party. I must go to that party."

"I understand," he had pleaded, "but I can't take you. It would look too suspicious. If we went together we'd blow everything."

"What else can we blow?" she screamed. "I didn't get the fucking hotel. What does it matter now?"

There was no way he could appease her. She screamed obscenities at him for five minutes, then backed off and tried to sweet talk him. Neither approach worked.

"There must be another way. Maybe Oscar can weasel another invitation. You'd have to go alone, but at least you'd be there."

"Alone? Are you fucking crazy, Sonny Fremont? No way. I'd be a laughing stock. Never mind your helping me, you cowardly bastard. I'll handle it."

And apparently she had. Diana had done it as only she could. There was no way anyone would have dared make a scene with her on the arm of the Sheik. It was ballsy, and he could only imagine how much it had upset Tiffany. He just hoped they didn't take it out on him.

Still, his hat was off to Diana Forrester. She was a woman who knew how to get what she wanted.

"You okay?" Val had sensed Tiffany's distress and broken free from some of her new admirers, promising to return shortly.

"Not really," Tiffany said frankly. "My insides are shaking. Just seeing her again has me crazy. I should have known she'd find a way to crash the party. And to add insult she was wearing a dress from the Paris Show."

"I know," Val said in amazement. "We had it delivered to a dress shop in Chicago. The owner said she had a customer who wanted it and didn't care what it cost. I thought maybe it was someone from the Friends Ball. I had no idea..."

Before they could discuss it any further Johnny joined them.

"I hope I'm not interrupting anything ladies.

"Mademoiselle Hostess, may I have this dance?"

"You certainly may," she said, her eyes thanking Val for having been concerned.

Tiffany pressed close to Johnny, needing him to put his arms around her and tell her everything was going to be all right. She needed to feel safe. Feeling the firmness of his body helped squelch her fears.

"I haven't had much of a chance to tell you how happy I am that you made it," Tiffany whispered as Johnny pulled her even closer. "It means a lot to me. Just having you here."

262

She wanted everything between them to be smooth again and she looked forward to spending the night in his embrace.

"The good news is I'm here," he said softly. "The bad news is I have to return to Chicago as soon as the party is over. I can't even spend the night."

"But there won't be any more flights by the time the party ends," she protested.

"I know," he said holding her even more tightly. "I've chartered a private plane. I'll leave whenever the party ends."

She was crushed.

It had been nearly two weeks since they had been together and she could feel tears choking in her throat.

"The Colossus is a beautiful hotel," Johnny continued, "but I would give anything if you weren't involved in it. I think you'll agree that I've been patient the past few months, what with all your flying back and forth to handle hotel business, but I'd really like you to do whatever you must to sell this place as quickly as possible."

"What?"

How could he ask her that? Johnny knew nothing of her father's letter. He had no idea how important the hotel was to her father. Or to her.

She was about to tell him why she couldn't do it. Why she couldn't and wouldn't sell the Colossus when he put his fingers over her lips to quiet her.

"I know you want to do what's right, what your father would have wanted you to do," he said. "The thing is, I just don't want my wife to be a casino owner in Las Vegas…"

She had not misheard him. He had proposed to her. She stopped dancing for a moment and stepped back to look at him. No words came to her lips.

Johnny smiled at her.

Still numb, Tiffany felt Johnny pull her closer. She was both happy and confused. Why now, when they had been having problems? Of course she was pleased, but she didn't like him practically ordering her to sell the hotel.

But then, if they loved each other what would it matter?

It was a night she would never forget.

When the song ended Johnny said nothing more about it.

"Hold that thought my love. I must mingle a little more. There are still a few things I need to discuss with Walter before the evening gets away."

Brian, Liz and Tom had replenished their beverages and had moved past the initial phase of small talk. They were all on the same wavelength, however each was reluctant to make the first move.

"I guess you know all the players here," Liz said to Brian as she scanned the huge ballroom.

"Not really. I know some of them, but only from gatherings like this where the most meaningful things you ever say are "nice to see you again" or "how've you been?"

Tom and Liz both laughed. Brian's salient observation diffused the tension and Liz used the opening to unleash some of her artillery. She had decided Brian was one of the good guys.

She figured him as a wise guy, but basically straight. How straight depended heavily on how straightforward he was with his answers.

"What kind of guy is Walter Thurston?" Liz asked, deciding bluntness was the best approach.

Brian wasn't sure exactly what Liz was after, but he was perceptive enough to know the ground war had begun, and the hair was off the dog. It was show and tell time.

"He's concerned about Tiffany. That much I'm sure of. And I think still grieving inside over the death of Adam Forrester." It wasn't all he felt, but it was all he was willing to say at the moment.

"Were he and Forrester still close?" Tom asked. "I mean, after Adam left Chicago, did they stay in contact?"

"It's my understanding they did. Adam asked Walter to keep an eye on Tiffany. To be sure nothing happened to her."

Tom Felton aimed his next questions at the Colossus and the rumors that Adam Forrester's death was a mob takeover attempt.

"What about the rumblings that Forrester was connected?" he asked.

Brian liked Felton. Maybe "appreciated" was a more appropriate term. He could understand why the man was a successful investigative reporter. He wasn't afraid to ask tough questions.

"First, let me assure you Adam Forrester was not a part of the mob or syndicate or whatever you want to call it. I'm positive of that." Brian paused as a group of revelers passed nearby, then continued. "He was killed because he refused to sell the hotel. The mob wanted the hotel and believed they could convince whoever inherited the hotel to sell it."

"Tiffany," said Liz.

"Wrong answer," Brian countered.

"Everybody in the world expected Forrester to leave the place to his wife Diana Forrester, the redhead who made such a grand entrance a few minutes ago. Even Tiffany expected Diana to get the Colossus. Remember, Tiffany and her dad hadn't so much as spoken in five years."

Brian could see where the conversation was going. They were going to keep pumping him for information and he would have to either tell them more than he felt comfortable doing, or be evasive. And he hated being evasive.

It was always better to take the offensive.

"Time out," Brian said aloud, at the same time using his hands to form a "T".

"My turn for a probing question."

"Fair enough," Liz said.

"Why are you guys here? No way you just dropped by for a social visit. So nat's the deal?"

All three knew that trust was on the line.

"We're here because we're afraid Tiffany's life could be at stake," Liz swered. "I don't think she has any idea how much danger she's in, or who the d guys are.

"My gut feeling tells me there may be a Judas in her own camp."

"And how do you know I'm not the Judas?"

"Because whenever you talk about her it's obvious you care for her, and not st as a friend," Liz smiled.

"And because you don't have any influence over her," Tom added. "The das would have to be someone capable of manipulating her."

Brian gave Felton a puzzled "and what are you doing here look", and Liz cked up on it instantly.

"I asked Tom to come because he's familiar with the mob and how it perates."

"Two weeks ago I knew virtually nothing about Tiffany Wayne," Tom rried on. "And if it weren't for Liz, I'd still think of her as no more than an tractive, and probably spoiled little fashion designer."

"Did she tell you anything about her close call in Paris?" Liz asked.

Brian shook his head.

"It wasn't all that serious but I knew when it happened there was more to her an fashion designing. Someone wanted to scare her. To send her a message.

"A car jumped the curb and nearly ran Tiffany, Val and I down while we ere walking back to their hotel in Paris."

He was not surprised that Tiffany hadn't mentioned it.

"Could have been accidental," Brian said, "or it could have been a oincidence."

"Maybe, but I seriously doubt it," Liz argued. "I turned around and looked irectly at the driver just as he started to swerve away. He did it on purpose. He idn't want to kill anyone, and he wasn't drunk or out of control.

"That got me to checking on Tiffany, which is how I came to call Tom in hicago."

Tom picked up the story.

"For the past two weeks I've been calling on old sources, trying to see if Liz' uspicions have any merit."

"And..."

"I've called in a few favors and leaned hard on some old sources and I've otten a rough picture of what's going down."

Brian was anxious to hear if Tom's information corresponded with his own.

"Insiders tell me the Chicago Syndicate is first in line for the Colossus, b they have to gain control of the hotel in the next few months otherwise it's up f grabs."

Tom Felton's next sentence was critical, and after he made it, Brian knew l could trust him implicitly.

"I think the key player is a guy named Mario Torino," Felton said boldl "He's the reigning king of the Chicago underworld. He's got the power and th hotel would be a big feather in his cap. It would keep him on top in Chicago. I could be the guy pulling the strings..."

"But you don't think so, do you?" Brian jumped in when he detected a no of tentativeness in Felton's tone.

"No I don't," Felton said quickly. "There 's a silent force one step u somewhere, but we don't have a name. He's the brains and I think he's a clea shirt. The legit end. At least on the surface."

Tom again let Liz take the lead.

"I have my own theory about who's been orchestrating this whole thing," sl said, pausing to let some of the statements settle.

Brian didn't know what to think. He had no idea that anyone outside himself, Walter, Tiffany and Sarabian was aware of the infrastructure of tl situation. Now two strangers were not only confiding their suspicions, they we adding new layers to the cake.

So far they really hadn't told him anything he didn't know, although he w impressed that they had come up with Mario Torino.

The only thing he was holding back was the tidbit about Walter's numb having been called from Sam's office. He decided to hold onto that nugget just little longer.

"I have to admit that even though I'm not ready to say for certain that Li prime suspect is our man, her theory does have some strong talking points." To Felton was measuring his words.

Their eyes met and there was a small silence, all three waiting for the oth shoe to fall.

Brian's gaze was riveted on Liz Mallon.

"Well..."

Liz was sure the name she was about to utter would come as a shock Brian.

"Keep an open mind for a minute and think this through," she said, holdi him in suspense for a few more seconds.

"As Tom said, a couple of key things are necessary for this whole operatic to work. We know this isn't the brainchild of some street punk or loose band hoods.

"Whoever is masterminding this thing is first of all smart. Second, he powerful enough to arrange a hit. Third, he is close enough to the Colossus now what is going on, and most important, Tiffany trusts him totally. He can also influence her judgment and manipulate her whenever he needs to."

She had put all the pieces together but Brian still didn't see the knockout punch coming.

"Everything I've outlined points to Walter Thurston," she concluded. And he was even more convinced about Walter's involvement after listening to her own argument.

A fire raged through Brian's soul.

Liz had said out loud what he was afraid to say.

He still needed more proof to be convinced.

"Impossible. Walter Thurston could not possibly be behind all this," he said strongly.

"And why not?" Liz asked." Just because you hope he isn't?"

"One other thing Brian. Walter is a criminal attorney. He defends criminals. That's no secret. And when you spend so much time defending them, and getting to know them, you sometimes get involved with them. And the truth is, some of them are very charming." Tom was fueling the fire.

"Walter knows everything about the Colossus." Tom was making the case now.

"He has the Chicago ties, he had inside information on Forrester, he talked to Adam on a regular basis and he has access to the ongoing details of the case. And no one has more influence over Tiffany."

"I'm even willing to bet the will was no surprise to him. And it expressly told Tiffany to let Walter decide on the new buyer."

Brain's eyes roamed the busy room, momentarily shutting out the cacophony of sounds as he searched for Walter. Finally, he located the lawyer, standing in the shadow of one of the giant palm trees that had been brought in to help create a tropical atmosphere.

Walter had returned to his conversation with Johnny Marciano, and Tiffany's boyfriend did not seem as cool and debonair as he had earlier in the evening.

Johnny's forehead was creased and a serious look covered his handsome face. He was beginning to look disheveled. He was listening. Walter seemed to be dictating the tempo.

Were they discussing Tiffany? The party? Chicago? Adam Forrester? The Colossus? Was Johnny a part of it? Was it really possible that Walter was behind the whole plot?

Brian recalled his mid-week meeting with Walter. He had told the lawyer about Sam and Laura and shown him Rita Mathews' letters. If Walter was the man behind the murders as Liz suspected, Brian knew both he and Rita Matthews were now likely targets.

It was easy to see how Liz had arrived at her conclusion. Everything fit.

Maybe Walter Thurston had not hired him by happenstance. It could all have been part of a pre-conceived plan. Hire a watchdog, then watch the dog. Have him report back to you with all the inside scuttlebutt.

And hadn't Walter made it clear from the beginning that he wanted to be the first to know whatever new information Brian was able to discover, either from his own sources or from his police contacts?

By knowing what the police had, what Tiffany was thinking and what Brian uncovered on the street Walter could block any path the authorities might choose or close it off and leak false information, causing the investigation to go spinning in a different direction.

Adam's personal letter to Tiffany came to mind. Brian wondered if it was real, then decided it was bogus.

Walter would never forward a letter he had not read. It was too dangerous and he would never take that kind of risk. The letter had asked Tiffany to try and keep the hotel, which would mean appointing Walter to take over permanent management or appoint someone of his choosing to run the Colossus.

The letter also advised her to sell out if there was any danger, and to trust Walter to choose the buyer.

It was too pat.

The lights dimmed and Sonny Fremont began a slow soulful ballad.

Nothing was what it appeared. At least not when you got up close and personal. Sonny did not recognize the man talking to Oscar but he could tell Bento was uneasy. Oscar's face was strained and the agent's constant shuffling from one foot to another indicated he was anxious to have the conversation end.

"We're getting real close on all this stuff Mr. Bento, and it's funny how your name keeps popping up?" Sarabian was laying the groundwork. He didn't for a minute think Oscar Bento would crack, but he wanted to make the weasel-like little man squirm.

"I don't have a clue what you're talking about detective. I'm just here keeping an eye on my client and trying to have a good time."

Oscar had taken heat before, and he knew how to handle it. He also knew the good detective was fishing, hoping he'd say something incriminating.

"The window of opportunity is closing fast, Mr. Bento. It might be a good idea to crawl through it before Sonny Fremont or some other flunky with a little bit of information to sell beats you to it."

Oscar smiled and turned to walk away.

"Enjoy the party detective."

"One last question Mr. Bento. Is it true that Sam Bradford was going to fire Sonny from "Morocco Heat" and would have done so had he not been killed?"

Bento's droopy eyes flashed, but he remained composed.

"I don't know how vicious rumors like that get started," he said shaking his ead. "Sam Bradford personally selected Sonny Fremont for the lead in that icture, and the way I understand it, he was thrilled with the early footage.

"Mr. Bradford's death caused Sonny a major career setback, not to mention a reat deal of money," he said harshly. "It doesn't take a genius to see that Sonny vas better off with Bradford alive. The picture would have made him the biggest tar of the decade. Now if you'll excuse me, I see some people I must talk to."

"Of course. And Mr. Bento…if you should run across any old photos or egatives of Mr. Bradford and his friend Boyd Matthews, would you be so kind is to send me a copy. We seem to have misplaced our set and I was told you night be able to help."

Oscar Bento had turned away, thus preventing the bulky cop from seeing very pocket of his fleshy face turn a bloody shade of crimson.

Sarabian wondered if Bento knew Boyd Matthews was dead, then decided here was no reason he should. The kid's death hadn't even merited a line in the Los Angeles Times and only a minor obituary in a weekly Santa Monica freebie.

Sonny Fremont was getting ready to take a short break so Sarabian moved nimself into position to catch the singer as he came off stage.

As he made his way down the backstage steps Sonny saw the Armenian cop's imposing figure but made no attempt to avoid him, thinking the man might be a friend of Oscar's.

"Can I talk to you for a minute, Sonny?"

Sonny eyed the detective warily, but relaxed when Sarabian flashed an easy smile.

"Sure. Do you mind if we talk in the dressing room? I gotta take a leak."

The dressing room was a small, makeshift little cubicle hastily constructed to give the entertainer a place to put on make-up, change clothes and relieve himself. It was a far cry from the star facilities Sonny was afforded at other venues, however Oscar had assured him they'd make the Colossus pay when he became a regular.

"What can I do for you?" Sonny asked, zipping his pants as he turned toward the cop.

"It's more a case of what I can do for you," said Sarabian, trying to sound non-combative.

"You trying to be funny?" Sonny said smartly.

"I don't think there's anything funny about murder, do you Mr. Fremont?"

"What the fuck are you talking about?" Sonny said raising his voice. "I didn't kill anybody. Are you nuts?

"What are you, some kind of cop?"

Sonny was sorry he had been so accommodating. Usually he wasn't. Now he was cornered. This big asshole had him trapped in the tiny dressing room and there was no way to force him out.

"Forgive me for not introducing myself earlier," Sarabian said flashing his shield. Detective Don Sarabian, Las Vegas Metro."

Sarabian decided to roll the dice a little, sensing Sonny was a bit unnerved.

"Look Sonny, we know all about how you got the lead in "Morocco Heat" and what happened between you and Sam Bradford in Atlanta.

"We also know about the connection between you, Oscar Bento and the Chicago mob guy Mario Torino."

"I have no idea what you're talking about," Sonny said defensively.

But Sarabian had interviewed a thousand Sonny Fremonts, and he knew from the way Sonny's eyes were darting around the room that he was on edge.

Sarabian decided to squeeze a little harder.

"I know you're a gutless piece of crap who's been fucking Diana Forrester, and that you're involved in this whole rotten deal up to your hillbilly eyeballs. How's that for starters?"

Sonny's eyes were wild, and he was staring over the detective's shoulder hoping someone would knock or come in and rescue him. Where the fuck was Oscar?

"Nobody's coming to save you. Not now and not later." Sarabian sensed Sonny's desperation. "When this goes down do you think any of them are going to make a move to save your sorry ass?"

"You've made some sort of mistake," Sonny said weakly. "I don't even know this Mario guy, and Oscar is my agent."

"And I'm the fucking tooth fairy," Sarabian said harshly. "Listen up, Fremont. In Nevada, the law says an accessory before or after the fact can get the same sentence as the guy who actually committed the crime. That would mean serious time for you and your girlfriend."

He had busted a thousand perps and Sonny Fremont was no different. He had more money and more fame but he was still an opportunistic punk looking for the elusive big score.

And he was weak. He'd never make it inside. Prison would eat him up.

"Face it. You're a pawn Sonny and before the last dog is hung they'll throw you to the wolves. Or they'll kill you. Like they did Sam Bradford and Adam Forrester."

Sonny had wanted to believe that Sam Bradford's death had really been an accident. He had made himself believe it was. Now this big fucking cop was telling him it wasn't.

He wondered if they had any proof or was the guy just blowing smoke.

"Why are you telling me all of this?" Sonny was digesting it all and regrouping. This detective was nobody. He hadn't come to arrest him, he wasn't reading him his rights and he had nothing. The man was just guessing.

Ignoring him would be the smartest thing to do.

Sonny made a move toward the door and Sarabian stayed his ground.

"This isn't going to go away Sonny. What's more I'm not going to go
yway. You're a little fish and you know what happens to little fish...they get
ten up by the bigger fish."

"Showtime, Sonny."

Sarabian silently cursed the rap on the door. He had Sonny on the run and
th of them knew it.

"Maybe we'll chat again on your next break. If you decide to cooperate I can
ake things a lot easier." The burly cop turned and exited first, leaving a shaken
nny in his wake.

Sonny poured a straight shot of whiskey then dumped it without sipping a
op. His lips were dry, his throat parched. He reached for a bottle of Evian
illing in an ice bucket and gulped a large swallow.

"Go find Oscar Bento," he screamed at Dawn, the wardrobe girl as he
nerged from the dressing room and headed for the stage. "Tell him it's an
nergency."

It was near impossible for him to concentrate when he returned to the stage
r his next set. The detective's accusations kept mixing with the lyrics.

A few minutes into the set his guitarist passed him a note. He thought it was
equest.

"Can't find Mr. Bento. He's left the party. I tried his room, but there was no
swer."

He needed to think, and the pounding of the drums was scrambling his brain.

"Here's something for the lovers in the house," he announced as the familiar
ains of "Unchained Melody" filled the ballroom.

It ticked him off to even sing the damn song because it reminded him of how
ky the Righteous Brothers were. He couldn't buy a god-dammed hit and they
d one twice with the same song, twenty years apart, thanks to Patrick Swayze
d that fucking ghost movie.

In the audience, Brian, his emotions a bundle of loose wires, was trying to
gain perspective.

"I agree, that all of what you're saying is possible," he said to Liz and Tom,
ut I'm having a hard time believing it. Only because I've been working closely
th the man for the past couple months and I think he's been up front with me."

Brian didn't want to heap any more suspicion on Walter but the time had
me for him to share the phone number information with them. Maybe they'd
me up with a different take on it, or a plausible explanation.

"There is one other thing you should know," he said cautiously. "And I know
only adds to the case you're building against Thurston, but I've got to tell you
yway."

They eyed him carefully.

"There was a phone call made by Mario Torino from Sam's cell phone to
alter Thurston's office." He knew what their reaction would be.

Ron Delpit

Liz' expression practically said "what more do you want", while Tom stare off into space, perhaps trying to come up with an explanation other than th obvious.

Tiffany glided over and interrupted the conversation, and Brian asked her t dance, wanting both a chance to hold her in his arms and an opportunity to clea his head about Walter.

"I hope you're having a good time," Tiffany said politely. "It appears yo and Liz and Tom have hit things off pretty well."

"They're nice people," he said mechanically. "Very down to earth and ver open." He wanted to talk to her about Walter, to get her thoughts, but didn't. H had known her for five minutes. She'd known Walter Thurston her entire life.

When the music stopped Tiffany was hustled off by some political aide t pose for a picture with the governor and some local dignitaries. She shrugge helplessly as she was led away.

He returned to Liz and Tom.

"I'm going to go up to Walter's room to snoop around," he said boldly. " won't condemn the man until I see something in black and white. Somethin about all of this just doesn't wash with me. Maybe it's because I don't want t believe I've been that blind, but neither of you knows him like I do."

"How will you get in?" Tom asked.

"I'll get a pass key from housekeeping. They know me so it shouldn't be problem."

"Keep an eye on them," Brian said, nodding in the direction of Walter an Johnny who were still deep in conversation under the palm tree.

"And if you get a chance, see if Sarabian got anything from Sonny or Osca I saw him talking to Oscar earlier and he had planned on intercepting Sonn between sets."

He had told them everything, including his suspicions about Sam and Laura deaths, how Sonny had gotten the movie role, and he had already made it clear t Sarabian that they could be trusted.

He managed to slip out of the room without attracting any attention.

Getting into Walter's room was easier than expected. Helen, the penthous floor maid, had just come out of the suite after turning down the bed. She was th same woman who attended his room and they had chatted on a number o occasions.

"How ya' doing today Mr. P.? Is the big party over already?" She was large, friendly woman with a gold tooth in the upper front.

"Not yet Helen. Mr. Thurston needed me to get something out of his roo for him. Do you happen to have the master key?" He knew she did.

"Yes I do Mr. P. Here, let me let you in. When you're done just close th door behind you. It locks automatically."

"Thanks Helen."

272

"No problem Mr. P." And she was gone.

Inside, he did a quick study of the layout, trying to picture where Walter might stash something of importance.

"Basics", he repeated to himself. "He's not the kind of guy to tape something inside the fireplace, or under the bar. And he has no reason to think that anyone is suspicious of him."

The big roll top desk, a wall safe or the suitcases were the most obvious hideaways. And he remembered Sarabian's advice to check the inside coat pocket of suits hanging in the closet.

If whatever he was looking for was in the wall safe Brian knew he was out of luck. He ignored the papers on the desktop, realizing the lawyer wouldn't be so careless with incriminating documents.

He was looking for anything that would tie Walter to Mario Torino or Oscar Bento. He flipped through the attorney's personal datebook, scanning it for notes, initials or dates related to Sam or Adam.

The double drawer at the bottom right side of the desk was locked.

"Crap." He grabbed at the solid brass letter opener, deciding to try and pry it open, then had the presence of mind to check the middle desk drawer. There were two small keys in the self-contained wooden tray, but neither fit.

He was attempting to force the drawer with the brass opener when he heard a magnetic key in the suite's front door.

The bathroom wouldn't be safe. Walter or Margaret may have come upstairs to use it, or to change clothes.

He darted for the far closet, closing the sliding mirrored wardrobe door from the inside just seconds before he heard the entry door open and close.

From his less than advantageous vantage point, Brian could not see who had entered, despite the closet door being ajar a full inch. His legs were suddenly weak and he was frightened. His adrenalin count was probably off the charts.

If he was discovered in the closet there would be no way he could explain.

The closet took up most of the far wall of the bedroom, and was adjacent to the terrace, so unless the visitor ventured out to the terrace Brian would not be able to get a clear look at him.

He stood erect, and perfectly still, amused he hadn't lost his bizarre sense of humor.

This would be one helluva time to come out of the closet he chuckled silently. He was definitely one sick puppy.

The clink of glasses being filled with ice alerted him that the person had moved to the bar. But he had heard only one person come in. Why two drinks?

He could not tell yet if it was a man or a woman, but he knew it wasn't Liz or Tom or Sarabian. They would have called to him. They knew he was in the room. And none of them would have been pouring drinks at the wet bar.

He decided it was Walter, and hoped the lawyer had not decided to turn i
for the evening. He assumed the other drink was for Margaret who would b
arriving shortly.

Less than a minute passed before there was a knock on the door.

It wasn't Margaret.

"What the hell is this all about Walter?" It was Johnny Marciano and h
sounded annoyed.

"It's about Adam Forrester. It's about the Colossus and it's about Tiffany
Especially about Tiffany.

"What about Tiffany?" Johnny challenged.

"She's just told me that you asked her to marry you." Walter's tone wa
anything but congratulatory.

"So? Aren't you pleased for us?"

"Pleased? I'm disgusted. You're a cruel sonofabitch. Why can't you jus
walk away?"

"What are you talking about?"

"The police may never be able to prove that you ordered the hit on her fathe
but I think I've put all the pieces together. I wasn't sure until a few minutes ago.'

"You don't know what you're talking about, old man," Johnny said wit
hostility.

"Really. It all started to come together when I learned about Sam Bradfor
and the way your associates blackmailed him into using Sonny Fremont in hi
movie.

"You do remember the director, don't you?"

"What does he have to do with all of this?"

"For most people, nothing. But remember I've been around Chicago for
long time and I have a lot of well-placed sources of my own.

"Mario Torino is your cousin. His uncle is some big shot in Sicily name
Don Fanzi and he's the man who helped you get to this country."

"Who told you all of this shit?"

"It doesn't matter how I know, Johnny? Or should I say Gianni, or mayb
you'd prefer Carlo Monetti?"

"You're crazy," Johnny said wildly. "My name is Johnny Marciano. Yo
know who I am. You've represented me for five years. You know I'm
legitimate businessman."

"I used to believe that Johnny. But there are too many coincidences, and
don't believe in coincidences.

"You took Mario under your wing as a favor to Don Fanzi, and it was th
perfect set-up. You had a front man to do all your dirty work. Torino is ver
slick, and well educated, but he's still a thug. It was up to you to be the brains. T
pull the strings.

"But I can't let you pull Tiffany's string any more. If you walk away now you may get away with it. I don't think they can link you to Adam's murder. But you'll never get the Colossus."

Brian couldn't believe what he was hearing.

Tiffany's boyfriend, Johnny Marciano was the man behind everything.

Johnny had stopped refuting Walter's accusations. His eyes were scouring the room, searching for unfriendly ears.

"You've got it wrong Walter. There's more to the story, some things you ought to know that will make you change your mind. Things aren't exactly the way you're laying them out."

"Then tell me, Johnny. Prove to me that I'm wrong."

"How do I know this room isn't wired?" Johnny said, his eyes searching the room for hidden microphones.

"It isn't?"

"I can't take your word for it, counselor? You're not acting as my lawyer right now, and there's too much at stake. Let's talk outside.

Brian saw only the back of Johnny's tuxedo jacket as he moved to the terrace door, unlatching it and sliding it open.

"Out here."

Walter crossed in front of the closet and moved out onto the terrace. Both men were now in full view of Brian's narrow line of sight.

Downstairs, Tiffany joined Liz and Tom.

"Have either of you beautiful people seen Brian?"

"I think he went to the men's room," Tom lied. "He said he'd be back in a minute."

"Seems like all the men in my life are slipping away from the party," she teased. "Is this shindig that bad?" she asked, hoping no one would agree.

Tiffany was aware that someone had come up on her shoulder and she turned to see the hulking outline of Detective Sarabian.

"Hello detective. Anything new?"

Sarabian seemed poised to say something, then hesitated.

"It's okay detective," Tiffany said reassuringly. "Liz and Tom are reporters from Chicago and by now they probably know more about what's going on than I do."

"I think Sonny Fremont's scared," Sarabian said dryly. "With a little more nudging he might be willing to give up Torino, but only if it meant saving his own ass."

"Mario Torino?" Tiffany said quizzically. "What does he have to do with all this?"

"Do you know him?" Liz asked.

"Not really," Tiffany replied, still not sure how any of it fit. "I think he's a friend or distant relative of Johnny's. He stopped by our table to say hello to Johnny on one of our first dates. His name stuck in my mind."

Sarabian's antennae went up.

"Really. Well maybe I should have a word with Johnny," the detective said soberly. "Anyone know where Mr. Marciano is now?"

"I'm not sure," Tiffany said. "He said something about needing to make a phone call."

"And where's Mr. Thurston?" Liz asked.

"Walter said he had to go to his room to get some papers he wanted Johnny to take back to Chicago," said Tiffany, beginning to feel nervous.

"I didn't realize Johnny and Walter knew each other," Tom said.

"He's Johnny's lawyer. It was Walter who sort of introduced us," Tiffany explained, "at the Friends of the Arts Ball in Chicago."

"I think we'd better get up to Walter's room right now," Tom said frantically.

"Brian's in Walter's room. There could be a problem." It was too late to keep secrets or worry about anyone's feelings.

"You're damned right there could be a problem," said Sarabian. Especially if Johnny's up there too. Torino might even be with them."

The four of them rushed toward the ballroom's entrance, almost breaking into a run as they raced toward the penthouse elevators.

"Tiffany, get a key to Walter's room. Right away." Sarabian meant it as a request but it sounded more like an official police command.

A bellman wheeling a luggage dolly emerged from the adjacent elevator and Tiffany virtually assaulted him, ordering him to give the detective his master key.

"But miss, I can't..."

"Don't tell me can't," Tiffany screamed. "I own this damn hotel. Give him the key now."

"Tiffany is an innocent and I won't let you do this to her," Walter said angrily once he and Johnny were alone on the terrace.

"There is nothing you can do about it," Johnny laughed. "Tell the police anything you want. No one can ever prove I had any knowledge of anything you've talked about. I never even knew Sam Bradford."

"You didn't have to know him to have him killed. You may never get convicted for any of the murders," said Walter, "but I know who and what you are now. Once you're exposed you'll be ruined in the social circles you love running in. And I have a hunch your underworld friends will find you a liability too."

Johnny lunged at Walter, knocking over one of the patio chairs as he pushed the older man against the small balcony railing.

Brian didn't know if he should go to Walter's aid or remain a bystander. He watched as Johnny drove a fist into Walter's temple, dazing the lawyer. With a acticed movement Johnny grabbed Walter and overpowered him, moving both them dangerously close to the edge.

As Walter tried to fight back Brian bolted from the closet, running full speed o Johnny like a fullback trying to smash through a goal line defense. The force his charge caught the startled younger man so unaware he lost his balance, ling through the railing, with most of his body dangling over the ledge.

Walter had a loose hold on Johnny's left hand and Brian was struggling to ng to the sleeve of Johnny's tuxedo jacket when the door opened and Sarabian rst in followed by Liz, Tom, Tiffany and a Colossus security guard.

Before they could reach the terrace Johnny Marciano escaped their grasp and inged 31 stories, plummeting through the night into the Colossus parking lot.

"I wish you could have held on to the son of a bitch," Sarabian said jectedly.

"I would have loved to see him burn."

Tiffany was devastated, virtually collapsing into Liz' arms. She was sobbing controllably.

Brian and Walter looked at each other hard, both searching for an answer or a e. Then they hugged. It was a long, comforting embrace.

The others still did not understand all that had happened.

In a quieter moment, two days later, Brian confessed his suspicions to alter, detailing the circumstances that made it seem like the lawyer had isterminded the conspiracy.

"One thing still isn't clear Walter. Why would Mario Torino have called your ice from the cell phone in Sam's office?"

"The attorney seemed perplexed. I really don't know," he said. "I've never ken to Torino."

Then a light bulb went off in the older man's head.

"I think I know how it happened," he said. "Johnny was a client. I handled ne business things for him. Legit stuff. The last time we met was four or five nths ago. We were in my office when my secretary buzzed and said Johnny d an emergency long distance phone call. He took it at a phone in the outer ice so I thought nothing of it."

Tom and Liz had concluded that since Walter had drafted Adam's will, he ew all along that Tiffany was going to inherit the Colossus. They figured it s too perfect. He was someone she trusted and he could influence her to do atever he suggested.

What they didn't know is that Walter hadn't drafted Adam's final will. It had en done by his Las Vegas attorney, and amended within three months of his th. It was then that he decided to leave the Colossus to Tiffany and not Diana.

Cause and effect. Everything in the universe had an explanation. Sometimes u just had to wait for the answer to surface. Sometimes you never found out. t there was always a reason.

Ron Delpit

It made Brian think of his mother, who had passed away a few years earlie
A devout Catholic and a big believer in prayer, she always encouraged Brian
pray when he had a problem.

"God doesn't seem to hear my prayers, or answer them," he had sa
cynically.

"He hears them," she scolded.

"Then why doesn't he answer?"

"He does answer," she smiled. "Did it ever occur to you he's saying no?"

It was more than a month before Sarabian finished filling out the paperwo
and unraveling the entire scheme.

In October, Oscar Bento was convicted of extortion, obstruction of justi
and accessory to murder. A month later, thanks in part to testimony from Soni
Fremont who was granted immunity, a Chicago jury convicted Mario Torino
second-degree murder, extortion and racketeering. He was given two li
sentences without the possibility of parole.

The bizarre sequence of events had turned into a heartbreaking nightmare f
Tiffany. The evidence linking Johnny Marciano to her father's murder seem
irrefutable, and Mario had sworn under oath that Adam Forrester was killed
Johnny's order.

She wanted to not believe it, a small part of her heart trying to convince b
brain that Torino was shifting the blame in hopes that it would bring him a light
sentence.

Believing that Torino was lying was the only way she could face life agai
Also, she knew that whatever part Johnny had played in her father's death h
been done before he met her. And before he knew Adam was her father.

It didn't make him any less guilty, or her hate him any less, but it did affo
her some small consolation.

For months she was an empty shell, limp, lifeless and confused.

Knowing Johnny had orchestrated the entire horrible plan, and discoveri
he was the actual head of the Chicago Mafia did not alleviate the emptiness sl
felt. She had given herself to him. And loved him.

Once again her world had been turned upside down.

But the cleansing sense of satisfaction and revenge she had expected to fe
after her father's murderer was caught, was sorely missing. It was a hollo
victory, dulled by the feeling that she too had lost.

Through it all Walter was there to lend his support, and Brian had been the
for her to lean on, to cry on, and to confide in. Brian had been wonderful, and I
patience had helped nurse her emotions back to health. Or at least near t
surface again.

And she had done something on her own. She filed to have her name legal
changed to Tiffany Wayne-Forrester. She did it for herself, and for her father.

Brian loved her. She knew that. And she loved him too, but she was so unsure of her own judgment she could not let herself say the words. She had been wrong about her husband, wrong about shutting her father out of her life, and horribly wrong about Johnny Marciano.

But she had been right about Diana. She was the consummate opportunist. She had avoided prosecution, moved to the Middle East and married Sheik Mohammed Gaddi. Eight thousand miles away still wasn't far enough as far as Tiffany was concerned.

Tiffany joined Brian in Las Vegas for Thanksgiving dinner, the two of them driving to Walter's new home overlooking the Legacy Golf Course in Green Valley.

She smiled contentedly as she eyed Brian in the driver's seat.

"I'm very happy you agreed to take over as interim president of the Colossus," she said, reaching out to hold his free hand. "It has taken a lot of pressure off Walter, and he says you're doing an incredible job."

"Just remember, it's only temporary," he said as he ran his fingers over her hand. "There's just too much corporate crap to deal with everyday. Running a hotel, even as president is too much like having a real job."

Tiffany laughed.

"I know you went through a lot for me on this one," she said, "what with the licensing and all, and I really appreciate it."

Getting licensed had been a little sticky, but Brian had survived. He had even hired "Suspect" as a shift supervisor in the surveillance department. It was the least he could do.

"What time are Liz and Tom getting in?" he asked.

"The Felton's should already be here," she replied. "They're meeting us at Walter's."

Liz and Tom's wedding at the Colossus was one wonderful memory of the hotel Tiffany could always hold in her heart.

"I'll bet that's their rental car," Brian said as they turned into the cul de sac where Walter and Margaret's rambling, single-level home backed up to the 14th green.

"It looks like the long vacation and the move to Las Vegas has done both of you a lot of good," Tiffany said to Margaret as they shared a glass of wine in the kitchen.

"It has," Margaret replied. "Walter seems at peace with himself, more so than he has been in a long time. Semi-retirement suits him just fine. He goes to the hotel two or three days a week, just enough to keep active, and to see if Brian needs any help. The rest of the time we do nothing, although I must admit I have begun to take a little interest in golf. We're planning to do some traveling next year. Maybe Greece. Or Rome.

"And it would be especially nice if you and Brian joined us."

279

Tiffany smiled. It was a warm, gentle smile.

"That might be nice," she said. "I guess you'll never stop, will you?"

"I can't help myself," Margaret admitted. "I can't figure out what's holdin
you back. I know you two love each other. It's written all over the both of you."

"I suppose you're right," Tiffany conceded, "but he lives in Vegas, I live i
Chicago and I don't want to live out here. Vegas isn't for me, but it sure suit
Brian."

"Well, I'm convinced that if you guys try, you'll be able to work it out,
Margaret said, determined no to give up.

Brian, Tom and Walter were standing on the patio, watching a foursome pla
the 14th hole, which was practically in Walter's back yard.

"You know Brian, it really was exciting, and a pleasure working with you.
don't think I need to tell you the case would never have been solved if not fc
your tenacity, and your contacts. I'm grateful for everything you did. For Adan
for me, and for Tiffany.

"Thanks Walter, but I did it for me too. Getting to the bottom of all this wa
good therapy. It gave me a new beginning."

At dinner, they gave thanks, expressing gratitude for their health and the gif
they had.

Later they enjoyed a toast.

"To your father," Walter offered. "He was a fine man, a great friend, and i
the end, a wonderful father who never stopped loving you."

"I love you all," Tiffany said, and she held Brian's hand more tightly. He
eyes were moist, but Brian's arm around her waist gave her strength.

"It all feels so strange sometimes, "Brian said as he and Tiffany drove towar
his home. "Being at the Colossus everyday, Thinking about all that went on, an
how we got to where we are today. So many things have happened and so man
things have changed."

In the end, Sonny Fremont had cracked. He gave up Oscar and spilled h
guts about Mario in exchange for immunity. And even more amazingly, h
managed to survive the bad press about his porno movie days, somehow playin
it off as if he were the victim. But not without paying a price.

As they motored along the 210 freeway Brian pointed to an unlit billboard s
about fifty feet off the highway shoulder. It advertised a small, second-ra
downtown hotel.

Tiffany stared at it for a moment, then looked away.

The sign read, $ 1 single deck blackjack. Then, in smaller letters
announced, "Shrimp Cocktail .99 cents." And in still tinier script, at the ve
bottom the sign proclaimed, "Sonny Fremont Show, midnight to 5 a.m."

There was a God.

As they came to a stop in his driveway, Brian pulled Tiffany close and kisse
her lovingly.

"Maybe Margaret's right," she said, seemingly thinking out loud.

"Right about what?" he asked, not having a clue.

"Maybe it's time I stop being afraid, and start trusting my own feelings again."

Brian kept silent.

Tiffany paused for what seemed like a long time.

"I want things too Brian."

She continued, without waiting for him to ask.

"Like happiness. Like freedom. The freedom to do what pleases me, instead of what might please my father or someone else. "He was listening attentively, and watching her every movement.

"When you hold me I know nothing can hurt me. You won't let it. I believe you will always be there for me."

"And I will."

"Even if I put you out of a job?"

"What do you mean?" he asked. "You just told me what a good job I was doing. Are you firing me?"

"That depends a great deal on how you answer a few important questions, Mr. Powers."

He shot her a confused look.

"First of all, would it break your heart if I sold the Colossus?"

She caught him by surprise and he stammered, searching for the right response.

"I'd miss being boss," he smiled, "but I'd get over it. More importantly though, are you ready to do that?" He had mixed feelings. Her selling the hotel would mean she'd have no reason to come to Vegas, except for an occasional visit. He also realized he was being selfish because her life was in Chicago.

"I wasn't sure until this very minute," she said. "But I've reached the point that I can move on without feeling any guilt about having let my father down. I think I've made my mark on the Colossus, and it will always be a living legacy to him. There have been some legitimate offers in recent weeks and I have to admit I've thought about them. And I know Walter can arrange a sale. He's just been waiting for me to say the word.

"The other questions are a little more personal," she warned.

He braced himself.

"Are you sure you love me, Mr. Powers?"

He was afraid the next thing she was going to say was, 'then move to Chicago so we can be close to each other', but he answered anyway.

"I've never loved anyone more," he said without a doubt. "You are my fantasy. The woman of my dreams."

"Will you marry me, Brian?"

It was his turn to be shocked.

Boy chases girl until she catches him. What an ending.

"You know what?" she asked, a smile on her face and tears on her cheeks.

"No, what?" he replied.

"Maybe Vegas isn't such a bad place after all."

ABOUT THE AUTHOR

Ron Delpit is a veteran entertainment writer who has rubbed elbows with everyone from Frank Sinatra, Elvis and Howard Hughes to real-life Mafia hit men during his twenty-five years in Las Vegas. *The Colossus Conspiracy* is his second book. His first, *By Blood Betrayed*, was a paperback best seller.

A former syndicated entertainment columnist as well as a critic for *The Hollywood Reporter* and editor for *Gannett* newspapers in New York, Delpit incorporates his wealth of knowledge about Las Vegas, its entertainers, its hotels and their ruthless Strip Wars into this fictionalized murder mystery that gives readers a rare glimpse behind the glitz, glamour and gaming that is Las Vegas.

Delpit is also an ex-sports writer and college athlete. An injury cut short a promising baseball career but gave birth to his entry into the business side of sports as a player agent in the early 1970's.

The late Sammy Davis probably summed it up best when he said, "Ron Delpit is that rare breed of cat who not only knows where the bodies are buried; he knows who buried them. He is as Vegas as neon and green felt."

Ron Delpit is also a past president of Nevada Special Olympics and currently resides in Las Vegas.

Made in the USA
Las Vegas, NV
26 April 2022

48044874R00173